Secrets of a Reluctant princess

Secrets of a Reluctant princess

Casey Griffin

Entangled Publishing, LLC
2614 South Timberline Road
Suite 109
Fort Collins, CO 80525

Entangled Teen is an imprint of Entangled Publishing, LLC.

Visit our website at www.entangledpublishing.com.

Edited by Lydia Sharp and Stacy Abrams
Cover design by Kelley York
Interior design by Toni Kerr

ISBN: 9781633755932
Ebook ISBN: 9781633755987

Manufactured in the United States of America

First Edition March 2017

10 9 8 7 6 5 4 3 2 1

Chapter One
Crowned

Spotlights blind me, lenses zoom in on my makeup-plastered face, and there is a collective holding of breaths, as though whatever is about to come out of my mouth next is television magic.

"Umm," I say. "What was the question again?"

And the breaths are released in disappointed sighs and groans.

The director leans forward in our new armchair, like this is an intimate little chat, just the two of us—except for the cameraman, the grip, the stylist, the boom operator, and my parents hovering in the background.

"Let's start with an easier one," he says. "Can you tell us a bit about yourself, Adrianna?"

My eyes dart to Mom, who's standing behind our living room sofa. She's already coached me on this part. She wants us to come off as fancy-pants sophisticated, "a family that wears their new money well," as she put it. Not like the people on the network's other reality show, *Lucky Lottery Lowlifes* (Thursdays, nine p.m. Eastern, eight p.m. Central).

No. We're the *Bathroom Barons*. Yeah, that's much better.

I open and close my mouth a few times, trying to think of something to say, but nothing comes out.

"Maybe we'll come back to that one later." The director consults his clipboard. "How do you feel about the recent success of your father's business, Bottom's Bathrooms and Accessories?"

Mom stands behind him, pointing to her bared teeth like she wants to know if there's something stuck in them. To make her happy, I attempt to smile for the camera. Mom makes a face so I stop and look back at the director, Corbin, I think his name is—because everyone in Hollywood seems to name their kids something eccentric just in case they become famous, so they won't have to make one up like Lady Gaga.

He waves his hands in a circular motion as if that's going to encourage me to think. "How does it feel to be insanely rich?"

"It's pretty cool to be rich, I guess. We get to live in a huge mansion with a pool, but it's not like I get a bigger allowance or anything. Or even a car now that I'm sixteen."

I shoot a look at Dad. He's standing nervously by our floor lamp in the corner. He gives a subtle shake of his balding head, clearly not pleased with my performance so far. I mean, come on. Dad bought himself an Aston Martin, but I can't even get a stinking Kia? It's so unfair that I want to scream.

Corbin moves on. "How do you like California so far?"

"Let me see," I begin to say, sarcasm dripping from my voice.

Mom gives me a warning look. I press my lips tight to prevent all the things I really want to say from falling out.

I should tell him that my life sucks. That I had to leave my whole world in Seattle behind, Mom's turned into a hungry socialite overnight, and now I live in a show home full of furniture I can't sit on or touch, with cameras shoved in my face at six a.m. Like I'm not going to be enough of a leper at my new school as it is. The heiress to the famed *Bowl Buddy*.

Corbin's arms are moving in giant circles now, like he's trying to smell his own cologne. I have to say something.

"California is…warm?" I glance helplessly at the front door, but it's too early to go to school yet. I take the next best exit. "Can I go to the bathroom?"

"Cut!" Corbin yells. He waves an impatient hand at me, and I take this as permission to escape.

Mom maneuvers in her stilettos through the equipment cluttering our living room, but I scurry out before she can get to me. I shuffle like a single-jointed robot in the designer skirt the stylist picked out that is two sizes too small for me. It's supposed to make me look slimmer, because for a small thing, I've got more curves than Hollywood prefers, apparently.

Slipping into the nearest bathroom, I flick on the dazzling chandeliers. I shut the double doors and lean against them, taking a deep, calming breath. The smell of scented potpourri makes me nauseous.

This can't be happening. A reality show about our family? Who cares about our personal lives and how different it is now that we're rich? Even I don't find it interesting. I slide to the cool marble floor and bang the back of my head against the door a few times.

Just because Dad sold a million of those stupid glow-in-the-dark toilet inserts, suddenly we're worth talking about? I mean, what's so great about them? Why can't boys just flick on a light to pee in the middle of the night? And now everyone on Earth is going to know that my dad invented it.

We couldn't be rich from something cool, like discovering a new fuel source or curing cancer. Nope. It's a luminescent pee target.

Someone raps on the door. "Sweetheart, are you in here?" It's Mom.

"No."

"Can I come in?" She barges in without waiting for an answer, pushing me along with the door. I don't know why she bothered asking. I should have locked it and shoved one of the overstuffed decorative chairs beneath the handle to barricade it.

"Is everything all right?" she asks.

"Mom. What if I'd been on the toilet?" I say, hoping she'll leave.

"Don't be so dramatic, Adrianna." She insists on calling me by my legal name now. Not Andy. *Adrianna.* Much more Hollywood.

I stomp over to the toilet. The motion sensor detects me and raises the lid in anticipation—yet another Bottom's Bathrooms accessory. I slap it back down and have a seat. Heat radiates through my skirt. I nearly leap off before I remember Dad installed the Hot Buns™ seat warmer on every toilet in the house.

I groan. "My life sucks."

"It's not that bad," Mom says. "You'll get better at this. You'll see. Eventually, you won't even notice the cameras." She stops checking out her makeup in the mirror to glance at me. "And just look at you. You're so lovely this morning."

"Lovely? This skirt is so tight it's going to take a crowbar to get me out of it."

"The stylist says it's the latest fall fashion."

"It isn't me. I miss refashioning thrift store clothes. I miss my patterns. I miss my sewing machine. It may not have been the latest fashion, but it was *me*."

The stylist can take away my nerd pins that I wear on my messenger bag and obscure sci-fi T-shirts, but at least she can't take my Wonder Woman underwear. Or can she?

Mom doesn't get it. Of course she doesn't. This is her Cinderella story. From rags to riches. She turned into a princess, while I feel like the pumpkin. Who am I to pee on her fairy tale? She can have it. Mom means well, but I just wish she'd keep me out of it.

"Trust me, sweetheart. This is every girl's dream. One day you'll be glad you decided to do this."

"You mean glad you forced me into it?" I say. "The stylist wants to dye my hair blonde, Mom. Blonde. She tried to stick a wig on me."

"Well, your hair is a little"—she tugs on one of the vibrant red curls springing from my head—"out of control. But you're going to be a TV star now. What girl doesn't want that?"

"Me. That's who."

"Think of all the new friends you'll make. You'll have a fresh start."

"Friends? Yeah, right." I wrinkle my nose at the reminder.

That was the plan. Why I was excited about the move in the first place. Leave Seattle, leave "Awkward Andy" and "Bowl Buddy Bottom." Leave all the teasing and snickering behind my back, or rather, backside. But the reality show hadn't been part of the original plan. Now that we're on TV, the bullying will be ten times worse.

"Things won't be different just because I get new hair and new clothes and because I go to a different school."

"You don't know that," Mom says. "You're a junior now.

Maybe it will be different. Just try something new." She tugs at another stray curl, wrapping it around her finger like she did when I was a kid. "I just hated to see how unhappy you were at your old school."

"I was unhappy because of all this." I wave a hand around the bathroom. Well, that's not entirely true. The teasing began way before Dad's inventions took off. It only gave the other students something new to focus on rather than the tired old geek routine.

"Who wants to watch a show about my awkward, freak-show life, anyway?" I cross my arms. But then Mom smiles with strained cheerfulness, and guilt claws at me until I feel like I should turn the attitude down a few notches. I unfold my arms.

"The cameras will be following your dad and me, too. Who knows? They might not even be interested in filming you that much."

"So now I'm not interesting?"

Another knock on the door and Dad's balding head pops in. "Hello? How are things going in here?"

"We're holding family meetings in the bathroom now?" I say. "Seriously?"

Dad leans against the counter and considers Mom and me for a second. "Why don't I tell the crew to wrap it up for the morning?"

"But they've hardly been filming for an hour," Mom protests. "You're having fun, aren't you, sweetie?" she asks, like she can convince me.

Dad folds his arms across his chest, more like he's giving himself a hug than anything. The new changes have been tough on him. Correction: Mom and I have been tough on him. Of course, Mom's been all for the TV show, but I've been as enthusiastic as a cat having a bubble bath.

I know Dad has to do what he has to do for the growth of his bathroom empire, and he's really happy they got the contract for the show, but he also wants me to be happy. Problem is, he also wants Mom to be happy. And with this whole moving to Beverly Hills and reality TV thing, we couldn't be on further ends of the spectrum. He's like an elastic band being pulled emotionally between the two females in his life. I wonder how long before my mild-mannered, peacekeeping father will snap. But at the end of the day, he's excited about the show, too. So it's two against one.

He glances at my mom's look of pleading, then back at me with a sigh. "You're probably just nervous about your first day at school," he suggests hopefully.

"Ugh. School." I fall against the toilet's padded, ergonomic backrest, and the footrest pops up. "I can't go to school. I'll be laughed out of there. You remember what they called me at my last school. Like it's not easy enough with a last name like Bottom."

Dad waggles his eyebrows. "You'll be the *butt* of jokes."

I give him my best withering glare. "You're hilarious. I'm serious. I'll be Bowl Buddy Bottom again. Or how about Andy Assho—"

Mom holds up a finger. "That's enough, young lady."

"What was it in grade nine?" Dad says. "Farty Freshman?"

"Dad! See? That's what I'm talking about. It's going to be Seattle all over again—but worse, because it'll be broadcast all over TV."

It took months for kids at school to find out about the embarrassing late-night infomercials that Dad had for the Bowl Buddy. Now our entire lives will be prime time. No escaping. No hiding the truth from anyone. No fresh starts. Let the teasing begin.

Not only did I become the laughingstock of my old school, but even my so-called "real" friends started keeping their distance once my dad's business took off. It's like they thought being a loser was contagious.

Dad sighs, giving up the cheerleader routine. "Princess," he begins what will surely be some positive pep talk.

"That's it," comes a voice from the hall.

A light blinks in the mirror on the wall across from me. Dad left the door cracked open. The camera lens wedges into the room to record my reflection. Mom stops rearranging her new boobs in the mirror and tries to act natural.

"Get that thing away from me," I say. And because there's nowhere else to go, I jump into the double-wide tub and tug the curtain closed.

"I've got the perfect angle to sell the show," Corbin says.

"What's that?" Dad asks. He just can't help himself. He thinks this whole reality show business is the best thing ever. A whole new audience to listen to his cheesy jokes.

There's a clamor outside my shelter, and I imagine the whole crew trying to cram themselves into the bathroom.

"I know what everyone will call you," Corbin says. "I present to you"—the curtain suddenly whips back, exposing me—"the Porcelain Princess."

My mouth drops in horror as the cameras zoom in to capture my reaction. Corbin's nostrils flare in triumph. Dad's chuckling at the clever name. Mom's got something stuck in her teeth again.

And with that, my life officially goes down the double-wide tub drain.

Chapter Two
AsSension

I open my locker door and stick my head in, wishing it were a guillotine. I wonder if I can fit my whole body inside, stupid pencil skirt and all, which I wore only because Mom insisted with her poodle-like enthusiasm. Have you ever said no to a poodle? You can't. They're too cute.

I'm not that big. Maybe I can shut the door behind me and hide in there until the day is over. But then the bell rings. Sighing, I dig into my bag to search for a pen, since I lost mine sometime around lunch.

I guess things aren't *that* bad. The world hasn't ended *yet*. Corbin said they were going to start airing commercials for *Bathroom Barons* at the end of the week. I have until then to enjoy a normal life and maybe try and make a friend or two before I get outed as the Porcelain Princess.

The first episode is less than four weeks away. Apparently there's been a big push by the network to pump out reality TV shows faster in order to remain competitive with their rival's latest hit, *Confessions of a Contract Killer*. So instead of waiting for the whole season to be filmed first, I have under a month to say good-bye to any hope of a social life, just like back in Seattle.

Why bother with the new clothes and makeup? They can't disguise who I am for long. Eventually people will see the geek hiding beneath it all. And I'm okay with that. I like superhero movies, and anime, and board games, and that's not going to change. But add that to the potential toilet jokes, and it's an unlimited supply of material. Like a Bullies-R-Us for high school ridicule and torment.

Giving up the search for my elusive pen, I close the door and consult the map I received in my orientation package. My last school didn't require a map. But Beverly Hills High is so big that I'm tempted to GPS my locker's position on my phone just so I can find the way back again.

I walk around with my map, looking like a tourist. If I'd arrived at my new school when fall semester started the week before, maybe I wouldn't have stood out like a supermodel at a comic convention. Only I'm not the supermodel. Everyone else is. I'm the geeky kid bumping into people while trying to read my map.

When I finally locate my biology class, the only seats left are near the front of the room. Everyone's wandering around, chatting with friends. Friends—lucky them.

People have been nice enough, I suppose. It's not like I haven't talked to anyone all day. Well, they talked to me and I responded, but that still counts.

Maybe it's the constant fear of everyone finding out what an embarrassing life I live. Who would want to be friends with me? It would be like boarding a sinking ship. I remind myself that I'm supposed to be making friends before that happens, to start over, to try something different, *be* different.

I turn to the girl next to me. "Hey, I'm Adrianna," I say,

because apparently that's the name I go by now.

She smiles—a good sign. "I'm Harper."

A future movie star, for sure.

"I haven't seen you around before," she says.

"I'm new here. My parents and I just moved from Seattle."

Out of the corner of my eye, I see something sail across the room. Before I can react, it hits me on the side of the head and bounces to the ground. It's a crumpled ball of paper. People are already throwing things at me—a bad sign.

The guy at the table ahead of us chuckles and picks it up. "Sorry," he says. "That was meant for me."

As he stands his laughing eyes are close to mine, and I swear he's so beautiful that I wish he were a centerfold in a magazine so I could take out the staples and pin him up on my locker door. He's tall, and muscular, and seems to consume the entire room with his presence, and he smells like spearmint hair gel.

"That's okay," I say. "I don't mind." I would take a million paper balls to the head for him. I would face a paper airplane firing squad. Dive on top of a paper-cut grenade.

He leans on the desk in front of Harper, like he wants to get closer to her. "New friend of yours?" He nods in my direction.

She just glares at him. "None of your business."

He sneers at her reaction, in an "I was only trying to be nice" way, then looks back at me for a second. A really long second, like maybe two or three. He finally turns away, and I think stars are blinking in front of my eyes. Then I realize it's just my oxygen-starved brain telling me to breathe.

I lean toward Harper and whisper, "Who's that?"

"Lennox." After she eyes me ogling him for a few more seconds she adds, "My ex," very pointedly.

I peel my eyes away guiltily. Daydreaming about her ex? So much for making friends. "Oh, I was just curious." I glance around the room like I have so many better things to be looking at right now than her ex.

She shrugs and her eyes involuntarily shift over me. A primitive girl instinct to size up the fresh meat—although I'm more of a bologna slice to her filet mignon.

Her sun-bleached blonde hair cascades like a golden waterfall over her slim shoulders, just like that hot, itchy wig the stylist tried to cram over my lion's mane. Under the perkiest nose I've ever seen is the biggest, prettiest mouth that would rival Scarlett Johansson's. Harper's one of those naturally beautiful girls who probably wakes up looking that way, no drool, or eye crusties, or anything.

When she's done giving me the once-over, she flashes me a friendly smile. Obviously she found no competition here. Nope, none at all. It makes me grateful for my torture session with the stylist that morning; I could have looked worse.

The teacher walks in. He's old—well, forty-something old—with short, stubby legs. He totters across the room like he has no knees. I check my itinerary. His name is Mr. Bigger.

He claps to get everyone's attention. "Okay, people. Take your seats."

"Oh, I almost forgot," I say to Harper. "Do you have a spare pen?"

She digs into her pencil case and hands me a sparkly pink one. "Here. Keep it."

"Thanks."

The class flies by, and I think I might actually make it through my first day without incident. One whole day that I've done nothing to be made fun of for. Like I'm a totally normal person or something. When nothing blows up in my face, I actually start to pay attention to class. My grades aren't half bad when I do that.

Mr. Bigger tells us to finish copying the notes on the board and leaves the room. It's exactly ten seconds before the place erupts with last-class restlessness, chatting, wandering around, texting.

Five minutes later, Mr. Bigger returns and begins to shout for everyone to settle down. Just when he's turning red in the face because no one is listening, he yells, "*Sit down*," really stern-like, and I drop the pink sparkle pen on the floor.

I look at him to see if the "sit down" applied to me, too. He waves his hand impatiently to go ahead and pick it up. I'm getting a lot of impatient hand waving lately.

It's really quiet now. Mr. Bigger stands there with his arms crossed while I slip off the stool as ladylike as I can in my too-small skirt, waiting all dramatically like he's making an example out of me. I wish he would just start teaching already, because all eyes are on me as I bend down to pick up the pen.

And then I hear it.

The tearing of high-quality fabric.

Time stretches out—the way my skirt didn't—and the sound seems to echo around the room for an eternity. Surely the whole school can hear it. My heart seizes in my chest. I feel the cold air seep in, and I know the entire class can see my Wonder Woman underwear.

The deafening silence erupts with laughter. People are howling, banging their tables. Screw the pen. I grab my notebook and hold it against my butt as I make a break for the hall.

The teacher yells after me, telling me class isn't over.

But I won't go back. Not for anything in the world. Not a bigger allowance. Not a date with a boy—not that I'll get one now. Not even for a Ferrari.

Endless hallways confuse me, and I feel like I'm trapped in a seventies cartoon with a revolving chase scene background: lockers, washroom, water fountain, lockers, washroom, water fountain. Finally, I track down my locker.

Yes. Almost home free.

Then the end-of-school bell rings.

Bodies press out of doors, and instantly the halls are teeming with students and teachers. I'm trapped. I back up against my locker, notebook squished behind me. If I can just get my backpack out, I can grab my sweater to hide the tear in my skirt.

Two students want to get into the lockers on either side of me, and I'm jostled out of the way. They look at me like, *What's your problem?*

I want to scream at them. Can't they see I'm having a crisis?

Maybe if I stay here, back against my locker, I'll act cool and pretend I'm waiting for someone until the place clears out. Then I'll make a run for it. Just act natural.

"Adrianna, there you are." It's Harper. Naturally, half the biology class has followed her. How did she find me when I barely found my own locker?

She stomps over to me. "That's *my* notebook. I just finished copying down all the notes. I need them."

"What?" Craning to peer behind me, I see the book now squished up against my backside is hot pink with little heart stickers pasted all over it. When I glance at Harper, she motions to my book under her arm. I feel my whole body sag with the impending doom of it all.

I press against the locker and grip the coiled book tight

like a safety blanket, knowing it's the only thing between the ten million students in the hall and my Wonder Woman underwear—or at least it feels like ten million to me. Maybe the stylist should have picked out my underwear, too. Or better yet, just left me and my jeans alone.

Reaching around me, Harper tugs my last defense away. My hand automatically reaches out for it, and my thumb snags in the skirt's gaping tear. As I bring my hand forward, the rest of the skirt gives way. It rips from zipper to hem…

Releasing the mighty Wonder Woman.

Some students give me no more than a curious glance. Others just ignore the debacle and keep moving. I even see pity in a few eyes. But it's not them I'm worried about. It's the ones who are laughing at me. Laughter from behind me. Laughter from all around. Bodies crowd and elbow in so there's nowhere to stand but the center of the hall.

I'm going to die of embarrassment.

The tone changes, hilarity turning to chatter. Then I see the light. No, not *the* light. I'm not dead yet—although I wish I were. A red blinking light. The cameras.

The film crew has gotten into the school somehow. That would have taken release forms, permission slips, authorization—next to impossible. I thought Dad said I would be safe here. That's just my luck. Or rather, my unluck.

I can't let the cameras see me. If they see me, so will all of America. Worse yet, anyone can find the show online. It might even become viral on the internet. The whole world will see. I try to shrink in on myself, to duck past pointing arms through the sea of bodies, but it's like a solid wall of shame.

Corbin sees me, and the whites of his eyes flash. He barks orders to the camera guy that I can't hear over all the jeering. His face transforms like, *it's go time*.

No. They can't be here. Not now.

While one camera takes in an artistic panorama of the mob, the other rushes toward me.

"Stop," I say. "Leave me alone."

But Corbin doesn't relent. This is the action he's been waiting for, the humiliation that sells TV. *My* humiliation.

I shove people away from my locker, trying to cover my butt with one hand and fumbling for the lock with the other. Ignoring the new wave of whistles and cheers, I grab my bag, toss it over my shoulder, and fight my way through the crowd.

I don't stop running until I'm out the door and can't hear the laughter anymore. But it still rings in my ears.

So much for making friends. And in a matter of days, my public humiliation will be advertised on every television screen across the nation.

The whole world is going to see Andy Bottom's bottom.

Chapter Three

Hellywood

The bell above the shop door rings, and I duck behind the checkout counter, pretending to look at the jewelry display. I peek around the corner. It's just some old lady with a fat Louis Vuitton shopping bag. My shoulders slump in relief.

"Will that be everything for you?" the shopgirl asks.

I scramble to my feet. "Yes, please."

She tosses my shredded skirt into the trash. As I watch, I make a silent vow to the fashion gods that I will never wear one again. She scans the tags for a hooded sweatshirt, a pair of sunglasses, and a new pair of distressed jeans, even though I prefer to distress them myself. But maybe this is what Mom meant by fancy-pants.

The shopgirl's letting me wear the new clothes out of the store, thankfully. After I left the school, I dug a sweater from my bag and tied it around my waist. Returning home wasn't an option. That's the first place Corbin would have looked for me. But I had to do something about my wardrobe malfunction, so I headed to the only place a

Hollywood newbie, such as myself, could think of: Rodeo Drive.

The shopgirl shows me the total. I blink at the number and feel my mouth pop open. After a mini heart attack, I close it again and remind myself that we're rich. I hand over the emergency credit card Mom and Dad gave me. If this isn't an emergency, I don't know what is.

After I pay, I wrangle my curls into a ponytail and tug up my hood. I suddenly wish I had the stylist's blonde wig.

Peering through the glass door of the shop, I scope out my surroundings. The sidewalk outside is bustling with afternoon shoppers. School has been out for almost an hour now. I press my face to the glass to see as far as I can down the street for any familiar faces, but since I've been in school only one day, I doubt I'll recognize anyone. It's Corbin and his crew I'm really worried about.

But Beverly Hills is a big place, and I could have gone anywhere. There's no way they'll find me. I'm just being paranoid, that's all.

Slipping on the pair of sunglasses I bought, I feel like a movie star who's left the house without makeup and gets caught by gossip-rag paparazzi. Only I'm just the Porcelain Princess. And I didn't get caught with a bare face. I got caught with a bare butt—or close to it.

I emerge from the store and head down the pedestrianized street. So far so good. I call Mom's cell to leave a message that I'm shopping on Rodeo Drive and that I'll be home for supper. If she knew what happened, she would want to talk about it, and all I want to do right now is forget.

The shops on either side of the street are just what you'd expect. Coach, Prada, Cartier, Harry Winston. And some are so expensive I've never even heard of them. You can tell they're pricey because they have only three articles of clothing on each rack.

Six months ago I wouldn't have been on the same street as these stores. Now, Mom's been begging to take me on a mother-daughter spending spree at them. But just because there are a few extra zeros in our bank account, doesn't change my taste in clothes.

I miss Seattle's back-alley boutiques and secondhand stores. The seventies and eighties may have had some strange tastes, but the clothes are great for revamping with a little modern fabric and a sewing machine. Mom tossed most of our old stuff, though, including my machine, calling it "old junk." She promised to buy me a new one, but things have been a little busy with the TV show and Corbin being so intrusive.

We didn't just upgrade the house and car, but our entire lives. I feel like I'm supposed to be Andy 2.0 now. When really, I feel like a complete zero. I'm still the same person I was back in Seattle. It wasn't like a new outfit and school were going to change that. But maybe there's something else that could—a new car certainly couldn't hurt.

Or maybe it has nothing to do with the clothes, or the car, or the show. I may not have been cool back in Seattle, but you fake it until you make it, right? I could just laugh off the whole underwear experience at school. Say it was totally staged for the show. I could pretend I'm an aspiring actress—who *isn't* in Hollywood? Now I just need to learn how to act.

I traipse down the street, my head tilted kind of nonchalantly. Very future-star-like. The newly reinvented Andy. World, meet Adrianna Bottom. Scratch that. Just Adrianna, like Madonna. I wonder if Mom and Dad will let me change my name.

Bright banners flutter from the sides of Victorian-style

lampposts—if Victorians used energy-saving lightbulbs. The heels of focused shoppers click across colored bricks, overstuffed bags knocking me as I pass. Even the storefronts are decorated in an old-worldy style, as though this will trick people into thinking they've gone back in time. A far cry from Pike Place Market in Seattle.

I come to the end of the street where the brick path gives way to traffic again. I stop in front of an ice-cream shop, contemplating one or two scoops, sprinkles or none, when I see a van in the window's reflection. It whips onto the sidewalk and comes to a screeching halt. The vehicle's suspension is still rocking when I turn around—a big mistake, I realize, when I spot Corbin.

Our eyes meet, and his lips curl up into a smug smile. He points in my direction, shouting orders to the crew, who then throw open the back doors and grab their equipment.

How did they find me? Did they plant a tracking device in my bag?

I don't give them the chance to get a shot. I turn on my heel and weave through people, shoving bags aside as I go. I'm small and quick, but the thing about film crews is that everyone makes way for them. In California they carry authority, like cops and firefighters. You don't mess with Hollywood.

While I struggle to make it back up the street, the crowd parts for them. They'll catch up in no time. I clench my fists, wanting to take swings at people so they'll back off.

At the next break in stores, I dart down the alley. Here I'm able to speed up, leaping over trash and puddles of… something that can't be water. The crew's stumbling footfalls echo behind me, right on my Wonder Woman tail.

I break through the other side, onto a quieter street. But there's traffic here. Traffic means stoplights, and the one up ahead is red. I'll have to stop for the crosswalk to turn, unless I want to be road pizza. They're closing in on me.

At the last second, I slip under a striped awning and into a shop. The bell rings. I slow down and step casually through, giving a cursory wave to the checkout counter. I beeline it for a display of boxes at the back and squat behind it just as Corbin and his minions tear by the front window.

I keep hidden until their shouting dies down. I even wait a few minutes until I'm sure they're not loitering on the sidewalk.

Once again, I wonder how they found me so easily. I glance at my phone, at my last call. There is only one way they could track me down in this huge city. Mom must have ratted me out. I called her so she wouldn't worry about me not being home from school yet, and she betrayed me.

"Can I help you look for something?"

From the floor, I glance up at the salesperson. He's a young guy in a Superman T-shirt, probably around my age, with black bed-head hair and the darkest, fullest eyelashes I've ever seen. It's like an artist smudged a charcoal pencil around his sparkly blue eyes. Light blue, like a winter's sky. A startling contrast to his dark hair.

"Umm. Just looking, thanks," I say.

He gestures to the display in front of me. "In the market for a snake?"

At the mention of a snake, I stumble back and fall on my butt. I stare at the pyramid of boxes and the picture of a tool on the front of them. I blink. "Oh," I say. "A toilet snake."

The guy chuckles. "Yes, but no less scary than the real thing, especially once they've been used."

Sliding my sunglasses on top of my head, I scan the

walls around me. The shelves are lined with rows of toilet paper, drain cleaner, pipes, tubes, plugs, and chains. Plungers stand at attention, faucets glisten on display next to toilet flapper thingies and scrub brushes. It's everything I want to avoid—right in my face.

"A bathroom store? God, no matter how far I run my life seems to follow me like a bad smell." I don't expect the clerk to understand what I'm talking about, but he pulls a package off the shelf behind me.

"A bad smell? We've got something for that, too." He holds up an air freshener.

I'm not sure whether to be annoyed or to laugh, but when he flashes me a grin, I know he's just joking. He holds out a hand to me. I take it, and he helps me to my feet.

I notice how cramped it is between the shower heads and the toilet lids. I'm close enough to smell him. He smells good. Not like Lennox-good, but still good. Fresh, like lemon and pepper, only it doesn't make me want to sneeze. And I don't think that's the air freshener.

I wonder if I should be worried that I'm smelling so many guys in one day, like some horny Chihuahua or something. It can't be normal. It's not like *Teen Vogue* has scratch and sniff centerfolds or anything. Maybe that should be a thing—Eau de Boy Band.

I feel a little awkward standing so close to him. I move to the front window and peek between the sale ads taped to the inside of it. Corbin and the crew are still out there. They hesitate at the next intersection, only a few shops away, looking up and down both streets in search of me.

The boy sidles up next to me. "Friends of yours?"

I inhale deeply, wondering if that's cologne or aftershave. A hot flush crawls its ugly way up my cheeks.

"No," I say. "Definitely not."

He raises his eyebrows in question, but I shake my head. "Long story." And I'm not quite ready to relive my humiliation.

"Well, it looks like you'll have to hang out here for a bit until your friends leave."

His mouth is nice, too, and when he smiles at me his cheeks wrinkle up like he's totally happy to be talking to me. He's cute. Definitely, way cute. Sort of different than Lennox, who is like, *Bam! Hot!*

This guy reminds me of when I boil a pot of water for hot chocolate, you know, the kind with mini marshmallows. One minute the water is still, but with each passing second it warms until it's bubbling and churning. And steamy.

"My name's Kevin."

"Adrianna."

He smiles and returns to his counter. As I take a moment to glance around, I realize I didn't unwittingly stumble into a bathroom store, but a hardware store.

Rustling noises draw my attention down an aisle where a guy in a denim apron is restocking work gloves on the shelf. The man sees me and waves. I wave back, like I totally belong in a hardware store, and continue to look around.

But my attention is drawn right to Kevin. He's got a book open in front of him on the counter, and it looks like he's doodling something. I catch him glancing up at me a couple of times before turning back to the page.

"What are you doing?" I ask.

He shrugs, closing the book before I have a chance to see. "Killing time. You're the first customer in about two hours."

"I'm not really a customer."

"No? I thought you mentioned something about

needing a bathroom store in your life." Again with the cheek wrinkles. Oh, so very steamy.

I snort, but before I can answer, the man in the apron cuts in like he's been eavesdropping.

"Looking for bathroom accessories?" His eyes light up behind his glasses. "Maybe I can interest you in a new soap dispenser. It's pink." He gestures to the display on the table next to him. "Oh, and there's a matching makeup organizer and mirror. And see? There's a light to help you apply your makeup." He flicks on the light and I wince as it blinds me.

"Uncle Gerald, she doesn't want the mirror," Kevin says.

"Why not? It's a good quality mirror. Maybe not a name brand like Bottom, but it's still good. Here, give it a try." He brushes away the layer of dust on it and shoves it into my hands.

"Bottom?" I take it numbly. My mouth goes dry, but I try to act casual. "As in Bottom's Bathrooms and Accessories?"

"You know it?"

"Not really," I lie. The last thing I want to talk about is my dad's business. I focus intently on the mirror in my hands. "I just heard that they're putting in a store near here."

Kevin's uncle huffs. "It's going to ruin us. *Ruin* us. A big-box store like that? How am I supposed to compete with that?" he asks Kevin and me, like we should know. "I can't carry that kind of volume. And rumor has it they're thinking of putting in a second one somewhere in the city."

I shrink in on myself like his company's ruin is my fault. I suddenly find the mirror much more interesting, like I'm really considering buying it. "Wow, this is really pink." I flick on the light. "And so bright."

"Just ignore him," Kevin says. "He's been obsessed about toilet stuff ever since the new store was announced."

His uncle pushes his glasses up his nose, like all the agitation is shaking them off his face. "I'll tell you what belongs in a toilet. That cheap Bottom crap."

Kevin snorts. "You're just upset because you can't get the contract to carry their products."

"What do I need to carry that junk for when I've got good quality merchandise like this?" He takes the mirror from me and raps on the plastic. The plastic cracks under his knuckles and he frowns. "Hmmm. This one appears to be defective. I'll get you another one from the back," he tells me, and disappears.

"Err, thanks."

I glance out the window again, searching for signs of Corbin. As much as I don't want that mirror, I'm not ready to risk leaving my sanctuary. I pull away from the window and begin to browse, staying within checking-out distance of Kevin. But it doesn't matter, because he slowly follows me, tidying up the tool section as he goes.

I hear voices coming from the other end of the store. I glance through the half-open door to a back room where two guys and a girl sit at a folding table. Pointy ears stick up through the girl's short black hair. The smaller boy hovers over his chair awkwardly, like he's leaning on one butt cheek. After a moment, I see that a sword is attached to his back, preventing him from sitting upright.

I stare too long, and they notice me watching them. The bigger boy raises a black-gloved hand, and I wave back. He's wearing black shorts and a black hooded shirt. I see an eye mask on the table. If he pulled up his hood, he'd look like an out-of-shape ninja.

I turn to Kevin in a whisper. "It's only September.

Isn't it a little early for Halloween? Why are they dressed like that?"

"Oh, they just came in to make a few adjustments to their costumes for this weekend. My uncle lets them use the stock room and our extra tools sometimes because they buy their materials from here."

"Materials? What's happening this weekend?"

"A game."

I glance at him, wondering why he's being so vague. "What kind of game?"

"It's called live action role playing. Larping, for short."

"I think I've heard of that. You dress up and fight battles and stuff, right?"

"Yeah. We do it on the weekends." He rubs the back of his neck like he's a little embarrassed to admit he does it too. The Superman shirt was a dead giveaway he's a fellow nerd, but larping sounds *über*-geeky. Then again, who am I to judge? I'm Bowl Buddy Bottom.

"It's more fun than it sounds," he says quickly. "There are rules and goals. Sometimes we give prizes to the winners."

I check out the girl again, with her pixie-like hair and pointy ears. She must play some kind of elf or fairy. She's wearing a big gold costume necklace over a pretty blue top and a quiver of arrows on her back.

Pretending to be someone else? Considering my life at the moment, that wouldn't be such a bad idea. "Sounds cool."

He seems to be waiting for me to laugh, but when I don't, he starts to tidy up again. Well, he's mostly picking up things that are already organized and putting them back in the same place, like he's looking for an excuse to hang around me in this part of the store.

And since I kind of want him to, I say, "So what were you drawing before?"

"Comic book stuff. Mostly superheroes, Marvel, that kind of thing."

"You're obviously a Superman fan," I say, pointing to his shirt. "So you must like DC, too."

His thick eyebrows arch in surprise, like he didn't expect me to have mad geek game. I grin inwardly, feeling very cool in my uncoolness right now. No acting necessary.

After a moment, he recovers. "Uh, yeah," he says. "Both franchises have their strengths. I'm a big fan of Deadpool, too, actually. It's great writing. You know, breaking the fourth wall and everything." His ears turn pink, like he's afraid he crossed some kind of geek line, and he looks away.

If only he knew who he's talking to. "Don't worry. I'm a comic fan, too."

Kevin keeps his gaze focused on the welding masks in front of him and bites back a smile. "Yeah, I know." It still looks like he's embarrassed, but I can't figure out why.

I smile, unsure of what he means. Thanks to my stylist, I have none of my usual geeky attire on to give my true self away. How can he know? Was it the DC comment?

Then he turns toward me and I see that his embarrassment is directed at me. His eyebrows crease, like it pains him to say what comes next. "I'm guessing you like Wonder Woman."

I think my heart just stopped. "Why would you say that?" It barely comes out a whisper.

"You know, because she's kind of on your, umm"—his eyes flick down then dart back up to the ceiling—"underwear."

Oh my God. He knows. He knows about my skirt malfunction. I can't look him in the eye anymore as my mortifying day comes rushing back to me. Was he there?

Is he a student from Beverly Hills High?

I want to grab one of those welding masks and hide behind it for the rest of my life. I turn away, but Kevin grabs my arm.

"Wait, I'm sorry," he says. "It's not a big deal. Wonder Woman's cool."

But I don't respond. I'm too busy wishing I could find a hole to crawl into and die.

The bell on the door rings, announcing a newcomer. I see a microphone boom and a tripod struggle through the door.

The film crew has found me.

Chapter Four

Hide and Go Geek

I'm trapped. Corbin pushes his way into the small hardware store, telling the crew to hurry up. I have to hand it to him. He's persistent.

I can't let Corbin see me. Who knows what I'll do. I might kick him in the junk. Or smash the camera. Or worse… I might just break down and cry right here in the store. In front of Kevin.

Before Corbin sees me, I drop to the ground. His footsteps scuff hesitantly into the shop like he's looking around. To stay hidden, I have to crawl on hands and knees to the other side of a display table, circling Kevin's legs like an oversized cat.

Even though I can feel his eyes on me, I swallow my pride and focus on the checkered linoleum. I'm practically curled up in a ball behind his legs, but there's nowhere else to go in the aisle, since it's so jam-packed with merchandise. There's nowhere to hide. I'm doomed.

Heavy footsteps thump on the linoleum close by. "Hello." It's Corbin.

"Hello," Kevin says. "Can I help you?"

"We're looking for a girl. About yay big. Flaming red, curly hair. Can't miss her."

Kevin sucks on his teeth and pauses for a moment. "Sounds kind of familiar. I think I might have seen her, but she took off."

Corbin swears. He obviously turns to talk to the crew, because I only hear mumbling for a minute.

Go away. Go away. Go away.

In the silence, the larpers' voices drift from the back room. My muscles stiffen as I wait for Corbin's response. There's a long pause.

"Do you mind if I have a look around anyway?" Corbin asks.

It's obvious he doesn't trust Kevin. I press my forehead against the cool floor. If he goes to the back, he'll pass right by me.

Kevin says, "Not at all. Go ahead. Check out the clearance items while you're back there." As he's talking, he steps closer to the table. Very casually, he brings one foot up, lifting the curtain that hides the underside of the display table.

A few storage boxes are crammed underneath, but there's just enough room for me to wedge myself between them.

As I hear Corbin's approach, I slip under. Kevin drops the curtain behind me. I twist and turn my body until it fits and I can lie down amongst the dust bunnies. I cringe. Perfect. It just gets better and better. I hold my breath, hoping I won't sneeze.

The crew shuffles around the store, probably to check out the larpers in the back.

Kevin's voice comes through the curtain. "Sorry. I figured if I told him 'no' it would seem suspicious."

"Thanks," I say.

Muffled voices filter up from the back. Corbin must be talking to Kevin's uncle. The voices become clearer as they wander out onto the floor.

"...was a girl up here," his uncle is saying. "She was just..." He pauses. "Well, that's odd. I didn't hear her leave."

"Yeah, that girl left in kind of a hurry," Kevin says. "Said she was running late to meet someone."

"Did she say where?" Corbin asks.

"No. Sorry."

Corbin swears before thanking him. The bell dings as they rush out, presumably to raid more stores in search of their princess.

I sigh with relief. My body turns to Jell-O, and I sprawl out among the stored paint cans and Slap Chops. But before I reveal myself, Kevin's uncle laughs.

"Do you have any idea who that girl was, Kevin? She's a Bottom. A *Bottom*," he says, like Kevin hadn't heard my stupid name the first time.

I freeze, unsure if I should come out or stay put.

"She's the daughter of the Bowl Buddy inventor. Imagine! In our store. Do you think she was here to spy on us? You know, size up the competition?"

"No offense, but I don't think we're any competition for them, Uncle Gerald."

"You're right." He groans. "And I called Bottom products crap in front of her. Way to suck up to the family, Gerald. I'll never get a contract now. I don't *really* think their stuff is crap."

"I know," Kevin says patiently.

"Well, I'm going to call your aunt. I just can't believe it. What are the chances?" His voice fades as he heads into the back again.

Kevin's feet scuffle as he kneels down in front of the gap in the curtain. He lifts the material and peeks under. "It's safe to come out."

"No it's not." I tug the curtain back down between us. I don't want to look him in the eye. The fact that he knew about my Wonder Woman underwear was bad enough. But Corbin showing up was the icing on my bad-day cake. "I think I'll stay under here if that's all right with you."

He laughs. "Okay. But you might get hungry eventually."

"Pizza delivery," I say. I know I'm sulking, but I think I deserve to right now.

I just can't escape my embarrassing life. Even when I thought I could pass as normal for half a second, it turns out Kevin knew all about my mishap at school.

"You'll get bored," he says.

I tap a stack of catalogs digging into my rib cage. "I've got reading material."

"You'll eventually have to use the bathroom."

"Got that covered, too." I pick up a roll of packaged toilet paper.

He snorts. "Sounds like you've got it all figured out. Except for one thing."

I lift the curtain just enough to peer out at him. He's sitting cross-legged, chin resting on his fist.

"What's that?"

"We close at eight. So you've only got about three hours."

Groaning, I accept my fate and crawl out. I brush the dust off my new clothes, and he picks a particularly big dust bunny—more like a jackrabbit—from my hair.

"That's some interesting hair you've got," he says, picking out another piece.

"It's naturally curly," I say, because no one ever believes

me. It looks like an eighties perm gone wrong.

"I was referring to the color."

"Maybe not for long," I say. "My stylist wants to dye it blonde and straighten it." A new pink mirror is lying on the table. His uncle must have grabbed it from the back. I pick it up and check to make sure there are no more dust bunnies—something tells me the store doesn't move that much product.

"Your stylist? Let me guess. Part of the long story?" He nods toward the street, where the camera crew just exited.

"Yeah."

I'm finally able to look him in the eye again. The flirty smile is gone and he's serious now. "For what it's worth, I like it the way it is. And I also like Wonder Woman."

Heat crawls up my neck, and I struggle not to look away again. "Well. Did you know that because I'm a redhead I'm more likely to die?"

He raises an eyebrow.

"It's true. Redheads are born missing a gene or something that makes blood clot, which means that we're more likely to bleed to death than other people."

"I'll have to keep you away from sharp objects." He ruffles his dark hair and it sticks up like an anime character. "Look. I'm sorry about the Wonder Woman...underwear... thing. That must have really sucked."

I cringe at the reminder. "How do you know about that, anyway?"

"I, well..." He hesitates. "I'm in your biology lab."

"Oh my God. You were there when it happened?"

His ears are pink again. "Actually, I sit in the seat directly behind you."

I plant my face in my hands to muffle my cry. "No. No. No."

"Oh, come on. It wasn't that bad." He pulls my hands away. "Not really."

I glare at him.

"Okay, so it was sort of bad. But people will forget about it. Eventually."

Then he doesn't know it was all caught on camera. He wasn't part of the flock of sheep that followed Harper to my locker.

Suddenly, I want to tell him about the show and my whole messed up, embarrassing life, but so far he doesn't think I'm a horrific freak, cartoon underwear and everything, and I want to keep it that way. After everything that's happened today, I still might have made a friend. A real live friend.

I buy the mirror because I feel kind of bad for his uncle, with our family business ruining his and all.

"Well, thanks for the refuge," I say. "I should get going." Before I screw something up.

"Sure. If you ever need a hiding place, you know where to come."

When I open the door and the bell rings, he calls out.

"Hey, wait!" He rips a piece of paper off a corkboard behind the counter and hands it to me. "This is the info for our larping group. You should try it. You know, if you're interested." He shoves his hands into his jeans pockets. His flirty confidence is gone and his self-consciousness is kind of endearing. "We do it every weekend. It might take your mind off things."

I read the flyer. *Come join us in the realm of Asdor*. I smile up at him. "I just might."

"In the meantime, Red, stay away from pointy things. And moving cars. And unusually large slivers," he calls out as I exit onto the sidewalk.

I salute obediently in response to his orders and wave good-bye. As I trudge home to meet my fate, since Corbin will likely be waiting for me, the idea of pretending to be someone else entirely, even for a day, seems like the perfect hiding spot.

Chapter Five

Andy 2.0

Dad pulls his Aston up in front of the school, slow as a funeral procession. It might as well be, since any potential social life I might have had has died a horrific, gruesome death.

The production van parks nearby, and the crew unloads their equipment while Corbin lights up a cigarette and watches. Whatever. There's no point in hiding it anymore. Besides, if the crew gets enough footage of the teasing I'm about to endure, I can use it as evidence to support my campaign to be homeschooled.

I turn to Dad and sigh, maybe a bit overdramatically. "At least they can't actually step into the school." There were some concerned parents who called the principal after the underwear fiasco. Now Corbin and his crew have been banished.

"Don't you worry about that," Dad says. "They can film around the premises but can't enter the building. I've made it clear that you're my daughter, not their comedic relief for the show."

"Ummm, thanks?"

He tightens his tie. He means business when he does that. I think that's a trick he learned from reading one of his confidence books, because my dad never means business.

"Besides," he says. "Corbin promised to show me the final cut of the first episode for approval. I'll make sure they *butt out* of my princess's life."

I roll my eyes. That must be his hundredth joke today. "Thanks, Dad. But I don't think you're the best judge of what's embarrassing."

He grins. "Don't worry. Mom will be there, too."

That's a bit of a relief. While she wants the show to be successful, she certainly doesn't want it to be at our expense. When I told her that the crew had chased me all over Beverly Hills, she called Corbin and canceled filming for the rest of the evening. When he said, "You can't do that. Those aren't the terms of the contract," she just snorted and hung up the phone. Go, Mom!

But still, she says I'm overreacting about the show in general. Dad thinks this is all "character building." I say we move to Alaska, to a town with no cable or toilets, and never speak of this again.

I glance at the school doors, unable to bring myself to step out of the safety of the car.

"Look on the bright side, kiddo," Dad says. "Things can only get better from here."

I recline my seat to hide from students passing by, on their way to check out the film crew. "That's what happens when you hit rock bottom." I cringe as I realize my poor choice of words.

Dad obviously caught it, too, because he snorts but tries to hide it with a throat clearing. "Oh, it's not that bad. You're a rich kid going to a good school and you're on national television."

"Rich kids have cars."

He ignores the jab. "It could be worse."

"How?"

"You could be a starving child in Ethiopia."

I groan. How can I argue with that? Nothing trumps the Starving Child in Ethiopia card. So I take a steadying breath, say good-bye, and step out of the Aston.

Next to the crew's van, Hugh hoists the camera onto his shoulder and takes a panorama of the school, ending on me walking toward it. I freeze, unsure if I'm supposed to wait for instructions.

Corbin waves me on. "Avoid looking at the camera. Pretend we're not even here."

"Yeah, right," I mutter. "Like that's even possible."

So far, the other students are focused on the film crew. They wave and joke around. Three guys break out into a fake fight to get some airtime, while a couple of girls on the steps tug down their tops an inch or two to show some cleavage. I take the opportunity to slip into the school unnoticed, but I'm only halfway up the stairs before eyes start following me.

It's a quiet sort of staring, like when you walk into a room full of people who, moments before, were talking about you. Or maybe that only happens to me. But this morning I made sure not to give them anything to talk about, besides the obvious entourage shadowing me to my first class. I initiated a no-skirt policy with my stylist, refused the inch-thick makeup, and I even wrote my name on every notebook I have so I won't pick up the wrong one again.

That doesn't stop the students from staring, though. I

feel like an alien that just landed on another planet and they're trying to decide if it's safe to make first contact.

I try to ignore it all. Pretend that nothing is wrong. Who's Wonder Woman? It's any other day, and I'm just a cool new student going to find my cool new friends. If I act like it's true, then eventually it might become true, right? At least that's what Mom's self-help books always say.

My eyes stay straight ahead, and I resist the urge to sprint through the doors and get lost in the endless maze of halls and stairs. When I reach for the door handle, that's when it starts.

"Hey, Wonder Woman!" a guy calls out from behind me. "Where's your Lasso of Truth?"

I spin to face him, but there are too many people staring, leering, and snickering to tell who said it.

"Go back to the Amazons!" a girl sitting on the steps yells, even though I'm only five feet away and can hear her just fine. But now so can everyone in the vicinity, lounging on the grass, lingering in the parking lot.

More eyes turn to me.

A guy in a letterman jacket next to her cups a hand around his mouth and makes a call like, "La-la-la-la-la-la-la-la-la-la-la!" He guffaws before he's whacked in the head with someone's messenger bag as they climb the stairs toward me. "Ouch!" He rubs his head and scowls at the student. "What's your problem?"

It's Kevin.

"Oops, sorry, man. I didn't see you there." Kevin holds up his hands with an apologetic look. "And that's Xena the Warrior Princess who calls like that, by the way. If you're going to make fun of someone, get your references right. Or you just look stupid."

The guy flips Kevin the bird. "Nerd alert!"

But people are chuckling at the guy in the letterman jacket now, so he shuts up and turns to the girl next to him. "Can you believe that guy?"

People are still staring at me, and I hear whispers of "Wonder Woman" drift throughout the grassy field in front of the school, but I don't really notice them much anymore because Kevin's smiling at me. He's wearing a Boba Fett T-shirt and his hair looks like he just survived a tornado, but in a good way, like how some guys try really hard to look like they didn't try at all. I suspect he's not one of those guys, but I secretly hope he was trying in case he'd see me at school.

That morning when I was with the stylist, Suzzy—with two zees, not one—I made sure she didn't straighten or subdue my hair at all. Since Kevin said he liked my natural hair, I asked her to emphasize its curliness. I even wore green so it would complement the color. After what happened to the skirt she insisted I wear yesterday, she was more than willing to cater to my requests. Both with my hair and the pants. But I gave in on a pair of sequined kitten heels.

"Hey," Kevin says.

"Hey." Because I can't think of anything original to say. "Thanks."

"Just ignore the peanut gallery." He nods to the students making fun of me—which is everyone.

He holds the door of the school open for me, and I glance over my shoulder to catch Corbin's sour look. I flash him a wide grin as I enter, and he's forced to stay put.

"How's the mirror working out for you?" Kevin asks.

"Best mirror ever," I say, heading in the general direction of my locker. I think. "It's so reflect-y."

"As good as a Bottom's Bathrooms and Accessories

mirror?" he teases. "I shouldn't even be talking to you, you know. You're the enemy." He ducks his head, whispering behind his hand like we'll be overheard. "I hear you guys are sending spies into our store."

"If we are, I couldn't tell you. Or I'd have to kill you." I eyeball him. "You're not spying on me right now, are you?"

"And if I am?"

"Maybe I'm feeding you false information."

He grins. "As in you don't actually like the mirror?"

"Exactly. And my name isn't really Adrianna," I say in my best Russian spy accent. "It's Boris."

Kevin breaks character, laughing. "And here I thought I wasn't attracted to men."

I trip over an invisible bump in the floor, replaying the last five seconds in my head, just to make sure I heard right. Kevin finds me attractive?

I'm not sure how to respond, so I just laugh, like I get that kind of thing every day (not!), and point down the next hall on our left. "I think my locker is this way."

"I'll walk with you."

"Thanks. I'm afraid I'll get lost in this place without a guide."

"This school is pretty intimidating at first." He cuts the next corner a little and his shoulder rubs against mine.

I feel tingles down my arm and I slow down just a little, umm-ing like I'm not quite sure if this is the right way. I want to draw out the moment, to see if he's walking so close by accident or on purpose. And also because I like the feeling of his arm against mine. When he doesn't give me any more space, I know it's on purpose.

The conversation kind of dies off, and I keep thinking about his comment, to make sure I understood it right. But what else could he have been saying? It's not like he actually *is* attracted to male Russian spies.

Maybe I should say something back. I mean, he *is* attractive. But it would sound stupid now.

By some miracle, we stumble upon my locker.

"Well, this is me," I say.

"I'll see you around," he says, backing away. "And try to avoid another striptease today. That's so been done to death already."

I laugh. "I'll try."

As I watch him walk away, I realize it's less than twenty-four hours since the incident, and Kevin already has me laughing over it.

Too soon he's out of sight, and I fish the books for my next class out of my locker.

"Adrianna!" It's a girl's voice.

When I turn around, I see Harper headed this way, perfect blonde locks bouncing like some shampoo commercial.

I get flashbacks of her grabbing her notebook back the day before when I was using it as a butt shield, tearing away my last defense. I back up until my butt hits my locker, subconsciously protecting it.

She doesn't seem to notice. Instead, she smiles like she did when we sat together in biology, like nothing happened, like I didn't moon the whole school—I wish—and hands me a notebook.

"Here's your biology book," she says. "I finished copying down the notes you missed. I feel really bad about what happened yesterday. I had no idea that's why you ran out. I didn't see it in class."

Hesitantly, I take the book from her. "Thanks," I say. I can't tell if she's being sincere. She *was* sitting next to me in biology, after all. Maybe she really didn't see. Kevin was the one who got the full shine from my moon.

"That must have been terrible." She frowns. "But don't worry. I heard there was a freshman who threw up during gym class yesterday. It got all over the volleyball nets." She grins like this is the best news ever. "And there was a senior who just got his license and drove his car into the principal's Suburban last week. There's always something. So don't worry. You'll be old news in no time."

"I usually am," I say with a hint of sarcasm. "But I think it's going to be hard to live down the underwear thing."

"It'll be fine. I promise. People just need to get to know more about you than what kind of underwear you wear."

I open my mouth to tell her that I own more than just Wonder Woman underwear, but before I can, she grabs my hand.

"Come on," she says. "I'll introduce you to some friends."

Chapter Six

Heartbroken Harper

Since arriving at school this morning, I've been shying away from funny looks and hearing people whisper "Wonder Woman" everywhere I go—or at least I imagine I do—but maybe that's just my paranoia. But now that I'm escorted by Harper, I'm suddenly swept through the school like Alice through the looking glass, into another world where people aren't staring at me like I'm a freak. They glance our way, but this time it's with curiosity, not total disdain. Some people even smile and say hi. I'm certain a few of them are the same ones who made fun of me earlier.

When the bell rings, Harper holds out her hand and asks for my schedule. I hand it over and she compares it with hers.

"Hey, we have Art together next. I didn't notice you in my class yesterday."

"I don't think anyone noticed me before *the incident*."

She rolls her eyes and smiles. "Well, soon enough they'll remember you because you're a star. Not for your underwear."

When she puts it like that, I'm not sure it's any better.

I can tell she's hinting about the cameras. That she wants me to tell her about the show. I wonder if that's why she's being so nice to me. Is she just a fame leech? Not that I think I'm famous or anything. But I hope that's not the case, so I keep my mouth shut instead and follow her to Art.

Harper tows me through the halls between classes, introducing me to all her friends; she's got a lot of them. Her besties seem to be Star, Amber, Prissy, and Mercedes—or SPAM as I like to call them, since I can't remember which ones are which. They seem friendly, and they don't even mention the underwear thing.

By lunchtime, I have more friends than I've ever had in all the years of my life combined. And it's the first time since I can remember that I'm not sitting alone in the cafeteria. I'm chatting with Harper when her ex, Lennox, sits across from me, and it's not even to speak to Harper. He's looking at me. *Me.*

"Hey," he says.

My mouth has gone dry and my "Hey" comes out all breathy.

"What happened to you yesterday must have sucked," he says.

"Obviously," Harper snaps at him. "So don't bring it up."

He holds up his hands to ward off her sudden attitude. I wonder how long they dated. Or more importantly, if she still has feelings for him.

"I'm just saying. It was crazy bad timing," he says, popping a tater tot into his mouth. "Like something from a movie."

"Yeah," I say. "An R-rated one."

He laughs, deep and kind of guffaw-sounding. Maybe a chortle. "Is that why those cameras were following you?

Are you in some kind of movie or documentary?"

Harper's head swivels to me, also interested in the answer. But I like that she didn't ask me first.

"It's for a reality TV show," I say.

"Really?" He plants his elbows on the table and leans in closer to talk, kind of like he did to Harper in class the day before. Right before she snapped at him. "That's so cool. What's it about?"

They're both staring at me like there's no one else in the room. Like what I have to say is totally important. I find I don't quite mind the attention as much when it's not because people are making fun of me.

I quickly tell them about *Bathroom Barons* and the whole Porcelain Princess thing. I cringe as I say it, but they don't look at me as though I'm a social charity case. In fact, Harper looks at me like she's kind of jealous. Only yesterday, I thought that was impossible.

"That's so cool," Lennox repeats. "You must be really interesting if they want to film you."

He hasn't stopped looking at me since he sat down. I shrug, a little self-conscious. "Not really. It's mostly to follow my parents as their business grows and to show how different our lives are now."

"Did you want something?" Harper asks Lennox a little coolly. "Because Adrianna and I were talking."

"Fine. I just thought I'd be nice and say hi." He gets up and grabs his lunch tray to move. "See you later," he says to me, like he doesn't mean "see you later" but "*see you later*."

Harper glares at his retreating back, but her stare lingers even after he finds a seat at another table.

I wave a hand in front of her face. "Hello. Earth to Harper."

She starts, like she didn't even realize she was staring.

"So, do you still like your ex, or something?" I ask.

Harper scoffs. "What? As if. I broke up with him." Her eyes flick back over to his table and her plump Scarlett Johansson mouth turns down. "Well, nobody really broke up with anybody, actually."

"What do you mean?"

"We sort of just lost touch over the summer. We got busy. He was at football camp and I was in Europe with my parents," she sums up, like everyone vacations in Europe. "When we both got back to town we were just sort of not talking anymore. School started last week and it's like nothing happened between us."

"Why didn't you just ask him what was up?"

Her nose wrinkles. "I guess I was afraid of getting dumped. Officially, I mean. I figured if he wanted to be together, he would have said something. Right?" She looks kind of bummed out. Not the confident girl I'd expect someone as perfect as her to be.

I slide my tray closer to her and say, "Tots?" Because comfort food fixes everything. She nods and dips one in a blob of ketchup.

"But maybe he's thinking the same thing," I say. "Maybe he's still waiting for you to say something to him."

I can't help but notice her eyes turn all puppy-dog when she stares across the room at him, like she secretly hopes he'll turn around and return the look. But he's too busy guffawing at something his friend said.

"You still like him. Don't you?"

She looks like she wants to deny it, but her eyebrows kind of raise helplessly.

I remember the way Lennox was staring at me across the table and how he said "*See you later.*" For some reason, I feel guilty.

"Then tell him how you feel," I say.

Harper's eyes get big, and she waves her hands. "No way. If he's not interested then it's like getting rejected all over again, if that's what really happened. Like I can't take a hint or something. I'd feel pathetic."

"Then set it up so you spend more time together by accident or through friends. You can see how it goes without having to say anything at all. Maybe you'll find he feels the same way."

She thinks about this over a couple more tots and finally nods. "Maybe you're right. Thanks." She wipes her hands on a napkin. It makes me think that I've helped, since no more comfort tots are needed. "So what about you?" she says. "Find anyone you like yet?"

"Me? No." I almost laugh at the idea. I couldn't get a guy to talk to me at my last school, far less date me. Then I remember Kevin's comment that morning, and I wonder if maybe it's not so impossible.

I glance nervously at Harper. I only just met her. My plan was to avoid revealing things that can open me up to ridicule. Then again, she just shared big-deal news with me, so I wince and say, "I've never actually been on a date before."

"Are you serious?" Harper seems shocked, but there's no laughter in her voice, so I keep talking.

"I wasn't exactly what you would call super popular at my last school, because of the whole bathroom business." And the whole being a geek thing, but I decide not to add that for now; one incriminating thing at a time.

But she still doesn't laugh. Finally she asks, "Is there anyone you're interested in?"

Again, Kevin pops unwillingly into my brain. But we only just met the day before. And while I've been imagining our next meeting during every boring moment in my classes today—which was a lot of the time—I'm not ready to confess my crush until I'm convinced that he likes me, too.

I shake my head but smile inwardly like I have my own delicious secret. "I just got here. Too soon to tell."

Her lips purse as she thinks. "Well, maybe we can do something about that. And the popularity problem, too. You've already made one friend." She bats her eyelashes, in case I didn't know she meant her.

I smile, because I think she's right. And she's not just one of those friends you wave to in the hall, but one you want to see outside of school. I just hope it's me who made the friend and not the Porcelain Princess from *Bathroom Barons*.

"And I'll try to help with your Lennox problem, if I can," I say.

Maybe Mom was right—not that I'd ever tell her that. Maybe things *can* be different in Beverly Hills. Maybe this is my chance to turn things around. But in order to avoid the teasing, does that mean I need to keep the new clothes, the new makeup, the new me? Or can I just be myself?

Chapter Seven

Ruthless

The bell rings, and Harper and I head for biology class. We stop by my locker on the way, and I see Kevin talking with a couple of people nearby. I recognize the swordsman and Pixie Girl from his uncle's hardware store.

Kevin turns and notices me staring, so I wave. He waves back and pushes away from the locker, as if to come over and talk to me. It feels like someone sucked all the air out of the hallway, because I'm having a hard time breathing. And it looks like he is, too, because he's turning kind of red the closer he gets to me.

I take an automatic step forward, but Harper grabs my wrist.

"What are you doing?" she whispers.

"I know that guy. He's really nice. I'll introduce you."

She laughs, but in a "so not funny" way. "Oh, I know who he is. You can't talk to him. To any of them."

"What? Why not?"

Harper drags me away and up a nearby set of stairs. I glance over my shoulder as we climb. Kevin stops in the middle of the hall and watches me go. I try to give him a look, but Harper tugs me around the corner and up to the second floor.

When we've gone far enough, she stops in front of a water fountain and turns on me. "What are you thinking? Those guys are major freaks."

Like I was about five hours ago? I nearly laugh, but she's being totally serious.

"We're talking the mayors of Geeksville, the Capitol of Loser Land."

I don't point out that Geeksville would have only one mayor, not three. "What's so bad about Kevin and his friends?"

"Look, you're new here. So I'll explain it to you." She takes a deep breath like she's making a real effort to calm down. "Fraternizing with that group would be social suicide. And after yesterday, I don't think you can afford to be caught dead talking to them. As it is, you've got major damage control to do."

I shrug. "But he seems nice. And don't I need all the friends I can get if I want to do damage control?" I use her words, but it feels like we're talking about war, not high school.

"Nice isn't the issue here." She holds up her manicured hands. "Okay, I get it. He's cute. Got that boy-next-door feel. But if you cross that line"—she jabs a thumb down the stairs where we left Kevin—"I don't think I can save you. That girl I told you about, in gym? The barfer? I hear she's already transferred to a different school."

"That can't be true."

"This isn't Seattle. This is Beverly Hills. You've got to be ruthless to survive." She takes me by the shoulders and stares into my eyes like she's hypnotizing me. "Ruthless. Look, you want me to help you fit in? This is the best advice

I can offer you. Avoid that guy." She shrugs. "I'm just being honest."

The bell rings, and she nods like that settles it.

I started the day convinced I was at the bottom of the social totem pole. Even worse. I was the bug crawling beneath the ground in which the totem pole is buried.

Now, it seems like there's hope. The cameras are gone, and Harper is still being nice to me. I've met a ton of new people who wouldn't have given me the time of day if it wasn't for Harper. She took me under her popularity umbrella, to protect me from the crap storm that might have happened after my underwear incident. No one at my old school would have done that. Especially not someone as popular as Harper.

Again, a little voice in the back of my head, the one that has been teased by countless people like Harper, wonders why she's being so nice. Is it really because she wants to be friends with me? Or does it have something to do with *Bathroom Barons*? But that little voice is getting smaller and smaller as the day goes on, as I begin to realize that my "fake it till I make it" plan might actually work. I don't have to be Awkward Andy anymore.

New house, new clothes, new friends, new life. Andy 2.0. Things are looking up. Only to keep it all, I've got to be ruthless, according to Harper.

But apparently being ruthless means being Kevinless.

When we walk into biology, I head for my seat at the front. Despite Harper's warning, I smile at Kevin as I walk by his desk. But that's it.

I want to talk to him, but Harper's waving me over. If I did talk to Kevin, it would be like openly flouting her wise popularity advice. I don't want to seem ungrateful, but I also don't want Kevin to think I'm ignoring him. Which, maybe I kind of am, but not really.

Sliding onto my stool, I maintain strict focus on the board at the front, but I know he's right behind me. I want to turn around. To catch his eye. Harper could be wrong. Maybe no one cares if I talk to one of the mayors of Geeksville.

I can sense Kevin's presence behind me, and it takes all my willpower—like donut-resisting kind of willpower—to not turn around. I remember how badly I wanted to talk to him in the hall, but Harper said talking to Kevin would be social suicide, and I'm not feeling particularly socially-suicidal. Not since the underwear incident anyway.

Mr. Bigger waddles into the room and claps his stubby hands twice. It makes me think of the Clapper—you know, the doohickey that turns off lights when you clap, like if he claps we'll all shut up.

He looks over his glasses at me. "Welcome back, Miss Bottom. Do you have any more entertainment scheduled for us today?" he asks dryly.

Heat flashes across my face until I'm certain I look like an oversized cranberry. "No, sir," I say. "I prefer improv."

This gets a few laughs—even Mr. Bigger chuckles—and suddenly my day feels perfect. Like sprinkles-on-your-ice-cream perfect. Or finding Mom's stash of the expensive chocolate perfect. A complete one-eighty from yesterday. I coast through the rest of class on a high.

Finally, the last bell rings, and I'm gathering up my books when a piece of paper slides onto the desk in front of me. I look up just in time to see Kevin wink as he passes by. But I'm supposed to be ignoring him around Harper. Ruthless, I remind myself. Must be ruthless.

My mouth betrays me and twitches into a smile. Stupid mouth.

He hasn't yet realized I'm being a total cow and kind of ignoring him, which only makes him seem so much cooler. Before Harper can see me blush, I turn away and glance at the paper.

It's a sketch. A really good one, like it should be in a comic book. It's Wonder Woman eating a slice of pizza. I reach for it, but Harper snatches it first.

"What's this?" she asks.

"Nothing," I say. "Come on, give it back." I don't think she knows who it's from, or she wouldn't be drawing attention to it.

There's something very private about the sketch. It feels like a special joke between Kevin and me, and if she sees it, she won't understand. She'll make fun of it. She'll make fun of *him*.

"Is that a note?" Lennox asks, his scent wafting my way.

"Is it a *love* note?" Harper asks. "Who's it from?" She holds it out of my reach. Star, Prissy, and a few others gather around.

Mercedes saunters over—I'm starting to tell them apart. "Let's see," she says.

Star peers over Harper's shoulder. "What does it say?"

"Is it from Mayor Geek?" Mercedes asks. Apparently this is a common name for him. "I saw him drop it on your desk. You're the *Princess*. Like he has a chance with you."

I can feel Harper glance at me, and I remember her earlier warning, but she says nothing.

Before anyone can see, I lunge forward to grab it out of Harper's hand—and it tears into two parts.

"It doesn't matter," I say. And so no one will see it, I crumple my half into a ball.

When I turn to toss it into the garbage, Kevin is standing by the exit, looking straight at me. His eyes slip down to my hand, then the garbage can, and then back to my face.

His jaw tightens for a second. Turning on his Converse heels, he pushes his way out into the hall. I just stare at his back, knowing I can't go after him with everyone there, because then it's like saying it really does matter.

Harper snorts and drops the other ripped half on the floor. "Well at least he won't be stalking you anymore."

"He's not stalking me," I say. But no one hears, because everyone's already leaving the classroom.

Harper heads out after them, but whispers as she passes me. "Just go with it. I'm trying to save you here."

I bend down to pick up the other half of Kevin's drawing. It's Wonder Woman's thought bubble. Tugging on the edges, I straighten it out so I can read it.

It says, *Even Wonder Woman needs sustenance. How about Friday, Red?*

Oh no. He was asking me out. A real boy was asking *me* out. Maybe he is the mayor of Geeksville, but what Harper doesn't know is that if there are numerous mayors, well, then I'm one, too.

The good-day feeling is squished, like grasshopper meets highway. Now *that's* what I call ruthless.

Chapter Eight
Ice-Creamed

Corbin snaps his fingers at me, and I realize I'm staring out at all the Sunday shoppers on the street. The afternoon sun glares through the store window, reflecting off all the bling on display. I blink the dazzle from my eyes and look into the camera.

"Not including my first day, the first week of school was great," I say, although, that's not entirely true. Kevin hasn't spoken to me since I trashed his picture. Although, this one time when I said "hi" to him in the hall, he said "hi" back. Kind of like a reflex. But then he didn't seem happy about it.

Corbin stands to the right of the camera, gesturing for me to expand on my answer, so I say, "I've made a lot of friends. They came shopping with me today."

The other camera sweeps around the store where Harper and SPAM sift through sparse, overpriced racks. I'm not all that interested in checking out clothes. It's not like I need to be when I have a stylist and personal shopper.

Our trip to Rodeo Drive couldn't be more different than the first time I fled to the busy shopping hub. The reminder of my humiliating striptease doesn't sting quite as badly anymore. Actually, it makes me think of Kevin. If my skirt hadn't torn, and I hadn't come here, I might not have met him. But now the problem is that I can't stop thinking about him. Nor can I be seen talking to him at school.

Across the room, Harper holds up a sweater that looks like it was used as a cat bed. "What do you think?" she asks in mock seriousness.

I give her a thumbs-up from my interview station. It wouldn't matter if she did wear a cat bed. She would look hot wearing a kitty litter box.

When I first moved to Beverly Hills, I just wanted a clean slate. To make friends. In the end, it wasn't as hard as I expected, even after the Wonder Woman underwear incident. But what I didn't expect was that there would be so many rules. If I want to avoid the teasing, the relentless torment like I had to endure from bullies back in Seattle, I have to make the "right" kind of friends. It's like I have to choose between being friends with Harper and her entourage as "the Princess" and grabbing a pizza with Kevin.

Corbin doesn't seem as interested in my interview as he does getting shots of SPAM popping out of the fitting rooms dressed in increasingly sexier outfits. I wonder if the girls really came to hang out or if it was just to be on TV, because Prissy and Mercedes seem to talk to the camera more than they do me, and nobody even buys anything.

When I suggest we leave the store, Amber complains that she never got to try anything on for the cameras. Star doesn't seem to mind either way; she gets easily distracted by sparkly things in the windows we pass.

Harper points to a bright sign at the end of the street. "Let's get some ice cream."

"Definitely," I say. "I'm starved."

"But I'm not supposed to have ice cream," Star says. "My agent told me that I need to lose two more pounds before my audition next week."

Mercedes looks up from her phone and stops texting for half a second. "It's not ice cream. It's gelato."

"Oh. What's the difference?"

"It's made of gelatin," I say, because I really want ice cream. "It's basically fat free."

Harper giggles but doesn't call me on the lie.

Star's forehead wrinkles. "Well, then I guess it's okay."

As we go to enter, Corbin holds up a hand. "One second. Let us go in first, we'll get a shot of you guys entering from inside."

Corbin holds the door open, and Hugh carries the camera into the ice cream parlor. Through the window, I watch him set up the shot. We all wait awkwardly outside until Corbin gives us a thumbs-up. Finally, Star opens the door so we can go in. Yeah, because this feels totally natural.

When I step into the shop, though, I want to turn around and leave. My eyes lock across the room to the only people in the place, and my face falls.

Kevin's here.

And he's wearing a cape.

He's sitting at a corner table with several other larpers. Among them I recognize the three from the hardware store. Pixie Girl is wearing that pretty periwinkle tunic again. They must have just finished larping for the day.

I want to run, but I also can't help staring at their table, hoping Kevin will see me. He's seated on a long bench that runs the length of the shop, facing toward me. His eyes finally shift our way, and he scowls. I wonder if that look is just for me or for all of us.

He turns away to listen to his friend tell a story. At least he isn't whispering bad things about us. Then again, he doesn't seem like the type. SPAM, on the other hand, is the type.

Harper and the others come through the door behind me and immediately spot them.

Prissy gasps. "No way!"

"Look at them," Mercedes says. She holds out her phone and takes a photo. "I'm so posting that."

"It's like a geek convention exploded in here," Amber says way too loud, so all the larpers can hear.

Harper elbows me and widens her eyes meaningfully, like "see?" And I don't think she's referring to Kevin himself, but the others' reactions.

I get it. She's trying to protect me from teasing, just like she promised. That's why she told me to stay clear of Kevin. I just wish it didn't have to be like that.

Star spots them last. "Oh fun! Is it a costume party?" I glance at her, expecting sarcasm like the other girls, but she seems genuinely curious.

I stiffen at the awkward tension around us. I order ice cream just so I can turn my back to the room. The girls giggle behind me, and I know they're shooting judgy glances at the larping table.

The guy behind the counter hands me a bowl of chocolate chunk ice cream with raspberry purée and sprinkles. I stand by the door to wait for the others, anxious to go. Only, when they get their ice cream, we don't leave.

Even though there are seats on the opposite side of the small shop, Mercedes sits down right next to the table that Kevin and his friends are sitting at. She waves us over.

"Why don't we go?" I say. "We can window-shop while we eat."

"We've been walking all afternoon," Mercedes complains. "I'd rather stay here." She grins mischievously. I imagine that's just how the evil queen smiled when she gave Snow White the poison apple.

I don't want to stay, but Hugh zooms in on me and Corbin snaps his fingers and points to the table, telling me to sit down. Harper turns around and widens her eyes at me in a secret message, like if I make a big deal about Kevin, then the others will start to ask questions.

Star, Prissy, Amber, and Mercedes are quietly eating their ice cream, so I hope that's the end of their teasing. Maybe they really do just want to sit down. So I slide onto the bench next to Mercedes, the only seat left at our table. Right next to Kevin.

Harper eyes me across the table. I can feel her gaze shift between Kevin and me. I wonder what my expression looks like, because it doesn't feel very good on my face. The camera hovers closer, and I flinch away.

When I look back at Harper, she seems kind of thoughtful but doesn't say anything. What is she thinking? Would she make fun of me like the others if she knew I have a crush on Kevin?

Kevin doesn't look at me, and I can't look at him. We are very decidedly not looking at each other, and I wonder if he wants to as badly as I want to. It feels like a not-staring contest. Who can look away the longest?

All I want to do right now is tell him that I kept his drawing. That I fished it out of the garbage and took it home. That I smoothed out the wrinkles with Mom's iron and taped the two pieces together from the back, so it looks whole again, and pinned it up in my room. That for the past week it's been a daily reminder of him, of how badly I want to talk to him. And how I can't.

But I don't. I just sit there and listen to Harper and SPAM babble about the commercial for *Bathroom Barons* that aired on Friday night and answer their questions about the show. Corbin and the crew lurk in the corner of the parlor, as though waiting to pounce at any sign of drama. It has me on edge and my muscles stiffen.

Finally, the larpers get up to leave. They grab their foam weapons, arming themselves to brave the streets of Hollywood. When their backs are all turned, I slump in my seat with relief.

Mercedes reaches over and dips her spoon into my ice cream. I assume she just wants to try it, but then she winks at me. Turning in her chair to face the group, she holds her plastic spoon backward and flings it like a catapult at the larpers.

The airborne dessert soars across the room and lands on Pixie Girl's silky top. It rolls down her back, dripping onto her light beige tights.

I gasp and cover my mouth. A couple of the girls snicker.

"Oh, no," Pixie Girl says.

Kevin pauses in the doorway to wait for her. "What's wrong?"

She grabs a napkin from the counter and twists to rub at the stain on her tights, but it only makes it worse. Kevin sees the sticky raspberry puree, sees the chocolate, and knows it can't be anyone else's doing but mine because there are sprinkles, too. For the first time in days, he locks eyes with me.

Mercedes ducks her head and laughs, and my hands are still covering my mouth, so it looks like I'm laughing, too. I pull my hands away and mouth the words "I'm sorry," but Kevin already turned to help the girl clean off the mess. She's crying over her pretty costume, and he's being so nice, trying to make her feel better. And I feel terrible.

That's it.

I stand up, nearly knocking over the table. Amber's dessert lands on its side, along with half the condiments on the table.

"Hey," she says. "What's the deal?"

"Why did you do that?" I ask Mercedes. "What did that girl ever do to you?"

Mercedes snorts and looks at the other girls, like, *What's up with her*?

Star isn't paying attention to anyone. Amber's busy trying to save her spilled ice cream. Harper puckers her lips and turns away. Her obvious disapproval of Mercedes's bitchiness reminds me why I liked her from the start.

It occurs to me that, unlike some of the other girls, she hasn't said one bad thing about the larpers. I just wish she'd stand up and say something to defend them. Like I should have already.

"That was mean, Mercedes." Reaching over to the toppled napkin dispenser, I grab a handful of them. I rush over to Pixie Girl and Kevin.

The camera pans to follow my movement. I don't know why this is so interesting to them, but I wish they would leave. Apparently humiliating me isn't enough. Now they need to humiliate Kevin and his friends?

"I am so sorry," I say, because I am. And not just about today.

Pixie Girl doesn't respond. She only raises an eyebrow like she's suspicious of me. I wave the bundle of napkins like a white flag. She bites the inside of her cheek, trying to make up her mind about me. Finally, she turns around, so I can rub the stain on the back of her tunic.

"You know," I say, "I have some stain remover at home that might get this out."

Kevin stares down at me through those super thick eyelashes, this time with an ounce less scowl. I give him a hopeful grin.

"You could bring the shirt to school tomorrow," I tell him. "I could try to fix it. Or you guys could come over tonight," I say hopefully. Then I look down at my work, and my hope bubble bursts.

Amongst the chocolate, and the raspberry, and the half-melted sprinkle dye are giant streaks of blue.

"Oh-oh." I pull the napkins away and turn them over to find Amber's vibrant, incredibly staining blueberry jelly topping. It must have gotten on the napkins when everything fell over on the table.

Kevin grabs my wrist to look for himself. I can feel the anger in the touch, and I don't blame him. But it makes my insides shrivel up. The girl's mouth pops open when she turns to see it, too. Throwing her hands in the air, she grabs her longbow where she dropped it and shoves the shop door open. The bell rings violently.

Kevin drops my wrist. "Nice," he says with disgust. "Really funny."

He turns and stalks out after the girl. I'm still staring at the napkins in my hand when the bell stops ringing. Corbin snaps his fingers, using some kind of director sign language, and Hugh zooms in on my expression.

Kevin thinks I did it on purpose. He thinks I meant to make the stain worse. Like I was playing along with Mercedes's trick. I just made things so much worse.

Star gapes at me. "Now, *that* was really mean."

I chuck the napkins in the trash. "I didn't mean to."

Mercedes giggles behind her hand. "But that's what makes it so funny." I glare at her, and she presses her lips together. "I'm sorry. It's so not funny."

"No. It's not." I drop back into the booth and bang my head against the table. "He hates me."

Amber snorts. "Why do you care?"

Star looks genuinely curious as she licks ice cream off her spoon. Harper's regarding me with that thoughtful look again.

I want to say, "Because he seems cool." But I hesitate. They may not be nice to Kevin and his friends, but they're nice to me. All I wanted was to avoid getting bullied at my new school, to make friends. And I've found some. With the exception of Mercedes, of course. I don't really want to hang out with her again. But does that mean that I have to be the bully?

I've lived through Monday meatloaf thrown at me as I walk through the cafeteria, a pudding-filled locker, being targeted by soccer balls—all kinds of balls, really—during gym class. And I don't want it again.

So I swallow hard and say, "I dunno," and shrug. But inwardly, the meatloaf-target me is screaming, "What's wrong with you!?" Am I suddenly crossing over to the dark side? The side that thinks it's okay to tease people and cause them emotional grief for no good reason? Just to protect myself? The disgust in Kevin's voice still lingers in my ears, and I feel the same disgust in myself.

SPAM all share meaningful glances with one another and pull faces at my expense. Mercedes eyes me like my standing up for Kevin and his friend borders on treachery. I just keep my head down and play with my dessert.

I watch the girls eat their gelato. Mine doesn't taste

so good anymore. It tastes like evidence in a trial, like a murder weapon. I say I'm full and throw the rest away. Corbin seems to have gotten what he was looking for, because he tells the crew to pack up, and they leave.

I don't feel much like shopping anymore, either. But then Mercedes sees a costume store across the street and thinks it would be hilarious to check it out. The rest of the girls follow her in, and Harper grabs my hand, dragging me along. When I resist, she squeezes my hand. I meet her eyes and she gives me a strained smile, like she knows what happened in the ice cream shop upset me, but she wants to cheer me up at the same time.

As the other girls try on costumes, they giggle behind the changing room curtains. I don't want to join in because I know they're doing it to make fun of Kevin and the others. Well, at least Mercedes, Prissy, and Amber are. Then I see a costume kind of like Pixie Girl's. Wondering what I would look like as a larper, I grab my size from the rack and duck behind a curtain.

Enjoying geeky things like larping, being like Kevin, like my real self, means social suicide. It means ice cream catapults and paper balls to the head. And it only gets worse from there.

I left that all behind in Seattle. The teasing, the feeling of dread every day I went to school. Some days I would even fake being sick just so I didn't have to face it. There was no way I was going back to that.

Here in California, I have the chance to do things differently, to be liked. Not despite my dad's crazy inventions, but because of them. *Bathroom Barons* was why people first started to take note of me in Beverly Hills High.

So am I in a rush to return to my normal geeky ways

and throw away my newfound social sanctuary with Harper and SPAM? Not likely. But just because I'm suddenly hanging with the popular crowd doesn't mean I stop liking the things I always have. I don't stop being who I am. I just have to hide it from them.

I fasten the leather belt and cinch up my gauntlets before stepping out to meet the others. I stand in front of a mirror and assess the getup.

It's actually pretty good. You can tell it's made of quality material and the stitching is sturdy, but there are details that I would have changed, had I made it. It was thrown together for a quick sale. No extra artistry. No love. I imagine all the things I could create for larping, the different characters I could invent.

I YouTubed larping after I met Kevin. I even glanced at some rules and pictures of larpers. Knights, fairies, elves, and orcs. What would I be? After the ice cream shop, I feel like a troll, or maybe a wicked witch. Certainly not a princess.

Harper dances her way out of the changing room as Cleopatra, and Prissy and Mercedes stumble out as twin hobbits. Harper grabs her phone out of her purse and snaps a photo before either halfling has a chance to react.

"Hey," Prissy says. "I thought we were doing funny costumes, not sexy."

Mercedes dives for the phone, but Harper twirls out of reach and hits a button. "Too late. It's already posted. I'll make sure to tag you in it later, in case anyone from school misses it."

Harper takes a selfie of the two of us and posts it online, too. Just another reminder that nothing goes unnoticed. One wrong move and the whole school sees, whether I'm at school or not. There's no escaping it. Heck, thanks to

Bathroom Barons, the whole world will see.

There's a golden mask on display next to the mirror, a magical thing cut from metal, as intricate as the patterns on a butterfly's wings. Green-tipped feathers splay out from each side. They ruffle gently as I pick it up and place it on my face. The metal feels cool against my skin. The swirling design curls over my brow and across the bridge of my nose, hiding most of my face.

If it weren't for my beacon-red hair, no one would know who I am. And then it hits me. The mask. The stylist's blonde wig. I can sew my own larping costume. Different clothes. Different hair. Different me. Only I'll still be Andy underneath it all. Maybe it's not impossible to avoid being a social pariah at school, while still doing the things I like outside of it.

I take out my phone and dial Mom. It rings three times before she answers.

"Hey, Mom."

"Hey, princess. How is the shopping going? Find anything?"

This gives me the perfect opening. I sigh dramatically. "No. Not really. It's all the same old stuff, you know?"

"What do you mean? You're shopping in one of the best locations in the country."

"Yeah, but it's all the same fashion from store to store. I miss Seattle. I knew where to shop there. I knew all the original, one-of-a-kind stores."

"I know, dear. But we could always order any clothes you want online."

"Do you think, instead, maybe I could have a new sewing machine?" I ask. "Since we got rid of my old one before the move? Maybe I could start making my own clothes again."

"I think that's a great idea," she says. She sounds surprised, like she didn't think I'd ever give up on the my-life-sucks attitude. "Let me just talk to your father." And by "talk" it sounds like she means "tell."

"Thanks, Mom. That's great. I'll be home soon." I end the call and pick up the mask again. Maybe I can have my ice cream and eat it, too.

Chapter Nine
Sew Screwed

Mom cups her manicured hands over my eyes as she leads me down our hallway and into the room at the end.

"You're going to love this," she sings. "I've been working on it all week long while you were in school."

The camera crew follows us. Or at least, I can hear their shuffling feet behind us on the hardwood floor.

Mom steers me to the right. I stub a toe and bump an elbow. When I'm sufficiently bruised, she releases me and stands back, arms wide.

"Surprise!"

I blink a few times and the bright room comes into focus. Sitting on a shabby chic, antique-looking desk is a brand new sewing machine. Not just any sewing machine, but the Cadillac of sewing machines with an ergonomic foot pedal and a leather chair to park my butt. Above the desk is a pink corkboard with the words DREAM BOARD at the top to post notes and ideas.

I spin, taking in the whole room. A rainbow of multicolored spools are spread across an entire wall, ceiling-high shelves burst with bolts of designer fabric, and rows of decorative vases overflow with buttons. It's a sewer's heaven.

"What do you think?" Mom asks.

"It's amazing." I shake my head, my mind blown. "I just expected a sewing machine. And you did all this in only a week?"

"I just couldn't wait for you to have it. Now you've got a machine to sew, one to hem, and one to embroider." She lands a kiss on my forehead. "You've taken the move so well, and being filmed for *Bathroom Barons*. And I think it's great that you want to sew your own clothes again. You know your father and I will always support your interests."

I cringe guiltily. Of course I didn't tell her the real reason I wanted the sewing machine. I suppose, technically, I want to make my own clothes. They just aren't clothes I'll wear in public, unless medieval makes a comeback on the runways.

Eventually I can use my mom's gift to make school clothes, too—I never had a wardrobe malfunction with my own designs. But first things first. The sooner I make my costume, the sooner I can join Kevin and larp.

It's not like I can tell Mom about the larping. She would understand as much as Harper and SPAM would. Besides, if Corbin finds out that I'm planning on larping then he'll want to film it. If I'm going to avoid the cameras, to get to do the things I really want to do, to escape my public life, even just for a few hours, no one can know it's me. Not even Mom. After the last time Mom betrayed me, I have no doubt she'll tell Corbin. She's too wrapped up in the show, in finally having the celebrity life she always wanted.

"Thanks, Mom. I love it."

"Good. I'm glad." Her smile starts to look a little plastic on her face, like when someone's taking your picture and you hold it for too long.

"You know," she begins. "I thought about what you said last weekend on the phone, about fashion and everything. And I got to thinking."

"Uh-oh." I don't like the sound of that. Dread starts to fill me.

"Hear me out. You'll be really excited," she says, but she's the only one getting excited. "I know you just want to make your own clothes, but what if you started a line of clothing for teens? You know, have your very own fashion label."

"Come again?"

"You could call it Imperial Apparel or Regal Rags."

"Me? A fashion designer?" My head is already moving back and forth, instinctually repelling the idea. "But I have a stylist. I can't even dress myself, far less hundreds of people."

"Thousands," Mom says. Clearly, this idea has been circulating through her head since I asked for the sewing machine a week ago. "In fact. I've had our marketing contacts speak to a few retailers. Some of them might be interested in carrying your line."

"Why would people want to buy my clothes?"

"Because you're an icon." She pinches my cheeks, but I hardly feel it. "Or you will be once the pilot episode airs next Friday." She whispers the last part quiet enough so the microphone won't pick it up.

I'm overly aware of the cameras in the room and Corbin just waiting for some kind of drama. I only wanted to sew myself a costume. But I told Mom I wanted to create my own clothes, so this news should be like a dream come true. I feel like I've just laid my own trap.

So I smile and thank her because that's what I would

do if I were telling the truth. Besides, I really am grateful for the entire sewing room.

"I'll think about it," I say.

Mom hugs me, and I'm consumed in her cloud of Chanel. She pulls back and gives a hesitant frown, or what I assume to be a frown, if not for all her recent Botox injections.

"There's one more surprise," she says.

I hold my breath, waiting for the blow. Her smile is even bigger for this surprise, and I know she's compensating. Like she thinks her enthusiasm is contagious. But after sixteen years, I've built up a hefty army of antibodies.

"Marketing has been working on our new promotional campaign for Bottom's Bathrooms. But your father and I have been discussing it, and we've made a decision." She pauses to build the anticipation, but it only causes my dread to spill over. "Who better to represent the company than you? Our Porcelain Princess."

I release the breath in a grunt. "Me? *Represent* the company?"

"Yes." She claps her hands like the look on my face is glee and not nausea. I clearly need to work on my facial expressions.

"With the airing of the show, you'll be a household name. Everyone will recognize you and associate you with your father's company. It makes perfect sense. Besides, the marketing team loves the idea of a good, wholesome image like a princess for our mascot. And because you're our daughter, it emphasizes the family friendly appeal."

I feel like she just pulled the plug on my good day, and it's all getting sucked down the drain. "You want me to be the poster girl for Dad's company? His *bathroom* company?"

"And accessories." She doesn't seem to notice my incredulity. Ever the optimist. “Of course, we’ll pay you. It will be like a part-time job. What do you say?”

Great, more cameras. Just what I want. I tug on a red curl dangling in my face, wrapping it around my finger over and over again. What do I say? That this is a terrible idea? The worst?

And yet, when I look around the room, at everything my parents did to support me, I can’t say no when they’re asking me to support them. Oh, the guilt. The incredibly annoying guilt.

She has those begging, droopy, puppy-dog eyes—her Botox doctor said that would clear up in a few days—and I just can’t say no, especially since I’m lying to her in the first place.

I make sure to roll my eyes dramatically like it’s a huge favor, because it is, and also so she won’t ask for another one. “Okay.”

She drags me in for another hug. “Just think, princess. Soon your father’s company will be world famous. And you will be the face of it.” She kisses my cheek then wipes away her lipstick smudge. “Whenever anyone thinks of a toilet, they’ll think of you.”

Crap.

Chapter Ten

Incognerdo

Cowering behind a bush, I watch two warriors locked in a fierce battle to the death. They're barely a hundred feet away from my hiding spot. In between the dull *thunks* of padded boffers clashing, the warring larpers murmur words of spells to supplement their strength and health.

There's another person, too. I double-check the larping notes I wrote on the back of my hand. He's the judge or referee, I think. He's dressed in plain black clothes, with a black band around his head.

I observe the game from my leafy cover as I fidget with my costume that I spent the last two weeks creating. Something between tough leather-clad warrior chick and feminine princess, with emerald gossamer and lace.

I'm not spying. Not really. I'm just waiting for the right opportunity to jump in. I arrived late, and the game was already in progress. I spent too long standing indecisively across the Costco parking lot, too nervous to stroll up and introduce myself to the larpers. Before I found the courage, they all headed onto the undeveloped land next to the big-box store, disappearing into the thick woods that grow next to it.

I'm worried Kevin will recognize me. Sure, the stylist's wig might fool my own mother into thinking I'm a natural blonde, but maybe my voice will give me away, my walk, my mannerisms. But I also want to see him today, so badly that it feels like I haven't thought of anything else for the last few weeks. Every stitch I stitched, every spool I changed, every alteration I made, I feel like I made it for him as much as myself.

The decorative gold mask covers half my face, and brown is a common eye color, but will it be enough? Will I be able to act like myself while still hiding my identity to protect my reputation at school? Things are already going to be bad enough on Monday morning since the first episode of *Bathroom Barons* aired on Friday night. The underwear episode.

Nearly a month has passed since the Wonder Woman underwear incident. I almost fell into a false sense of security. But the moment my butt came on TV, the humiliation burned as though it had just happened.

No matter how hard Mom and Dad fought, they couldn't prevent the network from airing the mishap. Apparently we signed away a lot of our rights. Corbin can do practically whatever he wants. And he wanted my Wonder Woman underwear.

Now that we're rich and Mom is able to buy everything that is supposed to make us better people, I think she expected the show to present us as the sophisticated family she believes we are. But it seems Corbin has the opposite planned, like he's making a joke out of us instead, trying to highlight how silly we look trying to be something we're not. And I'm the walking one-liner providing him with the material.

Harper keeps telling me that no one will care, that it's just cool that I'm on TV. But it doesn't feel very cool.

The longer I watch the larpers, the more I think that meeting a bunch of costumed gamers in the Costco parking lot before they headed into the woods would have been less intimidating than approaching fairies, warlocks, and knights battling for the throne of Asdor.

Maybe this wasn't such a great idea. Maybe I should leave. I could try again next weekend.

I move to sneak away. A twig snaps behind me. Something presses against my neck and I flinch.

Startled, I fall back onto the grass and find myself staring up a long duct-taped blade aimed at my throat. And on the other end is Kevin. So much for running away.

He looks like a hero should. Princely in his loose, long-sleeved tunic and leather waistcoat. It accentuates his wide shoulders and broad chest much more effectively than his usual worn-out T-shirts. I can't do anything but stare up at him, a little awestruck.

"State your business here," he says. "Or face my blade."

He's so serious and stern. I can't help it. I giggle.

"You mock my threat?" Then in a stage whisper he says, "You're not supposed to break character."

"Oh, right." I put my hands up in surrender. "I come in peace." At the last second, I remember to alter my voice before he recognizes it, so I finish on a higher note. It works okay because it makes it seem like I'm acting nervous for the role—either that or I sound like a teenage boy who suddenly hit puberty.

"Are you the guide my party seeks? Or are you here to take the amulet for yourself?" he asks threateningly. The blade inches closer to my skin.

"The amulet? I don't know what you're talking about."

He hesitates then removes the blade from my neck. He looks me up and down. "Are you lost?"

I get to my feet and glance back at the other larpers in the distance. "Yes, very, very lost."

"Clarify," he says. From my Googling, I remember that this is an official game word used to break character when someone needs to ask a question. In his normal Kevin voice, he says, "I didn't see you in the parking lot this morning. Are you part of the game?"

"I, ummm, was a little late. I'm kind of new to this."

Kevin sheathes his sword on his belt. "Well, then let me be of service, my lady. My name is Sir Kevin. A knight of Asdor." He bows low in a noble gesture. "It would be my honor to escort you."

"I'm A-Andy," I catch myself before I use my full name, Adrianna, what everyone at school knows me by. I bob in an awkward curtsy, taking his cue to revert back to my character.

"Well, A-Andy. The pleasure is all mine. Are you a lost maiden? Wayward priestess? A runaway princess, perhaps?"

I smile at the princess comment. "Something like that." I like the idea of a secret within a secret, so I adopt it into the character and backstory I'd prepared ahead of time. "But promise me you won't tell anyone."

"I will guard your secret with my life." He winks conspiratorially. "There's great evil out there that would use that information against you."

"Don't I know it." Like SPAM.

"Tell me, how does a princess find herself in a place such as this?" He gestures around us.

I try to ignore the square Costco building on the plot of land next to this one, even though I can see it peeking through the trees. I block out the sound of Jake-braking and honking from the road. Instead, I imagine the world of Asdor as he sees it. One of magic and mystery, where anything is possible, where my embarrassing life isn't scheduled to broadcast on TV every Friday night. A world where I can be myself. Where I can talk to Kevin freely.

"It was my life in the castle," I begin, thinking on my feet. "My entire life was laid out before me. I was told what to wear, how to act, what to say, and even who I was going to marry. I was engaged to an old, fat duke. I didn't feel like myself anymore. I felt suffocated. I wanted to be free to live my life. So I ran away." It's more truth than it is fantasy.

"Sounds dramatic," he says. "But your heart, dare I ask, is it still free for the taking?"

The way he asks it makes my toes curl in excitement, like he's asking for himself. I give him a daring look. "No. It is not."

He sighs in exaggerated disappointment.

"It is mine for the giving."

I'm surprised by his cheeky smile, and even more so by mine. There's something empowering about being in costume, about being able to use my own words and feelings while still hiding behind a character. To flirt with Kevin so openly and confidently, hidden beneath this figurative and literal mask.

"Well, Princess Andy. Since you're new, allow me to be your guide."

He proffers an arm and his cheek wrinkles as I take it. Something about that grin makes me equally giddy and achingly jealous. My plan worked. He doesn't recognize me. But he's so clearly flirting with pretend blonde me, when only a month ago he was flirting with real redhead me. Before I accosted his friend with ice cream, that is. It stings a little. Does he flirt with every new girl he meets?

I thought we had a connection.

Being on his arm softens the mixed feelings, and I relax into my role. I get to be myself and do something I'm really interested in. It's been a while since that's happened. A whole day where I can escape my life and no one will ever know. No social suicide for me. The best of both worlds—Earth and Asdor.

"You said you were seeking an amulet," I say. "What kind of amulet?"

"It is a very powerful magical item. The next step in our long quest. My party created a distraction so that I might sneak into the woods to uncover the treasure."

"Alone?"

"I am the strongest swordsman amongst the group, and there are tales that trolls lurk within this forest." He nods toward the short sword hanging from my belt. "I hope you know how to use that."

At the mention of trouble, I unsheathe my sword. I hold it in the hand not wrapped around Kevin's arm, which is pretty buff for a comic nerd. My weapon, or boffer, is just a PVC pipe with padding for the tip to soften the blow, but I grip it like it can really save my life.

"I have learned a thing or two from my princess defense training," I say. "Also, I gleaned some answers from a being called Google that resides within a magic metal box."

"The mythical Google." He nods sagely. "I have heard tales of its limitless knowledge."

The trees thin out as we walk, and we stumble upon a small clearing. Kevin takes my hand to help me over a fallen tree. When I jump down, I see an object on the ground ahead. It's a toolbox painted with swirls of gold. A Master brand padlock dangles from the lid. I wonder if Kevin got it from his uncle's hardware store.

"Is that what you're looking for?" I point to the box.

"Indeed," he says. "Well done. You must be my lucky charm."

He crosses the clearing to the treasure chest. As he bends over to pick it up, he pauses. Slowly, he reaches for the hilt of his sword.

"What's wrong?" I ask.

He points to a figure darting through the trees ahead of us. It's a troll, or as close as one can get in a Goblin mask from Spiderman, a knitted hat, and jeans cut off unevenly below the knees. The troll's skin is painted shades of green like camouflage. It's a non-player character, a person not participating in the larp but still roleplaying as part of the quest prepared for Kevin and the others to experience.

Hunkering low, it picks its way through the foliage and tall grass. It sneaks toward Kevin and me. At the edge of the clearing, it crouches and hisses a warning at us.

"Well, Princess Andy," Kevin says. "It looks like you are about to witness how things work in our world firsthand."

Chapter Eleven

Asdork

Kevin nudges me behind him, protecting me from the approaching troll. A twig cracks to my right, and I whirl around to discover one more creature. We're back-to-back as yet another one slinks amongst the underbrush. Three against two.

"How many hit points do you have?" Kevin asks me.

I glance at my cheat notes written on the back of my hand. When I was creating my character and backstory, I also had to decide on the character's strengths and weaknesses, including how many hits I could receive from an enemy before it killed me.

"Four." It seemed unrealistic to give a sheltered princess any more.

"Any magic?"

Again, I have to refer to the notes. "I can do healing and protection spells mostly. And a couple weak defensive spells like invisibility."

"Okay. These trolls are worth four hit points each. Focus on dodging their attacks. A hit to their torso is two points, the arms and legs only one each. But aim for the limbs. It will prevent you from having to get too close and risk your own life."

Kevin shouts a war cry, going for the nearest troll. I feel him move away, but I don't turn around to watch him. My opponent is crouched in front of me, waiting to attack.

I feint to my right. The troll cuts me off and lashes out with his boffer that's in the shape of a rough wooden club. I barely skip out of the way to avoid the hit.

Another enemy approaches to my right, its spray-painted Nikes shuffling through the loose dirt. Gripping my sword, I slash at the one in front of me. I read online that it was dangerous to swing at someone with a downward motion, so I make sure to follow the rules and hit at a ninety-degree angle. I catch him on the right shoulder.

"Hit one, right arm," the troll calls out the damage he receives. He transfers his club to his other hand and tucks the injured one behind his back to simulate the injury.

I circle around him so I'm facing both of my opponents. I lunge forward again, and this time my sword connects with the injured troll's leg.

"Hit one, right leg." Pretending that I really did sever it from his body, he begins to hop on his other leg. It doesn't last long. He soon stumbles and falls to his knees.

The second troll swings its club. I'm not ready. I try to block with my sword, but the club grazes my chest. I simulate the damage by grunting and staggering back.

"Hit two, chest," I say, like the troll did.

My new enemy is a girl in a brown knitted hat and a green tank top. She comes at me, striking again and again. I meet every blow to deflect them, but each time, I move a step back.

I'm taken farther and farther away from Sir Kevin

until I'm on my own. Out of the corner of my eye, I see he's got his hands full with three other trolls, so I need to warrior-up and defend myself.

Finally, one of the troll's attacks goes wide. I take a swipe at her leg and my blade connects.

"Hit one, left leg," she says.

The other troll is on his feet, or rather, his foot. He hops toward me, swinging wildly. I dodge his attacks and circle around a tree to throw him off. He braces himself against the trunk, but I keep maneuvering until I'm behind him. I get the last two blows in before he can get away.

He groans and drops to his knees. Eyes rolling dramatically into the back of his head, he flops facedown onto the ground and dies.

Something stabs my leg. I spin around. The other troll snuck up on me.

"Hit one, right leg," I say belatedly, and raise my injured limb.

Hopping around in the thick underbrush is harder than it looks, and I stumble back. My butt hits the ground hard. I stare up as my attacker growls and closes the distance between us. I've already been injured in the chest and the leg. That's three hit points. One more hit and I'm done for.

Standing above me, the troll raises her weapon for the final blow. I hold my sword up, for what little good it's going to do, and wait for death.

Just as the troll braces to bring her club down on me, a groan escapes her lips.

"Hit two, torso," she says.

She stumbles forward and I see Kevin behind her. He came to my rescue.

At the last minute, I lean forward to catch the troll in the stomach with my own blade, using up her last hit point.

She collapses dead at my feet.

Kevin rushes to my side. "Have you been injured, Princess Andy?"

"Yes. My leg and my chest."

He checks a key ring attached to his belt and counts the blue plastic tabs dangling from it. "I have very little mana left. Not enough magic to heal your injuries."

I recall that you need mana in order to perform magic spells. There are no set rules on how to keep track of mana, but it looks like this larping group uses tags as counters.

He checks my own belt, his fingers brushing against my stomach. "And it appears as though you haven't received any yet." He holds out his hand. "Come on. I will get you to my companions. We have a powerful warlock. He will be able to help you."

I take his gloved hand, and he helps me to my foot. To keep my balance, I lean against him, maybe a little more than I need to. Lemon and pepper mixes with the raw scent of his leather vest.

Once I'm steady, he pulls away. He wraps his arm around me, and we make our way through the carnage and green troll bodies scattered on the forest floor. When we reach the hand-painted treasure chest, he removes a key from a chain around his neck and hands it to me.

"Would you like to do the honors? After all, you were the one who found it."

"Sure." I bend down and unlock it.

The hinges squeak as I raise the lid. There, lying on a bed of purple velvet, is the magical amulet. The gold medallion embedded with colorful stones looks like something out of the seventies that I'd find in a thrift store. I reach inside to pick it up.

"Hold, there!" someone calls out.

I whip around. It's Pixie Girl, and she's got her bow trained on my chest. The bow is made out of light wood, but it looks a little less intimidating with no arrow nocked. Instead, she clutches a small red beanbag in her fist to represent the real thing. I didn't even hear her sneak up.

Moments later, three more larpers stumble into the clearing. There's the short swordsman, the ninja from the comic store, and the third is a wizard with a sparkling robe.

Kevin gasps. "No. Don't shoot."

Pixie Girl's eyes narrow at me. The beanbag draws back even farther. "She's stealing the amulet." She's not so small and cute now that she's holding a deadly weapon. Well, pretend deadly.

"This is Princess Andy." Kevin moves to shield me. "She's a friend. She's helping us."

"We don't even know her." Pixie Girl glares at me, and I'm surprised by the fierceness of that look.

Does she recognize me? Did something tip her off? Does she remember me as the ice cream flinger? She gets ready to hurl the beanbag at me as though it's an arrow.

"She could be a spy," she says.

Kevin shakes his head. "She's not a spy."

"That's exactly what a spy would tell you," the wizard says. He thrusts his staff in front of him, ready to cast a spell on me.

"That's true," says the swordsman. "How do we know we can trust her this far into our quest? And only just when you've found the amulet."

"We can't risk it," the wizard says.

The big ninja simply crosses his arms in silent agreement.

Pixie Girl nods. "It's settled then. Democracy wins." And then she lets the arrow fly.

Chapter Twelve

Parking Lot Potluck

"Sorry for killing you earlier," Pixie Girl, aka Keelie, says. She tosses her bow and beanbags in the back of a minivan with the rest of the larping supplies.

"That's okay," I say. "You did revive me after."

"My character's a bit of a hothead. Shoot first, ask questions later." She smiles, flashing tiny white teeth like perfect Tic Tacs. "You'll get to know her."

I hadn't even considered creating a different personality for Princess Andy. The whole point is to be myself for once. I can't do that if I'm pretending to be someone else. It's already complicated enough.

I notice that Keelie is wearing a new tunic. Or maybe it's old, since the seams look like they're unraveling around the sleeves and the material is pilling from wear. It's not as pretty as the one that was stained at the ice cream parlor. I look away guiltily.

Mostly everyone is still wearing their costumes, or parts of them, at least. I'm glad, since it won't seem strange that I'm still wearing my mask.

Ken, the middle-aged Game Master, puts the treasure chest and amulet in the back of his van and closes the door. To fit in the driver's seat, he removes the cone-shaped magician's hat, revealing a perfectly round bald patch.

He rolls down the window and leans out. "I'm glad you could join us today, Andy."

"Me too," I say. "I had a lot of fun."

"And remember, if you get a cavity, you know where to find me. I give good larping discounts." He passes me his business card. "Hope to see you next weekend."

We all wave good-bye and watch him leave. Dentist by weekday, dark magician by weekend. He's been doing this so long that he creates the story lines and quests with some of the other gamers. They make up the plot committee. There's also a lawyer and a social worker in the group. I guess when you do nothing but fill out paperwork and perform energy-zapping jobs all week, you need to escape to a little fantasy on the weekends.

Across the parking lot, one of the larpers jumps into the back of his rusty Chevy truck to call everyone's attention. His hair is long enough to brush his shoulders as he waves his broadsword in the air.

"Hear ye, hear ye. Gather round, gather round. I have braved the fearsome freeway, traveled to the nearest village in my chariot, and returned with a feast of cheese and bread." He jumps down from the pickup bed and opens the pizza boxes with a flourish. "Let us celebrate today's victory."

Everyone thrusts their weapons in the air and cheers.

"Are we supposed to be in character still?" I ask Keelie.

"No. That's just Eddie. He stays in character most of the time. Pretty much all the time, really. Even at his day job at the Stop and Shop."

I laugh, but then I realize she's not kidding.

Crossing the busy Costco parking lot, we join the others at the banquet table, also known as Eddie's rusty tailgate, and grab a couple of pizza slices. We lean against his truck while we eat, enjoying the view of the undeveloped land with its thick woods and hilly terrain: Asdor. Kevin comes up behind me and hands me a can of pop.

"Is my sister harassing you?" he asks.

"Keelie's your sister?" I glance between the two of them. While Kevin's pretty tall and Keelie is even shorter than I am, I can kind of see it. They have the same coloring. Like her brother's, her hair is a soft black. Her eyes are blue like his, but a bit darker, less shockingly light. But that's where the similarities end.

"Yeah, she's one lucky girl," Kevin says with a smirk.

Keelie shoves him. "You wish."

Kevin has removed the leather armor, and his tunic collar is splayed open, the strings dangling down his chest. I notice a few others have removed pieces of their costumes, too. Kevin's short swordsman friend from school, Chad, has tucked a napkin in his chain mail.

In the late afternoon sun, the metal of my mask absorbs the heat. Sweat forms around my eyes and nose. I wish I could take it off, but then they'll recognize me for sure even under the wig. Then someone might blab at school. I remember the way SPAM reacted to seeing the larpers in the ice cream parlor. I doubt even Harper could protect me if the truth comes out.

"I like your costume, Andy," Keelie says. "Where did you buy it?"

"Thanks, but I didn't buy it anywhere. I made it myself."

"You made it?" She runs a finger over the piping along the shoulders. "It looks so professional."

It did turn out pretty well, but I suppose that's what the best equipment money can buy gets you. And then I remember my promise to Mom.

"I'm thinking about starting my own business. Making my own clothes. I could sew you something if you like." I think of her tunic, ruined by my ice cream stains, and can't help but cringe.

I've been carrying stain remover in my backpack ever since the incident, hoping I'd have another chance to apologize. Since Keelie is a grade below me, we don't run into each other often, and every time I do finally see her in the halls at school, she glares at me and turns the other way.

"You'd look good in blue," I say. "It would bring out your eyes."

"Really? That would be amazing. I'll totally pay you."

"Don't worry about it. I have lots of spare material sitting at home. I enjoy sewing." And I would never accept the money. I'd feel guilty accepting a thank-you.

I turn to Kevin. "And I noticed your gauntlets have seen better days. I could fix them up for you."

"They're not so bad," he says.

I swipe them out of his pocket before he can object further. "They won't take any time at all. Some seam reinforcements and a few extra details."

"That would be awesome. But I use them for yard work." He slips them on and flexes his fingers a few times. "You'll have to promise to bring them back."

"Don't worry, I won't leave you without your armor."

His one cheek wrinkles. "It's not the armor I'm worried about not seeing again."

I stare at him for a moment before I understand his meaning. He means me. He's flirting with me. Again.

It's different now that we're not in character, and

suddenly I'm shy even behind my mask. I'm glad most of my embarrassing blush is hidden, and I turn to watch the cars filter in and out of the parking lot in search of bulk goods at warehouse prices.

"That's gross," Keelie says. "My brother's flirting. I'm going to go clean out my ears with soap now."

Kevin gives her a soft shove but says nothing. She continues to fake dry heave as she walks over to join the wizard who voted in favor of killing me earlier. His name is Finn, I think. I can't help but notice he tends to orbit around Keelie a lot during the game play. I wonder if that's because his character wants to or if he does.

I go to grab another slice of pizza, and that's when I notice something's off. Maybe it's because the other larpers are all looking across the parking lot. Maybe it's a dark premonition.

When I glance over Kevin's shoulder, all I see is a van at first. Then I recognize the network's logo on the side of it. And Corbin is jumping out of the passenger seat.

The pizza turns to cement in my mouth. I feel the blood drain from my face like a curtain dropping, and for a second I feel dizzy. I brace myself against the truck.

Nobody knew I was coming here. I made sure of it. I even smuggled my costume out of the house to change in a gas station bathroom. My fingers clench the metal tailgate, my nails turning a hot white. One day. I can't escape for a single freaking afternoon. My embarrassing life follows me everywhere.

I look for an exit, my motions feeling jerky and uncontrolled. Beyond running like a crazy person back into Asdor, there doesn't seem to be a way out that won't draw attention to myself.

Corbin scans the parking lot, his eyes roaming over us.

I duck behind Kevin, pretending to reach for my drink, but I keep my eye on the crew. Hugh the camera guy opens the sliding side door and starts to remove the equipment while Corbin gives the others instructions.

They don't seem to be in a rush. Corbin's lighting up a smoke, not chasing me down with a camera yet. Something's not right. That's when I see Dad get out of his Aston. He glances in the tinted back window to check his comb-over and straighten his tie.

My shoulders sag in relief, and I release the death grip on my drink. I get it. They're not here for me. It's got something to do with Dad. Maybe Costco is going to start carrying his line of toilet accessories.

I want to laugh at the coincidence, but people would think I'm a crazy person. Of course, it's not all about me. Even though it feels like Corbin follows me everywhere, they film Mom and Dad more than they do me.

I lean against the truck in relief. I'll be fine, as long as I stay out of sight and don't draw too much attention—which is difficult to do dressed as a warrior princess in the middle of a parking lot eating pizza.

The crew and my dad hang around until some other guy in a suit shows up and hands my dad a business card. The cameras start to roll. They make their way toward the tree line and the path where we exited the world of Asdor. Dad and the new guy slip on the loose dirt in their dress shoes. They're almost out of sight.

Tires squeal against the pavement behind us, and an engine revs. A bang, a splash, a high-pitched female scream.

When I look over, I realize it's not a female but Eddie screaming. He's dripping with something red. A slush cup rolls around at his feet.

Then I'm hit, not by a realization but by fries. Soggy

McDonald's fries. They pelt us and hit the side of the truck like rapid-fire bullets. Keelie squeaks, and Kevin shoves us behind him and around the truck.

When I look back, I see our shooters. Or rather, I see the car. A new black Mustang with red racing stripes down the center. Totally ostentatious. I'd rather have my Kia. And it's probably an automatic, which is like owning a toothless Rottweiler.

"Not these guys again," Keelie says.

"You know them?" I ask.

Kevin grabs my arm and pulls me down just as another slush cup sails overhead. "Yeah. We call him the Mac Attacker. He and his friends visited us a lot last year. They disappeared over summer. I thought we finally got rid of them."

I peek around the corner. The cameras are pointing our way, interested in the sudden commotion. Just my luck. For once it wasn't me who drew the attention.

Hugh trots down the path toward us with the camera on his shoulder aimed our way. He would be hurrying a lot faster if he knew it was me. It's only a matter of time. Why are they even here? They're going to ruin everything.

The Mustang tears through the lot. I think they're about to leave, but then they circle around again. Eddie closes the tailgate with a slam and tosses the leftover pizza in his cab.

"I must bid you farewell, my comrades," he says. "Let us make a hasty retreat and live to fight another day."

We back away from the truck as he gets in and starts the engine. It takes a couple of tries before it finally roars to life like a choking dragon.

Keelie scrambles around the front of the truck. "Eddie, wait. I'm coming with you." To Kevin, she says, "I'm having a sleepover at a friend's tonight. Mom and Dad already know."

Eddie puts the truck in gear. "Sorry, I have no more solace to offer the two of you. The back is full of supplies."

By supplies, I see he means old junk.

When Eddie takes off, Keelie waves out the open window and calls back to us. "Good luck."

We're the only two larpers left. The others scattered like water from my dad's shower head, Mister Misty (Patent Pending). We should have run when we had the chance.

Hyper-masculine engine sounds echo throughout the lot. The Mustang loops back. Both cameras now follow the muscle car. It sweeps around the corner, picking up gravel as it speeds toward us again. Following the action, the crew jogs after the car as best they can while burdened by the equipment.

"It's coming back," Kevin says. "That's a lot of food."

"They must have supersized," I say.

I'm not as worried about the car as I am my dad. Costume or no, parents just have a way of knowing their kids. Even incognito. Besides, he saw the wig when the stylist tried it on me the first day and so did the crew. They'll know it's me. My cover will be blown.

The Mustang's passenger leans out the window and draws back his next deep-fried weapon.

I grab Kevin's gloved hand. "Come on."

We run, hand in gauntlet, weaving through parked cars and barricades. The Mustang is forced to go around each row of cars and cut through gaps, while also watching for pedestrians. Kevin squeezes through a broken chain-link fence and turns back to hold the gap open for me. I think we're safe and start to slow.

While that was as adrenaline-inducing as fighting a horde of trolls, I start to laugh, and so does Kevin. Then the remains of a Big Mac rain down on us. I cover my wig and run until we're out of reach, until we're through the next big-box store parking lot and onto the sidewalk.

When we finally slow down to catch our breath, I notice we're still holding hands. And it's a good thing he's wearing gloves, because I feel like my palms are sweating. Not from our escape, but his nearness. Eventually we pull away, because that would be weird. We only just met, so far as he knows. But I kind of liked it. I feel like a balloon just inflated in my chest, but all the helium's gone to my head.

As we stroll down the street, we pass four bus stops, but neither of us joins any of the lines to wait for the next bus. People eyeball our attire, but I feel safe behind my mask.

"I guess I should bring my car next time," Kevin says. "Makes for a faster getaway."

"You have a car?"

"Yeah, it's nothing special. It's just an old Kia."

"Really?" I beam up at him. "I've been asking for a car, but my parents refuse."

"Why don't you buy one yourself?"

"Actually, that's not a bad idea." I remember Mom saying that they would pay me to be the face of Bottom's Bathrooms and Accessories. "I just got a part-time job. It starts next weekend."

He frowns. "You'll miss larping."

I like how upset he looks because he wants me to come back, but I also don't like that he's upset. "It's just on Saturday. I won't miss larping next week."

We come to another bus stop, and this time we join the lineup.

"Well, in the meantime, do you go to Beverly Hills High?" he asks. "Maybe I'll see you around at school."

Oh, he'll definitely see me, but I don't want him to be on the lookout or to start making connections, so I say,

"Actually I go to Hollywood High."

He frowns. "That's too bad. But at least you won't miss larping next week. Because I'm counting on you to fix up my gauntlets."

"Right." I bump my shoulder against his. "You can't live without them."

I notice he remains close, so our shoulders continue to touch. It reminds me of my second day of school when he walked me to my locker. And he's definitely doing it on purpose this time, because the sidewalk is more than big enough for the two of us.

My bus pulls up then. We quickly exchange numbers, and he gives me his gloves. When I turn to go, he grabs my hand again. Bringing it to his lips, he kisses it very prince-like.

"Until we meet again, princess."

Chapter Thirteen
High Horse

Pistil, meiosis, mitosis…

I'm not going to think about him.

Stigma, style, gametophyte…

I'm not going to think about his smile.

Anther, pollen…

Or his *Dragon Ball Z* Goku hair.

Germination…

Or his lips on my skin.

Reproduction…

Or that.

Harper waves her fluffy pen in front of my face. "Helloooo. What are you thinking about?"

"Reproduction," I say. "Of flowers, I mean." As evidence, I point to the front of the class where the reproductive cycle of plants is displayed for us to take notes.

"What did you do this weekend?"

I fought a horde of trolls, and died, and then came back from the dead, and met a knight of Asdor. "Nothing. Just hung out."

"Are you sure it was nothing?" She elbows me. "You've been daydreaming all day. I think it's a boy," she singsongs.

"What? No. No." Is it written all over my face? "There's no boy. I-I don't have a boyfriend."

Automatically, Kevin's face pops into my head, and I want to turn around to his table. I've been thinking so hard about him all day that I'm sure he can hear my cerebrum practically screaming his name.

Harper's eyebrow twitches and she smirks. "We'll have to fix that."

Lennox spins on his stool to face us. "Fix what?"

She sneers at him. "Fix none of your business."

"Oh, come on," he says. "Tell me."

He leans his massive arms on our desk. I'm surprised at how good he still smells after my day larping with Kevin. Not that I thought he'd smell like rotting garbage on a hot day or a carnival outhouse or anything. But when I've been thinking so much about Kevin lately, how can I be so fickle as to swoon over Lennox? I blame it on my teenager hormones.

But even though it was really fun to hang out with Kevin, Lennox's teeth are still just as dazzling, his eyes so ocean blue that I want to do a triple backflip and dive into them, and his hair is just as supple as the "after" shot of a shampoo commercial. It defies physics the way all that muscle packs into his shirt.

Harper hits his arms with her pen until he moves back. "We don't need your help."

"Hey. I'm a useful guy. I'm Mr. Problem Solver. I know people. I get things done."

I subtly kick Harper under the table. Her eyes shift to me, and I widen mine. This is exactly the kind of thing I was talking to her about just last night on the phone. If she wants to get Lennox back, she has to stop being so mean. I think it's because she's afraid of opening herself up to rejection. But her "screw off" attitude isn't exactly going to charm the pants off her ex.

She rolls her eyes at me. And then tickles her chin with the pink fur on the end of her pen, deep in thought. Finally she says, "You're friends with Conner, right?"

"Yeah," Lennox says. "So what?"

"Didn't he just break up with his girlfriend?"

"That's right. She was dating some college guy over the summer behind his back."

Harper flashes a toothy smile like the Cheshire cat from *Alice in Wonderland.* "Maybe you can help us after all."

I don't like that look, but I don't have time to dwell on it because the bell rings. I close my notebook and head for the door. As I pass Kevin, I can't help but stare at him.

"Hi," I say.

"Hey." And I know he means it this time because he pauses and eyes me for a second before responding.

It feels like his gaze is boring through me like a laser, but I soak up every second of it, hungry for his attention. It's been over three weeks since the ice cream incident. Maybe he realizes by now I didn't mean to stain his sister's shirt. Or maybe he just doesn't want to be rude. Either way I'm happy he's talking to me again.

"How are you?" I ask.

"Fine," he says, in a very neutral tone. Not overly friendly, but not hostile either.

Lennox is right behind me. He sees me talking to Kevin, but I don't care. Since the first episode of *Bathroom Barons* aired on Friday, everyone at school wants to be friends with me. Which I totally don't understand, since it was the underwear episode.

I've gotten a few butt jokes, but Harper has stuck close by me, shooting nasty looks that seem to shut them up right away. I hope she's doing it because she's my friend. But then again, she was in that episode, so maybe she wants the show to seem cooler.

I also think it helped that Corbin followed me to school this morning. The appearance of the cameras again had everyone excited, trying to talk to me, Wonder Woman underwear or not, just to get on TV. And if they're not teasing me about that, then I'm practically invincible. Right?

Maybe if I talk to Kevin, he'll be safe from bullying, too, the same way Harper did for me. I could be his insult shield. It's only fair. He was my McDonald's shield.

The urge to smile at the memory twitches my lips. I have to gnaw on the inside of my cheek to stop from grinning stupidly. It's like I've just overdosed on Pop Rocks and they're fizzing throughout my entire body.

I linger while Kevin gathers his books and pencil case. When he goes to leave, Lennox blocks him. Kevin ignores him and tries to go around, but Lennox's friend stops him from the other direction.

I yank on Lennox's shirt. "Leave him alone," I say, feeling brave. Invincible.

Kevin looks at me, kind of surprised, like he didn't expect me to say anything. Lennox shrugs me off and raises a fist in the air, and before Kevin looks back, it comes down, smashing the books from his hands. They scatter across the floor.

Lennox guffaws with his friend before grabbing Kevin's pencil case and slowly opening it. He stares him down as he does it, too, like he's goading Kevin to do something about it.

Kevin just crosses his arms and waits like *Okay, it's*

a few pens. So what? Super mature compared to the two Neanderthals in front of him.

When Kevin doesn't react, the pencil case is turned upside down. Pencils, erasers, pens, and highlighters clatter to the floor. Lennox gives it one last shake for good measure before dropping it on the pile. He even picks up Kevin's notebook from the floor and rips out a page. He crumples it up in his hand before leaving with it.

Meathead. I want to scream at Lennox and punch him in his oversized abs. Ducking in front of him, I give him a shove. I might as well be trying to stop a tank, but I stand my ground.

"Knock it off," I say. "What's your problem?"

"Leave it alone, Adrianna," Kevin says from behind me.

I glance back at him, confused. "What?"

"This is none of your business." He says it so matter-of-factly, but I still recoil, as though his words physically stung me.

Is it a boy thing? Too much male pride to let a girl stand up for him? Or is it because it's me?

Harper links her arm with mine. "Let the cavemen play their stupid games."

She leads me out of the room like we're shopping at the mall. I hesitate, but Kevin told me to butt out, so I'm not sure what else to do but follow her. Still, though, I feel terrible. First the fast-food attack on the weekend by the jerks in the Mustang, and now this. I know what it's like to be bullied, and I hate seeing it happen to Kevin.

When we step out into the hall, Mercedes and Prissy snicker together. They were watching the whole thing from the door.

"Standing up for your mayor boyfriend?" Mercedes says.

Prissy bats her eyelashes in fake sincerity. "That's so sweet."

"Come on, Harper." Mercedes tries to wedge herself between the two of us, cutting me off. "I'm starving. All this nerd flirting has delayed my lunch."

Now I've done it. Here I thought my newfound fame would protect not only me from teasing but also Kevin. I guess I overestimated my pathetic status. Harper warned me about this. Maybe I should have listened.

But Harper doesn't let go of my arm. She shrugs Mercedes off and steers us to the cafeteria. "No thanks. Adrianna and I are having lunch together."

Mercedes trips a little on her own feet before she recovers. "Whatever, suit yourself." She turns to Prissy. "Want to skip next class?"

Prissy nods and follows Mercedes toward the exit.

Harper doesn't even need to say anything. I can see the "I told you so" clearly on her face.

"Thanks," I say sheepishly.

I don't get it. Kevin's cute. No, he's hot. And funny. He could rival Lennox, in a geek-is-the-new-chic kind of way. So why isn't he considered cool? Because he does geeky things? Okay, yes, he's a total geek. But I don't care. I think his unashamed geekiness makes him even cooler. He likes the same things I do, yet he's not afraid to admit it.

When we're almost at the cafeteria, I jerk free of Harper's grip. "Sorry. I just remembered. I forgot something back in the classroom."

"What did you forget?" she calls after me.

"A pen," I lie.

"I'll lend you one."

"No. A special one. My dad gave it to me," I say so she'll give up. "Save me a seat in the cafeteria."

Back in the biology lab, Kevin's crawling under a table to reach his eraser. I pick up his textbook from the floor and wait, fidgeting from foot to foot. I'm not sure what to say.

When he notices me standing there, he starts and bangs his head on a chair. "Ouch!" he cries. "What, are you stalking me?" he asks, rubbing his head. "Oh wait. I forgot. I'm the stalker."

I drop my eyes to the book in my hands. "I never said that. That rumor came from the girls."

"Funny, you didn't correct it." I can tell he's totally annoyed. It's obviously about what Lennox just did, but I can't help but take it personally.

"I tried." My voice is weak, and I don't even believe it.

"Right. And I suppose you didn't fling ice cream at my sister."

My mouth pops open. So he really does think it was my fault. "I didn't. That was Mercedes. I swear."

He laughs, but I don't think he really finds it funny. "She wasn't the one holding the smoking gun. Err," he hesitates, "sticky spoon."

I reach for his arm, but he pulls away. "And I didn't tear your note," I say. "Well, I didn't mean to. I liked it."

"Don't worry about it." He snatches the book out of my hand and slams it down on the desk. "I received your message, loud and clear." His voice softens and he looks down at the floor. He kind of cringes, like he's swallowing glass.

For the first time, I get a glimpse of just how hurt Kevin is. He's not lashing out at me from anger, but sadness. I've really hurt him. And that can only mean it was because he cared. Cared about me. Maybe more than I realized. Maybe as much as I care for him. I feel hope balloon inside me, creating a desperation to fix things, to get us back to wherever it was we were headed before I messed everything up.

I reach out to him, hesitantly, like if I could only just touch him, he wouldn't be able to deny that spark between us. We'd just snap together like a couple of magnets, never to be pulled apart again. He'd wrap his arms around me and kiss me.

But as my hand lands on his arm, his fingers curl to make a fist. He doesn't pull away, not at first. His face contorts like he's arguing with himself in his head. But finally he jerks back like I'd burned him. He scowls. "I said don't worry about it."

I flinch at the venom in his voice. His ice-blue eyes are, well, ice, and his look gives me frostbite.

"Look. It's not like that," I say, becoming angry myself. I can feel the ugly red flush crawl over my pale face. "*I'm* not like that."

"Really? Let me guess. You've been framed."

"Well, sort of. It's all a misunderstanding." I drop to the ground where he's scrambling for a pen. I grab it before he does, and I hold it away so he looks at me. "I actually like you. And I think you like me, too."

"Yeah. I did like you when I met you in the hardware store." He stands up to look down at me. "Before I actually got to know you. You're just not the person I thought you were."

"You don't even know me." I get to my feet, wishing I was taller so I could glare into his eyes. "Maybe you're not the person I thought you were. Maybe you're just judgmental and pretentious."

"Pretentious?"

"Yeah. You act like you're better than me and my friends instead of giving me a chance. I'm a good person."

He draws back and shoves the last of his supplies into the case. Instead of looking mad or hurt, he shrugs all cool-like, which seems way worse. I can't reach out and touch him now. No matter how much I want to.

"Maybe you are a good person. Except when it counts. When anyone else can see." He grabs his stuff and heads for the door. "You're just like the rest of them. A sheep." He makes a shooing motion. "Run away now, little sheep. Your flock is waiting for you."

A sheep? A *sheep*? My fingers clench into painful fists, snapping the pen I forgot was in my hand. When I look down, my left hand is dripping with blue ink. After throwing it in the trash, I go to one of the lab sinks and turn on the tap. I scrub at the ink staining my skin.

He doesn't know what he's talking about. I'm still that same girl he met at the store.

Fists clenched, I stomp out of the lab. The cafeteria is packed, and I see Harper saving a seat for me, but I keep walking. I'll make it up to her later.

I storm all the way to the gym where I know Lennox works out during almost every lunch period. I shove open the door to an overpowering sweaty stench, the sound of grunting, and too much testosterone.

Across the room, Lennox bench-presses an impressive weight. He could probably bench-press me. I wait at the end of the bench until Lennox shakes with his last repetition, giant chest muscles quivering. With a grunt, he heaves it back onto the rack and sits up.

My "you've got a lot of explaining to do" look is ready on my face. He doesn't seem to notice, because he grins. Apparently I'm no better at facial expressions now than when Mom convinced me to be the business mascot.

"Hey, princess. What's up?"

I frown at the nickname. "Why are you so mean to Kevin?"

"Who? The supernerd?"

"He's not a nerd."

"I didn't say nerd. I said *super*nerd."

I roll my eyes. "He's not a supernerd. And yes, that's who I'm talking about."

Grabbing his towel, he wipes the sweat off his neck and face. He stares at my crossed arms. Hanging his head, he's quiet for a moment. I think he might actually apologize for his boorishness.

He balls up his towel and tosses it into the laundry hamper then walks toward the corner of the room. I follow, thinking he just wants to talk to me in private, but then he bends over the trashcan and riffles through it.

"I didn't pick on him for no reason," he says.

Pulling out the crumpled up piece of paper he ripped out of Kevin's notebook, he hands it to me. It's covered in squished banana and protein bar. I wrinkle my nose, so he opens it and holds it up for me to see.

"It's because I saw this."

I look past the discarded lunch smudges and can tell instantly it's one of Kevin's drawings by the drastic use of shadow and light and by the expressive faces. But it's not of Wonder Woman. This time, it's a sketch of me.

I'm bent over a dropped pen, my skirt bursting open at the butt. It's so detailed that he even drew Wonder Woman on my underwear. The other students are laughing and pointing in the background. He captured the most embarrassing moment in my life perfectly. But I suppose he did have a front row seat for it.

"Why would he draw this?" I say.

"Look, I've known Kevin since grade school," Lennox says. "We used to be good friends. But he's not as good of a person as he pretends to be."

I laugh in surprise. "I'm having trouble imagining you two getting along, far less hanging out."

"We were a lot younger. There was a time when I needed him, and he wasn't there for me. Instead, he pushed me away and forgot all about me. Started hanging out with new friends. Maybe I'm a little hard on him now because of it." He shrugs, like that makes up for the bullying.

But the new information certainly makes me look at the other side of things. Even after all these years, Lennox still seems hurt by whatever Kevin did.

"He's just not as great as he thinks he is." Lennox crumples the picture back up and tosses it away. "I know you must have thought I was kind of a jerk after class. But when I saw this on his desk, it just kind of pissed me off, you know?"

He reaches out and plays with the lace on my sleeve. I stiffen at the touch.

"And then you were so nice to him at the end of class, talking to him. I think you deserve better than that." His fingers trail down my arm. "I guess I just got protective."

"Protective? Of me?" I say.

Me? A guy like Lennox protective of Awkward Andy. I shiver under his touch, but I back away. Lennox is totally off-limits. Harper still likes him. And even if she didn't, they used to date, and she's my friend now. Friends don't date their friend's exes. That's like the unwritten rule of every friend everywhere in the history of all friendships. What is he thinking?

He moves in really close until my brain gets foggy with his heady smell, which only got better after his workout—I'm so weird.

He tucks a stray curl behind my ear. "Are you mad?"

"I guess you weren't the bully." My voice is all shaky. "Kevin was." Then why can't I get myself to thank him for "protecting" me? Because what he did seems just as wrong?

The bell rings to mark the end of lunch. Lennox pulls away and smiles, and it's so dazzling, like one of those toothpaste commercials.

"See you later," he says, in that way of his that sounds like a promise.

I watch Lennox leave, my head spinning from his side of the story. My legs feel weak, like my righteous energy has been zapped. I deflate onto a nearby bench-press machine.

It turns out Lennox wasn't the big bad bully I thought he was. In the end, he was my knight in shining armor today—or at least he tried to be. However, he doesn't know that I want to larp on the weekends. That maybe I'm even more of a "supernerd" than the people he teases. If he ever found out, would he be as mean to me as he is to them?

I was just angry when I called Kevin pretentious, but maybe there's some truth to it. He said I'm not the person he thought I was. Apparently the same goes for him. I had so much fun hanging out with him at larping on Sunday, but maybe Kevin wasn't so much a knight as he was some guy who rode in on his high horse.

Tears start to sting my eyes. With a shaking hand, I pull the crumpled picture out of the garbage can, then leave in search of Kevin, ready to throw his hypocrisy in his face.

Chapter Fourteen

Hardware Hubbub

The hardware store bell dings as I burst in. By the time Kevin stops scribbling in his notebook, I'm already glaring at him from across the counter. He might have been able to avoid me for the rest of the school day, but he can't avoid me at his work.

"What's your problem?" I demand.

He starts in surprise but recovers quickly, wiping his face clean of emotion. His gaze is cool. "I don't have a problem. But you came here, so I'm guessing you have one," he says sarcastically.

My anger spikes at his tone. I suddenly realize what a bad idea it was to confront him in a setting with so many sharp and dangerous objects laying around. "Yeah. My problem is you."

"Glad we figured that out. Thanks for shopping with us. Have a nice day." He dips his head back to the notebook like I'm just going to leave.

I slap his cruel sketch of me on the counter in front of him. "You want to explain this?"

He points to the wrinkled piece of paper. "Well, this is you. And…this is your underwear."

"Why would you draw this?" As angry as I am, I'm surprised at how hurt I sound. He seems to hear it, too, because he closes his book and regards me seriously.

"Do you have any idea how much this moment sucked?" I ask. "It was one of the top five worst in my life."

He huffs, his eyebrows rising. "If that didn't take the top place, then the others must have been catastrophic."

The sarcasm in his voice is gone. Actually, he sounds kind of sincere, but I'm annoyed that he's not arguing back. I'd prepared too many comebacks in my head on the way here not to use them.

"Well, it can't possibly beat the time that I was unknowingly offered toilet bowl water during gym class, and I drank it. Or there was the time a bunch of kids tied me to a chair in the middle of the hall with my dad's own toilet paper brand. I couldn't even tear myself free while people passed by and drew penises all over my face. It's incredibly durable toilet paper," I assure him.

His eyes drop to the counter and when they rise back to meet mine, I see Kevin. Not the icy Kevin from the biology lab or the disgusted Kevin from the ice cream shop. Just Kevin. It feels like too long since he's looked at me for real, with no barriers between us.

He frowns. "Wow, your last school sounds tough."

But I'm too fired up to let him off the hook that easily. "So you can imagine how I felt when one of the few people who I thought could actually be my real friend at this school drew something like this." I jab a finger at the evidence. "What? Were you planning on showing everyone? Maybe put it in the school newspaper for anyone who didn't catch it on national television last Friday night?"

He cringes, all trace of cool sarcasm gone. "It was on TV?"

"Like you didn't know." I narrow my eyes at him. "My parents tried to get them not to air it, but apparently we've signed our lives away and the network thought it was too funny not to air. Because my life is one big joke!" I throw my hands up in the air. "And now you're laughing at me, too."

His eyes close for a second, and he shakes his head. I don't think he's shaking it at me but at himself. "My uncle saw the show, but I didn't. I had no idea they filmed it. I'm not laughing at you."

Sadness touches his dark eyes in a flutter of thick lashes. God, how I hate the effect he has on me. How badly I want to believe him.

"Then what is this?" I wave the drawing in his face.

Kevin stares at his feet like he's got no argument. Of course he doesn't. The evidence speaks for itself.

"For someone who pretends to hate bullying," I say, "this was a pretty crappy move."

"I-I didn't mean it that way," he says, finally. "I never intended to show anyone."

I cross my arms, feeling slightly vindicated by the look of remorse on his face. "Then why would you draw it in the first place?"

With a sigh, Kevin flips open the notebook sitting on the counter. He turns it around to face me.

I glance down at the pages. It takes a moment to realize what I'm looking at. It's not a notebook at all. It's his sketchbook.

There's a jagged piece of paper sticking out from the spine where Lennox had ripped out the drawing of me. On the next page, there's another sketch. It's of Kevin's uncle. He's restocking the shelves in the store just like on the day I first stumbled into the place. It's very comic-like, heavy on the contrast between shadow and light. But it's so clear, right down to the few sparse hairs still left on his uncle's balding head.

I reach down and flip the page carefully. My hand freezes on the next drawing. It's me again. Only this time Kevin's in the picture, too, peeking under the table where I hid from Corbin that same day.

"These are really good," I say, my voice quiet compared to a minute ago.

"It's like a journal, but in comic form," he says. "I'm not much of a writer. I find it easier to communicate through drawing pictures, capturing moments in time."

He flips through the next few pages to show me. I catch glimpses of his sister, Keelie, of his friends from larping. Then I see a drawing of the ice cream parlor and I swallow hard.

A few pages later I see myself again, only he doesn't know it's me. I'm wearing my larping costume. It's all black and white except for the gold of my mask and the green tipped feathers framing it.

I peek up at him, but he's looking down at the drawing of Princess Andy. Heat crawls up my skin, and I hope he doesn't notice. For some reason, the fact that he took the time to draw me, not once but a few times, makes me feel not only ashamed for yelling at him, but also strangely happy at the same time.

I pick up the crumpled drawing that seemed so mean a few minutes ago. Now that I look closer, I see a familiar face drawn among the crowd of people laughing at me in the background. It's Kevin. And he's not laughing.

I suddenly wish that everything could be undone. That

we could just start over again. That I could reach out to him right now, but it feels like there's too much between us. I find where his sketch was torn out of the book and place it back in as best I can.

"Why did you have to choose this moment to draw?" It's embarrassing to know that when he thinks of me, this is what he remembers.

He closes the book reverently, and I feel bad that Lennox ruined his journal. "Because it was out of the ordinary. It was something different that stuck out."

I snort. "I do stick out."

"No. You're different in a good way." His hand slides across the counter, inching toward mine, like he wants to hold it. But then he freezes, as though it were an unconscious action, an instinct to be close to me like I want to be close to him. But he's fighting it, because he hesitates, dropping his eyes to the sketchbook. "Or at least I thought you were."

"Oh, trust me. I'm different," I say, my voice dripping with sarcasm.

"Why are you hanging out with those girls?" he asks. "Why are you trying so hard to be like them? I can see that you're not. None of them would wear Wonder Woman underwear."

I roll my eyes. "That's for sure."

"Stop that," Kevin says. The forcefulness in his voice makes me wince. "It's not because there's something wrong with you. It's because they're not individual enough to ever do something like that."

His head dips to try to catch my lowered gaze. He seems to be waiting for a real answer. And since he's lowered his barrier, I lower mine. "I guess it's because I don't get teased when I hang out with them."

"I get it. I do. Just look at what happened today with

Lennox and me." He rubs the back of his neck, and I can see his ears are turning pink. "Thanks, by the way. It's not like I didn't appreciate you standing up for me. I know you were just trying to help, but it wasn't about you. Lennox and I have been at it for a while now."

I nod. After speaking with Lennox, I can see why Kevin didn't want me stepping in for him. Curiosity nags at me to ask about what went down between the two of them, but it's none of my business.

"I liked how you had my back, though," Kevin says. "It just proves that you're different. When you're not being controlled by your friends."

Embarrassed, I glance down at the notebook again, because I'm not sure where else to look. Or what else to say. "You're a really good artist."

"Thanks," he says. "The journal's, like, a way for me to reflect. It started as a way to improve my drawing skills and it slowly became a regular thing, a way to convey the important things that happen in my day."

"Seriously?" I can't help but laugh. "And you chose to draw me? There must have been something more important to draw that day."

"Seriously?" he says. "No. There wasn't."

And by the emphasis he places on his words, I know he doesn't mean it was because the rest of his day was boring. It's because he thought I was important at the time. And I want to be important to him again. And I think he wants that, too, or he wouldn't still be standing here talking to me. He wants me. I feel it in his searching gaze, the way his body has unconsciously leaned closer and closer across the counter to be near me.

"Well, you captured one of my worst moments very well," I say.

"It wasn't meant to be a bad thing. I just like to capture it all. The good and the bad." He taps his pencil on the counter restlessly. "Look at it like a comic book. Every good superhero has to go through hard times to experience the great ones. Batman was orphaned. The Hulk, well," he waves a hand, "just look at him. He's big, green, and ugly. That can't be easy. Iron Man was held captive by terrorists."

Kevin is speaking my language. Finally, someone who understands me.

I smile a little. "Plus there was the whole nearly dying from shrapnel next to his heart."

He nods appreciatively at my geek knowledge. "There have to be bad moments. Sometimes they're what make someone's story worth telling. It's how you react to them that shows you who you are, what you're made of. And when you rise above the odds, that's what makes you super."

I think about the ice cream parlor, and I don't feel particularly *super* about that. I could have done more in that moment to stand up for Kevin and his friends.

"I really didn't throw the ice cream at your sister," I say, in case I don't get another chance. "Just so you know."

His cheek wrinkles sheepishly, and he shoves his hands in his pockets. "I wasn't 100 percent sure, but I kind of suspected it wasn't you. When you mentioned Mercedes, it made more sense. It does seem like something she would do."

"And I didn't really throw out the note you gave me. Well, I guess I kind of did, but I didn't know what it was until I fished it out again."

I wait for him to say something about it, as though the offer for grabbing some pizza together is still open. My heartbeat throbs in my throat as I stand there, but he doesn't say anything, and I wonder if it's not for the best. Maybe we both still have some things to make up for, to get back on track. But I think this might be the first step.

"Porcelain Princess!" a man calls out.

I shudder at the name and turn around. I spot a denim apron headed my way. It's Kevin's uncle.

"It's an honor, my lady, to have you grace this humble store with your patronage." He bows low, his bald patch shining beneath the fluorescent lights. He's wearing a Hawaiian shirt under his apron today.

Kevin groans like he's in physical pain. "Uncle Gerald, you're so embarrassing."

I laugh, wondering if he sometimes larps with his nephew. He'd certainly fit in. "I just popped in to say hi."

"Please, please. Don't let me disturb you." He holds up his hands. "Continue your visit. And if you want to have a look around the place, it's 10 percent off for royalty." He gives another gracious bow.

"Please stop," Kevin says. "You're killing me."

"I should really get going. But thanks anyway."

"Anytime. Anytime. And let the rest of your royal family know about the discount!" he calls after me as I leave. Even though the door closes, I can still hear his voice. "Way to get in good with the Bottom girl, Kevin!"

I turn back just in time to see Kevin banging his head against the counter. He catches my eye and waves to me. I smile back, and it's almost like we're friends.

Chapter Fifteen
Princess Perfect

I twist my body, crossing my legs at the ankles and jutting my arms out this way and that, but the photographer's sneer just gets worse and worse. He sighs and pulls the massive zoom lens out of my face, only to be replaced by Hugh's camera.

"I said provocative pose. Sexy." The photographer's French accent makes his scoff more pronounced somehow, more disdainful. "You look like a constipated pretzel."

"No she doesn't," Harper says from off to the side of the rented studio. She gives me a supportive thumbs-up.

"You are right," he says. "She makes a pretzel look relaxed."

I frown. Awkward Andy, that's me.

Mom crosses the studio and tugs at the ruffles of my princess dress to cover up my shoulders. She flashes the photographer her Mom Look. You know the one. Cocked eyebrow, pursed fish lips, twitchy eye.

"Sexy is *not* what we're going for," she says.

"She's right," Dad says, covering the mouthpiece on his

cell. "The company needs a clean image. We need sweet, innocent. A face everyone can trust while they sit on our toilets."

I groan. "Gee. Thanks, Dad."

"No problem, princess." He winks and gives me one of his usual goofy grins. I'm glad to see he's still himself. He seems so stressed out lately. He's been on his phone all morning but is determined to be around to support me.

"But sex sells," the photographer says.

"Not my toilets. And not my daughter." Dad tightens his tie.

"Very well." The photographer turns back to me. "Why don't you try sitting on the toilet this time?"

Sighing, I plop onto the toilet lid.

"That's right. Work it. You're the princess. It's your throne. You're royalty, darling. Royalty."

I follow his orders as best I can. It's torture. The lights are hot, and the dress is kind of itchy, not to mention outrageous. I look like Princess Toadstool. I half expect Bowser to show up and carry me away at any moment.

My giant pink dress puffs out like a balloon from my waist, there's so much blush on my cheeks and nose that I look like a drunken cartoon character, and my scepter is really just a golden plunger. At least I've got a prop toilet on hand if the photo shoot gets any more nauseating.

When Mom asked me to be the face of Bottom's Bathrooms and Accessories, I never expected this. Some headshots, a fashionable outfit, maybe, an awkward B-rate commercial. But not this. I look ridiculous. I'm a mascot. I wonder if they know I'm not a real princess. I can only imagine the kinds of pictures Kevin would draw about this. The thought actually makes me smile.

"Perfect," the photographer says, snapping away.

Of course now I can't stop thinking about Kevin, and the camera's going off like crazy. I remember how upset he became when he thought I wouldn't make it to larping tomorrow and how, when I promised I'd make it, he kissed my hand farewell. But he's not the only reason that I'm excited for larping. I can't wait to don my warrior princess leathers and kick some make-believe butt. But for now, I've got to spend what feels like an eternity sweating inside this humiliating pink parachute of a dress.

Harper's here, though. And she doesn't seem to be laughing at me. Okay, well, she is a little. But she's laughing with me, not at me.

The photographer pauses to change lenses. Harper comes over to feed me my latte through a straw—Suzzy, my stylist, doesn't want me to smudge the hot pink lipstick.

I'm glad Harper's around, for more than just the latte. Ever since I arrived at the set this morning, I've had this feeling. I can't really put my finger on it. It's like anxious hopefulness vibrating off everyone. Mom's chewing her acrylics, and Dad's pacing around the room with Corbin and the cameras following his every move. Every time his cell phone rings it's like he's waiting for someone to tell him the world is ending.

"Wave your scepter," the photographer yells. "Wave it."

I wave the toilet plunger back and forth, nearly taking out his expensive lens. With a tuck and roll, he dives out of the way in time. He glares at me. French disdain.

He waves Harper over without looking at her. "Let's try the crown now."

Hopping out of her seat again, she rushes over with the tiara. She nestles it into my curls that Suzzy swept into a half updo. She winks at me. "There. Picture perfect."

I hand her the scepter. "Here. Sit down. We need a few

pictures together."

Her nose wrinkles. "On a toilet?"

"Not just any toilet," I say, uber seriously. "A Bottom's Bathrooms toilet."

"Oh, well in that case." She rolls her eyes with a smile and drops down onto the lid.

I lean over her shoulder while the photographer takes a couple shots of us goofing off. Then Harper's phone buzzes in her pocket. She hands me back the scepter. When she reads the text, she makes an excited squealy sound.

"What is it?" I ask.

"It's Lennox."

"Oh. That's good. You two are talking again?"

She pulls a face. "Not really. We've just been working out the details of a double date for next weekend." Her eyebrows waggle meaningfully.

"How can you be going on a date with Lennox if you're not really talking?"

"It's a ruse," she says. "I'm setting it up like we're just going as fillers for the 'double' part of it."

My eyes widen at her clever deceptiveness. "Good thinking. So it's like you're on a date together, but he just doesn't know it."

I can see how excited she is, but her eyes drop like she's embarrassed. "I'm hoping it will give us a chance to reconnect."

"Well, if he's willing to do it, maybe he's hoping for the same thing." I give her a confident smile, and she returns it.

But then I remember the way Lennox was acting earlier this week at school. How flirty he got with me, the way he looked at me, how "protective" he was of me around Kevin. I swallow hard and face the camera again.

I never told Harper about it because I thought it was

probably all in my head. It's not as though a guy like Lennox would ever be interested in me. It was a miracle I'd caught the attention of one boy. Two would mean someone's playing a trick on me.

I kind of hoped that when Harper started showing a bit more interest in Lennox again that his weird behavior around me would go away. And maybe it has already. Maybe Lennox agreeing to the double date is a good sign for them.

I pick at a thread on my dress before speaking again. "I still don't get it, though. What exactly do you see in Lennox? I mean, he's so…" Several words come to mind, but I keep searching for something less mean—if true.

"Boneheaded? Dense? Cocky? Insensitive?" Even as she rattles off insults, Harper's grin grows bigger and bigger, like she's actually complimenting him.

"Umm, yeah." She said it, not me.

Her hands spread open, like *I have no idea*, but then she says, "Because when you get to know him and understand where some of those irritating qualities come from, you realize there's much more to him than what's on the surface. I guess he thinks he's supposed to be a stereotypical high school jock." She rolls her eyes. "Sometimes he overcompensates for the parts of him that he thinks don't fit the bill."

"I'm pretty sure he was born for the role," I say sarcastically.

She laughs but stares down at her phone impatiently. For the first time, I can see her home screen photo. It's her and Lennox together, probably from when they were dating.

"Maybe you're right," she says. "But beneath the hard shell, he's just a big softy."

"Like a Tootsie Pop," I say.

"Yes. Exactly." She looks up from her phone and her eyes are all glowy and reminiscy. "When we were together I knew the real him, the soft center, and he let me inside. And it was different in there, you know?" She points to her chest as though clarifying that she means inside Lennox, not a Tootsie Pop.

I nod but let her go on. It's hard for me to imagine this other Lennox. Listening to her is like getting a glimpse into a parallel universe, one I never thought I'd be on the cusp of. Where the popular people live.

"When we were together, we could both be ourselves," Harper continues. "And it was just him and me against the world." She stares at her phone again and shrugs. "Since we drifted apart, the world feels a lot stronger or bigger than just me."

I stop myself from laughing. Not in a ha-ha way, but because what she says sounds so familiar and I think maybe I'm not so crazy after all. Instead, I lean forward on my toilet and fix her with a stare. "I'm here too, you know. You're not alone against the world."

Those Scarlett Johansson lips curl into a half smile. "Thanks."

"Look at me, not the girl!" the photographer barks.

I do as he says, my eyeballs stinging as the flash goes off.

Corbin sidles over from the other side of the room. "Are you girls talking about boys?" I swear he has Superman hearing.

Hugh shoves the camera in my face, looking for something, anything worthy of teen girl drama.

"Boys?" Dad pulls his phone away from his ear and shuts it off. "Absolutely no boys."

"But she's sixteen," Mom says.

"Exactly." Dad's cell rings again, but he ignores it. He reaches up and tightens his tie. Is it possible to asphyxiate yourself with a tie? "No dates."

Mom's picking at her cuticles again. "She's not a little girl anymore, honey."

"She's still my little princess."

"I'm not a princess," I say, which is difficult to deny while wearing a ball gown and tiara.

Dad's phone rings again. He glances at it, then back at me, then at Mom and Harper. He grunts and then answers the phone.

Is that a yes? And why are we talking about this anyway? If I actually got a date with a boy, then I really would think the world is ending. I was close with Kevin, but I screwed that one up royally.

One thing that hasn't changed about my life is that my parents are still pretty strict. Dad doesn't think I should date until I'm eighteen. It's also why they won't buy me a car—not like they can't afford it. They just don't want to spoil me, or at least Dad doesn't. I've had Mom nearly swayed on more than one occasion.

Dad's yelling into the phone again and Corbin waves Hugh over. He scrambles across the studio with the heavy camera.

Mom fixes my tiara, tucking a few curls back into place. "Don't worry about your dad, sweetheart. He's just a little stressed out today."

"Why? What's going on?"

Her face twitches, and I think she's trying to frown. She hesitates like she's choosing her next words carefully. "Well, apparently this week's episode of *Bathroom Barons* wasn't well received by our consumers or our investors."

I frown, but the photographer wags his finger at me,

and I force a smile. "That's bad," I say through my bared teeth. "Is no one watching the show?"

"It's not that. It's, well..." She works at her nail color, chipping away at it. "We were hoping for a clean, family-oriented image for the company. But after what happened in episode two last night, with the ice cream parlor, some viewers perceived you to be a bit of a bully, which is not very family friendly."

My eyes bulge out of my head. After I watched the show with my parents they were furious at my behavior. Once I explained everything, they understood, because, let's face it, after what I endured at my last school, why would I ever bully anyone else?

"But I told you—"

She holds up her hands. "That it wasn't your fault. I know, I know." She squeezes my arms gently. "We believe you, princess. But the people know only what they see on TV, and well, it looked pretty bad."

I feel like the toilet just fell out from under me. "But that's not fair. It's Corbin's fault." I point the scepter in his direction. "It's his editing. He skewed everything to make it look like it was my fault. And then afterward, he refused to interview me about it to let me explain."

Harper was close enough to hear the conversation. So far she's been politely pretending that she can't hear, but she pipes up now. "It's true, Mrs. Bottom. It was really Mercedes's fault. Adrianna was only trying to help."

"I know it's not fair. But add that to the underwear episode—"

I laugh, but it sounds more like a gasp for air. "You think I wanted that to happen?"

"Of course not. It's not your fault." Her shoulders sag, like it pains her to say it as much as it hurts to hear it.

And it really does hurt. I can't breathe, like my princess corset is too tight. It would almost be better if I were in trouble. Instead, my parents are in trouble. And it's my fault.

Mom waves the photographer away, and he wanders over to his equipment bag, out of earshot. Once she checks that the cameras are still following Dad, she turns back to me.

"Our lawyers have gone through our contract with the network, and there doesn't seem to be anything we can do about our rights to control the show's content. It is what it is. In the meantime, we just have to be careful not to give them anything they can use against us. While it's been good for the show's ratings, it's been bad for business."

I tug at my corset ribbon to loosen it. "How bad is it?"

"It's worse than bad. Sales are down by 18 percent. Plus, one of the investors for the new store is trying to back out. That's who your Dad's on the phone with now." Her nose wrinkles like a bunny rabbit—practically the only facial expression she can make anymore. "Marketing is trying to do some damage control, but it all hinges on really driving this new image for the company."

"You mean me." I nod, beginning to understand. "The whole clean-pressed princess thing."

Corbin has been shadowing Dad for most of the day, but now he spots Mom and me having a heart to heart and signals Hugh to come in for a close-up. There are no secrets on national television.

This whole time I've felt suffocated by the cameras, afraid they'll ruin my life, discover my larping secret, and be the reason people tease me. But the whole world gets to watch Mom and Dad's mistakes and failures, too. And right now I'm the cause of it.

Mom starts biting her nails again. The fire-engine-red

paint is chipped on every one. "It's important to go forward even stronger, to make people forget the bad stuff that happened on the show so far. And with the grand opening of our central Hollywood store next weekend, a lot is riding on this." One of her acrylic nails snaps right off.

It's no longer just about avoiding things that can embarrass me, but also my parents. If not, Dad could lose his new store. Heck, an 18 percent drop in sales over a spoonful of ice cream? He could lose his whole business.

Dad opened his first store in Seattle. It was small, but once the business started picking up the pace and we went online, that's when things got crazy. Next weekend he's opening his second store. The first store in Seattle is doing well, but I know Dad's still nervous about how the new one will do. And it sounds like things aren't going very well already.

It makes me think of Kevin's uncle. Dad's worried about losing investors and sales overseas, meanwhile the hardware store is just worried about losing the few local sales they had to the new Bottom's store.

Mom's still nattering in her stressed-out fashion. "… not to mention, construction will be starting on our north store location soon. It's costing a fortune. If sales continue to plummet…" She peters off.

I pull her fingers away from her mouth. "Don't worry, Mom. I get it." So basically Dad's business is on the line here. Everything. The show, our home, our entire future. No pressure or anything. "I'll do my best. I promise."

"We really appreciate you helping us out, princess. Just keep focused on the positive things. The photos, the fashion line. Anything to gain some positive promotion and help increase the exposure of Bottom's Bathrooms."

"And Accessories," I mumble automatically.

"Your big public debut will be a few weeks from tomorrow at the grand opening of the new store." She tugs at my puffy sleeves. "Keep this dress ready."

"Public debut? On a Sunday?" I'll have to miss larping.

"Do you have plans? I know you've been hanging out with your new friends a lot lately, but this is really important."

It's not like I can tell her what my real plans are on Sundays. I glance down at my costume, and that horror-movie panic begins to set in beneath the lace bodice. But then I look at Mom's decimated nails and Dad pacing in the corner, and it worries me. I can't say no to helping them. Not when it can save their company. Especially when it's in trouble because of my actions.

I fake a smile, and the photographer takes this as his cue to start snapping again. "No. No plans. I'll be there."

"Thank you, princess." She kisses me, or rather the air around my forehead so she doesn't brand me with lipstick. "I know we're asking a lot of you, so we've already discussed your payment for all the work you'll be doing. Your father and I have decided that we'd like to buy you a car."

"Really?" I leap off the toilet. "That's fantastic. Thanks, Mom." I pull her in for a hug, and she smacks a big kiss on my cheek anyway. She kind of lingers in the hug, like she really needs one today.

"Thank your father, too. I should go see how he's doing." As she walks over to the corner where Dad's arguing on the phone, she glances back at me and points to her bared teeth.

I dab at the lipstick mark on my cheek until I think it's gone. At a gesture from the photographer, I take a seat on my throne again and smile for Mom—and for my new car, which isn't hard. I have to lift my feet since he's practically crawling on the ground to get another angle.

"Good. Fabulous. Now give me innocent. Bat those eyelashes. Wave that scepter. Wave it!"

Harper's cell phone jingles again. I can't help but try and sneak a peek at the screen, but she's too far away. "Lennox?"

"No. It's Conner. Just setting up a date with the two of them."

"But I thought you wanted to get back together with Lennox."

"They're not both for me, duh." She winks at me and lowers her voice. "They're for both of us. A double date."

"You want me to go on a date?" The scepter freezes in my hand. "Me?"

She nods enthusiastically.

I don't even know this Conner guy, but a nervous buzzing begins in my stomach. Whether it's a good nervous or a bad nervous, I'm not sure.

I've never been on a real date. And after losing most of my friends in Seattle, I never thought I would. Things sure have changed for me in Beverly Hills. I'm going on a date. *Me*. It feels good. God, next thing you know I'll be prom queen.

Then I think of Kevin, and I'm a little confused. I like hanging out with him, but it's not like I can go to the movies with him. Not yet, anyway. It still feels too soon since we mended things. I'm not even sure he would say yes if I asked.

The buzzing increases like a horde of angry bees trapped in my gut.

"I don't think my dad will let me," I say, because I'm not sure I want to go anymore.

"Let you do what?" Mom asks. Hugh is right on her heels with the camera.

Harper chirps up. “Go to the movies next weekend. It’s a group thing,” she says. “But there will be boys.”

Mom claps her hands. “A date! That’s so exciting.” She squeezes my shoulders. “Don’t you worry about your father. I’ll have a word with him. You two girls have fun.”

I sink down onto the toilet, and the photographer starts snapping photos again. I may not look like a pretzel on the outside anymore, but on the inside, my stomach is in knots.

I have a date. With a real live boy. But shouldn’t it be with Kevin?

Chapter Sixteen

Masked Mystery

"Attack!" The order comes from Game Master Ken as he slices his blade down the middle of the field. With that command, the battle commences.

A deafening cry goes up from the two armies that face each other, the red and the blue—which are the only color armbands they had at the sporting goods store. As though Ken's blade has severed some invisible barrier, the opposing armies surge forward, closing the gap between them.

I'm on a team with Keelie, Finn, Shawn, and about seven others whose names I still don't know yet. By the luck of the draw at the start of the game, I'm Kevin's enemy today—which doesn't feel lucky at all. I catch a glimpse of him amongst the advancing army, but I don't stare too long. I have to focus on the coming battle.

Our advance comes to a quick halt when our army collides with the red. Boffers boff, and both comrades and enemies cry out their hits. As warriors on the front line fall, the battle spreads out. Room opens up to maneuver, and

I search for my own fight. I pick my way through sparring warriors while I watch my back for arrows.

There's movement in the corner of my eye. I drop to one knee just in time to avoid a poleax to the chest. It sweeps wide, arcing over my head, narrowly missing me.

From the ground, I stare at the furry brown legs of a beast. I hop to my feet. My nose is nipple height to the muscular chest of a man covered in chain mail. I think his name is Mark.

The half man, half beast takes another swing at me. I see it coming this time and dodge again. It's a long weapon, not meant for close-range fights. Using that to my advantage, I tuck and roll next to him, sweeping my short blade across the beastly thigh. He grunts and stumbles back.

"Hit one, left leg," he says.

Lifting one hoof, Mark balances himself with his poleax. In a melee like this, he won't last long with dismemberment. I glance at his belt to check for magic, but his abilities rely on strength and power. He can't heal himself.

I back away closer to the tree line where there are more obstacles to put between us. He hops after me. I dart in for another hit, but he sweeps his poleax around, catching me on my torso.

"Hit two, chest," I say.

Wasting no time to heal myself, I circle around the big man. He's hopping around now, trying to keep his back to a tree trunk for cover. I keep him spinning until I get my shot. Since he's wearing chain mail, the hit is worth one point, instead of two.

"Hold!" Keelie calls out, loud enough for everyone to hear.

I freeze mid swing. Mark straightens up and stretches his leg out. Out of the corner of my eye, I watch a young couple walking their two wiener dogs right through the middle of the battlefield—or along the dirt walking path, I suppose.

They give us strange looks as they pass.

Ken nods his head, his wizard cap flopping a little. "Hello."

"Hello," the couple says back and carries on.

I take the brief pause to search the faces of the warriors around me. After a moment, I find what I'm looking for: Kevin. His dark crazy hair glistens with gel on the far side, catching my attention. He's facing off against Finn, and since the mana tags on Finn's sash seem to be deteriorating quickly, I assume Kevin's on the winning end of things.

Kevin's gaze flits to mine like he's looking for me at the same time—or at least I hope it wasn't by accident. I tilt my head in "hello," and he raises his sword in return.

I hope I don't have to fight him. And yet, part of me wants to, if only so I can spend a little more time with him today.

I wonder if he'll hold back. What if he does? What if I beat him? Or what if he doesn't hold back and he beats me? What would that mean? That he doesn't like me as much as I like him? Or maybe he just respects me too much to hold back?

I want to silently communicate a little longer, but the couple reaches the other end of the field to safety, and Keelie calls out again. "Three, two, one. Lay on!"

I begin my attacks on Mark immediately, catching him by surprise. Swinging wildly, I force him to use his staff to block instead of balance.

Taking my hits on the shaft of his weapon, he parries my blows. The next one sends him reaching. He overcompensates and struggles to stay on his one hoof. That's when

I cut it off at the ankle.

Once he's on his knees, legless, I stand in front of him. He spreads his arms wide, exposing his chest.

"Honor me with a warrior's death."

I nod gravely and bring my sword down on him over and over. He flicks his health tags aside to count down the hits. Eight in total. He was a strong warrior.

Groaning, Mark collapses to the ground. He then gets back up to his knees and interlaces his fingers behind his head. The death pose.

As I look back to the open field, I notice many have already assumed the same position. With so many players participating today, bodies sprawled everywhere would be a hazard. Assuming the death pose makes the most sense.

Among the fallen, I see my teammates Shawn the ninja and Keelie. From her death pose, Keelie nods her head slightly toward the trees behind me.

I spin around, expecting a sneak attack, but then I spot Eddie's tall, slim figure darting amongst the thick underbrush. He seems to have survived, but that's mostly because he appears to be running away from all confrontation.

Not for long. With a grin, I give chase. I weave through the trees and leap over rocks, following the flashes from the sun glinting off his armor. Eventually he tires and stops to lean against a tree to catch his breath.

When I get closer, he holds his sword at the ready and settles into a fighting stance. Eddie's character is experienced but clumsy, as I suspect Eddie is in real life, and the fight doesn't take long before he's in the death pose.

Turning my back on the dead body, I retrace my steps to the battlefield to see if any of my team survived. I'm about to round a gnarled pine tree when I hear fabric swish behind me.

I spin, bringing my sword up, but it's deflected. It flings from my hand and falls amongst the dried leaves with a crunch. I gasp when I see Kevin.

His eyebrow quirks, like "well, well." He brings his sword to my neck.

The duct tape feels cool against my skin as he backs me up against the pine tree's trunk. I flinch as he draws closer, but he makes no move to stab me.

I hold his gaze, daring him to do it. Instead, he takes a step closer until I can smell the leather of his vest.

His eyes roam over my face and mask, and for a brief moment I think he's going to kiss me. And I want him to. But then he asks, "How come you never take off your mask?"

I blink. I knew he'd eventually start to wonder, but this is only the second day that we've larped together so I didn't think it would be so soon. Maybe it's because I didn't take it off in the parking lot last time or because I showed up today with it on before we even officially began.

What am I supposed to say? That I'm hiding a grotesque birthmark? Maybe a giant scar?

Instead, I answer in character. "Because if I didn't, then someone might recognize me as the runaway princess and force me to go back to my stifling life at the castle."

"But you already revealed your secret to me. Surely, I can see your true face." He nudges the mask with a finger, pulling up on it.

I shake my head, grinning. "Then I'd have to kill you."

Kevin laughs. "Brave words for someone with a sword at her throat."

He tilts his head as though thinking, but in the same way one would do to kiss. We're certainly close enough to kiss. I suddenly realize how alone we are.

After a moment he shakes his head. "But I don't want to kill you."

"I don't want to kill you, either," I say. I glance down to his torso.

He follows my gaze. His smile vanishes when he discovers I'd pulled a knife from my leather bodice while he was acting all cocky. I press it against his leather armor. We're at a standoff.

"Well played," he says. "Truce?"

When I nod, he backs away carefully, withdrawing his sword from my neck.

"I wouldn't want to kill my gauntlet mender anyway." He holds up his gloved hand and wiggles his fingers. "You do great work. Thanks again, by the way. I'll never wear them for yard work again. They're too nice."

"You're welcome. And thanks for not killing me."

"Shall we return to the battlefield, Princess Andy?" He gestures for me to go first.

I automatically reach up to make sure my mask is secure before pushing away from the tree. With a wary eye on Kevin, I head back up the slope. "What if we're the only two left?"

"Then it will be my honor to be slain by such a beautiful girl."

"Beautiful?" I snort. "You don't even know what I look like."

"I don't have to see under the mask to know you're beautiful," he says. "You can look like Batman's Two-Face and I'd still think you were cute."

I make some noncommittal noise but settle on grinning like an idiot and staring at my feet as we climb up the slope. I can feel my cheeks burning beneath the mask. I'm pretty sure that was the sweetest thing a guy has ever said to me.

Which wasn't tough to achieve since the second best was probably something like "Can I borrow a pencil?" But still.

Embarrassed, I forge ahead, overtaking him on the hill. I'm too busy staring at my feet, so when I feel something hit my back, I don't know what it is until a red beanbag falls next to my boot.

"You can't move for fifteen seconds," Kevin says, sliding all his mana tags across his belt, draining his power.

I gasp. "But we had a truce."

"Don't worry," he says, circling in front of me. "I won't kill you. I just want to see who's under that mask."

Kevin grins mischievously at having outsmarted me. As he reaches around to the back of my wig, the air in my lungs solidifies, feeling thick and heavy. I think my heart has stopped beating, too. I would rather he kill me.

But as he tugs reverently on the golden ribbon holding it in place, I almost welcome it. Maybe it will be easier for someone to know my secret. Especially Kevin. He might understand. Or would he just be angry with me for duping him? He already thinks I'm two-faced enough as it is. What will he think when he sees it's me?

Frozen by his spell, I close my eyes tight and wait for the mask to come off. He takes his time, as though he's been waiting for this moment, imagining it as often as I have. I revel in the sensation of his hands so near my skin and yet not touching me. I swear my breaths are as loud as Eddie's screams were, and I want to gasp as he unties the bow.

I hear a *thunk* followed by Kevin's *umph*.

His hands freeze. I open my eyes to see confusion crease his forehead before he whips around to face the top of the crest.

Keelie's standing at the top, bow aimed at her brother.

After a stunned moment, Kevin says, "Hit two, chest."

Not wasting another moment, he bursts into action. He unsheathes his sword and sprints up the slope to close the distance, because close range makes Keelie's bow ineffective.

She releases another shot before he even gets close. Kevin tries to dodge the arrow, but it catches him in the side.

Kevin grunts and falls to his knees. His expression is shocked as he reaches up and interlaces his fingers behind his head for the death pose.

Keelie cheers. She sprints up to her brother to yell in his face. "Woohoo! We win!"

I laugh, more from relief that Kevin was interrupted than from surviving the battle. "Really? But I thought you were dead." The frozen spell Kevin cast on me wears off, and I run up the hill to meet them.

"Nope. I was faking it!" She gives me a delicate twirl in the new tunic I made her, beads and rhinestones tinkling against one another, flashing in the sunlight.

"Nice tactic!" I give her a high five.

When I glance back at Kevin, he's frowning bitterly at his sister in his defeat. Or maybe it's because he didn't get to see what was under my mask. I see his chest rise and fall quickly, as though he's panting, but I don't think it's because he was just murdered. As I walk away, he stares after me greedily. My body burns just from that look alone.

I got away this time. I'm safe to continue larping in secret, but I know it won't be long before he figures out what's up. How long will I be able to keep my secret?

Chapter Seventeen

Double-cross Date

I pace back and forth in front of the movie theater, popcorn-scented air wafting out of the front doors like buttery heaven.

"Can your knees sweat?" I ask Harper. "I think my knees are sweating."

"You'll be fine."

"I've never been on a date before."

"I know. You've told me a million times over the past week." Harper straightens the neckline on my dress that Suzzy said was imported from Europe. It's all flattering angles and tapering around the waist, cut to work with my curves, not against them this time.

Suzzy added a cropped jacket to dress it down a bit, and also to lessen the frown on Dad's face as I was about to leave the house. It fits like it was made for me, and for once, I don't feel self-conscious—about the dress, anyway.

I was so nervous getting ready for the date that I couldn't even match my socks, far less pick an outfit. I'll have to thank Suzzy again.

"Thanks for doing this, Adrianna." Harper bites her lip. I think she's nervous, too.

"Of course. It will be fun." I take a deep breath. "I can tell by the way I want to throw up."

I shock a laugh out of Harper, and she smiles gratefully. And I know it's her real smile because it's not her sexy fish-lips smile, or her I'm-too-good-for-you smile, or her I-didn't-do-anything-wrong smile. It's the smile she uses for me when no one else is around, and it's times like this that I think she's not hanging out with me just to be on TV. She might be my most real friend out of anyone from school. But then there are times when I still have my doubts, and I wonder if I'll ever truly know for sure.

I shake off the thought and focus on the night ahead. "Well, I hope tonight Lennox realizes what he's missing."

Harper flicks her blonde hair back. "Of course he will." She gives me a cheesy wink.

Right on cue, the camera crew pulls up in the parking lot. Thankfully they get only a few minutes of awkward close-up footage—too close, considering the size of my zit I tried to cover up on my nose. Before long, Lennox and Conner round the theater corner, chortling about something.

Lennox looks like he just walked out of an American Eagle or Calvin Klein poster. Conner's got on a pair of skinny jeans and has his hair slicked back like he's from the fifties or something, in a tried-too-hard kind of way.

It makes me think of Kevin's anime hair and how cute he looks without even trying. Or maybe it's because he doesn't take himself too seriously that he's cute. I remind myself that I'm supposed to be on a date with Conner, not Kevin.

"Hey," Lennox says to us, but he's looking at me.

"Hey," I say, because I can't think of anything else to say, or anything at all, really.

Lennox introduces Conner, because we've never met, and then we head inside. While we stand in line to buy snacks, Corbin berates our dates with a bunch of questions. The boys seem to love it, but it kind of gets annoying after a while. I feel like they're on a date with the cameras and not us.

Harper and I eventually drag the guys into the theater before the movie starts. I shuffle into the row first and take a seat. Lennox tries to follow, but Harper tugs him back.

"Wait, we should work out who sits next to who," she says.

Lennox looks confused and tries to inch toward the aisle. Harper looks at me for support, and back to Lennox. Suddenly I'm glad I went first; it's this kind of date stuff I'm not equipped to handle.

The lights go down, and the previews are about to start, so they have to decide. There's a brief moment of jostling bodies. It's totally dark now, but I hear whispered arguing and shoes crunching over the sticky, popcorn-littered floor. Someone crawls over my lap and steps on my foot.

"Ouch."

"Sorry." It's Lennox.

When the film starts rolling, I turn to find Lennox on my left. Harper is on my right, scowling at the screen, and Conner is sitting on her other side, looking a little out of place.

"Lennox," I whisper. "Why don't you sit here and I'll go sit by Conner?"

"Why?" he asks.

"Because I'm supposed to be on a date with him. Not you." Or at least, I thought so.

"Well, then I guess this is your lucky night." He gestures to himself like I've just won the lottery.

I roll my eyes and lean closer to Harper on my other side. She obviously heard what Lennox said, because her jaw clenches and her chin wrinkles like she's about to cry.

"Switch seats," I say.

She crosses her arms. "It's fine."

"But—"

"It's no big deal." And by the way she says it, I know it *is* a big deal. I want to turn and punch Lennox in the ear.

A movie sounded like a perfect date. A guaranteed two hours of being with a boy in a dark room—so he won't see my zit—where I wouldn't have to struggle to think of something to say. And best of all, no cameras. But it turns out I don't really get to enjoy it.

Harper's sighs, which at first are delicate huffs from her nose, soon become louder and more annoyed, the kind of sigh that she wants everyone to hear. I sit back and try to enjoy the movie, but now I'm hyper-aware of everyone around me, the noises, the movement.

Why would Lennox sit next to me? I'm not even sitting next to my date. And how are Lennox and Harper supposed to get back together if I'm stuck in between them? I can't even watch the screen because I keep stealing glances at Lennox out of the corner of my eye.

His hand is twitching a lot, and his knee is bouncing so much it's vibrating the entire row of seats. My butt hurts because I haven't moved an inch since I sat down, but at the same time I feel like I haven't stopped moving.

Lennox shifts beside me, and I think he's getting up to go to the bathroom. Maybe that's why he's been fidgeting so much. But then he lifts his arm like he's stretching, and when it comes back down, it's around my neck.

I freeze. Holy crap. I'm not sure if I'm supposed to look at him, or shove him away, or pretend everything is normal like maybe he really is just stretching. But everything isn't normal. Lennox is into me. He's supposed to be realizing that he misses Harper. What the heck is he doing?

Next to me, Harper has become a statue. It's like she's staring at the screen, but not really seeing it. She's kind of shrunk in on herself so no part of her body touches Conner or me.

My insides go quiet, my heart and stomach shrinking and shriveling up.

Harper said she set up a double date for us, but when she was texting with Lennox, did she say whose dates were whose?

"Harper," I whisper. "Can you go to the bathroom with me?" Which is a secret code, because that's the officially recognized meeting place for all women everywhere.

She keeps her eyes on the screen. "I don't have to go."

So I lean forward and move my neck this way and that, as though I have a kink in it, then I rest my elbows on my knees and my chin on my fists. I stay like that so Lennox can't put his arm around me, listening to Harper tap her nails on the armrest for the remainder of the movie.

The second the credits roll, Conner gets up, ready to end the date. I'm not sure if Lennox gave him the impression I was his date, or if he thought he'd be paired up with Harper, but either way we all ended up losing.

When we hit the parking lot, Harper whips out her phone to call her dad to give us a ride, but Lennox stops her.

"Conner and I both drove tonight. We can give you ladies a ride home."

Since I know it will only start another round of "who goes with who" and upset Harper more, I shake my head.

"That's okay. Harper and I were going to hang out tonight, weren't we, Harper?"

I link my arm with hers like we're inseparable, but she kind of goes limp and moves away, hugging herself. "Actually, I'm tired." She says it nice enough, so I know she's not mad at me. She even sounds a little sad.

I get it. She's just disappointed things didn't work out the way she'd hoped. I'm disappointed for her, too. But I wish she'd stop freezing me out. I came here tonight for her. If she wants to take it out on someone, then she should target Lennox since they planned the date together in the first place, and he's the one screwing it all up.

"Great," Lennox says. Even though it's kind of warm out, he puts on his leather jacket. I wonder if he just wants to seem cooler. But right now he doesn't seem very cool at all after what he pulled. "So I'll give you a lift, A."

Since when did he start calling me A? That's not a nickname. That's a letter. At least Kevin was semi-original when he called me Red.

Harper stiffens at the name and chucks her phone in her purse. "Fine. Conner, will you drive me home?"

I don't want Harper to leave mad. "Wait," I say. "Lennox, you live like a block away from Harper. It would make more sense for you to take her."

"Conner has to drive that way anyway," he says.

Conner shrugs. "It's cool."

"It's fine," Harper says. And because she grabs Conner's arm and starts dragging him through the parking lot, the conversation ends.

"Talk to you tomorrow?" I call to her back, but she doesn't answer.

Lennox gestures for me to go ahead of him, as if he's some kind of gentleman. We walk around the side of the building, and I look back in time to see Harper crawl into Conner's car silently.

I watch them drive away, wondering if I should have fought a little harder to leave with her. This date did not go how I expected. And now there's nothing I can do but go with Lennox.

He stops walking. "Here we are."

I turn around. In the dark parking lot, all I see at first is just a black car. But once my eyes adjust, my mouth pops open and stays like that.

"I know, right?" Lennox says, like I'm impressed by his wheels. "This is my baby."

But I'm suddenly having fast-food flashbacks from my first day of larping. I recall the muscle car the McDonald's attackers drove, as clear as if it were happening at this very moment. The humiliation and the senseless torment. Something I know too much about from my life in Seattle.

Lennox's "baby" is the Mustang with red racing stripes down the center. He's the Mac Attacker.

Chapter Eighteen
Kiss and Tell

The Mustang engine roars, but it's not that impressive, since I was right about it being an automatic. Lennox glances at me from the driver's seat and gives me a "what's up?" head nod.

Those lips don't look so luscious anymore. More like two turkey sausages. And I never noticed just how loudly he breathes. I mean, it's like he's snoring while awake. And sure he looks like a real version of a Ken doll, but maybe he's a little too perfect, like he spends just as much time getting ready in the morning as I do. Is that bronzer on his face?

He's not so Mr. Perfect, after all. What does Harper see in him? He's just your typical high school bully. Just a guy who has nothing better to do on his weekend than seek out and torture larpers.

The only reason he's nice to me is because he's apparently interested in me. Then again, I wonder about his motives behind the date. Lennox on a date with Awkward Andy? The movie *Carrie* flashes through my mind, and I wonder if I should be worried.

"I had a good time tonight," he says, reaching for my hand.

"Yeah. It was fun." I grab my phone out of my purse to keep my hands occupied, and Lennox grips the wheel again.

I text Harper. I'm not sure what to say. I mean, it's not like I wanted Lennox to make a move on me. She's probably just upset with Lennox, not me.

I'm so sorry. I text. **Are you okay? What the heck was up with Lennox, right?**

I study the neighborhood around us, but I have no idea where we are. If I tell Lennox off and jump out of the car, I'll have to call Mom and Dad for a ride. I'll never hear the end of it. Dad will be all "I told you so" and forbid me to date until I'm thirty.

I just want the car ride to be over already. I feel like I'm lurking behind enemy lines. I can't believe it was Lennox that threw McDonald's at us. That was just plain evil. And unprovoked. Was Conner in on it, too? Or was it one of his other mush-for-brains friends? I wonder if Kevin knows that it's Lennox leading the attacks. He must by now. The Mustang isn't exactly covert.

"Here we are," Lennox says as he pulls up in front of my driveway.

There's something in his voice that makes me clutch my purse, ready to bolt out the door once the car comes to a stop. When it does, the manicured gardenia bushes conceal us. Like we're hiding. He shuts off the headlights.

"Well, thanks for the ride." I reach for the handle, but the auto locks haven't released, and I fumble for a second.

Lennox leans over and moves my purse onto his own lap. "Not so fast." He takes my hand in his and pulls me away from the door. "I had a good time tonight."

"Yeah. Sure." I just wish it had been with someone else.

Kevin, to be precise. "It's too bad you and Harper didn't get more of a chance to talk." I emphasize Harper's name like I could hypnotize him into thinking about her.

"I don't want to talk to Harper. I want to talk to you."

I scoff, but he doesn't seem to notice. He's got as much chance with me as the 100 percent beef patties he likes to throw at people's heads. Not to mention he's an insensitive jerk for hurting his ex-girlfriend who is obviously still into him. He has to be blind not to see it.

Okay, well maybe not that blind.

Actually, come to think of it, he'd probably need ESP to decipher her feelings, because from what I've seen, Harper's only ever a cow to him at school. But just a little. Like a miniature cow, really. And first thing tomorrow, I'm going to call her on it. Tell her to just be up-front with him and stop letting her pride get in the way. If she really likes him, then she needs to just say it or else football-for-brains will never figure it out.

I reach across for my purse at the same time as he leans in. His lips connect with that little dip below my nose. After they drag down my face, he finds my mouth and slurps on my bottom lip.

Clamping my mouth closed, I press my fists against his chest, pushing him away, but his linebacker arms are wrapped around me.

"Lennox, stop," I try to say, but as I open my mouth to talk, he rams his tongue in. It fills my mouth like he's trying to perform a tonsillectomy on me, and my words come out as incoherent mumbles.

I back away, but now my head is squished against the door, and I've got nowhere to go, no way to fight but by trying to force his tongue out of my mouth with my own. I keep pushing at him, but he grabs my hand, like it's all romantic or something. He actually thinks I'm kissing him back?

Spit dribbles down our chins, and I turn my head to break his seal on my face. I gasp for air. That's when I see the lights glaring through the windshield.

There's a bang on the window behind me. I scream.

Hugh presses his lens up to get a close shot of the make-out session. Every gory moment of it. They were waiting for me to get home from my date. This time when I shove Lennox away, he moves back.

"Oh my God," I say. "They were filming it all."

"Don't worry about it. It's great drama." Lennox leans in for another kiss, but I shove him away again.

"Stop!"

"What's the big deal, A? We're making TV magic." He grabs me to pull me in, his hands like clammy chicken cutlets. "We're magic, baby."

"I'm not your baby, and it is a big deal. Get off me." I throw my hands up, catching him on the nose.

He yells and holds his face. It's dark, but I think I see blood dripping from between his fingers.

Purse in hand, I grope for the lock and fling the door open. Hugh stumbles and falls back on the grass. I step over him. Lennox calls after me, so does Corbin, but I sprint for the front door.

Dad's already got it open. He flicks on the porch lights, illuminating the crew behind me. He doesn't look happy.

"What's going on out here?"

I burst right past him and take the stairs two at a time. Once in my room, I slam the door and barricade myself against it.

I ignore the soft knocks from Mom. "Princess? Can I come in?"

Tears sting my eyes. I rub them away, glad Suzzy used

waterproof mascara tonight.

"It's safe to come out," Mom says. "The crew is gone now. Corbin said they just wanted to film you coming home from your date."

Of course he did. Innocent Corbin.

When I don't respond, she asks, "What happened?"

My first kiss. That's what happened. My terrible first kiss. And it was all caught on camera. No thanks to Lennox. He didn't even stop when I told him to, not even when he saw the cameras.

He only likes me because of the TV show, just like everyone else. Maybe he even planned this from the start of the night, wanted a big make-out session with me to be caught on film. Just to be on TV.

"Sweetheart?" Mom calls through the door. "Whatever it is, we can settle it tomorrow with Corbin. Everything will be okay."

Mom sounds worried. I know I should open the door, but I just want to be left alone, and the last thing I want to do is talk with my parents about what happened in the car. But I'll have to in the morning. It's either that or let them see it on television in a few weeks when it airs.

Eventually, I hear Mom walk away. Murmured voices drift under the door as she talks it over with Dad nearby. Soon, I hear a third male voice. By my parents' angry tone, I realize they're talking to Corbin on speaker phone. I imagine Mom's angry fish lips and Dad wishing he wasn't wearing his bathrobe so he could tighten his tie.

I crawl into bed just so I can bury my face in my pillow and scream and curse at Lennox, hands balled into fists around my blankets. A frog is supposed to turn into a prince when you kiss him. Not the other way around.

Instead, he turned out to be a big, warty toad.

Chapter Nineteen

Lying Two-Rhymer

I search my locker again for a book that doesn't exist. I'm running out of excuses to linger in the hall. I had hoped Harper would come by my locker this morning, like the double date with Lennox and Conner never happened. But she was a no-show. Which tells me a lot. As do my three dozen texts she ignored since Saturday night.

I'm so used to talking to her every day. I know how upset she must be, and I just wish I could talk to her and make sure everything's okay between us. It feels like there's a rabid raccoon trying to claw its way out of my stomach.

After Mom and Dad went ballistic on Corbin, the weasel promised that he'll edit the footage from our date tastefully. A simple telling of facts. We went to the movies, Lennox drove me home, he dropped me off. End of story.

I still haven't told my parents what happened in the driveway and why I was so upset. And if Corbin keeps his promise, I'll never have to. I'm still too embarrassed.

As I'm pacing by my locker, Kevin walks by with his friend Chad. They're taping up posters advertising the

Sadie Hawkins dance in November.

Kevin waves, and I wave back. We do that now. Sometimes we say "hello" too.

When I woke up yesterday, I had a hard time dragging my butt out of bed after my crappy double date. But the second I stepped into Asdor, all that went away. School, Corbin, Lennox, the Porcelain Princess—none of that exists when I'm larping.

For a few hours, I was Princess Andy of Asdor. The only thing I had to focus on was traveling from one end of the realm to the other without dying.

Kevin and I even got put on the same team, and we totally won. As we were cheering, he put his arm around me in a celebratory half hug. It felt nice. Not like when Lennox touched me.

It feels like Kevin and I are getting closer, but maybe that's just in my own head. While I've been spending a lot of time with him at larping, he doesn't know it's really me. He probably thinks we haven't done anything but a wave here and a "hello" there since he showed me his sketchbook journal at his uncle's hardware store a couple of weeks ago.

If I'm really going to get to know him, and let him get to know me, I need to do it as my school self. Not always hidden behind a mask.

I wait as long as I can before I head to biology, taking the scenic route by Harper's locker. When I get there, she's just grabbing her stuff to go. Maybe she was hanging around like I was in case I came by.

Stepping beside her, I cut her off before she can leave.

"Hey," I say.

And because she can't ignore me to my face, she has to say, "Hey."

"Why didn't you return any of my texts yesterday?"

Harper shrugs and starts walking to class. "I was busy."

She's walking too fast, so I pull at her sleeve, and because it's Prada, she slows down before it stretches. But she doesn't look at me.

"Harper. Talk to me." I say it a little harsher than I meant to. "Why are you mad at me?"

Instead of continuing to pretend that she's not, she spins to face me. "Because you knew how I felt about him."

I start at the accusation in her tone. "Which is exactly why I went on that double date with you. So you could spend time together."

"That date was supposed to be—" She stops and glances around. Students on their way to class are slowing down, lingering in the hall around us. They stare at us like they're waiting for a catfight.

"Carry on." I wave my hands. "Nothing to see here."

When no one looks like they're going to move any time soon, Harper walks down the hall to an alcove and waits for me there. She holds her book in front of her like a shield, scowling at me. Not exactly a "let's be friends" gesture. But then again, I guess I have my arms crossed as I stomp toward her.

"That date was supposed to be my chance to get back together with Lennox," she says in a hushed but sharp voice.

"I know that," I say. "Now tell *him* that."

"What's the point when he's obviously into you?" Her eyes narrow like she's trying to be scathing and cold, but her voice shakes.

I rub a hand over my face, unsure of why we're getting angry with each other and not Lennox.

"Look," I say a little calmer. "I'm sorry the date didn't go as you expected. But that was Lennox's fault and not mine. I did nothing to make him think I was interested in him."

It looks like she's hugging her book now. Her eyes drop to the floor.

"Harper. You're my friend," I say. "I wouldn't do that to you."

She closes her eyes and sighs. "I know you wouldn't." She gnaws on her lip for a few seconds before she finally looks at me. "It's just, when it happened, I didn't know what to feel. It really hurt, especially because it was you he wanted. And not me."

"And I'm sorry it happened," I say. "But you have to know I'm not interested in him at all. Like, at all." I make a giant swiping motion with my hands to show there was no chance in the whole wide world.

A hint of a smile appears as she slowly starts toward class again. "I guess, at the time, I was just too angry to think. I should have realized you didn't want him. But I mean, who wouldn't be interested in him?"

"Me, that's who." I laugh at the thought of it. "Harper, he's not a very nice person. I'm not sure what you see in him." I say it hesitantly, because if she's this hurt, I know she still likes him a lot despite what happened at the movies.

I frown, trying to figure out how to let her know what I know without blowing my larping cover. "Just look at the way he treated Kevin that one day at school. How he tore up his notes and picked on him after class."

She blinks like she suddenly remembered something. "Oh, yeah. I meant to tell you. Apparently Kevin drew something really mean about you, and Lennox didn't want anyone to see." She frowns. "Obviously because he likes you."

I shake my head. "No. That's not what happened."

"It is." She nods. "Lennox told me himself because I gave him crap for it."

I stop walking and turn to her in surprise. "You did?"

"Sure. I mean, mayor of Geeksville or not, it did seem like a jerk thing for Lennox to do at the time."

I stare at her. I know she would stand up for me, but the fact that she stood up for Kevin suddenly makes her seem…different. Like she's not just a good friend to me. She's just, well, good. I remember how I wished she'd stood up to Mercedes when she flung ice cream at Keelie. Maybe it bothered Harper more than she let on.

"But Lennox told me what Kevin drew," she continues. "So obviously he deserved it. Aren't you glad I warned you not to talk to him?"

I want to tell her the truth. Tell her that Kevin didn't mean it that way. But then I'd have to admit that I've been talking to him. I don't really want to start a big disagreement over Lennox and the whole Kevin issue now that Harper is talking to me again.

"Besides, that Kevin guy isn't that nice, I hear," Harper says. "Lennox told me that they used to be really good friends and when his Gram-Gram Mary was in the hospital dying, he wouldn't even return Lennox's calls. And he was so upset. How harsh is that?"

"That does sound pretty harsh," I say. And not at all like Kevin. I know there has to be more to that story, but again, while hiding behind so many personas, it's hard for me to argue that one. "And you believe Lennox's side?"

"Of course. It's Lennox," she says simply.

I try again to tell her what I know about Lennox. To show her that he's not worth her pining over. "Well, I heard, from someone," I say vaguely, "that Lennox bullies these geeks who do some kind of weird make-believe dress-up game on the weekends. He throws food at them and chases them in his car and stuff."

Harper just rolls her eyes and laughs. "Those are just rumors. Don't believe everything you hear."

I want to remind her that she believed hearsay about Kevin. But then again, it came from Lennox, and she seems to know a Lennox that I don't and obviously trusts his side of things. How can I make her see?

"People at school are afraid of Lennox because he acts all tough. But half the stories about him aren't true." She hugs her book again. "He's a lot softer than he lets on. You just need to get to know him better to see that side of him."

I grit my teeth, wishing I could tell her that I know this story is true, because I'm one of the geeks! But no one can know the truth. Not Mom, not Kevin, not Harper. It's the only way I can continue to enjoy what I like to do and avoid being teased about it at school.

She sighs, like she's missing out on a great catch. "Did I ever tell you how Lennox and I got together?"

I shake my head.

"He asked me out in a poem."

"Lennox writes poetry?" I laugh, maybe a little too loudly, because I'm surprised he can even spell, far less rhyme.

"I got poems all the time when we were dating. He was actually a really great boyfriend. He did lots of sweet things." The bell rings and we start to walk to class again, this time picking up our pace.

"Lennox would sit through chick flicks for me, let me pick the restaurants, opened doors for me like a gentleman. Not a lot of guys do that anymore. Oh, and when I sprained my ankle last spring, he carried me literally everywhere. It was really cute." Harper smiles kind of sadly.

Pulling aside her collar, she reaches in and draws out a pendant. I've never seen her without the white gold chain around her neck, but since she keeps it tucked under her shirt, the pendant's always been hidden.

When I blink at it under the florescent lights, I realize it's not a pendant, but a ring.

"I kept the promise ring he gave me. Just in case," she says. "Until Saturday night, I didn't think it was really over. I hadn't given up hope. I just thought we could get it all back, you know?"

Harper gives me this wistful, hopeless look that makes me decide not to tell her about what happened when Lennox dropped me off on Saturday night. Not right now, anyway. Not when it's so raw for her. According to Corbin, that footage will never see the light of day. I'll have time to tell her when things settle down.

"Harper," I begin hesitantly, "have you ever wondered why he's been acting so distant since school started?"

"Because he's not into me anymore, obviously."

"Or maybe it's because he doesn't think you're interested. Have you ever considered, I dunno, being nice to him? You've been pretty standoffish yourself." I give her an angelic look that I hope says "don't kill the messenger."

When she responds, she speaks more to her feet than me. "I just don't want it to seem like..."

"Like you're into him?" I suggest.

She laughs and rolls her eyes like she knows how crazy it sounds. "Yeah. I suppose you're right. I could give him a little slack."

"Then who knows," I say. "Maybe there's still a chance. There's always the Sadie Hawkins dance coming up in November. You could ask him to go." I wrap an arm around her as we head through the doors to biology. "Maybe you won't get things back the way they were before. Instead, you could start over. Make it better than ever."

She smiles, but she still looks kind of sad. "Maybe."

I make a promise to myself to tell her about what really went down at the end of our double date, just to make sure she really wants a guy like Lennox. Harper is my friend. I want to see her happy. Even if it's with a guy like him. Besides, from what she says, it sounds like there's a lot more to Lennox than I understand—not that I care to.

But if it's what she wants, then who am I to judge what kind of person he is when I've seen only one side of him? I certainly have my own hidden side.

Chapter Twenty
Seeing Red

Hairy, bloodthirsty monsters prance around their capture, celebrating the feast to come. The feast is Keelie, and she's tied to a tree. She struggles against the rope, but even if she were to get free, she's surrounded by the pack of werewolves.

Kevin and I crawl to the edge of the dry riverbank. From this vantage point we can see the entire pack below. The river has long since dried up, cleared of all the rocks and debris that could be tripped over during the inevitable battle.

"This is all my fault," Kevin says.

"Don't beat yourself up," I say. "How were you supposed to know that guy was the king of the werewolves?" "That guy" meaning Tony Chang, the manager of the IT department at the mall. One moment he was a tradesman we were haggling with over some magic stones, and in the blink of an eye he became a ferocious monster. And by "blink of an eye," I mean we paused the game so he could don a costume wolf head.

"Finn will be here soon with the silver arrows," Kevin says.

"The silver arrows that can be used only by the person currently tied up? How very convenient."

"Yeah, that might be a problem."

We're silent as we wait for the rest of the group to join us. But a good silent. While we may not be speaking, it's as though our bodies are, like I can feel the thrum of energy coursing between us. My senses are on alert, monitoring his every move, calculating when he gets farther away, when he draws closer. And he seems to find plenty of excuses for that.

Kevin suddenly reaches toward me, brushing his fingers gently over my cheek and down my neck. I shiver under his touch, both surprised by the move and excited by it. He's never touched me before without some little excuse, like pulling me away from danger or "accidentally" brushing up against me.

When he draws his hand away, a ladybug is crawling across his long finger. I'm a little disappointed, but smile as I watch him set it down on a leaf. When it flies to safety, Kevin reaches over again and brushes my hair, or rather my wig, aside. I feel his fingers trace a gentle line from my jaw to collarbone.

"Another bug?" I ask, a little breathless.

He shakes his head, but his eyes are following that same line. "No."

I bite my lip to stop from squealing from pure glee, but I can't control my skin as it tightens into goose bumps. I close my eyes and enjoy the designs he draws over me like I'm his human sketchbook. Instead of a pen, though, it feels like he's using a hot, flaming torch.

It feels nice to be with Kevin. It feels right. At least, it does when we're larping and I'm wearing my mask and wig.

I consider my dual personality and think of Lennox. For the rest of the school week, I watched him closely, searching for that person Harper described as her ex-boyfriend. The only other person who would know his other half would be Kevin, since they used to be friends way back, but I can't outright ask him.

When I've been quiet for a while, Kevin asks me, "You okay?"

I quirk an eyebrow in question. "Clarify?" I say in order to break character.

He nods. "Yeah, go ahead."

"Who were those guys in the Mustang the other week?"

He scowls, pulling away from me. My skin feels cold now that he's not drawing his imaginary pictures on it. "Don't worry about those guys. They're just some jerks from my school." He tugs on a blade of grass next to him. "It's not the first time. Won't be the last."

I hoped to get more of an explanation, to hear his side of the story. I try again. "But what's their problem? Why would they do it?"

Kevin shrugs. "It's always been like that. They're jocks. They think they're better than everyone else. Just ignore them. I do."

They're tough to ignore when one of them is shoving his tongue down my throat and my BFF is hung up on him. "How do you act so cool about it? Why aren't you pissed at them?"

"Because they're *not* better than us. I know that, and that's all that matters." He plucks the blade of grass and tickles the back of my hand with it, trailing it up my arm and across my shoulder. "To make themselves feel good, they need to make others feel like crap. At least we're being who we want to be. We're doing what we like and we're not ashamed of it. We don't hide it. We shouldn't have to run away from people like that or hide who we are."

I wince beneath my mask at his words. My heart thuds guiltily in my chest. Crawling closer to the bushes that line the crest, I move out of his reach, so he can't touch me, so I don't have to meet his gaze.

I'm hiding this part of my life from my friends, my family, from the whole world. I can't show Kevin the real me, not really. I'm not any one person. I'm not fully Adrianna or Andy. I feel like a bunch of scattered pieces of a whole person.

The only person I know who would accept the real me is Kevin, only I can't tell him who I really am in case no one else will. And even if I did, he may not even want to talk to me once he discovers I've been hiding my identity this whole time.

He inches toward me. "You're so different than anyone else I've met. You're comfortable just being you. Those guys in the Mustang only care about what everyone else thinks of them. Of being cool. How many social media friends they have." He scoffs and shakes his head. "There's this one girl at my school who's on a TV show— "

My head snaps toward him. "Really?"

"Yeah, they call her the Porcelain Princess." He snorts, and it suddenly feels as ridiculous as it did the first day of school. Before I had all my new friends, before I was the kind of girl who went on double dates.

"She and her family are on some reality show. I thought she was kind of cool at first, but I think she might be just like the rest of them."

I'm trying to act natural, but my expression feels plastic on my face, my limbs too twitchy. "Why? What did she do?"

"I don't know." He shrugs. "It's just that she doesn't stand up for what she believes. She's only into guys with letterman jackets, and she probably dreams of being prom queen." He makes a noise like the French photographer. Disdain.

I stutter for a second, not even sure what to say. When I do speak, my voice comes out all squeaky. "I hate people like that."

"I know. But you're totally cool. You're not afraid to be you."

I look away, but this time he reaches up and grabs my chin. He turns my face toward him. "I know we met only a few weeks ago, but I really like you, Andy."

The plastic expression melts, and the smile on my face is so automatic. Of course I knew it, like I knew oxygen belongs in lungs—even if my lungs can't find any at the moment. The way he looks at me like someone drew an extra twinkle in his eyes, how any time we're in a crowd and I catch sight of him, he's already staring at me, and when we say good-bye at the end of larping, he looks at me like we'll never see each other again. But knowing it and hearing him say those beautiful words are two totally different things.

There's a look in his eye. You know, *the* look. And then he starts to lean toward me. He's going to kiss me. And it's so tempting to lean in and kiss him back, but something makes me pull away before his lips can touch mine.

My heart starts beating so fast my chest feels like it has a cramp. I try to shuffle over, distance myself subtly. My foot catches an exposed root. I yelp as I'm sent thrashing into the bush in front of us.

Twigs scratch me and knot themselves into my wig. I grab onto it as Kevin tries to fish me out of the tangled mess. We wrestle with the branches until he pulls me free. I stumble into him.

"Are you okay?" he asks.

I straighten my tunic. "Yeah. I'm fine."

No. I'm not! What's wrong with me? It's not like I haven't daydreamed about kissing Kevin. Of course I have. So why don't I want to kiss him now?

Howls echo through the ravine below us. The wolves heard me. I guess there's no more time for romance.

We both turn to peer over the crest. Eight of them crawl up the slope, licking their lips with hunger and barking in excitement. Only two remain to guard their prisoner. The rest are coming straight for us. Kevin grabs my hand and we begin running.

"We'll have to split up," he says. "I'll distract them. You circle around to take out the two remaining werewolves and save Keelie. Then when the others return with the arrows we can take out the rest."

"But what about you?"

"Don't worry. I'm a fast runner."

"We'll follow you as quickly as we can," I say. "If you get tired, come back this way and we'll help you fight them off."

He points to a blind corner just ahead of us. "Hide over there. I'll lead them away."

Squeezing my hand, he lets it go and sprints in the other direction. I dive behind a fallen log. Not a second later, I see the werewolves' furry heads appear over the riverbank crest. I curl into a ball, hiding until they all leap past in pursuit of Kevin.

The soil smells rich and moist as it soaks through my tunic. I wait until their howling and barking fade into the distance before I scramble to my feet.

Carefully, I sneak down the slope to where Keelie is

being guarded. Avoiding the dried leaves and sticks that go *snap*, I keep to the exposed dirt that softens my footfalls. I take it slow, watching over my shoulder for any beasts that decide to come back to their base.

The two guarding werewolves are curled up on the ground with their backs to me. One's busy gnawing on a stick. I recall what Game Master Ken said at the beginning of the day. Only three hit points are required to take a werewolf down, since their main strength is that they travel in packs.

My hand on the hilt of my short sword, I inch my way toward Keelie. When I tug at her ropes, she flinches in surprise but remains silent. I untie her as fast as I can, working out the knots with shaking fingers.

When I've unraveled the last knot, the ropes fall around her ankles. The rustling makes the two creatures look up. They spot me and begin to growl, snapping their long wolfy jaws.

Keelie dives for her bow. By the time the werewolves hop to their feet, her bow is already in hand.

She counts out loud to simulate nocking the arrow and aiming. "One Mississippi. Two Mississippi. Three Mississippi."

The first wolf lunges at her, but she takes aim and the beanbag flies true. The creature takes two to the chest. I stab at its leg for the third hit. It goes down with a whimper of pain.

Keelie's not fast enough to nock another one before the second wolf pounces. I step in to protect her. My blade slices off its hind leg at the knee. As my foot lands, I sweep around, spinning to take another strike at its torso in one smooth movement.

The wolf collapses. But neither of them is dead. They're

just down for thirty seconds. Only the silver arrows will take them down permanently. I hope Finn gets here soon.

Keelie turns to me and curtsies. "I owe you my life, Princess Andy. I am forever in your debt."

"Well, you better wait to thank me. Your brother sacrificed himself so I could help you."

Her blue eyes widen. "He's dead?"

"Not if we can help it." I flash an enthusiastic smile. "Come on, let's go find him before these two wake up."

She scrambles up the bank ahead of me. Once she's at the top, she nocks an arrow and covers my back. "You know, my brother really likes you."

I feel myself grin. "I like him, too."

"He's one of the good ones. Just don't hurt him, okay?"

I crest the bank and heave myself to my feet. When I stand and look up, she's got an arrow aimed straight for my heart. She closes one eye and looks down the side of the bow for accuracy.

"Or I will kill you."

I raise my hands in surrender. I'm surprised by her seriousness, the coldness in her eyes. I suddenly feel guilty—not for the first time—like I've been found out.

I eye her up and down, searching for a sign. "Is this your character speaking? Or you?"

She winks and smiles before skipping ahead on the path.

Relieved, I shake my head. "For a small thing, you sure are scary."

I start to follow her, but then I hear our names being called. We turn to find Finn, along with Eddie and Shawn. They're on the other side of the bank.

Finn holds up a quiver. It shines silver in the sun peeking through the trees. It's really more of a sack filled with beanbags, but at least those are silver, too.

"You did it," Keelie says. "Hurry. Bring them over."

Finn lifts his wizard robe and begins to descend, but then a howl echoes down the riverbed. The two werewolves are awake.

Getting to their feet, they pace back and forth below us. There might as well be a raging river separating our group. The only thing that can kill them are the arrows, but Keelie must use her bow to shoot them, or they won't work.

"How do we get them to you now?" Finn asks.

"There's no other way," Keelie says. "You have to fight your way across. I don't have enough arrows left to take them down again."

But even I can see that descending takes too much concentration. Eddie would need both his hands to steady himself on the narrow path. He couldn't use his sword, especially since it requires two hands to wield it. The creatures would have him before he even made it to the bottom. And a glance at Finn's belt tells me he has no mana left to spell-cast. As always, Shawn remains silent.

"We have to think of something," I yell to them. "We've got to help Kevin. He's got the entire pack on his heels."

Finn's eyes widen. "I know." He points behind us.

Keelie and I spin around. We see a dark figure sprinting toward us, cape flapping in his haste. It can only be Kevin.

As he gets closer, the shadows move behind him. At first I think it's just the dappling light through the forest canopy. Then the shadows solidify into a pack of crazed werewolves, yipping and howling, snapping at his heels. And headed straight for us.

Chapter Twenty-One

Princess vs. Princess

Keelie and I back away from the approaching pack as far as we can go. Our heels are practically at the edge of the dry riverbank. The two werewolves scratch and claw at the bank walls below, trying to get at us. But they know as well as we do that if they climb up, we will have the advantage and kill them. Just like if we climb in there, they will have their feast.

Kevin's getting closer, the rest of the pack right behind him. Talk about a rock and a hard place.

"Keelie," Finn calls from across the ravine.

We turn just in time to see him spin the quiver over his head and toss it across the twenty-foot gap between us. I think it's going to make it, but it snags in the bushes along the crest and tumbles back down.

Kevin's already yelling for backup. His voice is harsh as he's gasping for air.

I look at Keelie. "I'm going in. I have an invisibility spell."

She glances at the blue mana tags dangling from my

belt. "No. You can't. You don't have enough mana to get you back out of there again. They'll tear you to shreds."

"There's no other way. I've got to take one for the team."

"Keelie!" Kevin yells as he runs. "Hurry!"

She turns back to me. Biting her lip, she barely thinks a second before nodding.

I begin my descent down the side of the riverbank. I mouth the words to the incantation, which I haven't invented yet, so I say, "You can't see me. You can't see me. You can't see me," over and over again.

The sentence takes about a second to repeat. I slide one mana tag across the ring on my belt for every second that passes.

The werewolves continue to growl at the others still up on the bank, their teeth bared. Their claws rake the air close to my own body as I sidestep past them.

I face them, too afraid to turn my back. One sniffs the air, as though it detects me. But then it snorts and continues to look past me. I can't wimp out now. I'm so close to the quiver.

I continue to recite my incantation as I reach down and grab the quiver. Keelie spreads her arms wide, ready to receive it. Taking an extra step, I heave it up to her. She barely catches it by the strap.

One by one, I slide my mana tags across, already rushing for the path out of the shallow ravine. I grope for my next tag. My spell catches in my throat. They're gone. I'm out of mana. The magic wears off, and I materialize again.

The first werewolf notices me and howls, alerting its brother. Grasping my sword, I unsheathe it, but a battle between a level four princess and two werewolves won't last long.

The first lunges at me, snarling. I dodge its dirty claws,

but the other shadows my move. It bites me on the arm, teeth grazing my skin.

I cry out. "Hit one, left arm."

I backpedal, careful not to trip. I see Finn and the others coming to help me, but the animals work well as a pack. My team won't be fast enough to save me.

When I block one wolf's attack, the other is there, claws grazing my torso.

"Hit two, chest."

Back against the bank, I have nowhere to go. The wolves pace in front of me, ready for the kill. One lifts its furry maw to howl, but the sound is cut short. A silver arrow falls to its feet. The wolf gives a pained whine before it dies. This time for good.

I look up to find Keelie standing above me on the bank. She reaches back and draws another arrow from her quiver. The other werewolf tries to scamper away, but Keelie's aim traces its retreat. She releases, and it soars true. The creature falls dead.

With all of us united again, we make quick work of the rest of the pack. We slice through fur and dismember limbs, stunning them for thirty seconds, plenty of time for Keelie to prepare her next arrow. And the next. And the next.

Before long, we have rid Asdor of the werewolf plague, and we return to the parking lot as heroes. Although we are all fearless warriors, everyone searches the area, wary of the Mustang.

"Maybe we should celebrate another time," Eddie says, rubbing at a dark mark on his costume. "Slush is hard to get out of unicorn hide. Especially cherry." He sounds strange when he doesn't speak in his fake Ye Olde English accent.

"Why don't we all go over to my house," Kevin says. "My

mom already said it was okay. Anyone feel like Chinese food?"

Everyone agrees and begins to pile into cars. Anything to avoid another fast-food attack. But I hang back.

"Come on," Kevin says. "You can ride with me. I brought my car this week." He indicates to the blue Kia parked under a blank billboard across the lot.

Still, I hesitate. If I go to Kevin's house, that would mean I need to take off my mask. I can't keep wearing it. That would be weird.

I want to go, to hang out with him, to be closer to him for longer. But then I remember the way he spoke about me earlier, about what he thinks of the Porcelain Princess. Would his feelings for this half of me, the Princess Andy half, be enough to overcome that? Or would he just hate me more for tricking him?

That's why I couldn't kiss him. Not like this. Not when he dislikes half of me.

Guilt is burning at my insides, for lying to him, for deceiving him. I now realize it's been there the whole time, growing worse with each week that I put on my mask and fooled him just to escape my own life for a few hours. Growing worse as my feelings for him developed, and as I've watched his feelings for me flourish.

What did I think? That when he found out the truth, we could just have a good laugh about it, like the end of some poorly thought out B-rated movie?

I shake my head. "No thanks. I promised my parents I'd come home straight after."

The words hurt to say. I think that if my heart had legs, it would kick me. But I can't take off my mask for him now. First I need to make things right between Kevin and the Porcelain Princess, to get to know him better at school.

"Okay. No problem." He looks as disappointed as I feel. "I'll text you my address later, in case you change your mind."

I watch him go before heading for the nearest gas station to change.

The more I hang out with Kevin, the more I realize his sister's right. He really is one of the good ones. He's true to who he is, both on the larping battlefield and at school. I feel like I can be my true self only when I'm hiding behind a mask. Maybe it's time I take off the mask for him.

Chapter Twenty-Two

Peking Plan

On Monday, my make-Kevin-like-the-real-me plan is over before it begins. When I enter the biology lab, he's not in class.

Hoping he's just late, I take my seat as the bell rings. Lennox spins in his chair and gives me a dopey grin. Harper glares at him—if looks could kill. I kick her under the desk to remind her she's supposed to be nicer to him and stare at my textbook as though biology is the most interesting thing in the world.

"Eyes forward, people," Mr. Bigger says, and Lennox turns around.

For the rest of class, every time someone passes by in the hall, I glance back. But Kevin never shows.

When Mr. Bigger steps out to go to the "photocopier"—I'm beginning to suspect he's sneaking out for smokes—I pull out my phone and text Kevin, as Andy, of course, since I never exchanged numbers with him at school.

Hey, thanks for inviting me to your place on Sunday. Sorry I couldn't come. Wasn't quite feeling myself, anyway.

Which was truer than he could ever know.

It's only a few seconds before the reply comes.

No problem. It was probably for the best. Must have been some funky Peking duck.

Oh, no. You're not sick are you?

Yeah. Food poisoning. In the doctor's waiting room now.

Hope you feel better.

Mr. Bigger comes back, so I have to put my phone away. At least I know why Kevin isn't at school. It kind of puts a kink in my plan to spend time with him if he's not around. I need a plan B. If he's not coming to school, then I'll have to go to him. Just a concerned fellow student checking in.

After class, I hang back and wait until all the other students have left. When Mr. Bigger is done wiping the board, he notices me.

"Can I do something for you, Miss Bottom?"

"Umm. I noticed Kevin wasn't here today."

"Your powers of observation astound me. What of it?"

I ignore the jibe. He's seen me as a class clown ever since the first day of school, so he dishes it out on a regular basis.

"I was going to take his homework to him. I live close by." Which I know from my alter-ego me. "Can I get a spare handout?"

He slides out an extra copy from his folder and hands it to me. "Here you go. I didn't realize you were friends."

I smile but say nothing.

"Check with the secretary at the end of the day. The rest of his class assignments will be there."

"Thanks, Mr. Bigger."

After school, I hop on the bus and head to the address that Kevin texted me yesterday after larping. My finger hovers over the doorbell as I mentally practice all the things I want to say to him when he opens the door.

Maybe I should act all aloof, like, "Hey, what's up?" Or maybe, "I was just in the neighborhood." Will he think it's weird that I was the one who delivered his homework?

I check my hair in the frosted window next to his door for the tenth time. Taking a deep breath, I ring the bell. My heart throbs against my rib cage. It speeds up when I hear footsteps approach.

The door opens. It's Keelie.

"Can I help you?" she asks. Her eyes roam over me briefly. Recognition flickers across her face. Her eyes narrow, and her jaw tightens. I know how bad-tempered her larping character can be. I just hope that isn't part of her real character.

I want to tell her I'm sorry about the ice cream. That it wasn't me. That I'm the one who made her the new tunic to replace the stained one. I hope Kevin already told her that it was Mercedes.

But I don't really know where to begin so I start with, "Hi. I'm Adrianna. I'm here to see Kevin."

"I know who you are." She doesn't open the door or move, so I stay on the porch, shifting from foot to foot.

"He's sick today," she says when I don't leave.

"Yeah, I know. He wasn't in class. I brought him his homework." I pull the bundle out of my bag and hold it up as evidence.

"I was wondering who picked it up. It wasn't in the office when I went." She reaches for the stack.

My fingers clamp down, but she yanks it from my grasp.

"I can give it to him," she says.

Now I have no excuse to see Kevin. My mouth opens to protest, but I can't think of any other reason to stay. I stare blankly at her, frozen on the porch. Suddenly, I remember the bottle of stain remover I've been carrying around in my bag.

I dig through my backpack and pull it out, but as I look up, the door is already closing in my face.

"Thanks," she says and shuts the door.

I stare at the door for a couple of seconds, the sun beating down on my shoulders. At least she didn't try to shoot me with an arrow.

I turn around to trudge back to the bus stop when the front door squeaks open behind me.

"Porcelain Princess!" It's Kevin's uncle.

"Hi." I blink up at him from the front steps; I didn't expect him to be there. "Actually, it's just Adrianna."

"Gerald." He thrusts out his hand, as though he's delighted that we're on a first name basis, and I shake it. "What brings you to our humble abode?"

"I heard Kevin is sick. I just came to drop off his homework."

"How thoughtful of you. Come on in." He opens the door wide and waves me inside.

I step through like I've somehow won a small victory, and he closes the door behind me. Their home is bright with daffodil yellow walls and oak wood. Warm and inviting. Not at all like my show home.

"What do you have there?" He points to the bottle in my hands.

"Oh, it's stain remover." The contents slosh as I hold it up. "Really good stuff from my dad's company." Because apparently the laundry room is just a short step from the bathroom. "I've been meaning to give it to Keelie. It's for her costume. I feel really bad that it was ruined. I didn't mean for that to happen."

Considering his obsession with *Bathroom Barons*, I

suspect he's seen the episode. I wonder if he believes Corbin's version of things. Maybe he thinks I'm lying. That I bullied his niece.

But if that's what he thought, Gerald smiles at me now. And I think it's not just to "get in good" with my family and me, because his smile looks so much like Kevin's. Genuine.

"Well isn't that nice?" he says. "Come on this way. Kevin's in his room. I'll just tell him you're here."

Slipping off my shoes, I follow him down a hall lined with family photos.

"How's school?" he asks over his shoulder.

I shrug even though he can't see me. "It's school."

"And business?" He sounds funny, like he's trying too hard to sound casual.

"It's good," I say, even though it's not. "How's business for you?"

"Oh, hanging in there." And I can tell he's lying, too. "Say," he begins in a not-so-offhand way. "Do your parents ever talk about expanding their distribution network? You know, selling some of their products through other already established stores? They could really decrease their overhead."

Like your store? "Ummm. I don't think so. They've got the one store in Seattle and the two planned for here in L.A."

"Oh, the rumors are true, then? A second store?" Gerald tries to sound lighthearted, like he's just making idle chitchat. But his voice kind of sounds like Eeyore from *Winnie-the-Pooh*. From behind I can see his shoulders deflate like a week-old helium balloon as he reaches up to knock on a door at the end of the hall.

"Come in." Kevin's voice filters out from inside.

Gerald opens the door and sticks his head in. "Are you feeling up for a visitor?"

Kevin must have nodded, because his uncle steps aside.

I move for the door, but Gerald holds up a finger. "If your parents ever do decide to branch out, let me know. I might be able to help them." He rolls his eyes, like it would be a huge favor. "I'd have to move stuff around and create some room, but I could make it work."

I try really hard not to laugh at his poor acting abilities. My face is totally serious when I nod and say, "I'll keep it in mind."

"Great!" He claps his hands together, his face bursting with enthusiasm. "I'll grab you a card."

When I walk through the door, Kevin bolts upright in his double bed. Then he immediately holds a hand to his forehead like he's dizzy. "Adrianna. What are you doing here?"

"Hi." I hover awkwardly in the doorway. His room smells like him, in his good lemony-scent way. "I brought your homework for you. The school gave me your address," I say as a cover story, so he doesn't wonder how I found him. On second thought, maybe they wouldn't have, for confidentiality reasons.

Kevin doesn't question my lie, though. His mouth is still agape at the sight of me in his house, and he looks down at my empty hands.

"Keelie took it," I explain. "I just wanted to see how you were doing."

"I'm okay." He stares at me for a moment, like I'm not a girl but a pink elephant that just walked into his room. Finally, he gives his head a shake, which seems to make him dizzy again. "Please, come in."

He begins to clean up, tossing books off his desk chair. He wipes a few crumbs onto the floor and gestures for me to sit down.

"Are you sure?" I ask. I'm suddenly shy, second-guessing myself only now that it's too late.

He props himself up in bed with his pillows. "Don't worry. I'm not contagious. It's just food poisoning."

I laugh and stare at my feet. "That's not really what I meant."

He regards me for a second, and I fidget beneath his gaze. His cheek wrinkles. "I know. And yeah, it is all right."

Those words seem to feel just as good as when he flirted with me before. Despite our rocky moments, he actually wants to hang out. Trying not to smile like an idiot, I plop down in his desk chair. My body is on high alert now that I'm this close to him as my school self, and not just near him, but alone, in his room. No mask, no barriers between us.

"How are you feeling?" I ask.

"Like I've swallowed an atomic bomb."

"Well, on the bright side, maybe you'll develop superhuman powers from the radiation."

Kevin laughs suddenly and clutches his stomach in pain. His eyes are all droopy, and I wonder if he's feeling up for company, but I can't bring myself to leave.

After a minute, the pain on his face clears. "If you could choose any supernatural ability, what would you choose?"

"Invisibility," I say. "Definitely invisibility. Corbin can't film what he can't see."

He lets his head fall back against the wall like he can't hold it up anymore and stares at me for a moment. "What's it like being on the show?"

"You'd think it would be cool. But it's not. It's awful." I frown. "They follow my every move. They always seem to be around for my most embarrassing moments, which for me, happen frequently. Sometimes Corbin even creates his own embarrassing moments."

"Like with the ice cream incident."

"Yeah." I look for signs of lingering doubt or sarcasm, but I don't see any. "I'm glad you believe me."

He shrugs. "No big deal. It's definitely a Mercedes thing to do."

It is a big deal. I hope that his faith in me is a sign that he still has feelings for me. I want to tell him about what Corbin pulled last Saturday night. About the date from hell, but for some reason, I don't want him to know I went on a date at all. Because I wish I'd gone to the movies with Kevin instead. And we're actually having a real conversation for once, and he hasn't asked me to leave yet. I just want to keep it going. So instead, I say, "What would your superpower be?"

"Super strength," he says. "Nobody messes with a guy who can turn you into a pretzel."

"Am I right in guessing the first person you'd beat up would be Lennox?"

"I wouldn't abuse my powers. 'With great power comes great responsibility.'" He holds his head high. "But yeah. It would be hard not to pretzelfy him."

A knock on the door makes me jump. I turn to find Gerald's head poking into the room.

"Here's my card." His arm snakes inside as he passes me the slip of paper. "If your parents have any questions, or need a favor, or any hardware supplies, or you know, since they're new to the neighborhood and all… Hey, there's an idea." His eyes widen behind his glasses. He has eyes like Kevin's. "Maybe we should have a barbecue and invite the Bottoms over. What do you think, Kevin?"

Kevin groans and clutches his stomach. "Don't talk to me about food right now."

His uncle pulls a sympathetic face and turns to me.

"Well, think about it, anyway."

"I will," I say. "It sounds fun."

Gerald lingers in the doorway for a second longer, totally natural-like, glancing from Kevin to me. After several seconds of awkward silence, he taps the doorframe like a drum and says, "Well, I'll let you guys get back to it."

Kevin sighs at his uncle's retreating back. "Sorry, he's a little eager when it comes to you and your family. He's just worried."

I nod. "About his business. That's okay. I get it."

"We'll be okay."

"Does your uncle live with you?" I ask. "Or is he just here looking out for you while you're sick?"

"My uncle and aunt help out a lot. It's just my mom raising us. She's at a work conference in San Diego for the week, so my uncle's staying with us."

I bite my lip, wondering if it's overstepping some line to ask the obvious question. "And your dad?"

"He lives in New York. My parents divorced when I was in middle school."

"I'm sorry."

"It's not the kind of hardship that makes superheroes." His mouth pulls down and he automatically glances at his bookshelf lined with comic books. "But yeah, it sucked. We see him for special occasions and in the summer. It's probably for the best, though. I think they're both happier. But you should be glad your parents are still together. Especially now that they're big TV personalities."

I laugh at that. "Yeah, they're okay. Things have been really stressful around the house lately with the business, but I think they really enjoy the whole reality TV thing. Maybe that's why I haven't opposed it as much as I really want to."

"The show must be good for their business."

My nose wrinkles. "Yes and no," I answer vaguely.

"What do you mean?"

"It's okay when I'm not screwing up. Like the underwear thing or the ice cream incident."

He pulls an incredulous face and leans forward on his pillows, like there really is something between us, an invisible winch drawing us together, impossible to resist. Even if he doesn't realize it yet. "But the underwear thing wasn't exactly on purpose."

"I know, right?" I throw my hands up in the air, like *Thank you!*

"And I thought the ice cream was Mercedes's fault. If it's not what really happened, how can they air it that way on TV?"

"Corbin likes to take creative license with the footage," I say. "Apparently our lives just aren't as dramatic as he'd like. Each time the show airs, I feel like the whole world is waiting for me to screw up."

"Well, I'm not," he says seriously, in a way that makes me take a restorative breath.

It feels so good to finally vent about the show to someone. Harper hears it all the time, but she still thinks it's really cool, so she can't see where I'm coming from. Talking to Kevin feels good. Like he gets me. Both versions of me.

Kevin closes his eyes for a second, then a few more, until I eventually wonder if he's fallen asleep. When he opens his eyes again, he looks really tired.

I stand up and head for the door. "I should probably get going. I can drop your homework off again tomorrow if you'd like," I say really casually. But I hope he says yes, because that would mean he wants to see me again.

"Sure," he says, and I smile. "Thanks for coming by, Adrianna." He hesitates. "Do you go by anything short for Adrianna?"

I can't exactly tell him that I used to go by Andy. He might start making connections that I don't want him to. I'm surprised he hasn't already recognized my voice by now. But he's probably dismissed any subconscious connections, what with my lie weaving and all.

"My mom wanted me to go by my legal name. It's part of the whole reinventing ourselves thing now that we've gone Hollywood."

He snorts at the tone in my voice. "And have you become all you thought you wanted to be?"

I think about that. Really think about it. "I'm still working on it. I'll let you know."

Kevin yawns, squirming his way under the covers for a nap. "But Adrianna's a pretty big mouthful."

"I'm a pretty big handful," I joke. I think about the name for a second then shrug. "I don't know. I kind of like the name Red."

His eyes are already closed, but he smiles. "I like Red, too."

Chapter Twenty-Three

Slushie Shutdown

After my last class on Friday, I head straight to the main office to pick up Kevin's homework. I've been worried all week that Keelie might try and beat me to it so that I wouldn't come over to their house. I never gave her the chance. I practically sprinted to the office after the last bell.

As the week went by, Kevin and I even started to do our homework together. The new plan to get to know him worked better than seeing him at school. It allowed us to be ourselves, to be more relaxed, to not have to worry about anyone watching. I could finally be myself. It felt good for once.

The secretary recognizes me by now, and the moment she sees me come through the office door, she hands me the stack of homework. I thank her and turn to leave, but something grabs my eye. It's a poster taped to the wall for the Sadie Hawkins dance coming up. I stop to read it.

"Are you going to ask someone?" the secretary inquires pleasantly.

I don't go to school dances anymore, since I can't

remember the last time anyone asked me to actually dance. "I don't think so."

"Well, if you change your mind, you can pick up your tickets here."

"Thanks," I say, and leave.

It's quieter in the faculty hallway. Most of the students have left for the day or are loitering in the parking lot, except for the ones headed to the principal's office. So I jump when someone grabs my hand and yanks me into an isolated corridor.

Lennox's body spray accosts my nose before I even look up. And when I do, his face is inches from mine. I back away until I hit the wall. He moves closer, and I have to push him away.

"Lennox, stop."

"Why?" he asks, but backs off. He takes a giant slurp of his grape slush. "I thought things were cool between us."

"Cool? How could you tell? From all your texts that I didn't return?" He doesn't seem fazed by my cold response. "What are you doing in here, anyway? And where did you get that?" I point to the 7-Eleven cup in his hands.

"7-Eleven."

"No kidding."

"I skipped last class. Got caught when I came back to get my stuff out of my locker. That's why I'm headed to the principal's office." He leans closer. "Don't I get a last request before I'm sent to detention?"

"No, Lennox." I hold my books in front of me like a shield. "What you did on the double date was *not* cool. You stepped over the line. Besides, Harper's my friend, and I don't want to hurt her."

He takes a few steps back. "Harper? What does she have to do with this? We broke up months ago. She doesn't even care." His eyes drop to his shoes and his mouth twists. I wonder if it's with regret, or maybe it's just the chill of the Slurpee, because when he looks back, the cocky grin is firmly in place.

Of course she cares, I want to tell him. But I can't. I promised Harper I would keep her secret.

Instead I just shake my head. "In case I didn't make myself clear enough before, I'm not interested. And I don't want to ruin my friendship with Harper, so back off. And promise me you won't say anything to her about that night." I jab a finger into his chest and stare him down, trying to take a page out of Keelie's book. "Or anyone else, for that matter."

He doesn't seem very intimidated. He takes another sip from the straw. "Well, you can't hide your feelings forever, A. Eventually our kiss will air on *Bathroom Barons* and the whole world will know. Then you and I can go to the Sadie Hawkins dance together. What do you say?"

I remember the kiss and can almost feel the slither of his tongue in my mouth. I shudder. I can't believe he did that when he saw the cameras were there. Like he wanted his big scene in my embarrassing life story.

Thankfully, Corbin promised not to air it. And since my parents lost it on him and threatened to go to the network executives to complain, I can't see him going back on his word. But I don't want to tell Lennox that or he might try something even more extreme to get on TV. Hopefully by the time he realizes his big debut has been cut, Harper will have caught his eye again—not that I think he deserves her. Then the last thing on his mind will be a take-two.

"That's not how the Sadie Hawkins dance works," I say. "Girls ask guys and I'm not asking you. End of story."

"But—"

"Do you have any idea what kind of damage you could do if you keep this up? To my life? To my parents' lives? How much damage you could have done with the stunt you pulled on our double date?"

"A..." He hesitates.

"For some reason, people actually watch our stupid TV show. They care about what I do. Customers care. And after the last time the director made me look like a jerk, my parents' business suffered for it," I rant on, unable to stop. "I can't even imagine what your stunt might have done to the business's reputation. It might have destroyed the new store's grand opening."

"I didn't think—"

"Well, then think next time," I snap.

"I'm sorry." He honestly looks ashamed, so I think I might have gotten through to him. Then he says, "I can see why you want to keep our relationship a secret."

Leaning in, he plants a kiss on my mouth. His lips are wet and cold from the slush. It feels like a kiss from a mackerel.

I shove him away. He stumbles back with a smile on his face, like he thinks I'm playing around. Reaching for his slush drink, I grab the frosty cup out of his hand, rip off the lid, and toss it at him.

The purple ice crystals splash across his chest, his face, his letterman jacket, and down his designer jeans. Of course I don't come away unscathed, but I don't care. I think I made my point.

A big guy like him I kind of expect to get mad, to turn all red and Hulk-like, or I suppose that would make him Red Hulk. But instead, his eyes grow wide like a big puppy dog.

"A?"

The cup crumples in my hand as it curls into a fist. God, he has muscles for brains. Groaning, I toss the empty 7-Eleven cup at his feet and turn back to the secretary's desk. Because I've changed my mind. I *do* want to go to that dance. And Lennox just made me realize I couldn't choose anyone better to go with than Kevin.

It isn't until I turn to storm away that I see we have an audience. I trip over my own feet and stumble into a wall when I see who it is. Keelie.

She's suddenly her larping character, with her cool, calculating gaze flicking from me to Lennox. I half expect to see her whip out a bow and arrow.

How much did she hear? How much did she see?

Keelie moves past our hallway and disappears from sight. I run to the end of the hall and look both ways, but she must have gone into one of the offices. I feel sick, like I've eaten some bad Peking duck. What will she tell her brother?

My brain rewinds and replays the last five minutes, but I can't think of anything too incriminating. She doesn't know exactly what we were talking about. And Lennox might have kissed me right then, but I did throw a slush drink in his face, so I think I made it pretty clear I wasn't interested.

By the time I get back to the secretary, I've calmed down. Maybe I have nothing to worry about after all.

"You're back," the secretary says. "Did you forget something?"

"Actually, I think I will buy those tickets."

She gives me a coy look over her thick glasses. "Are you going to ask the boy you've been picking up homework for all week?"

Heat rushes under my cheeks and I duck my head into my bag for spare cash. "Ummm. Yeah."

"Well, that's nice." She smiles like she's genuinely happy for me. "I hope he says yes."

I hand her the money. "Thank you. Me, too." I really, really do. Because I plan to tell him everything first. So if he says yes, he's saying yes to the real me. All of me.

"Hi, Andy," a girl says behind me.

I turn and smile. "Hey."

A knee-jerk reaction. Like blinking or when your mouth waters at the sight of pizza. Then I see it's Keelie, and I realize what she called me: Andy.

Chapter Twenty-Four

Caught in the Act

Keelie's got one hand on her hip and a look on her face more suited to her larping character than Kevin's little sister. She raises a judgy eyebrow. With that simple look, I know that if we were on a battlefield, I'd be toast.

I've been frozen for too long, my reaction too slow. I try to act natural anyway. "Actually, my name is Adrianna."

She crosses her arms. "Andy. Adrianna. What difference does it make? I still know who you are."

Her glare makes me want to slink behind the secretary's desk and hide. But I hold her gaze. There's no point in denying it.

I sigh and nod to the office door. As though by silent agreement, we leave together.

Neither one of us speaks until we've reconvened outside in the school parking lot. I turn to face her, feeling surprisingly calm. There's nothing I can do about it. No way to deny it. She knows. Now it's just a matter of waiting to see how everything I've built with Kevin will fall apart. And I can't be mad at her because there's no one to blame but myself.

"How did you know?" I ask.

"You wrinkle your nose when you smile. Plus, when we were fighting together on Sunday, I noticed you were wearing a wig." She begins to count each point on her fingers. "I'm a girl. I know hair. Finally, when I saw you toss the slush at Lennox, I remembered the day you first larped with us. Something just clicked. Also, I'm not blinded by hearts in my eyes like my brother."

I clasp my hands, ready to get on my knees and beg if I have to. "Please, please, don't tell Kevin."

She crosses her arms. "Why are you doing this? Is this some kind of stunt or undercover thing for your reality show? To make fun of us?"

"No. Of course not. I'm not like that."

Her head tilts to the side. "Aren't you?"

The question takes me by surprise. She's asking me in total seriousness. And seriously? Well, maybe there's some truth to it, whether I intended it to be like that or not. I consider the situation from her perspective and how bad it must look. But maybe that's because it really *is* that bad.

The fight whooshes out of my body like a Whoopee Cushion. "I don't want to be. I really don't. Larping was just a way for me to escape the show. To be myself without anyone finding out."

"So you're using us. We welcome you and accept you into our group and you've been lying to us the whole time?"

"No, it's not like that." I keep my voice hushed, hoping she will, too. "Well, okay maybe it is, a little. But if I told anyone the truth, the cameras would follow me. And I swear I didn't throw the ice cream at you. Mercedes did," I say, glad to finally have the chance. Glad to finally be so honest with someone. I resist the urge to spill my guts about everything with sheer relief, regardless of the consequences.

"And I felt so bad about it. That's why I made you the new tunic. You deserved better than that."

"And Kevin doesn't?" Keelie crosses her arms and looms closer. I take an automatic step back. "He likes you. Well..."—she looks me up and down before sneering—"the you he knows from larping. But it's just a lie." She turns to leave.

I scramble around the car next to us and cut her off. "It's not a lie. It's the real me. Please don't tell Kevin."

"Why shouldn't I? I overheard you talking with Lennox. I could talk to your director, go on the show, tell the whole world on social media about your larping, your lying, and your deceit."

I flinch at the emotional detachment in her voice. "Why would you do that? I mean, I know you're mad. I get it. But my parents' business—"

"Would be finished," she says. "I could take down the Bottom Empire before it gets a foothold in the neighborhood. My Uncle Gerald's neighborhood."

"Your uncle," I repeat numbly, thinking I won't be able to talk my way out of this one so easily.

"Times are tough." Keelie shrugs, emotionless as a hit man. "He helps our mom a lot. He's our family. You want to protect your family's business? Well, this is how I can protect mine. If what you say is true, the key to taking down the empire is the perfect Porcelain Princess. What will your fans think of the secret you? What will the customers think?"

I raise my hands like the hit man in her is holding a gun. And her threat certainly feels that way. "I'm trying to make up for everything, and I planned to tell Kevin tonight. But if you tell him, if he finds out that way, he'll hate me more than ever. Please. Just give me a chance to make things right first."

She chews on a fingernail and stares at me for a few seconds. “I don’t know. This all seems a little sitcom-scheme to me. The mask, the dual identity.”

“All I know is that I feel more myself when I’m pretending not to be, well”—I wave a hand at the outfit Suzzy dressed me in that morning—“this.”

People are heading to their parked cars, watching us with interest. I’m practically whispering now. “And I have more fun. With Kevin, and you, and Finn, and all the others. I know I should have been honest up front, but I don’t think Kevin would have let me join in the first place.”

“I wouldn’t have blamed him.”

She tries to leave again, but I hold up my hands in surrender. “I’ll tell him. I will. I really was going to before you found out. I was planning on asking him to the dance tonight. Please, just let me tell him myself.”

Keelie frowns. “This is crazy. I’m not cool with lying to my brother.” I can see her conviction wavering. I think it’s more for her brother’s sake as opposed to mine, but I’ll take it. She bites her lip. “If you don’t tell him by the first bell on Monday morning, then I will.”

I want to hug her, but I stop myself. She’s my friend, but I haven’t exactly been hers. “Thank you so much. I swear I’ll make this right.”

“You better,” she says. “Or I’ll tell the world your secret.”

Chapter Twenty-Five

Above Average Andy

When I knock on Kevin's front door, his uncle Gerald answers.

"Hi, Princess Adrianna!" He beams down at me.

At least he'd lost the "Porcelain." I've brought Kevin his homework every day this week, but it seems we still need to work on the "Princess" part.

Gerald waves me inside. "Kevin's just jumping out of the shower. I'll go check to see if he's decent."

When he leaves, I pace around their living room. I'm nervous. What will Kevin think of my secret? Will he understand? Or will he feel hurt by me? Or maybe he'll feel hurt by the other me. I wonder if I didn't tell him but still asked him to the dance, would he say yes?

But I have to tell him. Of course I do. It wouldn't be right otherwise. For the tenth time, I check my back pocket to make sure the tickets are still there.

As I wander restlessly, I scan the room. The mantle is loaded with family photos. I notice a team photo. Football. The players are lined up, posing in their uniforms and pads.

I reach for the frame to take a closer look. Scanning the faces, I recognize Kevin kneeling in the front row. Then I notice Lennox standing just behind him. They both look a few years younger. They were once teammates, and now they hate each other. Not exactly what I would call team spirit.

I recall how Kevin spoke about me at larping, about how I'm only interested in dating guys with letterman jackets. Awfully judgmental considering he used to wear one himself.

"Hey, Red," Kevin says from behind me. His hair is still wet, sticking up even more than usual, like he'd just dried it with a towel. Or a 797 jet engine. It makes my stomach do somersaults, and so does the way he smiles at me now.

"Hey." I point to the football photo on the mantle. "I didn't peg you for a jock."

He glances at the football team and rolls his eyes. "That was the old me. I was in middle school when that was taken. That was when Lennox and I used to be all right. Actually, we used to be pretty close. We'd hang out all the time. He was one of my best friends."

I remember Lennox telling me his version of the story. That Kevin wasn't a good friend. So whose story is the right story?

"What happened?" I ask.

"My parents separated near the end of middle school. My dad was the one who always encouraged me to join football every year. Once high school started and my dad moved to New York, I didn't try out for the team."

He sighs and flops down on the love seat where I spot his homework laid out for us to work on together. I notice he didn't choose the larger sofa, but the couch where we'll be forced to sit close enough so our bodies touch. "I drifted away from my teammates and made new friends. Lennox just didn't seem to have time for me anymore. When I needed him most."

According to Harper, the two had a falling out because Kevin wasn't there for Lennox when his Gram-Gram died. They both feel wronged by the other, when it might all be due to poor timing.

"Why do you think Lennox is such a jerk to you now if you used to be friends?" I hedge.

He picks at the loose thread on the armrest. "I guess it was easier to shun me than understand why I wouldn't want to be the popular jock. And maybe it made him feel more secure, like he was proving he wasn't about to defect like I did. So he could distance himself. Or…" He flips out the footrest and leans back. "Maybe he's just a massive, immature jerk."

I'm not entirely certain it's any of my business to interfere, or if it will even help. I think I should tell him eventually. It might make things easier for him at school and larping. But then again, I have bigger fish to fry today. One thing at a time.

I put down my backpack and take a seat next to him. "I prefer the term meathead."

He considers me for a moment as I start to take out my homework. "Is it true that you went on a date with him?"

My hand freezes over my textbooks. I blink, hard, if that's possible. "What? Where did you hear that?"

"From Lennox himself," he says, kind of quietly, like he hates to ask, or maybe because he hopes it's a lie. "He was telling some guys in the locker room after gym class last week."

"You're kidding?" I laugh, but not in a "ha-ha" funny way. "No, it's not true," I practically yell.

I don't want to betray Harper's confidence, but I want so badly for Kevin to believe me. To have no doubts about my feelings for Lennox.

"Can you keep a secret?" I ask, and he nods. "Harper and I went on a double date with Lennox and a guy named Conner because Harper is still totally in love with Lennox and she wanted a way to spend more time with him."

"Then why didn't she just tell him how she feels?"

"I think it's because she's embarrassed. Maybe a little afraid of being rejected by him." I have a sudden fear that the information will get out, and she'll be even more embarrassed. And I would have been the one who caused it.

"Thanks for telling me," he says. "I'm happy that it's not true."

I stare at him. "You are?"

It feels like the love seat is a lot smaller than most love seats. My whole side is practically squished up next to his. Even through my jeans, I feel the warmth from his thigh touching mine. I sense each one of his breaths and can tell when they start to get faster as he stares back at me.

It's like he wants to say something more, and he's preparing himself for whatever's about to come next, but then he looks away and grabs a book from the pile next to him.

My body, which had been growing tenser by the moment, deflates in disappointment. I grab my own textbook. "Please don't tell anyone. I don't even think SPAM knows."

His forehead wrinkles. "Spam? As in the canned meat?"

"Star, Prissy, Amber, and Mercedes."

"That's a mouthful. I can see why you turned them into an acronym." He laughs. "And don't worry. I promise I won't say anything."

I relax in my seat, leaning against the backrest. "Thanks."

Kevin's head rolls to the side so he can look at me. "You know they're just friends with you because you're on TV."

"Maybe some of them are. Lennox absolutely is. And just to be clear, he is *not* my friend." I look back at the last two months at school and I hope that there is one person who likes me for me. "But I think Harper's different. At least, I hope so. I guess time will tell."

He picks at the thread again. "In my experience, they're all the same."

"I'm not."

I remember how he called me a sheep at school, but this time when he looks at me, it's like he's looking at me. Not one of them. Not a sheep. *Me*. It feels as though he's trying to decide for himself.

"Then prove it," he says. "Actions speak louder than words. If you want to be someone, then you have to be that person all the time. Not just when your so-called friends aren't looking. Or else you're no better than them. No matter what's inside."

I swallow hard at the penetrating look he gives me. I'm grateful more than ever that Keelie gave me the opportunity to tell Kevin the truth myself.

When I told her that I kept my larping a secret because I wanted to avoid the cameras, I was being honest. But only partly. The other part is because I know firsthand just how accepting people can be of "different." Of how understanding SPAM would be of my extracurricular activity.

I consider how different my life is in L.A. compared to Seattle. The shopping trips with friends instead of being a target for teasing. The movie dates versus food fights. Princess status instead of Geeksville mayor.

Now that I've experienced both sides of the social fence, I'm beginning to think that it's not worth hiding myself anymore. I'm tired of bending over backwards to please everyone else. To be their perfect princess. I want to be a proud geek once again, to larp, to not have to calculate every move, to be with Kevin. And hopefully I'm getting closer to that possibility. The dance tickets are burning a hole in my pocket.

Kevin finally looks away. Whatever conclusion he came to, he's not about to share. He grabs his books from the side table. "Do you mind helping me with yesterday's assignment?"

I take this to be a good sign, because he still wants me to hang around. Maybe because he hopes that I can be that person, inside and out.

"Sure," I say.

For background noise, Kevin flips on the TV with the sound turned low. As he sets the remote back down on the side table, a notebook I've never seen before flops open onto his lap. I recognize his drawings right away, but this time they aren't just rough sketches. The images are lined and shaded with ink. Some are even colored.

"What's this?" I pick it up, flipping to the last drawing. It's me again. I'm standing in front of two guys in ski masks and there are waves radiating out of my head.

I laugh. "Now, I'm sure I'd remember this happening."

Kevin realizes what I'm holding and reaches for it. "Oh, it's not my journal. It's an idea for a comic book I've been working on."

I snatch it away and take a closer look. In the picture, I'm wearing normal clothes like jeans and a light jacket, but they've been altered to look like a superhero uniform. I now realize that the waves pulsing away from my head represent some kind of power.

I gasp, a smile spreading across my face. "You made

me into a superhero?"

He reaches for it again, and because his arms are longer than mine, he's able to take it away. But he has to lean over me to get it, his body pressing against mine as he sinks into the cushions. He smells really good, and I itch to simply reach out and wrap my arms around him, but I keep my hands to myself.

I notice his ears are turning pink as he shuts the book with a snap. "Well, the comic isn't really about *super*heroes. They're just regular teenagers with above average abilities."

"Above average? Sounds intense," I joke.

"Well, it's better than that," he says. "They're like really, *really* good at stuff. Like some people have a talent for sports. I have a character that stops bad guys by throwing baseballs at them or by hitting them with golf clubs. And there's Gossip Gaby who talks so much that she brings foes to their knees with mild migraines."

"And what's my power?" I ask, unable to hide the excitement in my voice. When he doesn't answer, I poke him in the ribs.

He flinches like he's ticklish and grabs my finger playfully. Instead of letting it go, his grip relaxes, and he stares down at my hand in his. And I hope it's not sweaty, because simply being near him makes me ten degrees warmer. But he doesn't seem to notice, or if he does, he doesn't say anything. Instead, he considers my hand, maybe wondering what it would be like to hold it all the time, because our hands stay like that.

"Well, it's not really you…"

"Just a short girl with super curly red hair, and a nose just like mine, and—"

"Okay, okay, so she's sort of based on you." He laughs and smiles, but at the ceiling instead of me because he can't quite look at me now. "I like to take inspiration from everyday life."

He took inspiration from *me*. I inspired him. "Then what does this redheaded character do?"

"She, umm..." Now Kevin looks at the door, kind of like he wants to escape. His ears are redder than I've ever seen them. "She can make anyone fall in love with her," he says, finally. "And while they're under her stupor, she can convince them to do things."

"Like what?" I say through my grin, but my voice kind of shakes. If I was his inspiration, does that mean he can see himself falling in love with me? "Convince the bad guys to hand over their guns?"

"No. None of the characters are that powerful. Just above average. So instead she might convince them to loosen her bonds, or flick the lights on and off three times to alert her friends outside that there's danger."

"How incredibly above average." But the feeling building inside of me is anything but average. I feel lightheaded and my palms are definitely sweaty now, but he doesn't seem to care, because his hold on my hand has tightened, like he wants to keep it there longer.

"She could influence someone to spill important information," he says. "Or for bullies to turn on one another. Or suggest people forget she's in the room."

"I'd like that power," I say.

I remember the tickets in my pocket. This discovery of my comic self, Kevin's imagined ability for me, makes me feel powerful. Or at the very least, above average.

With my free hand, I pull the tickets out and hold them up between us, struggling to meet his gaze. "Could she also convince someone to go to the dance with her?"

Kevin stares at the tickets in my shaking hand. His

surprised gaze flicks to my face. I suddenly wish I was wearing my mask, to hide the blush I can feel crawling over my face, and my disappointment if he says no.

But I hope he says yes. And my hand still held in his feels like a yes. And every powerful surge of electricity coursing between our connected bodies is screaming yes. I focus on that word, "yes," as hard as I can, as though I really do have the ability to make him fall for me. To make him be my date.

By the sudden creases on his forehead, he looks confused, and his eyes crinkle warily. But those little wrinkles in his cheeks seem like they want to say yes, and his hand is already reaching for the tickets.

He plucks them from my grip. His mouth opens to say something, and his eyes soften beneath those long, feathery eyelashes.

"Wait!" I say, before I even realize I'm speaking. I slap a hand over my mouth, but it's too late. It's come out. "I have to tell you something first."

I do? Oh, yes, of course I do. I need him to know the truth. As badly as I want to go with him, it won't mean anything if he doesn't know.

But a voice on the TV stops me. Even though the volume is low, I recognize the throaty, guffaw sound right away. It's Lennox's voice.

Chapter Twenty-Six

TV Treachery

Kevin must have recognized the voice on the TV, too, because he puts the dance tickets down and lets go of my hand to reach for his remote. He turns up the volume.

"Here we are," TV Lennox says.

"Well, thanks for the ride." It's my voice. My heart clenches in my chest as I see a black Mustang with red racing stripes pull up to a house on the TV. My house.

My mouth falls open. It's the footage from when Lennox dropped me off after our double date. The footage that Corbin promised he wouldn't use for the show.

The black Mustang idles in front of our driveway. Lennox kills the lights. At the time, I thought it was so my parents wouldn't notice, so he could steal a kiss before I went inside. But as the camera zooms in, I realize he did it to reduce the glare for a better shot.

A cold shiver rushes through my body, freezing me to my seat. Lennox knew the cameras were there.

"I had a good time tonight," he says.

"Yeah," I say. *"I'm glad we did this."*

Our voices are as clear as if Hugh had been right in the car with us. Yet the windows are up. That can mean only one thing: that Lennox was wearing a portable mic.

The whole thing was a setup.

I jump to my feet. "Oh, God. No."

Kevin glances at me uncertainly. I want to run from the room, but my legs have turned to mush. I can only watch with increasing dread. Like I'm witnessing a train that's lost its brakes and is about to plow through an intersection. An intersection crowded with mothers pushing baby strollers, headed straight for an orphanage for really cute children with ridiculously endearing lisps.

Corbin lied. He lied to me. He lied to my parents. It was a setup. Premeditated. And what's worse, Lennox was in on it. He's even more of a jerk than I thought.

Of course, they cut the part where he pulls me in with his grabby hands, and the part where I try to push him away. From this angle it looks like any other sloppy teenage make-out session. You can hear the sounds coming from inside the Mustang. It's like a Labrador retriever licking up peanut butter.

It's too much to process at once. My anger at Corbin, regret over Lennox, complete embarrassment that everyone I know, everyone watching this show, will see everything.

And Harper! God, Harper will see this. She'll think I betrayed her. I haven't told her yet. I thought I'd have more time to explain when things between them calmed down, to have a good laugh over it. She probably isn't laughing now.

So many thoughts run through my head at once that I'm not sure which one to focus on.

My parents will be furious with Corbin. They'll be disappointed in me. I'll explain, and because they already know part of the story, they'll back me up. They can help make this right.

But to what end? The damage is done. It's out there in TV land now and nothing can take it back. And the business, the new store. If a spoonful of ice cream could drop sales by 18 percent, what would this do?

One second I feel desperate to fight, and the next, I feel weak and useless with emotion. It makes me dizzy with helplessness. So I just stand there. Stunned.

I keep waiting for the part where I say "stop," or when I give Lennox a bloody nose, but instead, there's a sound like I'm eating a chocolate fudge sundae. But I know my voice, and those cheap porno sounds aren't mine. They're somebody else's.

Another wave of dizziness hits me when I realize what's happened. Corbin dubbed me.

I sink to my knees. "This can't be happening."

Kevin points the remote at the TV. His knuckles wrapped around it are white. "I thought your BFF was still in love with him. And that it wasn't a date." His voice shakes, like he's restraining his anger. He probably thinks I lied to him earlier.

My response is barely audible over the dubbed sighs and moans. "It wasn't." Like that makes it any better.

Kevin shifts in his seat and pushes his footrest down. He holds out the tickets to me. "Maybe you should go."

There's a sharp pain in my chest and I imagine my heart just shattered. I don't take them. My arms won't move. "But…"

I can't stop staring at the TV. At the girl who looks like me, and sounds like me, but doesn't quite feel like me.

"But…" But what?

I can't deny it. There it is in full digital HD. I may not

have wanted it, but there I am, in Lennox's car. And the way Corbin made it look. It looks so, so bad.

I knot my fingers through my curls and tug at them until my scalp screams. Who is going to believe me? Certainly not Kevin. Not when the foundation of our do-over is still so fresh.

The voice-over man comes on. "Well, that was a royal treat," he says. "Has the princess found her prince? Find out next week on *Bathroom Barons*."

I shake my head disbelievingly. "But *he* kissed *me*. I-I didn't want to."

"Yeah. It sure seems like it." But he's not looking at me anymore. He's staring at the tickets.

I'm still shaking my head, wishing I could press the rewind and erase button. This feeling of desperate helplessness is going to tear me apart. Or maybe it's the sobs I can feel working their way up to my throat. I choke them down.

"It's not true," I say, willing Kevin to believe me. "Th-That was edited. That's not how it happened."

Kevin turns off the TV and stands up. "Thanks for the homework." He still hasn't looked at me, and his response sounds so distant, so emotionless. That barrier is back up between us again.

The tears come now. I can't hold them back, and everything becomes a blur: the credits rolling on the screen, the tickets, Kevin.

He finally looks at me, and he's not emotionless at all. He looks hurt. And I'm now certain he was going to say yes, that he was going to go to the Sadie Hawkins dance with me. And now he may never speak to me again.

I open my mouth, but instead of an explanation, a plea, an apology, a sob comes out. I cover my mouth.

Even if I could speak, I don't know what to say, so I leave. Stumbling out of the living room, I blow past Kevin. I run by the kitchen where his uncle is carrying two bowls of ice cream.

"Anyone want… Adrianna? What's wrong?"

But my legs are on autopilot and they carry me forward, out the front door and down the driveway. I run three blocks before I start to slow. But I can't go any farther, because between my getaway, and the crying, and the wanting to die, I can't breathe.

I reach a hand up to wipe the tears from my face. My phone vibrates in my pocket. It's a text from Harper. My hand shakes as I open the message to read it.

I thought you weren't interested in Lennox. Forget about hanging out tomorrow. Or EVER!

Chapter Twenty-Seven

Royal Pains

The hiss of flushing toilets plays through giant speakers across the parking lot. Blasts of regal trumpets interrupt it every thirty seconds. I know the timing exactly, because it has been drilled into my brain over the last few hours. The only way it would be more perfect is if there were a gentle peal of farts. Because my life stinks.

I sit on a comically oversized toilet and wave my golden scepter—or plunger, if you will—at the shoppers streaming through the front doors. They push and fight over grand opening sales like twisty toilet tissue with 100 percent more absorbency.

"Our prices will really *bowl* you over!" I smile big for the customers and give a queenly wave.

The crinoline under my princess dress itches like a bad rash, and the tiara pinches my head, but if that was the only thing I was dealing with this weekend, I'd be golden.

When I got home from Kevin's on Friday night, Mom and Dad were waiting. They'd seen the episode. We had a talk. A very. Long. Talk. I told them how things really went.

Of course, they know their own daughter's voice, so they'd already guessed about the dubbing. And they saw how upset I was when I got home from my date. They didn't doubt me for a second.

I've never seen Mom's mouth purse that much. It was like someone strung an elastic band through her lips and cinched it tight. Her face got all red and her eyes big and round, but she was really quiet. Dad's face was nearly purple, but I think that was because his tie was too tight.

When I was done explaining my side of things, they both hugged me and sent me to my room. At the bottom of the stairs, I glanced back. Mom grabbed her phone, to call Corbin, I guessed. Dad took off his tie. He took it *off*. I didn't even know what that meant. After that, I ran up to my room to listen at my door. Then the screaming began.

I thought Dad was going to be the worst, but Mom sounded like a banshee. She was yelling into the phone, threatening to sue, to call the police. Dad finally had to take the phone away from her. In the end, Corbin arranged a meeting with his producer. His fate hangs in the balance until then.

Things have been tense. Mom refuses to even acknowledge Corbin's existence. Dad knows we have to fulfill our contract with the network, but every time he looks at the scummy director, it looks like he's going to strangle him with a shower hose.

Hopefully everything will change after the meeting with the producer. Hopefully we'll get a new director. Or better yet, the show will be cancelled. Not that it will help much with the damage already done. Both to Mom and Dad's business, as well as my life.

Customers mill about the shiny new store floor, but not as many as Dad projected. And I suspect most of them came only to get on TV, because they just hover around the cameras. They're not even carrying shopping baskets or anything.

As embarrassing as it is being associated with a toilet empire, Dad's inventions are actually pretty great. But people aren't showing up to check them out. *Bathroom Barons* has made a mockery out of Dad's hard work, making the whole business seem gimmicky. I've made a mockery out of it with my lying, and hiding, and bad choices, instead of just being myself, the person Kevin was obviously looking for. On Friday night, that girl was nowhere to be found.

Unable to resist checking my phone for the millionth time, I reach into my fuchsia velvet cape. I peek to see if Harper has finally responded to one of my desperate texts. The only new message is from Kevin. I open it.

Where are you? Are you coming to larping later today?

I consider texting back, but I'm not certain yet. I brought my stuff with me in case I got off princess duty early. I'd show up late, but at least I'd get the chance to hang out with everyone, maybe help out the non-player characters.

However, if I go to larping, I know I have to come clean to Kevin. To tell him the truth. I'd wanted to on Friday night, but I didn't get the chance, what with the world watching as I slutted it up with Lennox, my budding romance with Kevin coming to a screeching halt before it started, and losing my best friend because she thinks I want the guy she's in love with.

Regardless of what Kevin might think of me now, I still want to tell him the truth, and not just because I'm afraid Keelie will out me to the world. Because I want to stop hiding. But do I do it as Adrianna or Andy?

"Who's Kevin?" Corbin's voice comes from behind me, his ashtray-like breath coating my neck.

I shut off my phone, but it's no use. He's already seen it.

"And where are you going this afternoon?" he persists. "Is it, per chance, the same place you escape to every Sunday?"

Hugh sticks the camera in my face, but I cover the lens with my hand. I glare at Corbin. "Haven't you done enough damage already?"

"Are you still mad about the show on Friday?" He waves a dismissive hand. I notice a few extra rings have been added to his flashy collection over the last two months. At least someone is benefiting from it.

"That's show business, sweetheart," he says like it's no big deal. Like he hasn't totally ruined my life and possibly my parents' business. "It was the first half-interesting thing you've done. My producer would have killed me if I hadn't run the footage."

"So instead, now everyone wants to kill *me*. Sure. That sounds fair."

"Everyone meaning Kevin?" He waggles his eyebrows and reaches for my phone, but I slap his hand away and shove it back into my cape.

"Back off."

"Kevin who?" This time the question comes from Lennox.

I didn't even see him approach through the jumble of shoppers. Of course he'd turn up today. Ever since Friday, he's been calling and texting nonstop. It was only a matter of time before he cornered me. He probably thinks we're an official couple now. He doesn't get it.

Corbin snaps his fingers, and the sound guy clips a portable mic onto the back of Lennox's Levi's.

"That's what we're trying to find out," Corbin says. "Do

you two have plans this afternoon?"

"No." Lennox turns to me. "I was hoping to take you out for a ride in the Stang when you're off work."

"The Stang?" My nose wrinkles. "As, umm, tempting as that is, I've already got plans."

"With Kevin," Corbin says.

"Kevin who?" Lennox asks again.

"I'm going to try to get Harper to talk to me again," I lie. No one will check with Harper to corroborate my story. Certainly not Lennox.

I know I'm supposed to start with the whole truth-telling thing, but I clearly can't tell them the truth. Not yet, anyway. Larping will be hard enough, what with revealing my identity to Kevin. It's not like I need an audience.

Hugh the camera guy closes in on Lennox and me like a shadow, the lens in our faces.

"So what else is new?" Corbin asks. "Any comments from the happy couple? How does cloud nine feel?"

Lennox slings an arm around my shoulder. "Couldn't be happier. I'm so glad I found my princess. It's like a real-life fairy tale."

"Yeah." I roll my eyes. "It's a dream come true."

"Now, now," Corbin says to me. "You don't want to make a fuss on your dad's big day, do you?" He gestures around us. "Smile for the customers."

People have gathered below our little stage, lingering around my toilet throne, for a chance to get caught in the background of Hugh's filming. Maybe they didn't come to buy anything, but either way, I don't want to do any more damage to the grand opening than I already have.

Gritting my teeth, I flash a big smile at the customers. Hugh scans the crowd with the camera, giving them what they want. People wave and jump around, shouting whatever they think will get them airtime.

Giving a royal wave with one hand, I use the other to grip my scepter. I jab the pointed end right in Lennox's armpit. He yelps and pulls his arm away from me.

I keep my smile plastered on my face, but through my teeth I hiss at Corbin. "You stay away from me. Do you hear me? Or I swear I'll get a restraining order."

I turn my fake smile on Lennox. "And *you*. Maybe I wasn't clear enough. We are *not* dating, we were never dating, nor will we ever date. Not interested. Not now. Not ever. Can you get that through your thick skull?" I feel like bashing him over the head with my scepter to see if that will help hammer it in.

A big stupid grin spreads across his face. "This is just a little rocky stage we're going through, babe."

"No. This is harassment."

Batting my eyelashes delicately, I turn and descend the red-carpeted stairs, *accidentally* catching Corbin across the face with my scepter as I go.

I nod and say hello to the onlookers, as if to say, "Carry on. Nothing wrong here." Ducking through the crowd, I search for a refuge.

Dad looks busy. He's by the Power Plunger display, giving a demonstration to a group of elderly customers. The oversized king's crown is still balanced on his head. He bought it for the opening weekend as a marketing gimmick. Personally, I think it's an excuse to hide his bald spot.

Finally, I catch sight of Mom—which isn't tough considering she's wearing a fake-fur–lined queen's capelet.

Footsteps thud on the stairs behind me. I don't bother to see who it is. Lifting my skirts, I shuffle across the store in my silk high heels.

Mom spots me and turns away from the well-dressed

man she's talking to. She's got that fake smile she wears when she's trying really hard to impress someone—which is all the time. Suddenly, I get the feeling that I've jumped out of the bidet and into the toilet.

"Oh, here she is now." She waves me over. "Princess, this is Mr. Carson. He's the fashion investor I was telling you about."

He holds out his hand, and I shake it. Right, the fashion line Mom wants me to start. The one I said I'd give a shot. Because it's a dream come true—for someone other than me. Yet another half-truth I've told, a promise I've cornered myself into that I need to fulfill. What else can go wrong today?

The man is what you would expect for someone in the fashion industry. Well put together but in an effortless way. As though he wears Armani to shop in bathroom stores all the time, like it's a runway.

I am in way over my head. Suddenly, I wish I was wearing something Suzzy planned for me, not a Princess Toadstool dress.

Mr. Carson looks down his horn-rimmed glasses at me. "Your mother has been telling me about your recent designs. I can't wait to see them."

"Great." Just great, great, great.

I clench my scepter to prevent myself from fidgeting with my dress. Mom's obviously been stretching the truth because I haven't let her see any of my projects. Because they don't exist, unless you count a few larping costumes.

I put on another big fake smile. My cheeks are starting to hurt. "Thank you for the opportunity," I say. "I'm interested to see what you have to say about them." I'm sure it will be something like, "have you lost your mind?"

Mom starts talking me up to this guy, her high-pitched

giggle giving me a brain ache. He's asking a bunch of questions about nonexistent designs. Then Lennox comes over and introduces himself as my boyfriend. Of course, Dad shows up and he's all frowning at Lennox's efforts to hold my hand in front of the cameras. I keep flicking his sweaty ham-hands away, but Corbin just pushes us together. Mom is ignoring the sleazeball, while Dad looks like he's trying to melt him with his glare. Meanwhile, no one wants to say anything about it in front of the cameras, and the crowd, and Mr. Carson. And velvet was such a bad idea in this California heat. I just want to scream!

"Excuse me," I say, before I explode.

Mom tugs on my puffy sleeve. "Where are you going?"

"The bathroom," I say, so no one will follow me. But I zigzag through the aisles just in case I have a tail.

When I think I've gone far enough, I duck into a Bottom's shower stall on display. I frantically tuck and gather my poofy dress into the small space so I can shut the frosted glass door behind me.

The outside world becomes blissfully muffled. I soak up the solitude, the privacy. I wonder how long I can stay in here. Maybe forever. To avoid the chaos outside these plastic walls. How did I let things get so crazy?

I'm in the shower for only a minute before a blurred figure appears on the other side of the frosted glass and brings up a fist.

Knock. Knock. Knock.

I squeeze my eyes shut and lean my head back against the plastic wall. "Occupied."

But the door cracks open anyway, my dress spilling out. I reluctantly open my eyes. And for a second I wonder if I nodded off and I'm now dreaming, because Kevin is standing at my shower door.

Chapter Twenty-Eight

Toilet Tumult

My mouth falls open once I realize I'm not dreaming. Kevin's actually here. He showed up to the grand opening. After Friday's Lennox episode, I didn't think Kevin would ever speak to me again, but here he is.

He glances both ways down the aisle before assessing my shower stall hiding spot. "How are those powers of invisibility coming along?"

"Kevin?" I gape. "What are you doing here?"

For a second, my hopes soar. Then I see the extendible shower rod in his hand and they drop into my high heels. Maybe he's not here for me.

"Let me guess," I say. "Your uncle sent you here to spy."

Kevin leans the rod against a nearby rack. "Yes." His eyes flick back to me. "And no."

"And you also needed a curtain rod?"

Kevin shifts his spiky head aside like he wants me to come out. I fold my arms over my body and hug myself. I'm not ready yet.

He considers my expression for a moment. Maybe it's

the panic on my face, or the fact that I'm cowering inside a display shower stall, that makes him give in. He glances down the aisle before shoving my crinoline skirts aside and wedging his way into the already cramped space—it's the extra compact city loft edition of the Bottom shower stall.

We jostle and shift and I bunch up my dress until he can close the door. Once it's sealed again, the hissing toilet sounds are muffled. We stare at each other with nothing between us, well, except for a lot of princess dress.

"It's nice in here," he finally says. "I like what you've done with the place."

"It comes in eight colors," I reply automatically. "Kevin, why did you come?"

It looks like he doesn't want to meet my gaze, but there aren't a lot of other places to look. Finally, his eyes meet mine, and it's like he doesn't want to look anywhere else, because his expression softens as he searches my face. "Because I wanted to. I wanted to see how you were doing. You looked really upset when you left my house on Friday night."

Kevin is worried about me. Not only is he still talking to me, but despite the Lennox episode, and the look on his face when he watched me make out with Lennox, he's come to check on me.

The shower has filled with Kevin's scent and it makes my head spin. All I can focus on is how close we are right now, how alone, that there are no cameras, no Uncle Gerald, no customers, and that I just want to kiss him. To tell Kevin it's not Lennox that I want. It never was. It's him.

"I mean," he continues, "I don't know why you like Lennox. I just didn't think it was right, them putting it on TV like that."

I shake my head. "It's not what it looked like. Corbin

changed what happened."

His eyes narrow, and he gives me a look, like how can I really be asking him to believe that? "Just like he did with the ice cream?"

"Yes!"

But he still looks skeptical. "What were you doing in Lennox's car in the first place?"

"I told you. I went on the date for Harper. Because she still likes Lennox."

"Then why wasn't he giving her a ride home?"

"Because Lennox insisted, and it all got so turned around. It was a setup with Corbin all along. They'd planned the whole thing. To catch the moment on film."

"But you still kissed him. You kissed Lennox. You can't deny that."

"No. He kissed me." I reach up and grip Kevin's shoulders, and they stiffen beneath my touch. "Those noises, that voice. It wasn't me. They dubbed me. I was trying to push him away. I even gave him a bloody nose."

Kevin frowns and looks away. I squeeze his shoulders tighter, wanting to keep him from leaving. How can I make him believe?

"It seems a little strange that all these misunderstandings keep happening," he says, but in a way that seems like he wants to believe me, he's looking for a way. "That it's never what it seems. It's still hard to believe that Corbin is always setting you up. That he's behind it all."

"But he is."

Kevin's hands reach up and settle over my own. They're gentle and hesitant, but then he cringes like he's fighting with himself again, and it pains him. He grabs me by the wrists and holds my hands away from him, like he can't stand to be touched by me right now. "But you seem to make it pretty easy for him. You put yourself in these situations."

I grunt, finding it harder and harder to breathe, but I don't think it's the small space. "I didn't ask for any of this."

"But you're not exactly fighting it very hard, or it wouldn't keep happening." He hasn't let go of my wrists. Whether we're friendly or fighting, it seems like we can't seem to resist touching each other. Our brains just haven't caught up with what our bodies know already. That we're supposed to be together.

"I'm doing the best I can!" I yell. "I'm trying to keep everyone happy."

"And how is that going?" he asks sarcastically. "Are you happy?"

"No!"

"Good. Because neither am I!" He's practically yelling. I'm yelling. Our voices echo off the plastic walls.

He's not happy. But he's still here. After everything, he's still here, and I know in my heart it's because he feels the same as I do about him, but there's so much in our way right now. And it's my fault.

Letting go of my wrists, Kevin reaches for his back pocket and pulls out the dance tickets. "I also came here today to give you these back." He hands them to me with stiff movements, and I take them numbly. "Now you can go with Lennox."

I clench the tickets in my fist. "But I don't want to go with Lennox. I want to go with you."

"It doesn't matter. I think I want to go with someone else anyway." He's staring at the showerhead now.

My stomach tenses and churns like I've just been punched in the gut. But then I realize who he means. He wants to go with the other me. With Andy. Would it help how he feels if I told him I'm her? Does it even matter?

Either way he needs to know. Now. Before things get any worse.

"Sometimes I feel like I don't even know you, Adrianna."

"You do," I say. "You know me better than you think you do."

"What do you mean?"

"I'm—"

The door suddenly pops open and the real world floods in like cold air after a hot shower: flushing toilets, cameras, customers, Corbin's gold rings flashing beneath sample bathroom lighting, and Lennox.

Meaty hands reach in and grip Kevin's T-shirt. He's torn violently out of the shower stall. He trips on the frame and sprawls across the linoleum floor.

"What the heck are you doing with my girl?" Lennox demands.

I squeeze out of the shower like a Nerf ball out of a gun. "Lennox, stop!"

Lennox looms over Kevin with clenched fists. I grip his muscular arm from behind, but he shakes me off like a fly. Kevin barely gets to his feet before Lennox is on him.

Kevin is tall, but Lennox is thick and strong. He shoves Kevin against a shower. There's a crack as the glass shatters into a spiderweb behind his back.

Kevin grunts and gasps for air like it's been knocked from his lungs. He shakes his head as though he's in a daze. Lennox moves in on him again.

Reaching out, Kevin grabs the shower rod he leaned up against the rack earlier. As Lennox rushes him, Kevin thrusts the end at him. It connects with his torso.

Lennox doubles over, clutching his stomach. Kevin twirls the rod like a knight would a staff and brings it down on Lennox's back. He grunts, his face twisting, but doesn't fall down. Spinning, he grabs the rod before Kevin can back off and rips it from his grip. Taking it in both hands, he bends the aluminum metal and tosses it aside.

Lennox turns to me. "Was this loser harassing you?" His voice is loud, like someone might speak on a stage.

"He's not a loser! He's my friend."

"So he was the Kevin you were talking about earlier?"

"It's none of your business."

But he ignores me and stomps toward Kevin again, his eyes a little glazed, his face red with anger.

With a running jump, I leap onto his back, pink silk enveloping him. I wrap my arms around his thick neck. He tries to pry me off, but I clamp tighter. It gives my dad the chance to step between them.

Just as Kevin surges toward Lennox, my dad throws up his hands between them, royal cape flaring out dramatically.

"That's enough!" he yells. "You"—he jabs a finger into Lennox's chest—"you're banned from this store. Get out!"

Lennox quails, despite the fact that Dad is like half his size. He seems to come to his senses—or sense, since he can't have more than one—and blinks at the gathered crowd around him. He turns to Corbin. But Corbin is conveniently not looking at him, even though that's where all his precious "action" is.

"I'm sorry." Lennox points to the shower door. "I'll pay for that."

"Yes, you will." My dad is red in the face, too, and I don't think it's because his tie is too tight. "Now go before I call the police." He straightens the crooked crown on his head and holds up his hands to the crowd. "Nothing to see here. All part of the show, folks." He tries to laugh it off, but Dad was never a very good actor.

No one listens anyway.

I reach out to Kevin to see if he's all right, but he pushes me away.

Lennox tries to grab my hand like he's in a game of tug-of-war, only Kevin's not fighting back. "Come on, babe, let's go."

"What is wrong with you?" I snatch my hand away. "I'm not your babe!"

I turn back to Kevin in time to see him disappear into the shower curtain section on his way to the exit. "Kevin, wait!" I run after him, but as I pass a bathtub, the giant bow on the back of my dress snags on the faucet. It rips right off, partially tearing the skirt from the bodice.

"Your dress!" Mom cries. She grabs the silk in her hands, assessing the damage, but it didn't just tear at the seam. It tore the fabric itself.

"Are you happy now?" she asks me. "You've ruined the grand opening. It's all ruined." Her filler-injected bottom lip quivers, and her eyes turn red.

"Mom…" I reach out to her, but she turns away and heads for the bathroom. I look to Dad. "Dad," I begin. "I'm so sorry."

He holds up a hand. "Enough, Andy." And because he didn't call me princess, I know he's mad. Or worse. He's disappointed in me.

I feel the same way.

Turning on my pink heels, I run out of the shower aisle. Picking up my larping duffel bag from the front counter, I keep running, away from Lennox, away from the cameras, away from all my mistakes, and head for the only place I feel like I can be myself right now: Asdor.

Chapter Twenty-Nine

Imperiled Empire

I stomp down the sidewalk, my heels clicking sharply on the pavement. Lennox follows me in the "Stang" like a stalker, yelling at me, telling me that he's sorry and to get in the car.

Yeah, right!

I ignore him and try to blend into line, waiting for the bus—not an easy thing to do in a giant princess dress. The person in front of me is holding a Bottom's Bathrooms and Accessories shopping bag. At least someone bought something.

Curious eyes scrape over me, but I stare blankly ahead, tuning out Lennox's voice. When the bus pulls up, Lennox is forced to drive away to make room. His Mustang's engine roars as he stomps on the gas and speeds off.

I cram myself through the narrow door and into the bus, not even caring where it's headed. All I want to do right now is get as far away as possible. I grab a window seat—or rather, both seats, since my dress spills into the aisle. The glass is cool as I lean my pounding forehead against it.

As we pull away, headed for who-knows-where, I see Corbin pulling onto the street after the bus. The crew tries to be all discreet, keeping two cars back, but with the network logo on the side of the van, they're not exactly ready for undercover ops.

I need to get away, to disappear. But most importantly, I need to find Kevin.

After the day I've had, telling him the truth doesn't seem quite as monstrous a challenge. Who knows? Maybe he'll understand. I snort. Yeah, right. But at least the truth will be out there. All of it. I can stop being so afraid that it will blow up in my face.

My week spent hanging out with Kevin was amazing. Not above average, but *super*. And yet we did nothing more than do homework and read comics together. He was him, and I was me. Like I didn't have to be anyone else, not Princess Andy, not Porcelain Princess, not part of the SPAM parade at school, and that was okay with him. I can be myself around him.

There was a moment in his living room on Friday, when him liking me and going to the Sadie Hawkins dance with me didn't seem so impossible. Until *Bathroom Barons* came on TV and ruined any chance of that. Now I just have to tell him the truth before Keelie tells him first and he hates me more than he probably already does. I'm no longer aiming for a happily ever after. Just damage control.

Distracted by thoughts of Kevin and the speech I would give him when I finally reveal myself, I find the nearest corner store and change into my larping costume. I stuff the ripped princess dress into the duffel bag as best as I can. I have to sit on the bag to zip it up. It will be wrinkled once I pull it out, but I don't really care right now.

In my anticipation, the next bus ride goes by quickly.

Too quickly. Every second that passes is one more second closer to Kevin either forgiving me or hating me forever.

When I hop off and make my way to Asdor, I repeat the main points of my super convincing plea in my head like a mantra. But I don't have to look very hard to find Kevin. He's standing where he normally parks his blue Kia beneath the blank billboard, along with all the other larpers. The non-player characters look like they're dressed as vampires, ready to create the scenario for the larpers to play out. However, no one looks ready to suck any blood.

I pull out my phone, which has been going off nonstop with texts from my parents and Lennox. I ignore the notifications and glance at the time. Twelve o'clock. I'm surprised they haven't started larping yet. Taking a deep breath, I head over to the group.

My footsteps slow as I see their expressions clearly. They look distraught. A range of emotions plays across their faces, from anger to dejection. At first I wonder if they're getting in character. Then Keelie's eyes land on me and her face twists with disgust.

Did she tell the group my secret? Are they all waiting to confront me? Maybe I should turn around now before the rest of them see me. Then Kevin spots me, and it's too late.

He pulls away from the group to meet me first. I hesitate, my legs freezing in indecision, as though I instinctually want to make a run for it. But I know Kevin could outrun me.

I'm worried for nothing. The second he gets to me, he wraps his arms around me, pulling me in for a hug. Only a couple of hours ago, he was pushing me away—the other me.

"Good, you're here," he says into my wig. "I was worried you weren't coming."

I sink into his embrace, committing it to memory, absorbing comfort from it after the crap day I've had. And possibly am about to have, once I tell him the truth.

"And miss seeing you? Never." I try to infuse the words with as much sincerity and meaning as I can, hoping he'll remember how I really feel once he finds out.

Kevin grabs my hand and pulls me toward the group. No one is throwing things yet, or glaring at me—with the exception of Keelie—so I relax a little. Maybe the depressing mood has nothing to do with me.

"Are we going to start soon?" I ask, because no one is saying anything.

"What's the point?" Keelie snaps at me. "There is no more larping."

I frown, both at her statement and at her hostility. "What? Why?"

She narrows her eyes. "As if you don't know."

Is she mad that I haven't told her brother the truth yet? That I didn't tell him Friday night? But if she was that mad, then surely she would have revealed my secret by now.

"Keelie," Kevin says. "I know you're upset, but stop taking it out on other people. It's not Andy's fault."

Keelie's jaw clenches, probably to hold back all the things she wants to say to me right now. I can almost hear her teeth grinding. But still she doesn't expose me.

"What's going on?" I ask.

"Asdor is no more," Mark tells me, kicking loose gravel with his hoof. "We can't larp here anymore."

I drop my duffel bag on the ground. I open my mouth to say something, but too many questions rush to my tongue at the same time. No more Asdor? No more larping?

Ken the Game Master scratches his balding head. "There's always the Anaheim group. We could join them."

Chad whacks his sword against the billboard's metal post. The *ting* echoes across the parking lot. "That's too far away. Most of us take city transit. It would take us half the day just to get there and back."

"They larp on Saturdays in Anaheim," Kevin says. "I work for my uncle on Saturdays."

"We'd lose half our group," Finn says, leaning heavily on his wizard staff.

Shawn the ninja says nothing, but I can see the intense contemplation on his pudgy face, like he's trying to solve the world's problems.

"No!" Eddie wails. He curls up in a ball beneath the billboard, rocking back and forth. "We can't larp anywhere else. Asdor is our home."

They're all caught up in the debate, going round and round, their frowns deepening. I feel like I've missed the big picture.

"Hold on a second," I say. "Can someone fill me in? Why do we have to leave?"

"Someone bought Asdor," Mark tells me.

"How?" I ask, incredulously.

"They're going to demolish it and build a store here," Finn says.

"What? Can they do that?" Then I remember that Asdor is just a made-up world, and it's really just a plot of land. It certainly doesn't feel that way to me. It feels as though my homeland is really getting dug up. The only place I feel like I belong right now. My heart is racing, and a panicky sensation flutters in my chest.

Ken picks at a silver string on his wizard hat. "It's been an empty lot for years. People have been using it as a park. We assumed it belonged to Costco or the city."

"Obviously not," Keelie snaps. She's still glaring at me,

as though she's blaming me for losing Asdor, and I still can't figure out why.

Everyone grows quiet and somber, like they've all just accepted their defeat. But I want to fight. I want to defend Asdor.

"Maybe we can, I don't know, petition it or something." I know I sound stupid, but I suddenly feel like my world is falling apart. "Who does it belong to? What's the store going to be?"

Keelie laughs, like I just said something funny. "I'll give you one guess."

When I frown and shake my head, like "how can I possibly guess?" she jabs a finger up at the sign above us.

Kevin steps aside, clearing my view of the billboard behind him. It's been lording over the busy parking lot ever since I joined the larping group.

But it's no longer blank.

I suddenly feel like joining Eddie in the fetal position. Spread across the entire sign is a ginormous picture of me sitting in my princess dress on a toilet.

I blink at it for a few seconds before I finally remember how to read. My legs give out, and I flop down on my duffel bag.

The sign reads, HOME OF A FUTURE BOTTOM'S BATHROOMS AND ACCESSORIES.

Chapter Thirty

Masked Mayhem

My blade slices through the cold flesh of the undead, separating limbs from bodies. My fellow warriors and I hack and slash our way through the swarm of bloodthirsty vampires, taking our frustration out on their lifeless animated corpses.

Keelie and I tag team one. I lop off a rubbery gray arm, and she serves an arrow to its gut. It keels over, but the undead don't die quite so easily. We must kill their master—or so a non-player character informed our group when she appeared as an old hag from the woods.

Kevin and Chad race by, brandishing their weapons like maniacs. They charge down two more vampires who are in turn chasing Shawn. Eddie's high-pitched screams echo in the distance somewhere.

"We can't keep this up forever," Kevin calls out. "We need to work together. Try to corral them."

No one questions his orders since he's the leader of the group today. And quite frankly, killing the same non-player character over and over again is getting exhausting.

We wrangle them up and begin the massacre, which is much easier when we're all cooperating. I make sure to aim for the limbs, which take longer to grow back. This will give us more time to come up with a plan before their bodies reassemble and we start all over again.

When the undead fall, we relax for the moment, but no one celebrates. There's a heaviness about our group of warriors. We're weighed down by the depressing news that Asdor will soon fall at the hands of an enemy we can't defeat. My own father and his big-box store.

The billboard said that construction on Dad's new store will get underway two weeks from now. However, knowing this might be our last battle, we also didn't want to waste our day together, so we forged on.

I had hoped to spend one last afternoon with Kevin not hating me for lying to him. But once everyone finds out that it's my dad's store that's ruining their Asdor lives, they'll hate me, too.

This larping group is for everyone to come and vent their frustrations, to step out of their boring, stressful realities and escape. This hobby is important to all of their lives, my life too, and in Eddie's case, this *is* his life. And they won't be able to come here again because of Bottom's Bathrooms and Accessories.

Keelie leans closer to me so only I can hear. "You haven't told Kevin yet."

I cringe. "I thought we weren't supposed to break character."

"Which one? You seem to be playing a lot of characters lately."

"I told you I would. Friday just turned out to be bad timing."

Keelie addresses the group. "I think Kevin and Andy

should go look for Lord Veracchi's coffin alone."

It's put to a vote, and everyone seems to be in agreement. Keelie shoves the silver stake into my hands. I guess there's no more putting off the truth until the end of the game. It's now or never.

No one questions the plan as we walk into the thick woods together to vampire hunt. Everyone's used to Kevin and me going on quests alone, like we're some kind of larping couple. I want to hold on to that just a little longer. I grab his hand and squeeze tight.

He misunderstands my sudden anxiety, because he says, "Don't worry. We may not be able to larp anymore, but maybe you can come over and hang out at my house."

"That would be cool," I say.

We carry on down the hard-packed trail through the trees. A whiteboard dangles from a low branch up ahead. Scrawled in red dry-erase marker is the word GRAVEYARD, with an arrow pointing off the path. We follow it.

I try to act normal, to control my shaking hand in his, to slow my breathing. But the truth is coming, and I'm going to blurt it out any second, because there's a big pink elephant in the forest with us, and it feels like it's sitting on my chest. I can't breathe right.

My legs stop moving, even though I didn't tell them to. I feel dizzy, sick, like I've come down with the flu. "Kevin. I have to tell you something."

He sighs and turns to me. "Me, too." He looks down at my hand in his. "I've had a really bad weekend so far."

I wince beneath my mask as I catch on that he means because of me.

"But it's made me realize something."

He reaches up and traces the edges of my mask, his fingers tickling my skin, leaving behind trails of fire. It burns me sweetly until I think his touch is going to leave permanent marks, beautiful scars or tattoos that will brand me as his forever. Just the way he's already branded my heart.

I swallow hard. "What's that?"

"That when we're together, none of it matters. I can be myself when I'm with you. I don't feel like I'm being judged for who I am or what I like to do, because you're right alongside me, doing it, too."

His smile makes my insides ache like a boa constrictor is wrapped around them, and I wish he would just stop talking. Stop saying such nice things.

"And I realize that I want to do other things with you, too," he continues. "I want to hang out, and read comics together, and go to the movies…and my school's dance is coming up. I mean, it's Sadie Hawkins, so technically girls ask guys." He closes his eyes for a moment, as though redirecting his darting thoughts. "Those are the kinds of things that I want to do. We might not have larping anymore. But at least we can be together. I like you, Andy."

I take a deep breath, like a drowning victim breaking the surface for a gasp of sweet oxygen. "I like you, too."

The truth sticks in my throat like dry soda crackers. I want to tell him. I really want to, but it hurts to even try and pull the words from my throat, because he likes me. He likes me, and he's looking at me with those clear blue eyes, and I automatically tilt my face up toward his.

His eyes close and he meets my lips with his own.

They're like kissing gummy bears left out on the car dash on a sunny day. Soft, and warm, and sweet. This should have been my first kiss. Because he's not trying to devour my face. Instead, it's like he's savoring my lips, tasting them, or maybe my root-beer–flavored lip gloss.

Kevin cups my face like they do in the movies, and I'm lost in the sensation of my bottom lip sandwiched between both of his. I drop the stake on the ground. His fingers move over my wig and to the tie at the back of my head. He pulls at the ribbon and the bow comes undone. I let him. There's no going back.

My mask is pulled away, but our kisses barely stop for even a second. He doesn't yet know who I am. I wish he never would. And at the same time, I wish he did know. I wish he was kissing me now, the real me, the whole me. Adrianna and Andy.

I wrap my arms around his neck, like I can keep him there. Can keep him from pulling away and discovering the truth. But it hurts because I know I can't. And then noises bring us back to the real world. It sounds like the forest is falling down around us. Bushes thrashing, branches crashing, twigs snapping.

We both draw away at the same time, hands reaching for our swords. It could be vampires.

No. It's the worst bloodsucker of them all: Corbin.

Chapter Thirty-One
Dethroned

Corbin's attention scrapes by me at first, but then his head snaps back. He takes in the wig, and the costume, and the whole scandalous scene. His eyes glint. They actually glint, like the very idea of money is reflecting in them.

"My Porcelain Princess," he says.

Kevin doesn't seem to hear. He hasn't looked at me yet. There are cameras all around us now. The forest is alive with movement as the crew converges on us. Even some of the other larpers are closing in, having followed the commotion through the forest out of curiosity.

Corbin has drawn quite the crowd. I see Keelie, Finn, Ken the Game Master. Even Lord Veracchi has crawled out of his coffin to witness the action. Corbin must have searched all of Asdor, trying to find us.

No point in hiding anymore. I grip the wig and rip it off, bobby pins tearing at my copper roots. Kevin finally sees me, *really* sees me. He backs away. I can feel his eyes boring into me, but I can't seem to meet them. Instead, I stare down at his hand that's still ready to draw his sword. His knuckles turn white around the hilt.

When I finally meet his look, I expect to see fury. Because the girl who drove him away is also the one he ran straight toward. But instead, I see hurt, pain, like I'd taken the silver stake and driven it right through his heart. Is that look for Andy or Adrianna?

My heart, which had been so full moments before when we were kissing, now feels like it's breaking into a million pieces.

He closes his eyes for a second, and when he opens them, the whites look a little pink.

"Why?" he whispers, his voice cracking. Maybe because he doesn't want our audience to hear. Maybe because it's all he can muster.

I reach out to him, but he takes a step back and drops my mask in the dirt.

"I wanted to tell you," I say. "I was going to."

"Then why didn't you? You had every opportunity."

"I was afraid for anyone to find out, for the cameras to find out." I wave a hand at the crew. "I wanted us to get to know each other more. For you to get to know me outside of larping and see who I really am."

"So you waited until I fell for you to stomp on my heart?"

Kevin fell for me? My breath catches and I choke like I swallowed a bug. I take an automatic step forward, wanting to close the distance between us. "Fell for who?" I ask. "Which one?"

He scowls. "'Which one?' Do you hear yourself? Does it even matter now?"

"Yes," I say. "It does, because I like you."

He grimaces, like he's swallowing his own bug. Then he

shakes his head and begins to back away. "I can't believe a word that comes out of your mouth. Or either of your mouths. Both of you have been lying to me this whole time."

He spins on his heel and crashes out of the clearing. The two cameras stick close by. I want to yell at Corbin to leave us alone, but I know it won't do any good.

"Stop!" I yell. I catch up to Kevin and tug desperately on his arm. "I've never lied. Not about myself or us. You know me. It's still me, Kevin. I just kept my identity a secret. Like a superhero," I say, thinking of a way to get through to him. To make him understand. "If anyone can understand that, it's you."

His nose wrinkles, like he smells something bad. "There's nothing 'super' about this. Villains also hide behind masks. Why didn't you tell me sooner, before it came to this?" He gestures to the clearing around us, but he's looking at me like there's no one else there. The desperate look on his face feels so private, meant just for me. Not the whole world that will see this on TV.

He waits patiently, as though he wants a reason, an excuse that will absolve me from any wrongdoing. Like there was some kind of sorcerer's spell that prevented me from telling anyone. Maybe he still has hope and wants me to be innocent.

But there is no magic spell. It was yet another bad decision I made. "I was just so afraid you would hate me."

This obviously isn't enough for him because he throws his head back and makes a sound. I think it's supposed to be a laugh, but it sounds too empty. When he turns back to me, his gaze is cool and emotionless. I've lost him.

"And why would you possibly think I'd hate you?" he asks sarcastically, a new fire in his eyes. "Was this some joke to you? A setup for an exciting episode? To get good ratings? Like every other time you were supposedly set up, or made to look bad?"

"No." I shake my head. I can already feel tears forming. "That's not it."

When he turns away and begins to climb over the rise, I call out to his rigid back. "I only wanted to escape my life. I wanted to hide from the cameras and be with you."

He pauses by a tree and kicks at its trunk before turning back to me. "And to you, those two things are mutually exclusive. Because you were too embarrassed to be with me on camera. I get it. I'm not the arm candy Lennox is."

"Lennox? That's not it at all. Please. Let me explain."

"No. Let me explain something to you." He closes the gap between us and draws up really close. The cameras are practically pressed against our cheeks, but even he doesn't seem to notice in his sudden anger.

That boy who was kissing me five minutes before is gone, but I can still feel the memory of his lips on mine. I wonder if the cameras weren't here, if things would be different. If we could talk it out. Maybe my entire life would be different.

"You wanted to show me who you really are?" he asks. "I don't even think you know yourself. But from what I've seen, I don't want to know."

The fire in his eyes has died to cold ashes, and I know he means what he says, because he's not yelling anymore.

His Adam's apple bobs as he swallows hard. "Stay away from me."

And when he turns to trudge away, I obey. I can't seem to find the energy to follow. I can't even cover my face or turn away from the cameras as my tears spill over and run down my face. What's the point? They'll only follow me. I can't escape Corbin. He'll only find another way to ruin my life, or catch me ruining it myself.

After an unreadable glance back at me, Keelie follows her brother. Maybe she's disappointed. Maybe she pities me. Either way, I don't think she's mad. I got what I deserved and that's enough. She must have lost her patience and made good on her threat a day early. Maybe she called Corbin to rat me out.

I'm not mad; I deserve this. But my parents don't. It could mean the end of Bottom's Bathrooms and Accessories.

One by one the other larpers scatter. I think Corbin feels bad because he finally calls, "Cut!" even though I'm still crying, which is TV drama gold—footage to really drive that teen angst and pain home for the viewers.

If only it were all an act, I could shut off these painful emotions. But the emptiness inside lingers long after the cameras are gone, the feeling of helplessness. I wish someone could write me a script, tell me how to fix this mess, what to do next. But Corbin turns his back on me and leaves the clearing.

I feel something nudge my hand. It's my mask. Hugh gives it to me, and I automatically take it.

"You dropped this," he says, kind of sheepishly.

"Thanks. But I don't need it." I let go, and it falls in the mud. I reach up and rub at my chest. It aches, as though my heart has been ripped out.

Kevin was right about me. It doesn't matter how many masks I wear. I can't hide who I really am.

Chapter Thirty-Two

Princess to Pauper

I slam the door to the toilet stall and bang my head against it. I don't have to pee, but I sit down anyway and pretend. Anything to get a moment away from my entourage, SPAM. Through the crack in the stall, I can see Star, Prissy, Amber, and Mercedes vying for the mirror with the best lighting.

The first school bell hasn't even rung, and already the vultures are converging, fighting over a piece of me. Star wants to post a picture of the two of us, probably for self-promotions Prissy wants to be my study partner, Amber wants to borrow my new jacket, and Mercedes wants me to come to a party next weekend.

News travels fast, apparently. And since Harper is no longer talking to me, the members of SPAM are lining up like I'm holding auditions for the part of BFF. I'm pretty sure Star would start singing and dancing if I told her to.

The second I step out of this stall, they'll gather around me like flies on old meat. I peek through the crack in the door again. They check their hair and makeup in the sink mirrors, glancing back to confirm they can see my feet beneath the door, like they think I might escape. I'm trapped.

Trying to block out their endless bubbly chatter, I read the graffiti etched into the painted cubicle walls to pass the time. The first one I read is for a "good time" and gives Star's name and number. Maybe she would do more than start singing and dancing to be my BFF.

When usually they're clustered around Harper's locker before first class, SPAM was camped out at mine when I arrived at school. Maybe it was their blatant ship-jumping that finally proved they're not my real friends, or even Harper's friends. I mean, where is the loyalty?

And maybe it's because of Harper's refusal to forgive and forget so easily despite hundreds of texts over the weekend and me banging on her door three times, that makes me certain, more than ever, that she was the true friend. Corbin even approached her about an interview this morning, but she said, "No comment" and kept walking. If she'd only been hanging out with me for a few seconds of airtime, she would have jumped on the drama train. But she didn't.

She was my real friend. And now she's really hurt.

"Did anyone see Harper this morning?" Mercedes asks, like she can read my mind. "She was wearing yoga pants, a hoodie, and no makeup. Has she just totally given up on finding a guy?"

Amber giggles. "Well, she couldn't get Lennox back, so maybe she gave up."

I blink. What does she mean "get Lennox back?" How does she know she even wanted him back? I lean forward to hear them better.

"I thought she broke up with him," Star says.

"Yeah, right." Mercedes snorts. "It was the other way

around. But I mean, can you really blame him?"

"She's needy enough to drive anyone insane," Prissy says. "This weekend she called me three times, asking to hang out. Like I don't have my own life?"

"That must have been after she called me," Mercedes says, like she needs to be at the top of the social ladder.

"Me, too," Amber says.

The news that Harper has been calling everyone stings. She even called Mercedes, and she can barely cope with her at the best of times. Maybe she was desperate for a friend, to talk to someone about what happened on the show. I just wish she'd called me, so I could have explained everything.

Harper was obviously hurting. And here her so-called friends were laughing at her for it. I peer through the crack in the stall door.

Prissy throws her mascara back in her bag. "Harper's so needy."

"Pathetic," Amber agrees like the parrot she is.

"She called me, too," Star says. "We hung out yesterday."

Mercedes's head snaps her way. "Why?"

Star shrugs. "I think she was bummed out. I'm not sure why." She continues to make "dying" faces in the mirror, probably practicing for her bit part in that horror film next month.

"Because the focus isn't on her," Mercedes says. "We all know how self-centered Harper can be. Remember when she got upset that none of us could come to some house party in July? It's always about her."

I'm tired of listening to them. I flush the toilet and step out. The door slams against the wall. SPAM jumps and turns to me.

"It's because her birthday's in July," I say. "She probably wanted you to be there for her birthday party."

No one quite seems to know what to say to this. Finally, Prissy says, "Like we don't have lives?"

I roll my eyes. I don't even get to the sink before Star's snapping off photos of the two of us besties.

I wash my hands, answering their rapid-fire questions while only half listening. Most are about Lennox. The whole school thinks we're official now that our "date" episode aired.

"So did you spend the whole weekend with Lennox?" Amber asks.

"No. I spent it working at my dad's new store." Which is not entirely a lie. I was at the store yesterday until I ruined everything.

My parents haven't even grounded me yet. They're barely speaking to me. They say they still haven't decided on my punishment. The waiting is almost worse than any punishment they can give me.

"Lennox says you had a hot date," Prissy says.

What date? The five minutes I spent avoiding him in the store? "We're not really a couple, you know. It was just a stunt for the show."

"That's not what Lennox is telling everyone," Mercedes says.

I scrunch the paper towel into a tiny ball and aim for the trash, imagining it's Lennox's head. "I'm sure it's not."

"Don't worry," Mercedes tells me. "We're on your side."

"My side of what?"

Prissy wraps a comforting arm around me. "What Harper tried to do to you was awful. Trying to steal Lennox like that? When you're so obviously meant to be?"

I laugh, but I'm not smiling. "What are you talking about? Harper didn't try to steal Lennox from me."

Amber jumps on the counter, kicking her feet back and

forth. "That's not what Conner told me. He said that you were on the date with Lennox, and Conner was supposed to be Harper's date. Only, when Lennox made his move on you, she became a psycho jealous ex."

Star shakes her head. "Poor Conner."

"Poor Harper!" I say. "That's not what happened at all. This was all Lennox's fault. I was supposed to be Conner's date. Lennox was the one who got all handsy with me."

Prissy grabs me by the shoulders and clicks her tongue, like she's comforting a child. "You're such a good friend. But you don't have to make up excuses for wanting what you want. Conner told everyone what really happened. The whole school is talking about it."

My mouth falls open, but I don't even know where to begin. Conner was on the show for maybe only five minutes. He was obviously trying to get the rest of his fifteen minutes of fame from bragging about it at school.

Before I can explain the real story, the bell rings for class and the girls filter out of the bathroom.

On her way out the door, Mercedes flashes me a smile in the mirror's reflection. "Don't worry. We've got your back."

My life seems to have run away without me, or rather, it's dragging me along by my ankles, knocking my head on every speed bump along the way. I can't believe I let this happen. That I let it get this bad. I've been so focused on making friends and trying to please everyone else at the same time, I've forgotten to consider what I want.

Star strokes my silky smooth hair, each frizzy, curly twist flattened and straightened by Suzzy's tools this morning. "I like your hair today," she says, before skipping out the door.

I tug on a lock of it. I guess I gave in to that, too. Next thing I know, it will be dyed blonde. Will I even be recognizable?

In trying to be too many people, I've completely lost myself.

I stare at my reflection in the mirror. At the fashionable, popular girl who appears to have it all: the jock "boyfriend," the horde of so-called friends following her around, a television show about her sensational life.

Fake, fake, fake.

Where is the awkward girl with the wild red hair and a crush on the boy next door? The girl who just didn't want to be bullied at her new school? Is there any Andy left in there?

On the way to biology, my arm gets tired from waving to all the people whose names I only half remember or don't know at all. Even the seniors know my name. *Bathroom Barons* is really picking up, especially since my date with Lennox on Friday. The hits on our website have doubled in a matter of a single weekend. Apparently that French photographer was right. Sex does sell.

It's strange to have so many people be friendly with me and yet it feels like I have no friends at all—groupies don't count.

I keep my eyes peeled for Lennox in the halls. When the lab is in sight, I think I'm home free. My shoulders relax. As I pass through the door, a heavy arm crashes down around my neck, half choking me like a python.

"Hey, babe." Lennox drags me into the classroom like he's marking his territory, as though his tongue down my throat on national TV wasn't enough. He might as well just pee on my leg like a dog.

I'm trying to shrug Lennox off when I see Kevin. He notices me come in with my two-hundred-pound fame leech. He scowls and turns before I'm able to swat Lennox away.

At least Harper didn't see. She's not even sitting at our usual table. She's in a deep discussion with another girl near the back. It looks like they're solving the world's problems. SPAM snorts derisively as they pass her, except for Star who tries to catch her attention with a wave.

I notice Prissy, Amber, and Mercedes aren't the only ones who have suddenly turned their backs on Harper. Eyes all over the room dart toward her. Smiling eyes, gossipy eyes, mouths whispering behind hands. Probably saying the same things her ex-friends were in the bathroom.

As I try to catch her eye, a paper airplane soars across the room and hits her in the side of the head. She winces and rubs where it hit her. Instead of storming over and demanding who threw it like she'd normally do, she kind of shrinks in on herself.

When I first got to Beverly Hills High, I thought Harper was invincible, that being around her meant protection from teasing and bullying. It turns out not even she's safe. No one is. Maybe none of it mattered, my trying so hard to be different, hiding my geeky side from everyone. Pretending. Faking. Lying.

I sit down at our usual table alone. Lennox plops down next to me as though that's the way it's been all semester. My phone vibrates a couple times in my pocket, but I can't check it without getting caught.

When Mr. Bigger leaves for his smoke break, Lennox slides his stool closer to mine and tries to grab my hand. It's like he's trying to shove it in Harper's face. I take my pen and jab it into the back of his hand. He doesn't touch me again after that.

My phone vibrates three more times, but I don't get a chance to check it since high-pitched squeaking announces Mr. Bigger's return. He's pushing a metal trolley with a pile of neatly stacked stainless steel trays.

"Hope you skipped breakfast this morning!"

He starts handing out the trays from the front of the class. When mine slides in front of me, I recoil. The hard green lump on the tray stares back at me.

"Frog dissections!" Mr. Bigger announces.

I try not to look at the tray while Mr. Bigger gives instructions at the head of the class. The smell, however, can't be ignored. I try to breathe through my mouth instead. Since Lennox is sitting at my table, apparently that makes us partners. I hand him the scalpel, ignoring the desire to stab him with it.

As he makes the first cut, I spin on my stool to look away. Kevin's gaze is focused very intently on his frog, but when his mouth turns down, I'm certain he knows I'm looking at him. Because I don't think it's the frog that he hates.

I sigh and scan the room. A couple rows back, Mercedes and Prissy have completely abandoned their dissection for what's obviously a very interesting conversation at the table beside them.

"Mercedes! Prissy!" Mr. Bigger calls them out. "Are you done with your dissection already?"

"No," they respond with a sweetness I know they don't have in them.

"Then eyes on your own frog."

They giggle and pretend to pore over their notebook. He assesses their progress with a grimace before moving on to the next table. The moment he's far enough away, the girls lean back over to continue their conversation.

I decide to check on the progress of my own frog. A second later, I hear a "Psst!"

I spin around in my seat again. Mercedes is leaning forward in her stool. She hides her mouth behind a hand like she wants to tell me a secret. But since she's two rows back, it won't exactly be a secret.

"Adrianna," she yell-whispers. "Apparently a rumor's going around." She glances at her sources as though for verification, and they nod. Her face turns red like she's trying really hard not to laugh. "People are saying that you play some kind of weird role-playing game. Like Dungeons and Dragons, where you dress up and fight with swords."

Prissy snorts next to her, and they both succumb to giggles.

Next to me, Lennox shifts uncomfortably. "Is that true?"

Oh my God.

My eyes automatically flick to Kevin. He's no longer pretending I don't exist. He's watching my reaction.

When our eyes meet, his shoulder twitches in a shrug. I know he didn't spill the beans. And it's too early for Corbin to be airing commercials of future episodes already. Was it Keelie?

And then it occurs to me: does it even matter? Didn't I decide to start being honest with everyone? With myself? It's not like the truth was going to end with Kevin when I finally took off my mask. I'm tired of hiding, of pretending I'm something that I'm not. And it was Kevin who helped me figure out who it is I want to be. He helped me find myself again.

So I turn back to Mercedes and Prissy, and I be that person. "Yeah," I say. "It's not Dungeons and Dragons. It's called larping."

"OhmyGod," Prissy blurts like it's one word. "Are you serious?"

The entire class is listening now because she's forgotten to fake-whisper. I keep my focus on her like I don't even notice.

"I am. So what?" I give her a "what's your problem" look, like she's the weird one for overreacting, not me.

Before I turn back to my disgusting work, I catch a

glimpse of Kevin's expression. He doesn't even try to hide his surprise. His wide eyes are locked on me, as though he's seeing me for the first time.

Pretending I don't notice, I turn around again, if only so no one can see the panicked expression on my face. What's going to happen now? But Lennox can see. He's staring at me strangely, kind of like I just sneezed, and he's afraid he might catch a cold.

"What are they talking about?" he asks.

I ignore him, mostly because I'm not sure I can find my voice again. My phone has been vibrating nonstop in my pocket for the last fifteen minutes. I wait until Mr. Bigger makes another round and then slip it out of my pocket. The screen is filled with notifications. I scroll through them. *A lot* of notifications.

I've been tagged, re-tagged, and hashtagged on practically every social media outlet. One headline catches my eye. *Porcelain Princess: True Identity Revealed.*

With a shaking finger, I open it.

A photo pops up on my screen. A photo of me larping. And there's no denying it's me, because it's a perfect shot of me without my golden mask.

Another larper must have snapped the shot while Kevin and I were being filmed in the woods. And here I thought there were no cell phones allowed on the battlefield.

I clench the phone in my hand until it hurts. I knew the truth would come out eventually once the footage aired, but I expected more time. More time to prepare, to maybe start telling people on my own first, especially my friends, explaining what it is and why I do it before they started to judge me. Or maybe more time to apply for a one-way mission to Mars.

I look up to find eyes on me, and not the reptilian kind.

Everyone's staring, smiling, laughing. I remember eyes looking at me just like that back in Seattle.

Glancing from face to face, I search for a friendly one. Kevin's staring at his frog, deep in thought. At least he's not laughing like the rest of them. Of course he wouldn't be.

My desperate gaze lands on Harper. She's staring straight at me, but she's not laughing, either. I'm not entirely sure what her expression means before she frowns and looks away.

I feel numb. This is a hundred times worse than the underwear thing, because that was an accident, something they could pity me for. This is of my own doing. I can already tell by my classmates' expressions that they won't feel pity. They won't show mercy. I feel myself shake as my imagination runs away, dreaming up all the things they might do to tease me—and I have a pretty wide range of past experiences to fuel those thoughts.

But I won't back down. I'm going to stand behind the person I am. I'm in this mess in the first place because I wasn't honest, because I hid behind a mask. No more hiding. For better or worse.

I take in their scorn and sneers, and my fear of what's to come dulls as I feel a hint of pride. Pride that I've finally stepped up and started to do the right thing. That I'm standing up for myself and who I want to be, not running away from it.

So I raise my chin in defiance of those whispers and stares and laughs. Then something cold and hard hits me on the side of my face. It stings like I've been slapped with a wet rock.

I cry out and clap a hand over my stinging cheek. Lying at my feet is someone's half-dissected frog. When I pull my hand away from my face, it's covered in formaldehyde and frog juices.

Bile rises in my throat. Or maybe that's my humiliation and dread rising like hot fire up my throat. My breaths start to come in panicked gasps. I've had lots of things thrown at me in my life, but never a carcass. Who would do that to another person? Or maybe that's the point, because it makes me feel less than human.

Someone yells out from the back of the class. "Kiss your frog, Princess!"

"Yeah!" someone else says. "Maybe he's your prince."

These are the same people who waved at me in the hallway, who pretended to be my friends. I feel myself flush with fury and indignation, but it quickly turns to shame and then self-loathing. I realize that if I'd just been myself from the start, hadn't relied on my newfound Hollywood stardom to set me apart, to make me invincible, no one would have cared about my nerdiness that much. All I've done is paint a giant target on myself.

My eyes fill with hot tears, from the pain in my cheek and the pain I know I'm about to endure. I try to keep my head high as I slide off my seat, but my guise of self-dignity slips as the tears start to fall. Out of the corner of my eye, I see Kevin reach for me. But I'm already running to the hallway.

And so it begins all over again.

Chapter Thirty-Three
Restroom Revelation

The lunch lady is staring at me. I think she said something to me. She definitely looks like she's waiting for an answer, but I was too distracted by all the names being called at my back. Only because I have my back to the cafeteria. Once I turn around, the other students will have no problem calling them to my face. They have been since I was outed on social media last week.

"I'm sorry," I say. "What did you ask?"

"Did you want cheese sauce on that?"

"Oh. No thanks."

When the lunch lady gets to the tater tots, she glances over her shoulder before dishing me up two scoops. "You look like you could use some extra tots today," she whispers, like she's just handed me top-secret government documents.

I smile because extra tots do sound comforting. "Thanks."

The skin around her mouth wrinkles, like a half smile, half frown, as though she wishes she could give me *all* the tots.

The cafeteria is crowded today. I wanted to get here earlier, but after a guy in chemistry class dumped a truckload of pencil shavings over me, saying it was fairy dust, I had to clean them out of my hair—and shirt, and bra. The larping jokes are just getting better and better as the days go by.

I weave in and out of tables, searching for a spare seat. I pass by Harper's table, but she won't even look at me. Kevin's table is in the corner, but I can't look at him. And out of the corner of my eye, I can see Lennox waffling, like he has been for the last week, unsure if he should invite me to his jock table or not, but I don't even want to look at him.

I spot SPAM, who are obviously still not talking to Harper, because they're on the other side of the cafeteria. Mercedes has taken over as the leader of the group. Everyone is hanging on her every word.

Star waves at me, and I hesitantly head in that direction. Even sitting with Mercedes would be better than sitting alone right now, with the entire school throwing daggers at my back. But as I approach their table, Mercedes, Prissy, and Amber give me a look that says "over their dead bodies."

Star gives me an apologetic look. I get it. I've learned that Star is nice to everyone, but she wants to avoid persecution. Didn't I basically do the same thing to Kevin when I first got to Beverly Hills High?

I stumble slightly as I redirect my steps. I spot a girl I recognize from English class and pretend that I was already headed in that direction. We worked together on a Shakespeare essay earlier in the semester.

As I get close, I can tell she recognizes me. I lift my tray and smile as I approach, as though to ask if it's all right if I sit with them.

She tucks her hair behind her ear and ducks her head to whisper to her friends. They all glance up at once, like a creepy pack of meerkats. They not-so-subtly shift along the bench to take up the extra space.

I keep moving, forcing my chin to remain high, but the same thing happens at every table until I finally run out of places to try. Trudging over to the garbage, I dump my tray, tots and all, and leave.

On my way out the door, I feel something swish through my straightened hair. I run my fingers through it, and my hand comes away covered in ketchup.

Sighing, I head for the girls' bathroom. There's no point in retaliating. I learned that a long time ago. It only makes things worse.

Turning on the tap, I hold my head over the sink to wash out the condiment with hand soap. Once the water runs clear instead of red, I dry it with the hand dryer, but now my naturally curly hair has taken over, poofing out in just the one spot when the rest stays smooth.

Maybe it can be a new look. I can start a trend. Mom did say I was supposed to be an icon by now. I laugh, thinking of her idea for my very own fashion label. Who would buy clothing from me?

Mom and Dad haven't really gotten mad. Not *mad* mad, anyway. Just sort of disappointed in me and my decisions. They are furious at Corbin, however. They're meeting with his producer tomorrow. I hope he gets sacked.

The new store is still doing moderately well, but not well enough to support the second store being built on top of Asdor. Dad's gotten tons of stressful calls. There's been lots of tie tightening around the house. Mom even had to go for an early Botox treatment since she was frowning so much she was actually creating whole new lines.

And as for punishment? I'm on total lockdown. Not that it really matters much; I have nowhere to go anyway.

No friends left. I've basically spent the last week sketching concept designs for my supposed fashion label.

I carry my sketchbook everywhere now. I'm determined that I won't be a total failure in helping my parents' business. But I'll probably screw this up somehow, too. Because every time I try to imagine a trend-setting outfit, it turns out a little, well, medieval. A cute, knee-length dress transforms into a tunic beneath my pencil, a coat into a cape, a vest into chain mail. And eventually, I just give up and let my creativity take over, transforming the mundane into magical.

Over the last week, I've created a wardrobe to outfit an entire army—our larping army, to be exact. There's a wizard's cape for Finn, with embroidered flames licking across the shoulders, a capelet of felted butterflies and lace flowers for Keelie, and a cloak of invisibility for Shawn made of organza fabric, a swirl of iridescence in the light.

For Kevin, I've designed a costume fit for a prince. It has a fitted vest with flowing coattails of blue and gold paisley to match his eyes, a cream cotton shirt, and navy breeches.

I hear someone come into the bathroom. Swiping my sketchbook off the counter, I instinctively back into a stall, just wanting a few more moments of peace. I lock the door and quietly step onto the toilet seat, hoping they'll go away.

Whoever it is goes into the stall next to me and closes the door. To pass the time, I open my sketchbook and review my drawings. I quietly flip through the ideas, searching for something useful for the upcoming fashion show. But they're all larping related. None of it is useful for day-to-day wear.

I have less than two weeks to have an entire fashion line not only conceptualized but also created to show Mr.

Carson, the fashion investor. And I haven't sewn a stitch. Regular fashion just doesn't inspire me.

"Hi." A voice comes from above me.

I jump. My foot slips and dunks into the toilet bowl. Water splashes into my shoe, soaking my sock and pant hem. Typical.

Groaning, I shake off the excess water. I look up to find Keelie's heart-shaped face peeking over the stall. She's biting her lip like she's trying really hard not to laugh.

"I'm sorry," she says. "I didn't mean to scare you."

I scowl. "Then why are you peeking into my stall?"

"A better question would be why are you hiding in a stall?"

I glare up at her, the same way she glared at me on our last day of larping together. The day it all fell apart. "I'll give you one guess."

Keelie's eyes drop, and she actually looks a bit sheepish. "How are you doing, anyway?"

"Do you care?" I shove my way out of the stall and attempt to dry my shoe and sock under the hand dryer.

Keelie follows me. "I didn't tell anyone!" She yells over the dryer. "And it wasn't me who posted the photo online! I didn't tell anyone your secret!"

I pull away from the dryer, and after a few seconds the bathroom falls into silence again. "And Corbin? Did you tell him where to find me last Sunday? Did you tell him to come and film me at larping?"

"No."

I think back to that day. I was upset after what happened at the grand opening and nervous about telling Kevin the truth. I thought I lost Corbin on the bus ride to Asdor, but maybe I was just too distracted to notice him.

After a minute, I ask Keelie, "Why not?"

She hops onto the counter, watching me cringe as I pull on my soggy sock again. “Because we all get teased. It’s not like I don’t understand why you wanted to hide your larping. Not that we have to worry about that anymore since we can’t even larp,” she adds.

“You don’t get frogs thrown at you.”

She pulls a face. “Yeah, I heard about that. It seems a lot worse for you.”

“Why?” I ask. Although, I don’t really expect her to know.

“Maybe it’s because they expect it from the rest of us geeks. It could have nothing to do with geeky or cool. Maybe it’s because they had this certain image of you and it turns out you’re nothing like that at all. Maybe they feel a bit lied to.” She gives me a look, and I know she certainly feels that way. “Now, because they feel foolish, they’re taking it out on you.”

“I’m sorry I lied to you,” I say. “I just wanted to escape my life on the weekends and have fun. I didn’t mean to hurt anyone.”

“People will get over it.” And by that I hope she means her, too. But she’s so good at acting and hiding her true feelings, both on the field and off, that I can’t tell yet. “Once the initial shock wears off. It can’t be any worse for you than the rest of us larpers.”

I raise an eyebrow at her. “You forget about the whole toilet business thing.”

“Okay,” she relents, “so it will be a little worse.”

But I’m still not convinced she didn’t have a hand in my downfall. “What about your uncle’s business?” I ask. “I thought you wanted to take me down and all that?”

“I wasn’t really going to do it. I was mad, and I just wanted you to be honest with Kevin.” She shrugs. “He’s a big idiot. Someone has to look out for him. Might as well be me."

"What about everyone from larping? Do they all hate me because my dad is building his store on top of Asdor?"

"Well, they're not happy about it. Eddie's devastated. They say he'll never speak again." Keelie shakes her head sadly like she's making a dramatic joke, but knowing Eddie, I'm not entirely certain she's kidding. "They know it's not your fault"—she pulls a face—"mostly. But it doesn't exactly make it any easier to accept. Fair or not, I think you're kind of lumped in with the whole 'our Asdor lives are being ruined' thing."

I stare at my sodden shoe. "I wish I could make things better. For everyone."

"Well you're not going to do that hiding in a toilet stall, are you?" By the way she says it, it feels like one of the stupidest things I've done since arriving in Beverly Hills—and it has a lot of competition for first place. "Actions speak louder than words. So what are you going to do?"

I laugh as I recall Kevin telling me the same thing. "I could switch schools, change my hair again, pretend to be someone totally different. Porcelain Princess who?"

Keelie gives me a hard stare. "Do you really think that will help?"

I've already changed schools once, and it ended up exactly like Seattle. I think of the way Harper is still being teased about Lennox. If someone as pretty and nice as her can get teased, there's no guarantee.

I remember how nervous Harper got when she told me not to talk to Kevin the first day we became friends. At the time, I thought it was a bit overly dramatic. I now realize it's because she feared the same thing I did. She was never invincible, and she was aware of it as well as I was.

I already tried starting over, and that failed miserably. But most of that I brought on myself. I want to say it's all a misunderstanding. A combination of unfortunate events, uncontrollable forces set on my destruction. But if actions speak louder than words, then what were my actions?

I shunned Kevin at school, I posed as someone else at larping and lied, I let my own actions nearly ruin my parents' business, I let my BFF's ex-boyfriend, who she still liked, kiss me. Well, I didn't *let* him, and I did give him a bloody nose. But from her perspective, she believed I did it. And I still haven't convinced her otherwise.

I bite my lip hard as I begin to see things a little differently, a little less woe-is-me. The thing all those events have in common is that they start with "I." Not Corbin, not the crew, or Bottom's Bathrooms and Accessories, or *Bathroom Barons*. I did this to myself. Maybe not because of my actions, but my lack of them. My fear of standing up and saying what I feel and what I really want.

I slip on my shoe, cringing slightly at the squelch it makes. What do I want? I want to be with Kevin. I want to larp. I want to be Harper's friend. I want to sew costumes, not designer clothes.

I glance at my sketchbook again and flip through the pages of my inspiration. "Maybe there is something I can do," I tell Keelie. I stop at the page with Kevin's costume and smile. "I think I have a plan."

Keelie frowns. "To what?"

"To fix everything."

She closes her eyes and takes a deep breath, like "god of Asdor, help me." "Not another sitcom scheme. Your last harebrained idea didn't exactly pan out well for anyone involved."

"Maybe not everything then. I just want to make things

right. The things that count. With the people who count." I give her a pointed look to know that means her, too. "I know I have no right to ask you this, but if it's going to work, I could really use your help."

She crosses her arms and shakes her head adamantly. "I won't help you. Not this you." Her eyes rove up and down me, from my straightened hair, to my outfit picked out by Suzzy. "But that girl I knew from larping? The one who sewed me a tunic to make up for my ruined one. The one that makes my brother happy. She was kind of cool. I liked her better. I'd help her."

I smile. "Good. Because I like her better, too."

Chapter Thirty-Four

Deal with the Devil

I bang so hard on the back of the network van that it hurts my fists. They've been parked outside my parents' house practically twenty-four hours a day since the grand opening last weekend. My parents have refused them access inside until they meet with Corbin's producer to discuss an "alternative arrangement"—whatever that means. Hopefully it means nothing good for Corbin.

The door squeaks open, and Corbin's face appears. When he sees me standing there, he frowns. Pulling the cigarette away from his lips, he opens his mouth to speak.

Before he can get a word out, I haul myself inside and push my way into the back, nearly knocking Corbin over. Now he'll have to listen first if he wants to get rid of me. Either that or remove me by force. Which is a likely possibility.

Hugh's sitting in front of a laptop on a built-in metal desk. The Dorito in his hand freezes halfway to his mouth as I take a seat next to him on a stack of equipment cases. Behind a pair of thick-framed glasses, his eyes flick from me to Corbin.

"You can't be in here," Corbin says.

I settle into my seat and cross my arms in case it's not clear already that I'm staying right where I am. "What are you going to do? Fire me?"

He sighs. "What do you want, kid? We've got work to do." He waves a hand at Hugh like a magician, cigarette ashes fluttering to the floor.

Hugh obediently dips his head to the laptop and keeps working.

"I want a retraction," I say.

"A retraction for what?"

"You know for what. For the date episode. For the fiction you made up about Lennox and me."

He scoffs. "I didn't air anything that didn't happen."

"But you sure left out some important parts."

He shrugs, the chain around his neck jingling. "Creative license."

"And the voice dub?"

"Sensationalizing the truth."

My eyes narrow. "You and I have a very different concept of the truth. It was wrong, and you know it. Now everyone at school thinks I'm a slut, Bottom's Bathrooms and Accessories is suffering, I've lost my best friend, and the boy I really like won't talk to me." I'm starting to run out of fingers to count off the crappy things happening in my life, so I stop there. "It didn't happen that way, and you need to make it right."

"Not my problem." Corbin flicks his cigarette butt out the back door. "A retraction is impossible. I'd lose my job for sure."

Clearly he's not worried about the hot water he's in already—he must be used to it. "Because what you did was wrong?" I suggest through gritted teeth.

He doesn't answer that, but his mouth twitches to one side, like *Eh, what are you going to do? That's life, kid*.

I glance at Hugh, but he's studiously staring at the monitor that's playing footage from my parents' store today. I notice there aren't many people shopping. Hugh doesn't glance at me. No help there. I feel like I'm playing mental tug-of-war with Corbin, and I'm on the losing end.

"You need to help me fix this," I say to him.

"Why should I?"

I was wrong to try to appeal to his humanity. He has none.

Instead, I try to speak his language. "Because if you don't, I'll tell my parents what you did at larping on Sunday. After the Lennox episode, that will be the last straw for you. You've pushed things too far. Maybe I'll even do a little *sensationalizing* of my own." I let the implication hang in the air.

He sucks on his teeth for a second. "*Bathroom Barons* is the best thing that's happened to your dad's business. It's gotten them the exposure they needed. It's the best kind of advertising. You wouldn't want to ruin that for your parents, now, would you?"

I scoff. "You mean it's the worst thing that's happened. You've made a joke out of them, using me as the butt of it. Their business is suffering." I wave at the footage of their poorly populated store. "I bet it would do better if we had a new director. I mean, isn't that what tomorrow's meeting with your producer is about? To hear Mom and Dad out? To hear what you did on the double date. To decide what to do with you?"

He frowns and rubs his hands together. Finding them empty, he reaches into his pocket and lights up another death stick. "They can't decide what goes on the show. It's in the contract."

"They can if what you've done to me borders on criminal harassment."

"Criminal..." He sputters and puffs, trying to dismiss it like it's absolute crap. I see a flicker of uncertainty pass over his face. Finally, he glares at me. "Prove it."

"I'm sure there's plenty enough proof caught on film."

Corbin eyes the laptop like it might snitch on him, but Hugh wraps his arms around it protectively.

"That episode wasn't my fault," Corbin says, his voice suddenly rising, maybe even sounding a little desperate. "The producer had the final say. He's the one who approved those edits."

The rope on his side of the battle slips from his hands, and I feel myself gain the advantage. I jerk harder. "And I'm sure you had nothing to do with it," I say with sickly sweet innocence. "Did he even know you altered the footage?"

He just glares at me. A little vein rises on his forehead, pulsing faster with each second.

"Either way, it doesn't matter," I say. "They're my parents. They'll do what's best for the family before the business. Who do you think they'll side with, you or me? And this is Hollywood. You can't throw a rock without hitting ten up-and-coming directors who would jump at the chance to fill your shoes." Or so Star tells me.

I wait for Corbin to come back with a smart reply, but he just drags on his smoke. Hugh's still hunkered in front of the laptop, but his fingers hover frozen above the keyboard. There's a faint grin beneath his ginger beard.

Finally, Corbin lets out a long breath, smoke billowing from his nose. My nose wrinkles, and I cough. Shoving a hand into his pocket, he pulls out a nicotine patch and slaps it on his arm next to the two others already there.

"What do you want?" he asks, finally.

Ignoring the urge to break out in a super-mature victory dance, I hand him Ken's business card for his dentistry office. "This is the larping Game Master. You're going to work with him to organize an event."

He tries to hand it back. "I'm just an observer. I don't interfere with the show's subjects."

"You're a pretty aggressive observer."

He rubs a hand over his face. "Okay. I'll bite. What event?"

"The final battle for all of Asdor. Next Saturday."

"Next Saturday? Do you know the kind of permits we'll need to host that?"

"Well, then it's a good thing the landowner's my dad," I say sarcastically. "And you'll need to advertise. I want this to be huge. Like West Coast huge. And prizes. Lots of prizes." I'm not even bothering to smother the giant winner's grin off my face.

"What TV show does this look like? *Housekeeper Hustlers*?" he says. "This is season one of *Bathroom Barons*. The ratings have been good, but we have a tight budget." He rubs his yellowed fingers together in front of my face. "Where is this money supposed to come from?"

My smile melts on my face. I hadn't considered that. I mean, this is Hollywood, where TV magic happens. Where stars make more for a single movie than most people make in their whole life. I just assumed Corbin could snap his wizard fingers and it would happen. Magic.

"I can't pay for it," Corbin says. "Are you going to pay for it, princess?"

I'm too deflated to react to the condescension in his voice. I bite the inside of my cheek. "No. I still get the same allowance I did before we were rich. And it's not like I can get a job."

A job. That's it. I already have a job. Only, instead of money, Mom said I'm getting paid with a car.

My precious car. The freedom to leave this crazy life whenever I want. But where would I go? To see all the friends I don't have? To go on dates with my nonexistent boyfriend? Kind of a Catch-22 situation. When the money can help me make amends with everyone, a car doesn't seem all that important anymore.

"I have money," I say. "Not a lot, but enough. And maybe we can charge a small registration fee for the event, and get some advertisers, then maybe that will do it."

Hugh isn't even pretending to work anymore. He's staring at Corbin, who looks like he's sucking on a lemon.

"And what do I get out of it?" Corbin asks.

"My help," I say.

He sneers. "What do I need your help for?"

"To save your butt," I say. "Tomorrow my parents are going to try to get you fired with the network. I can help convince them to give you another shot. And by helping me with this event, it will go a long way to making amends. That's if you want there to be a season two of *Bathroom Barons*."

"Do you have any idea the kind of planning that goes into events like this? How long it takes?" Corbin asks. "Months. How am I supposed to pull this off in under two weeks?" But his argument sounds less sure than before, and more whiny.

"That's your problem. Not mine." I jab a finger his way. "You owe me one."

"And what will you be doing while I'm pulling off this miracle?"

"I have another miracle to perform. I need to sew an entire clothing line by next Saturday." And drop Lennox once and for all, and make up with Harper, and convince Kevin and all my larping friends not to hate me, and save my parents' business somehow. No big deal.

Corbin just stares at me and shakes his head for a few seconds. But he must have run out of excuses, because he lets out a groan and mutters, "I'll call my people."

Whipping out his cell phone, he leaves the van. I'm about to follow him when I feel a tug on my sleeve. I turn to Hugh. He holds a Dorito-orange finger to his lips.

I nod silently and glance out the van door, but Corbin's not facing us. Hugh clicks his mouse and types on the keyboard for a few more minutes. I can hear Corbin talking to Ken while he paces outside the van door. He's got his director's voice on.

When he's out of sight again, Hugh yanks a flash drive out of the laptop and slips it into my hand. I shove it into my pocket before Corbin walks by again.

"Maybe that will help you," Hugh whispers. "But no one can know you have it. And you most definitely didn't get it from me."

Corbin strolls by, his phone to his ear. He halts at the open door and snaps his fingers. Hugh gives me a withering look before turning back to the laptop to work.

I wave good-bye and race back to my sewing room. I close the door and plug the USB stick into my computer. My heart throbs like I've just gotten away with a crime. I glance at the door, half expecting Corbin to burst through and bust me. When the file opens, a smile tugs at my lips.

It's the original footage from my date with Lennox.

It's not a retraction, but it might be enough. I don't care about what everyone thinks about me so much anymore. Just the people who matter most to me. Now, if only I can get Harper to watch it.

Chapter Thirty-Five
School Snub

The next morning, I show up at school with a plan. A lame one, but a plan nonetheless. I borrowed Mom's tablet, I uploaded the original video footage Hugh gave me onto it. Once Harper sees how things really went at the end of our double date, I know she won't hate me anymore. I just have to get her to listen to me long enough to watch it.

Before the bell rings, I head straight to Harper's locker with my mom's tablet in hand. As I round the corner to her locker, I run face-first into Mercedes.

When she sees it's me, her face screws up. "Watch it, dork!"

Prissy and Amber laugh before all three of them shove past me, pushing me aside. When Prissy's shoulder bumps me, it knocks Mom's tablet from my hand. It clatters to the floor.

I gasp and drop to my knees to pick it up, hoping it's okay. When I flip it over, it's got a giant crack down the middle. Like I'm not in enough trouble as it is.

I hit the power button. At least it still works. But it's

one more thing I'll have to answer to Mom for. I add it to the growing list.

Hoping to check off the first thing on that list, I continue on to Harper's locker before she heads to class. Thankfully, she's still there. She doesn't see me coming. Her head is buried in her locker as she grabs her books.

I'm stealth. I'm ninja. She won't get by me.

She slams her locker door and turns. I jump in front of her, blocking her path.

"Hey," I say casually.

She scowls and tries to go around, but I stick to her like toilet paper on a shoe. "Please, Harper. Just hear me out."

"Why should I, when everything that comes out of your mouth is a lie?"

"I wasn't lying. Not about Lennox. I really don't like him."

She budges by me, clipping my shoulder. "Is that what you told him while you were tongue wrestling in his car?"

I keep on her, walking backward in front of her so she has no choice but to look at me. "That's what I came to show you." I wave my mom's tablet. "What really happened that night. Not Corbin's edited version."

"Oh, good." She gives me her fake smile. The one where she wants you to know it's fake. "So I get to watch the uncut footage of you making out with my ex-boyfriend? Thanks, but no thanks. I saw enough on the show."

I try to stop her from leaving, but I'm not exactly bouncer material, so she pushes past. "I need to get to class."

Sighing, I toss the tablet into my bag. How is she going to forgive me if she won't even listen? I need to get her alone. Corner her so she can't escape. So she'll have to hear me out. But that won't happen at school.

Feet skip along the linoleum behind me. It's Star. For

once, she's alone. As usual, she smiles and waves like she's not even aware the whole world hates me.

"Star, what are you doing after school?"

"Nothing." Her big eyes blink slowly. "Why?"

"I need your help with a plan. I was hoping you would ask Harper to go shopping with you."

"Harper? Why?"

"Because she's your friend," I say. "And you want to hang out."

"Okay. But what about you? What are you doing?"

"That's the other part of my plan."

"For your show?" Her eyes widen even more. "My agent says it's good for my acting career to get exposure."

"Yes, for the show." Technically that's true, but I don't tell her the cameras won't be there.

Corbin said he'd help as long as I didn't rat him out publicly about how he took creative license with his "observations" of my date. That's fine with me so long as Harper knows the truth. And hopefully Kevin. But one hurdle at a time.

"Okay, sounds fun," she says. "What do you want me to do?"

"All you need to do is take her clothes shopping. Better yet, bra and lingerie shopping. That's her favorite. I'll take it from there."

Star nods excitedly, her buggy eyes determined, like this is the role of her life. "It's like I'm an undercover spy. I won't let you down."

Chapter Thirty-Six

Double-Oh-Zero

My phone buzzes in my pocket, and I duck out of the continuous stream of Rodeo Drive shoppers to check the caller ID. It's Star. Operation "Trap Harper" is underway. I open her text.

H has a load of stuff to try on. She's about to go into the changing room. This is so exciting! LOL!

I cross the street toward the underwear shop, feeling like 007. Or maybe more of a zero. I'm gripping the door handle to the store when my pocket buzzes again.

Sidetracked by sleepwear. Hold on!

I peer through the glass door and spot Harper's blonde locks above a rack. Jumping aside, I dive below the storefront windows and flatten myself against the low wall. If she gets too close, she'll easily see the top of my flaming red head. I crouch down lower.

A few shoppers give me strange glances. Hopefully no one will recognize me and talk to me about *Bathroom Barons*. You can't exactly be an effective spy when people know you wherever you go. I bet James Bond never has to deal with that.

I check my phone again. How many pajamas does she need? Glancing at my cell reception, I begin to worry that something's gone wrong with my plan. It buzzes again.

Okay. Now!

Resisting the urge to duck and roll through the door, I enter the frilly lingerie store.

"Hello," the shopgirls sing in unison.

"Can I help you find something today?" one asks. "Our pasties are on sale."

I don't want to know what pasties are. "No, thanks."

"How about some crotchless underwear," the other girl says. "Two for one."

"I'm just meeting my friends." I point to the changing rooms at the back.

The two girls nod and return to their conversation.

Wandering into the back, I glance under each stall door. There are five customers trying on merchandise. I recognize Star because she's painted little stars on her big toenails.

Her door cracks an inch, and she grins at me through the opening. She points to the changing room across from her. I check out the feet under the door. Harper's toes are magenta. Her favorite shade of pink.

Taking a deep breath, I knock on the stall.

"Yes?" Harper calls.

When I don't answer, she slides the lock and pokes her head out. Grabbing the door, I yank it open. She squeaks and stumbles forward.

She's got a pair of skimpy striped pajamas on. Her hands fly up to hide her bare skin, so she doesn't fight as I corral her back into the changing stall.

When she sees it's me, her hands ball into fists at her sides. "What are you doing, you perv?"

Her clothes are hanging on the wall pegs. Before she thinks to get dressed and storm out, I unhook them and toss them out over the door.

"Now you're not going anywhere." Reaching into my bag, I pull out the tablet and thrust it at her. The video footage is already cued up on the cracked screen.

"Not this again." Harper grabs the complimentary robe from the back of the door. "When are you going to give up? Are you just trying to rub it in my face?" I can see the hurt in her eyes.

"Please, Harper. Just watch it. And I won't ever bother you again." I push it into her hands. "I promise."

She stares at me for a few seconds, considering. There's a knock on the door behind me.

"Excuse me. Only one person in a fitting room at a time." It's Pasty Girl.

"Please," I say again, and this time she takes it.

"Fine. If it will get you to leave me alone." I notice the whites of her eyes are turning pink. She blinks and looks away.

I step into the main room and toss her clothes back over the door. I wait. For a moment, I don't think she's going to watch it. Then I hear my voice. My real, non-porno voice.

"Lennox, stop!"

The rest is mumbles and sounds of rustling as I try to shove him away in the confines of his "Stang." Next is when I see the cameras, and then I'm yelling at him. He grunts as I whack him in the nose. I relive all of it just through the sounds.

The embarrassment of that night still stings. Kevin was right to question why I keep putting myself in these situations. I've been worrying about what everyone else thinks rather than worrying about what I want. Well, I know what I want now, and it's time to stand up for it.

Better late than never.

Hugh's mic picks up my sniffling as I run into the house and past my dad. I hear the door slam and then Corbin says, "We got it. That's a wrap."

The changing room goes quiet except for the sounds of material rubbing as the other shoppers continue to change behind their doors. I'm suddenly conscious of the extra audience. I wonder if they know what all this is about, if they'd seen the episode, or if they even cared.

Could I make things worse for Mom and Dad? It's one thing for me to not care what everyone thinks of me. My parents' business is a different story. I've already done enough damage. At least the two shopgirls don't seem to be paying attention. They're out front, organizing what I assume are the pasties.

Finally, Harper emerges in the robe. When she hands me the tablet, she still can't look at me, but this time I don't think it's because she's mad.

Maybe she's a bit humiliated by the whole thing, too. She still likes Lennox, or she did, anyway. I'm not so sure anymore. And I just forced her to watch evidence that he didn't feel the same way about her. I was so focused on my plan that I hadn't stopped to think what that would feel like for her.

She leans against the stall and rubs the magenta toes of one foot over the other. "So. You really didn't like him?"

"No offense, because I know you like him, and you've told me a lot of nice stuff about him, but not in a million years."

She nods but says nothing.

"I didn't even want to sit by him in the theater. I didn't want his arm around me, and I definitely didn't want him to drive me home that night."

"Well, it doesn't matter, since he likes you now and not me."

"Lennox doesn't like me. He likes being on TV." I wave the tablet in my hand.

"Yeah, I thought it was kind of weird that you could hear everything being said. I didn't think you had a mic on you."

I shrug. "Corbin must have given it to him when they interviewed the boys before the movie. I had no idea."

"The way they made it seem on the show"—she finally looks me square in the eyes—"well, it seemed bad."

"I know. And I should have told you about it right away, but Corbin promised not to air it. I was just embarrassed about the whole thing, and I knew you'd be upset, so I wanted to wait until some time had passed. And then he altered the footage, and everything went down the toilet. I'm sorry. I should have told you right away."

"It's not your fault. I shouldn't have made you go on the date in the first place. I just wanted to see if we still had chemistry, if he still had feelings for me. And I thought it would be fun, since you aren't dating anyone else."

When I promised I would tell her the truth, I meant the whole truth. I gnaw at my lip. "That's sort of the problem. I do really like someone."

"Who?"

"Well, it's only the kind of thing I'd tell my BFF." I smile. "Can I have her back?"

Harper smiles, really smiles, and moves in for a hug. The changing room door next to us bursts open. Star sashays out in a full red leopard-print bustier and garter belt getup, like a desperate, middle-aged cougar.

Her head swivels around the store and then she finally

looks back at us.

"Where are the cameras?"

I shake my head but try not to laugh. At least she's honest about her desire for stardom. A little too honest.

"Not here. But they'll be around this weekend," I say. "Actually, I've got a big fashion show on Saturday, and I need some models. Are you in?"

"Model in a fashion show? Absolutely." Star looks around again and pouts. "So, no cameras?"

"Not today."

"Cool. Well, I've got to get to the tanning salon. So I'm going to get dressed and take off."

Harper ducks back into her dressing room to change into her normal clothes, too. When Star leaves, she finally asks, "Who's this mystery boy? Do I know him?"

"You know him. But you don't really *know* him, if you know what I mean." I lean against the stall door so she can hear me better. "And if you're really my *real* BFF, you'll be open-minded."

She holds up a Girl Scout salute over the door. "No judgment. I promise."

I tell Harper everything. From my first day at school and the hardware store, to larping, to Sunday when it all went horribly wrong. I make sure not to leave out any details about Lennox. And as it turns out, I had nothing to worry about all along. She understands, because she's my friend.

Harper's for real.

Chapter Thirty-Seven

Feel Like a Tool

Since I've been bordering on stalkerish lately, I've practically memorized Kevin's work schedule. So when I walk up to the hardware store, grab the door handle, let it go, grab it again, hesitate, and finally open it, I know he's on the other side.

He's rearranging levels on a display table when I enter. "Hello," he calls over his shoulder as he works. "I'll be right with you."

He's so focused on making sure all the bubbles are in the middle of the glass vials—which might be hard since I can see the table is lopsided from here—that he doesn't see me walk up behind him.

"Can I help you?" he asks over his shoulder. When he turns and sees it's me, he looks like he's sucking on a sour candy.

"Yes," I say, glancing around the store curiously. "I'm looking for a hammer. Can you recommend one?"

His eyebrows shoot up. "A hammer?"

"Yes. A good one," I say. "Because I think we've got a

lot of things we need to hammer out."

There's a moment where his mouth twitches at the lame joke, but he fights it and continues to restock. "All out of hammers. Sorry. Try another store. We're closed."

"I thought you were open until eight."

"What can I tell you? New hours," he says over his shoulder as he disappears down an aisle.

I follow him. "Well, how about a measuring tape? Since as a friend, I just haven't been measuring up."

I hear him groan a little, but he doesn't slow. We pass the cleaning supplies, and I spot a mop hanging from a hook. I slide it off and pretend to assess it.

"A mop. Perfect." I grin. "Because I've got a real mess to clean up." I start to push it around the floor between us.

Kevin glances back and sees the mop in my hands. He spins around and snatches it away, returning it to its place on the shelf.

"Don't you have anyone else to bother?" he asks. "I'm trying to work here."

"Work?" I bat my eyelashes innocently, like I'm just not getting the hint. "But I thought you were closed."

He rolls his eyes and heads for the back. We pass the lawnmowers, the rakes, the gardening gloves. When I come across a shovel, I pluck it out of the holder. Kevin hears the scraping and turns around impatiently to find me holding it over my shoulder.

"Look," I say. "I'm just trying to dig my way out of this mess I made, okay?"

"Well, you're digging yourself a deeper hole." Kevin grabs the shovel and slides it back into the holder. "Why won't you just leave me alone?"

When he turns around again, I'm playing with a squeaky hinge. "Because you really unhinge me?" I know I'm reaching with that one, but I throw in a cheesy smile.

His nostrils flare as he grabs me by the wrist and drags me back up to the front of the store. “I’m asking you to leave. Please.” His voice cracks, and I can hear the emotion he’s been hiding peek through for just a moment.

I want to reach out to him, to comfort him, to break down the rest of that barrier he’s hiding behind, even if it releases nothing but bad things. Swear words, screaming, yelling, accusations. Because maybe, just maybe, we can work through it all if he opens up to me. If he lets himself be that guy who kissed me in the woods. That guy who never held anything back and who has always been himself.

I imagine I can feel that kiss even now, and I wonder if I throw myself into his arms and kiss him again, if he’d push me away. Or would he gather me up, despite his anger, and hold me close and kiss me back. So I can smell his lemon pepper scent, can feel the warmth and acceptance in his touch. Acceptance of me, and hopefully of my apology.

But I don’t kiss him. Because I’m too afraid of being rejected. I imagine it’s the same fear that Harper felt with Lennox.

I try one more time to get a laugh out of him, to joke around like we used to. I lean on the table he was organizing when I came in. “Will you just level with me already?”

The movement jiggles the wobbly table, and half of his levels come crashing down. I cringe.

Kevin closes his eyes and takes a deep breath. “Are you just about done?”

“Nope. I’ve got a few more.” I pretend to think. “Something about a nail and a saw…”

“Enough, Andy! Adrianna. Whoever you are.” He shakes his head as though I’ve really confused him in the last couple of months. “Yes, you have made a mess, but I don’t want to level with you. I don't care if you want to dig your way out, and I don't need a measuring tape to know that you've fallen short, really short, of the person I thought you were."

I fiddle with the hinge in my hands, finding it suddenly hard to breathe. I knew this wouldn't be easy, that he probably wouldn't want to talk to me, but still I'd hoped.

I miss talking with him, I miss larping together, and I miss how easy it is to be myself when we're hanging out. He not only helped me to accept my real self, he made me want to be a better me.

"Well. Okay," I finally say. "I just thought I would drop off this flyer." Reaching into my back pocket, I pull out one of the neon-pink ads Corbin made for the larping event. "I was hoping you could post it in your window."

When Kevin doesn't take it, I place the ad on the level display and turn to leave. I push the door, and the bell above it rings before he finally speaks.

"Is this for real?"

I turn back. He's holding up the pink flyer like it's going to bite him.

"Forty people have already RSVP'd," I say. "Some larpers are coming from as far as Montana. Pretty good for a last-minute event."

In fact, as part of his payback, Corbin called his "people" to advertise the event all around the West Coast. I don't know who these "people" are, but they're good.

"Why are you doing this?" He brandishes the paper at me. "Why don't you just give it a rest?"

"Believe it or not, I *like* larping. And if I can help it, I don't want to ruin it for the group. Maybe after this weekend we can attract more members and afford to reserve another space to larp."

"We?" He laughs without humor. "Well, I won't be coming."

I nod, fighting back my tears. "Please think about it. I've already talked to Game Master Ken. He's preparing a quest and battle plan with the plot committee as we speak. I saw Chad at school today. It sounds like most of the others are coming. And for what it's worth, I hope you come, too."

He's silent as he stares down at the flyer, and for the first time I see his wall collapse. His shoulders slump, his face twists with some kind of emotion, and this time I know it's not anger.

Maybe he misses me as much as I miss him.

Hesitantly, I reach out to him, but the moment my hand lands on his arm, he crumples the flyer and drops it at my feet. Spinning on his heel, he trudges into the back of the store and slams a door.

I blink rapidly, feeling tears sting my eyes. That's when I spot Kevin's journal lying on the counter.

I know I shouldn't. I know it's wrong. But something inside me just has to know what Kevin's thinking, what's on his mind. And he certainly won't tell me himself.

I strain my ears for noises in case he's coming back. When the store remains quiet, I creep over to the cash register and turn the sketchbook toward me.

As I flip through the newest entries, hope begins to build inside me, greater than any magical spell a high mage of Asdor could cast. Every single page is consumed with sketches of a single subject. Just one.

Me smiling. Me frowning. Me larping. Me walking. Me talking. Me eating tater tots. And Kevin and I together, kissing in the woods. Drawing, after drawing, after drawing.

There are entries of things that have never even happened before, like Kevin and I lying together on a couch, eating at a restaurant, holding hands in the movie theater, partnering up together for biology lab.

It's like proof that he's not only been thinking about me, he's been dreaming about me, too. Dreaming about us.

I stare, eyes wide, flipping one page after the next to experience a story about us. A story that tugs at something deep inside me, makes me yearn for it like an insomniac would sleep. I study each drawing greedily, wanting to be this couple that Kevin's created, needing to be. I want to crawl inside the pages and into his HB graphite arms.

In this imaginary world, Kevin looks at me so openly, so happily, so lovingly. Joy soars through my veins like a sugar rush, causing giddy laughter to bubble up inside my lungs. But it quickly turns sour, like a double cheeseburger heartburn, because right now that world seems so far away.

I close the sketchbook and hug it to my chest like it's my last lifeline. I could have all of this. It's not impossible. If the dozens of pages filled with my face is any indication, he doesn't just want me. He needs me. As badly as I need him. I just have to find a way to make him see it, to know there's a reason to fight for it.

But how am I supposed to do that if he won't let me apologize?

Chapter Thirty-Eight

Humble Highness

The metal stool hurts my butt. I shift uncomfortably as I wait for the cameras to start rolling. Harsh lights glare down on me, hot, unforgiving, exposing. No more hiding for me.

The crew is staring at me as they get ready to film, because I'm all there is to look at. My surroundings are entirely devoid of any decor. It was Corbin's artistic interpretation. He wants to strip away the glamour and facade, to shoot this interview in a way that represents the very "essence" of my gesture, to reveal it for what it is—the cold, hard truth.

And actually? I really like his idea.

I think Corbin gets it. He finally gets it. He sees what I'm trying to do. To remove the Hollywood and leave just me. And I'm definitely all that's left, because my hair is piled on top of my head in a crazy mess of curls like when I'm doing homework, I'm wearing my TARDIS T-shirt, and I have the bare minimum for makeup—and what I do have on is only because Suzzy said it would be too much shine for the camera if I didn't wear powder.

So I sit on the stool with a blank wall as my background, just me, in all my me-ness, to be 100 percent honest with the world. And most important, to apologize to Kevin.

Corbin stops barking orders at the crew long enough to take a seat in the director's chair across from me, just to the side of the camera. He gives me the once-over. "Are you ready?"

"To start repairing the damage to my life? Yeah. I'd say so." I laugh, but it sounds kind of like I'm choking on a Life Savers candy. I'm so nervous I feel like throwing up. "So what's the plan?"

He crosses his leg, very casual like. I get the feeling he almost enjoys seeing me squirm; after all, I did blackmail him. Or maybe it's just because my stress makes for good TV, and he definitely knows how to take advantage of that.

"I'll be asking you a series of questions that will hopefully get to the heart of things, will help the audience really connect with what you're going through and why you did what you did."

I narrow my eyes at him, but the effect might be lost since I'm squinting against the lights anyway. "And what about the things you did?"

"This show is about you and your family." He waves his pen in my direction like a wand. "I'm a nobody. Besides"—he leans forward in his chair, lowering his voice so only I can hear—"my ass is on the line here. I only agreed to do this if I'm absolved of any wrongdoing. Remember our deal?"

"I haven't forgotten."

"Good, because I've got a family to provide for, kid. You know, real world problems."

He's got a family? I'm not sure what I thought. Maybe

that he's a robot developed by the network? That he's a soulless demon?

To me he seems so unlikeable. But apparently there are people, real people out there somewhere, who like, maybe even love this man. I suddenly realize that there's probably a lot more to Corbin than I thought. I mean, I've somehow found my own excuses for making bad decisions along the way, so maybe he has some pretty good excuses himself. But that still doesn't make the things he's done okay.

"Don't worry." He leans back in his chair, obviously not very worried himself. "I'll be doing my part behind the scenes, working my editing magic, using all of our past footage for some montages, some sappy music, etcetera, etcetera. I'll be taking full advantage of your larping-Kevin drama." And the sleazy director I know is back. "The viewers will practically taste your teenage angst."

That's fine with me, since no amount of his creative editing could actually do my real angst justice.

Hugh steps away from his camera. "Okay, boss, we're good to go here." He gives me a wink and an encouraging smile before turning his attention back to his view screen.

"Great," Corbin says. "Let's get started. Know what you want to say?" he asks me.

The question causes my heart to jump into my throat, and I can't seem to talk around it, so I nod. Hopefully I can find the right words once the camera's rolling.

"Just keep your answers as honest and candid as you can," Corbin says as Hugh counts down on his fingers. "Don't hide the emotions, kid. Give me the works. Anger, grief, tears."

I snort. "No problem there."

The light on the camera goes green, and Hugh gives Corbin the hand signal. It spikes my nerves instantly. My heart is racing, my hands, no, everything is shaking. I hope Suzzy's powder is super strength, because I think I'm sweating through it.

After a dramatic pause, Corbin gives me a serious hard-hitting interviewer look. "Adrianna, what is it that you want to say to the viewers today?"

I straighten in my seat. "I'm here today to say that I'm sorry."

"For what?" His hand moves in a circle. "Go on."

"For..." I hesitate. There's so much. Where do I begin? I'm overwhelmed by the guilt, the desperation. "For everything." My voice wavers as I struggle to find the words.

He gives me a sour look and spreads his hands in an impatient gesture.

So I take a deep breath and try again. "I want to apologize for my poor decisions, for my actions, for not standing behind what I believe, for pretending to be something I'm not." Once I start, it all falls out of my mouth. I stop there, but I feel like I could keep going until they run out of memory on the camera.

"And what kind of person are you really?" Corbin asks.

"I'm a geek," I say, and this time my voice doesn't waver. I keep my focus on the camera. "I've never been very popular. I'm usually the one getting picked on, not the other way around. I don't know the latest styles or haircuts." I try to think of the things I do like. The things that make me *me*, an individual. Special. "I like anime, and comic books, and video games, and I like to live-action role-play. I like dressing up in costumes and pretending to be someone else in another world. Because I don't like the world I've created for myself here."

Corbin sucks on the end of his pen for a moment, his gaze boring right through me, as though he can tell if I am lying. He seems to decide that I'm not, because he asks, "And why do you think you've created this world you don't like?"

"I just thought maybe things could be different here in California. That I could change all the things I didn't like about my life in Seattle."

"And how did these changes turn out?"

"It only made me realize that I don't want to change anything. I don't want to be popular, or stylish, or a girl who goes on dates with the popular jock. I don't want a ton of friends who aren't really my friends. I just want a few really good ones. And I started to have that. But I'm not sure I've been a very good friend to them."

"Why not?"

Wow, he really is getting down to the hard-hitting questions. I take a gasp of air before answering. "I've hidden things from Harper that hurt her in the end. I've lied to Kevin, the guy I actually do like. I've deceived so many people both at school and larping." I count each offense on my fingers as I go. "Not to mention, I've damaged the reputation of my parents' business through my behavior."

I blink past the bright lights. All the crew who would usually be on their cell phones are staring at me, which must mean we're now getting to the heart of it.

Corbin leans forward on his chair. "So what do you want?"

I look down at my lap for a moment to stop focusing on everyone around me, the cameras, the crew, to think about me. What do I want? This is about me and my desires now. No one else's.

I look up again when I'm ready. "I want everyone to know that I'm done pretending to be someone I'm not. And that I want to make it up to my family and friends, to everyone at larping who's about to lose something they love. And I want Kevin to know how sorry I am. That I wanted to hurt him least of all."

"Is that all?" Corbin's eyebrow rises slightly, as though there's a right and wrong answer.

My resolve flickers as I second-guess myself. I scan the room like the crew can give me the answer, but even if I've left some things out, I know in my heart I've been as honest as I can be. I truly want to make things right. And that's why I'm here. Besides, it's only an hour program. I'm not sure they could fit in all the things I really want to say now that I'm warmed up.

I kind of laugh, but I'm serious when I ask, "Isn't that enough?"

Corbin stares at me for a really long time. The room of people collectively leans forward as though his answer is going to make or break the series. He takes a deep breath, and his nose rises as though he's testing the scent of my interview to see if it stinks.

He finally nods, like it smells good. "It's enough." Over his shoulder he yells, "Cut!" and everyone sighs in relief, myself most of all.

I slump over. It seems my tension and anxiety were the only things keeping me from fainting. "Do you really think so?" I ask him seriously, now that the rest of the room has picked up in a whirlwind of activity.

Corbin is already reviewing the footage with Hugh, but he turns back to me now. For the first time since I met him, he looks at me like I'm a real person, not just a means to good ratings. And for a second, I think that maybe he's not the worst person ever. He's just a guy trying to do his job. And I suppose he has gotten the show good ratings. If only good ratings meant good business for Mom and Dad.

Hopefully this episode will be the first step to helping turn things around.

"Leave it to me," Corbin says. "By the time I'm done with this episode, you'll be a hero. And I'll get the directing contract for season two."

"So this is a selfless act then," I say sarcastically. Okay, not the worst person, but also not the best.

"We've all got something riding on this, kid."

"You're not kidding."

After summing it all up like that for the cameras, I'm overly aware of everything relying on my plan being a success. Corbin intends to put a rush on this interview footage so he can air it next Friday, timing it better with the larping event. He probably wants to build up the anticipation, the drama of this particular story for the viewers.

I just hope Kevin will be watching. But will it even do any good after everything that's happened between us? Can Kevin forgive me? Corbin said "it's enough." But is it?

Chapter Thirty-Nine

Break a Leg

The heavy stage curtains hide the growing crowd. I pace nervously behind them, my anxiety growing with each passing moment. I peek between the part in the fabric. Beyond the temporary stage and the long runway, a crowd of humans and supernatural beings has gathered.

It's not just larpers here today. Friends have come, and fans of the show, people naturally drawn to cameras, and other curious passersby. And sitting front row center is the fashion investor Mom introduced me to at the store. Mr. Carson. Won't he be surprised by my fashion lineup today—and probably not pleasantly.

I spent every spare moment in the last two weeks in my sewing room working on my new designs. Not even Mom has seen the results yet.

I step away from the curtain, overwhelmed by the turnout. My heart flutters in my chest like fairy wings. I try to forget they're even out there, but they sound like a thousand bees buzzing. I just hope my unexpected fashion show won't get me stung.

"Let the battle begin," I hear someone call out. A larper, obviously, gearing up for today's event. There are answering roars and hoots that circulate throughout the crowd of warriors, beasts, and otherworldly creatures.

It took a lot of convincing and begging to get my parents to give Corbin another chance. I downplayed a lot of the crap he pulled on me and told them that this weekend was his idea to try and make it up to me. They made it clear to Corbin that this was his last chance. It gave him a little extra incentive to make this weekend amazing. And so far it has turned out great.

Once I put Corbin in touch with Game Master Ken, between the two of them, they got the licensing and paperwork for the event. And with Corbin's Hollywood know-how and network connections, he got the whole thing rolling, including the food vendors, props, and the stage I am now standing on. He even rounded up some volunteer actors desperate for exposure to be the non-player characters. Our enemies will be more convincing than ever.

As I peek out again, someone taps my shoulder. It's Star, and she doesn't look happy. In fact, she looks downright scary, and it's not just the green makeup and warts Suzzy applied to her face.

"Look at what your stylist did to me."

"You look great," I say. "The prettiest troll there ever was. Go on. Put on the hat."

She sighs but pulls the crochet hat over her tightly braided hair. Long, perky green ears stand erect on either side of her head. "When you said it was a fashion show, I kind of expected cocktail dresses and stilettos. Not mesh vests and leaves."

"It's a tunic," I say. "And it's made out of mesh fabric

to keep you cool. Larping is hard work. And trolls are forest dwellers." I pick at the leaves adorning the top to make sure they are well attached. "You need camouflage to sneak up on your prey."

She's wearing only a bra underneath, so bits of skin flash under the mesh. I let it go, since I did trick her into being a costume model.

"You make a very sexy troll," I say.

"I know." She rolls her eyes and stomps away, but she looks a little less like someone peed in her Cheerios. She joins the rest of the trolls in the corner, making up a gaggle, or a horde, maybe.

The changing room curtain whips back and Harper emerges. She's wearing a cute burgundy leather getup, one I made especially for her when she agreed to model for me. She gives me a little twirl, the skirt of leather pleats lifting. Very Xena Warrior Princess.

The rest of the larpers wander around backstage, dressed in the costumes I slaved over for the past two weeks. I look at the battle scars on my hands, the needle pricks on my fingers—which are more like pincushions now. But it was all worth it.

Finn showed up, and Shawn, Chad, Mark, Eddie, Keelie. Actually, pretty much our entire larping group showed up. Even some who I've never met before. I didn't have costumes prepared for all of them, but I have plenty of help backstage.

Everyone is here. All of them. Except for one.

Kevin's princely garb hangs lifeless on the rack, still in its protective cover. I take off the wrap, just to let the fabric hang naturally. Smoothing out the wrinkles, I check the sizing again, imagining how Kevin would fill it out. And since he's probably not coming, my imagination is the only way I'll get to see it.

I know he misses me. I know he's been thinking about me like crazy. The drawings in his sketchbook told me that much. But will it be enough for him to forgive me?

I hope he saw the episode of *Bathroom Barons* last night. Heard my apology. Plus, there was the additional footage Corbin threw in along with it. I have to hand it to him. The episode summed up the situation pretty well. It even had a dash of Hollywood romantic flair. And for once, I didn't actually look like a total bad guy. Just a slightly misguided girl crushing hard on a guy.

But today isn't only about Kevin and my broken heart. It's about everyone else. It's about fulfilling my promise to Mom about the fashion line, even if it won't be quite what everyone expected. It's about saving the larping group, and it's about putting on a great show to help Dad's business. But most importantly, it's going to be on my terms, and I'm going to be me and not who everyone else wants me to be.

I trace the embroidery around the collar of Kevin's costume and rearrange the vest on the hanger for the fifth time. When I look up, Keelie catches my eye from next to the refreshment table. She sees me beside the only remaining costume and has probably already guessed it's her brother's. She shrugs and half smiles.

Keelie's been a good friend to me in the last two weeks. She's acted as my advocate, convincing the larping group to show up today, smoothing things over. People might still make fun of me at school, but I've felt lighter ever since my real friends have started talking to me again. They're the only ones who matter. Not the bullies, not the haters, not the people out there in TV land who have never met me. If only she'd managed to convince Kevin.

It's not like I expected him to come. But I had each

one of my pinpricked fingers crossed.

Corbin swishes the curtains apart and steps backstage. He claps. "Places, everyone. We're about to start."

My heart leaps into my throat. I swallow it back down. "But we're short one model."

The music blasts through speakers out onstage. It sounds like something from *The Lord of the Rings*. The larping models line up next to the curtain, ready to strut their mythical stuff down the runway.

Corbin hands me a microphone. "The show must go on." He nudges me toward the curtain. "Break a leg."

With my luck, I probably will.

Keelie gives me a wink as I pass, and Eddie bows. I give one last hopeful glance at Kevin's costume before ducking between the curtains and onto the stage. The buzzing turns to applause. I wait for the clapping and the music to die down before speaking.

"Thank you for—" The speakers squeal from feedback and the audience grabs their ears. I wait until it fades before speaking softer into the mic this time. "Thank you all for coming. I'm glad there was so much interest in this weekend. We've had a great turnout."

The microphone shakes in my hands, and it feels like I'm trying to talk around an apple core stuck in my throat. I'm breathless. My words come out all weak and squeaky-like.

"I'd like to thank my mom for encouraging me to start designing my own line of clothing." It's true. I'm happy. Now that I'm doing what I want to do.

"It may not be what you expect." At this, I look to the fashion investor in the front row. "But it's what I'm passionate about, and I hope that comes across in my designs. Please enjoy the show."

The music gets louder, and the curtains part a few feet. I can hear Corbin urging some models out. A moment later, Star stumbles onto the stage, followed by the rest of her horde. I read from my cue cards that I prepared ahead of time to describe each costume's features and material.

They take their time, working the crowd because I have only so many designs to display. They claw and growl a bit at the front row while Star struts and spins like it's a New York catwalk.

Next, Eddie runs out onstage, waving his two-handed sword, challenging members of the crowd to a duel. His chain mail flashes in the light. I spray-painted his kneepads and elbow pads silver to match. The cape I created for him is long enough to flow behind him, but not so long that he'd get caught up during his wild movements.

Chad and Ken come out in turn, each in a variation of the medieval warrior style. Two girls, who I'd just met last week, follow them. They wear black spandex suits and boots, simplicity, in order to display the full effect of the fairy wings I constructed from chicken wire and coat hangers. Split into multiple sections, the iridescent fabric shifts color in the morning sun. Trails of wispy crepe fabric flutter as though the wings move on their own.

Shawn kicks the curtain aside and somersaults down the catwalk, too slow to be all that stealthy. Instead of a plain ninja, I've added some magical flair, like a black, flowing cloak of invisibility, leather belts, and armguards.

Special pockets hide his beanbag weapons that he now shoots out at the onlookers like throwing stars. Before leaving the stage, he pulls up his peaked, shadowy hood and wiggles his fingers at the crowd in a "you never saw me" kind of way.

Harper whips the curtains aside, a fierce look on her

pretty face. She makes her way to the front of the stage where she's greeted by loud whistles and hoots from the boys in the crowd. The leather sashays around her thighs. From watching her work the costume, I'm thinking the enemy would be too distracted to even fight back. She blows a kiss to her admirers before she exits.

The curtains part to reveal a gruesome lizard-like creature. It crawls out, hissing at the crowd. It skitters across the stage and takes a swipe at me with its shiny claws.

Even though I know it's really Mark, I still jump. He's given up his fur and hooves for scales and a tail. His reptilian skin glistens beneath the morning sun as he makes his rounds and then disappears backstage again.

Next, Finn and Keelie come out in full battle mode. Keelie fires off rapid beanbag arrows from her bow. Finn ducks, his pearly cloak shimmering with the movement. His new magician's hat stays put, thanks to the elasticized band I'd thought to sew inside.

He counterattacks with powerful defensive spells, but Keelie is aggressive and quickly finds holes in his magic. The butterflies on her capelet flutter as she moves, as though they're really alive, ready to take off on the breeze. She spins to avoid a spell, the layers of her tunic swirling around her like a dress.

Just when it looks like Keelie has Finn beat, he takes her by surprise and hits her with a love spell. This gets a few chuckles from the crowd. I'm glad to see that Mr. Carson is one of them. As she swoons, he catches her and drags her offstage in a lovestruck state.

I'm still giggling when I lift the microphone to my mouth, ready to end the show. The curtains shift behind me. When I turn around, I nearly drop the mic. Maybe Finn cast a spell on me, too, because I think I'm seeing things.

Dressed in my design, a prince sweeps heroically onto the stage to save the day. Kevin.

His focus remains forward as he glides onto the catwalk with his warrior's grace, tall and confident. He looks as amazing as I thought he would. The perfect balance between noble and powerful.

I blink at the sight of him, as though I'm dreaming about him again. This can't be real. I've imagined this moment so many times in the last two weeks that my fantasy must be leaking into reality. I'm losing my mind. I'm sure of it.

But the painful feeling like my heart has stopped dead in my chest is real, and the crowd gasps at his arrival, meaning they see him, too, so I can't be dreaming. When I spin around to the stage curtains looking for answers, I spot Keelie through the part in the curtain. She gives me a thumbs-up, and I realize she must have lined him up with the costume.

My eyes scan the cue card I'd prepared just in case he showed up, but the words look German to me, and my voice is caught in my throat anyway. So I just watch him, amazed and relieved that he came. But I still don't know why. Did he come for his last chance to larp today? Or did he possibly, maybe, hopefully, come to help me?

There's murmuring throughout the crowd, and it seems more than a few of them saw the episode of *Bathroom Barons* last night. They watched our relationship develop, blossom, even during moments that I hadn't realized the cameras were filming.

Corbin put it all together like a compilation of events, a miniature movie of our hopeful romance, which climaxed in the forest when my identity was revealed. The audience heard my plea, my apology, me spilling my heart out on television to the entire world. And apparently so did Kevin, because he came. But does that mean he accepts it?

Kevin makes a couple of broad swings with his sword to display the mobility of his new garb. Then he spins in an arc. The split tails of his flowing vest twirl like a fan around him. When he comes to a stop, for the first time since I spoke to him in the hardware store over a week ago, he's looking straight at me.

When I'd imagined this moment, over and over and over again, he was smiling at me, his face soft with acceptance, with openness. He was the same guy who kissed me in the woods again. But as I take in his charming features, I can't find that guy anywhere.

Kevin's emotions are locked behind his expressionless face, his eyes unreadable, the wrinkle next to his mouth neither a smile nor a frown. After a few seconds, which drag on like it's the last five minutes of school, he rises to his feet and strolls backstage. I hold my breath as he passes me, but he doesn't flinch, he doesn't blink, and he definitely doesn't look at me.

Suddenly, I'm no longer worried if everyone will clap at the end. If the crowd will love or hate my designs. If my fashion show is a success. Because what I'm really worried about is what Kevin's last-minute arrival means. Most importantly, what does it mean for us?

Chapter Forty
Capture the Prince

The tree bark is rough against my back, even through my tunic. I worry about ants crawling down my top, but I don't move an inch. Move and I die. Move and we're all done for. Our little scouting group is deep in enemy territory. A sneeze, a rustle, and they'll know we're here.

I can hear two of the sentries marching behind my wide oak tree. Back and forth they go, across a section of the perimeter to meet in the middle. They must have sentries placed every hundred yards or so doing the same.

The war has been raging for most of the day, ever since the fashion show ended. Now there are only three teams left: Yellow, Red, and Purple. We're Purple. Unfortunately, Kevin is on the Yellow team.

It's not like I thought I would be lucky enough to be on the same team as him, to be able to confront him, ask him why he came today. So many larpers showed up for the weekend event that Game Master Ken had to split the teams into seven groups. To be known forevermore as the seven Kingdoms of Asdor.

Food and pleasures fit for a king await the winners of the capture-the-flag scenario. The last remaining team receives gift certificates for movies, pizza, or bigger prizes like televisions and laptops. Also up for grabs is a grand prize weekend at Disneyland. And most important, the results will determine the ruler of all Asdor. At least, for this weekend, until the land is bulldozed to build another Bottom's Bathrooms and Accessories.

It makes me wonder if that's why Kevin came today, if he showed up only because it was his last chance to larp in Asdor. The way he looked at me at the fashion show gave me no clue about where we stand. Or maybe it did. Maybe his frostiness was answer enough.

It's not like he's given me the opportunity to talk to him since then. After the show was over, I ran backstage to see him, but he'd already slipped away. Once he was placed on the Yellow team, it was impossible to corner him without risking death.

As I wait in hiding, I wonder if Kevin's still alive, if I'll meet him on the battlefield. I've tried to put him out of my mind since I watched him march away with the rest of his army, to lose myself in the game, to enjoy my last few hours larping with my friends.

It's easier to pretend that the only thing that hangs in the balance is Asdor, not my apology to Kevin, my relationship with my parents, the success of their business, or my deteriorating reputation at school. Instead, I've been focusing on my next step, my quickly beating heart, the feel of the sword as I swing it at my enemies. I'm Andy of Asdor, here to defend my country until my last breath.

Dry twigs and leaves crunch as marching footsteps approach. The two soldiers come together and chat for a second. I recognize Eddie's Dick Van Dyke–inspired accent.

I wait until their footsteps fade before relaxing my stance again. I scan my surroundings for the rest of my recon party that Queen Keelie dispatched. A warlock from San Diego appears from behind a large boulder, stroking his nonexistent beard in thought. I glance at a depression about ten feet in front of me, just another dip in the forest floor, and Finn's head pops up.

I shrug as if to say I'm not sure what to do now.

"They're too spread out," Finn says in a hushed voice. "Yellow was given the largest piece of land. There aren't enough of them to hold their flag and secure the perimeter at the same time."

"I counted a full two minutes round trip for the sentries," the warlock says. "That means that for sixty seconds, they're marching away with their backs to us."

"We could slip by them," I say. "Sneak past the perimeter and take the flag from behind. They won't know what hit them. What do you think, Harper?"

A bush off to my right rustles. The thick green leaves part to reveal her pretty face. "I just want to kill someone already. When can we fight?"

"I think this is our best option of winning right here, right now," I say. "They won't expect it. We have a good chance. If we wait much longer then we lose that advantage."

"Imagine Queen Keelie's face when we bring her the yellow flag." Finn's expression gets all dopey, like he's imagining handing it to her himself. And maybe imagining other things that I'm not certain I want to know about.

"What are we waiting for?" Harper asks, leaping to her feet.

"Get down," San Diego hisses.

We all take cover just as we hear the footsteps approach. The moment the sentries' footsteps fade, I peek around the tree trunk to double-check that they're gone. "Okay. Now!"

The four of us scramble from our hiding spots and surge forward. We weave through the trees and thick underbrush, stepping as lightly as we can until we're on the other side of the sentries' path.

The forest soon swallows us, and we're hidden from sight. So deep into enemy territory, our pace automatically slows. We place our footsteps carefully in case someone is hiding close by and hears us.

"Where is everyone?" Harper asks.

Finn's head swivels back and forth, on the lookout for danger. "Maybe they're attacking another team as we speak."

"I hope it's not ours," I say.

"Let's not waste the opportunity," San Diego says. "Look. There's the yellow flag."

We follow his wand to see the yellow piece of fabric. It hangs from a stick wedged into a pile of boulders and rocks.

Finn raises his fist in triumph. "Let's go."

He takes off, the others close on his heels. I follow behind, my heart pounding, afraid the Yellow team will return at any moment. It can't be this easy. Only a few sentries to guard their flag? It doesn't make sense.

The yellow flag is so close. It's just a matter of grabbing it and getting it back to our land safely. If I can't manage to win Kevin back, then at least I might feel like I've come out a winner one way this weekend.

Over my boots scattering stones and my heavy panting, I hear footsteps scurry behind me, swishing through the grass.

My body tenses like I've been electrocuted. I grip my sword, but before I can spin around, I feel something dig into my back.

"Freeze," a voice behind me commands.

I gasp and do as he says. The others turn around, weapons at the ready, but they're too far away to help.

My Yellow enemy presses his weapon into my back. "Drop the sword."

Reluctantly, I let it fall to the ground and raise my hands. He circles around me until I can see him clearly. A flare of sapphire, a glitter of gold piping and details. It's Kevin.

Out of the corner of my eye, I see Harper's stance shift, like she's calculating if she can get to me fast enough.

"She'll be dead before you can reach her," Kevin says. His expression is unreadable as he holds the point of his blade to my neck.

San Diego's focus moves between us and the yellow flag, like he's considering sacrificing me for the win.

But Kevin anticipates this, too. "Don't even think about it. If I yell, I can have backup here in less than ten seconds."

"I don't suppose you'll show me mercy," I say.

His eye twitches. "Give me one reason." But he says it like he really means it. Like he wants an excuse to spare me. He's breaking character.

I search his hard expression for some flicker of warmth. I recall his sketchbook, filled with drawings of me. "Because you like me."

His mouth turns down, but more with sadness, I think, than anger. His blade lowers slightly. "I feel like I hardly know you."

"But you do know me." I move toward him, and the sword twitches in his hand. He's not ready to let his guard down yet. I don't blame him. "You've known me all along. At the hardware store, at school, at your house, at larping. I was always the same person. You just got to know me in different ways. Are you telling me you didn't like any of those versions of me?"

His mouth twitches like he wants to deny it, but he can't. Because it's true. I know it, and he knows it. "I liked them all in different ways."

"So then if you add all those girls together, you must really like me, right?" I ask hopefully.

But he's not smiling. "You sure made it difficult to get close to you."

"Okay, so I may not have wanted everyone at school, the entire world, to know about larping. I felt like I had to hide who I am so I would fit the perfect princess image for the show, so my parents' business could be a success, so I could avoid getting bullied at school."

The San Diego warlock is glancing between us, not sure how to react to the break in character. I can feel the minutes pass. The Yellow team could return at any moment. But I don't care right now.

"And how did that turn out for you?" Kevin asks me.

"Not well," I say. "I'd rather be teased as me than teased as someone I'm not. Then at least I'm happy with who I am as a person."

"And are you happy with yourself now?" Warily, he searches my face.

For once I'm glad I'm not wearing a mask, so he can see my sincerity. "Yes. This is me. All of me. No more mask. No more SPAM."

Finn wrinkles his nose, probably at the thought of Spam. San Diego looks like he's been hit with a confusion spell, Harper looks like she's both amused and proud of me, and Kevin, well, I'm not sure. He's got this blank look on his face, and he's really quiet. I can't tell what he's thinking.

The blast of a horn makes me jump. Turning away from Kevin's sword, I search for the source of the sound. My eyes bounce across the forest, which seems to be moving. They finally rest on an axe, a mace, arrows flying.

An army of larpers surge toward us like a tidal wave crashing through the forest, their battle cries like the violent froth hissing. Eddie and the other sentry lead the pack straight for us. The Yellow team has returned, carrying the red flag that they've stolen. Now it's down to Yellow and Purple. Them against us.

My comrades start to back away from the encroaching enemy. Harper hesitates, like she doesn't want to leave me behind.

Kevin looks from his Yellow team to me. His jaw clenches as he holds my gaze. "I don't want to kill you."

Despite the blade at my throat, I reach out to him. This time, he doesn't pull away. "Then come with us. Come over to my team."

His eyes finally soften. The blade drops away from my neck. "I've always been on your team, Andy. I'm just glad you finally realize what team that is."

San Diego raises his magical hands, ready to cast a spell, which would work as well as trying to blow out a house fire. "What should we do?"

Harper raises her mace. "We fight!"

She takes a step, but Kevin lunges forward and pulls her back by her leather vest.

I pick up my sword, and we all start sprinting in the other direction.

Finn lingers behind, staring at the cairn of rocks where the yellow flag flutters in the wind teasingly. "What about the flag?"

"Leave it!" I yell.

The full force of the Yellow team is bearing down on us. They scream for our blood, weapons raised high, eyes wild with savagery.

We're now down to the last two teams, and tensions are high. There won't be a peaceful surrender. The wave will swallow us whole.

Kevin rips the yellow band from his arm and drops it on the ground. "Run!"

Chapter Forty-One

Dark Knight Rises

My legs burn. My lungs burn. At any moment, I might collapse and let the crowd chasing us consume me. But I keep moving. One foot in front of the other.

We break through the tree line and onto the open field. Kevin and San Diego are on either side of me. Whenever a Yellow warrior breaks away from the mob and gets too close, Finn and the San Diego warlock cast spells to ward them off. But they're running low on mana.

Why am I torturing myself for a game? Why not turn around and give up? Or go down guns, err…swords blazing, like Harper did soon after we began running?

I want to. Or at least, my body does. But it's not that easy. It's not just a game. Not to me. I couldn't care less about prizes, about winning, about a big climax for the episode. *This* is my climactic moment. My last big hurrah. It might all be pretend, but the most important part is that *I'm* not pretending anymore.

So I keep running with beasts and enemies at my back because I'm having fun. I'm finally doing what I want, and

I don't care who knows it. In fact, everyone knows it, and the best part is, they're doing it, too, and having fun.

And if we stop, then it is a game, and we're all just a bunch of silly people running around in homemade costumes in a field. Those people aren't carrying swords and shields, but foam and duct tape covered PVC pipes and metal trashcan lids. They don't wear armor, but tinfoil-wrapped cardboard.

So it's not a game. It's real. I am a real warrior princess, and the enemy is on my heels.

Kevin spins to avoid a confusion spell. His vest tails flutter in a fan of velvet and silk. "We're almost there."

I can see the gentle grassy knoll of the Purple team's land. On the other side lies the parking lot, or rather, the impenetrable black ocean of doom. Stretched along its shores is the line of spectators, cameras, and food and merchandise vendors.

At the sight of us, the crowd perks up. I can hear Mom and Dad cheering me on from the sidelines. They stuck around after the fashion show to watch. So did Kevin's uncle, it seems.

I imagine they're peasants, villagers, and farmers who we're fighting to protect. Reaching deep, I tap into the last ounce of energy I have to reach the safety of our land.

We climb the slow rise, hoping to find our team waiting at the top, ready to come to our rescue and drive the enemy back. When we crest the hill, our purple flag waves gently in the afternoon breeze. However, there's only a sparse contingency left to guard it. Certainly not enough to save us.

San Diego waves to them, his long bell sleeve falling around his elbow. "Help. Help." One of our guards notices and raises the alarm.

"Where did they all go?" I say, between pants.

"There's not enough of them," Kevin says. "We've led the Yellow team straight to them. It's going to be a slaughter."

The few of our purple kinsmen who remain raise their weapons and charge forward. Those skilled at hand-to-hand combat form a line, blocking the path to our precious flag. They bang their shields with their weapons, gearing up for the approaching fight.

The archers and magic wielders remain safe behind the front lines, where they can do the most damage and still be protected. When we're close enough to avoid friendly fire, they begin their attack.

Arrows sail over our heads and into the crowd behind us at random. Spell casters throw their beanbags and bespell their successful targets. I hear grunts of pain behind me, but I don't turn around. They're too close; the air shifts behind my back as weapons whir and slice at me.

The moment we break through our own line and into safety, our Purple warriors rush the enemy, meeting them head on. There's a sudden clamor, dull thunks of plastic and foam weapons, a murmur of spell casting. But the loudest sound is the rushing heartbeat in my ears. I imagine if someone put their ear up to mine, it would sound like ocean waves, like my head is a seashell. And as empty as one.

I collapse on the ground and close my eyes against the sun. A shadow falls over me, and when I look up, I expect to see some goblin or knight perched above me, waiting to plunge its sword into my chest.

I squint against the light. It's Kevin. He holds out his hand to me. I take it. He pulls me to my feet and puts his hands on my shoulders like he's steadying me, only I feel sturdy.

"Let's finish this fight," he says. "Together."

I know it's just a small gesture and it shouldn't mean that much, but it does, and my chest suddenly feels full, and only now do I become unsteady. Maybe it's the way he said "together," or the emphasis his eyes made, as though it wasn't just a normal word. It was italicized. It means something more. Much more, I hope.

I nod and reach for my sword, but his grip on me tightens. His lips part, like he wants to say something, what could be our final words before we're slaughtered.

He settles on, "Promise me, Andy. No more hiding."

I nod fiercely. "No more hiding. This is me. Just me, like it or not." I give him a faint smile.

Kevin's flushed face finally softens, like he's the boy who kissed me in the woods again. It feels like so long since I saw this Kevin.

"I like it," he says. "And it's not *just* you. It's more than enough."

His hand cups my face and he brings his lips to mine.

I breathe in as we draw closer, as though I can have more than just his kiss. I greedily take in everything about the moment: the warmth of his lips, the scent of the sun on his handsome face, the sweet taste of Life Saver candy on his tongue.

It's just a fleeting kiss, and yet it feels as though the whole world has changed.

I wish it could be longer, but there's no time. He pulls away. My hand automatically moves to my lips, as though his kiss is a gloss that I can spread around and keep there just a little longer.

I beam up at him, and he grins back. A surge of energy courses through my body. I suddenly feel like I can take down the entire enemy army by myself.

Grasping our swords, with a roar that says "it's all or

nothing," we charge into the melee side by side.

Foam meets foam in soft squishes, tinfoil flashes in the sunlight, and the sickening sound effects of gruesome, bloody deaths fly from the mouths of our comrades. Our scraggly little group stands united, circling around our flag. We are ready to protect it until our last breath.

Working together, we hold our line, but the enemy keeps coming. Cut one down and two more appear. They gang up on us. It takes two forest dwellers and a centaur to bring San Diego down.

Next to me, Kevin grunts and falls to his knees. "Hit two, chest."

It's a serious wound to the stomach. I block him while he recovers. Meanwhile, a leather-clad thief throws a dagger, or rather, a beanbag, at me. It grazes my chest. I stumble back.

"Hit two, chest."

The thief draws back to attack again, but this time when the beanbag sails toward me, Kevin swings his sword like a bat and knocks it away. A home run.

I quickly heal myself with my remaining mana. The two of us tag-team each Yellow team member who comes at us. But it's only a matter of time.

One by one, our comrades fall. Bodies litter the ground. It's a bloodbath. Our human barrier between the Yellow team and our flag thins out. Soon they will have it. I imagine the crowd will swallow us whole. But at least we'll go down fighting. There's no surrendering for us.

I think it's all over, then I hear the bugle blast of a horn. Heads begin to turn away. The bodies that were about to crush us moments before back off. I'm so focused on keeping all my limbs that I can't see what's happening.

The chaos around us escalates, the pressure building. The referees can't seem to keep up with the mediating. I see more fighting now, but among our attackers. Confusion. Anarchy.

I see flashes of purple mixed in with the newcomers. Our teammates.

"They've come back for us!" I yell.

The remaining soldiers protecting our flag hear me and increase their efforts. It's not over yet.

My attention slips. My next block comes up short. A staff glances my hand and slides down my forearm. I barely have time to recover before a spear jabs my leg.

I collapse onto one knee. When I look up, a long sword draws back and cuts toward me.

I hold my own sword up to block my body, and our weapons connect. But the masked warrior before me is stronger. His arm ripples, and the pressure intensifies. I grit my teeth and press harder, but his blade inches closer to my chest.

Suddenly, his body jolts. A beanbag falls to his feet, as though hit from behind. The pressure on my sword relaxes and I pull back. Not wasting a moment, I swipe his leg, and he falters. Next, I take his arm, then the other.

The sword drops from his hand, and he falls to one knee. That's when I see Keelie standing behind him, bow held out before her. She was my savior.

She counts to three and releases another beanbag. The masked warrior collapses on the grass. His body convulses once then becomes still.

Keelie lifts her bow over her head and hangs it around her body. She grins at me before cupping her hand around her mouth.

"Attention, Yellow Kingdom," she calls out in her no-nonsense character voice. "You have been conquered."

She picks up what I thought was someone's staff laying

at her feet and thrusts it into the air. It's a smooth wooden pole. Tied to the end, flapping triumphantly in the breeze, is the Yellow Kingdom's flag.

Keelie waves the spoil back and forth so everyone around can see. "You have been vanquished. Surrender, or die a violent, bloody death."

A cheer rises from those of us saved by the turn of events. At the same time, a thunderous noise of objection rises from the Yellow team. Some throw down their weapons and raise their hands in surrender. The ones who choose to fight to the bitter end are quickly overpowered and receive a warrior's death.

Silhouetted by the violence and mayhem, Keelie approaches Kevin and me. "I'm glad you're still alive, Andy," she says. "I thought you were a goner when you didn't come back from your scouting mission."

"We almost were," I say. "But we got away, thanks to Kevin."

"What happened?" Kevin asks. "Where were you guys?"

Keelie leans on her bow to catch her breath. "We were going to wait for news from my scouts before attacking Yellow, because a head on ambush would have lost many people on both sides. But then suddenly, half of their numbers disappeared into the forest."

"Yeah, they were chasing us," I say.

"Well, it was a perfect distraction," she says. "We had no trouble circling around their territory and overpowering the few warriors they left behind to protect their flag."

We high-five each other. It feels good to be on the same team again. All feels right with my world.

A hyper-masculine roar interrupts us, startling me. It's nearby, and closing in on us. The three of us spin around to find a knight clad in dark armor, just in time to see him raise his sword against Kevin.

As he brings it down, the blade comes within inches of Kevin's face, completely against regulation target areas. Kevin barely has time to block.

"Hey, man. That's against the rules," a referee calls out, but because he's half the attacker's size, he seems reluctant to interfere.

"Yeah," says a merman. "Bad form."

The newcomer ignores them all and continues to attack Kevin with forceful, two-handed swings. Over and over again, Kevin manages to block them, but backpedals in surprise.

I don't remember seeing this warrior at all today, nor can I see his face. He wears a matte black suit of armor. His helm is painted the same, a nose bar bisecting his face. It's a professionally made costume, and not at all scuffed from a full day of battling.

While the cameras have been in the background for most of the day, keeping to the sidelines, they've honed in on the one-on-one fight now. Three lenses shadow the encounter like magnets.

The black knight makes an illegal jab to Kevin's stomach. It connects. He grunts and doubles over. His sword doesn't even look like a padded boffer, so I know the pain creasing Kevin's face is real.

Then the black knight raises his weapon high, ready to bring it down on his back. There are angry yells from the other larpers. A couple step forward to intervene, but Kevin twists out of the way, parrying it in time.

The fighting between the Purple and Yellow teams has come to a dead stop. All attention is now on Kevin and the mysterious dark knight. A few larpers stand on guard, weapons held at the ready in case they need to jump in, but Kevin seems to be doing just fine on his own.

Spinning on his heel, Kevin's light blade smacks the knight's weapon with precision. Obviously inexperienced, the knight blocks sloppily, unable to keep up with Kevin's speed.

Kevin is relentless in his advances. The costume I sewed him allows him to move freely, since it's made to fit his perfect form. Finally, the blade is flung from the knight's hands, and he's unarmed.

The other larpers are clapping now. For the first time all day, I see Corbin standing among them, off camera. He's watching the fight intently, like he's hoping something big will go down. Apparently, a war between the Seven Kingdoms of Asdor wasn't enough action for him.

Kevin raises the tip of his blade to his attacker's dark chest. "Yield."

Somehow, he's remained in character, despite the total lack of sportsmanship shown by the knight.

I think it's over, but then the black knight grips Kevin's sword by the blade and yanks it out of his grip. Grasping it with two hands, he raises it up before bringing it down on his knee. The PVC pipe cracks in two. It bends at a weird angle, held in place by only the duct tape.

Kevin throws up his hands. "What's your problem, man?"

In answer, the dark knight reaches up and slides off his helm.

I gasp. "Lennox."

Chapter Forty-Two

Lummox Lennox

Murmurs trickle through the crowd from the local larpers who know the Mac Attacker. Even the out-of-towners seem to know about him and his fast-food attacks from the connections Corbin made on the show, once he put all the puzzle pieces together.

Of course it's Lennox. Who else would it be?

"Lennox," I say, "What are you doing here? Stop it."

Lennox ignores me. His focus is on Kevin. "You think you can steal my girl?" He pokes Kevin in the chest with his broken sword. "Don't think I don't know about the little rendezvous you have with her every Sunday."

And because I know Lennox couldn't spell rendezvous, far less understand the meaning, I know he's following a script. This reeks of Corbin. I turn my glare on the slimy director, but he's watching the scene intently.

Instead of being smart or sane and denying that he even knew that it was me he was larping with, Kevin says, "Well, if you were a better boyfriend, maybe she would have spent that time with you."

"Dumbass," Keelie mutters under her breath. Which is a pretty fair assessment, because next thing I know Lennox picks him up by the collar of his princely vest. And while Kevin's as tall as the stupid quarterback, Lennox is meatier.

With a grunt, Lennox tosses him aside. I gasp and automatically run forward. Kevin tumbles several yards down the hill, toward the impenetrable black ocean of doom, before he slides to a halt.

For a nauseating second, he doesn't stir. I swallow the fear churning in my stomach and yell, "Kevin!"

I'm suddenly breathing hard, and I'm shaking even though I didn't run very far. My imagination spirals out of control, conjuring fears that he's unconscious, has a broken and bloody nose, or that he'll wake up with amnesia and won't know his own name.

Just as I get to his side, I see his fist clench. He bangs it on the ground before getting to his feet. Brushing the grass from the costume I made him, he notices some green stains and tries to wipe them away.

"Are you okay?" I ask.

"I'm fine, thanks." His scowl softens as he gives me a smile, which also looks a little bit like a wince.

The small group of onlookers, including the food and merchandise vendors, stops what they're doing. They join the larping crowd, everyone shoving to get a better look, a strange mix of old world and new world. I spot Mom and Dad among them. They look ready to intervene. Kevin's uncle pushes to the front of the crowd. Gerald's usually goofy expression has turned severe, his laugh lines creased with anger.

Some larpers are calling for Lennox's blood, raising their weapons in the air. But most are eyeballing the cameras and Corbin's hungry stare. I suddenly realize they probably assume this is all staged for the show. Even Mom and Dad hesitate. People look to the rest of the crowd for cues, but no one interferes, probably all coming to the same conclusion.

Dressed in his dragon costume, Game Master Ken storms up to Corbin, tail trailing in the grass behind him. "What's going on? What is this?" I'm not sure if he looks formidable or ridiculous in his costume.

Corbin raises a hand to silence him, unable to look away from the action. He waves his fingers at the scene before him, as though that's answer enough. Magic.

Lennox trudges down the slope toward Kevin. This isn't about me at all. It's just an excuse to pick on him. An excuse to get more airtime.

Kevin pushes up his puffy linen sleeves and plants his feet. As I suspected, even with Lennox barreling down on him, he's too mature to make a move to fight, but he doesn't back down, either.

Unfortunately, Lennox isn't as noble, and his fist draws back like a battering ram. It connects with Kevin's cheek with a meaty *thunk*.

To his credit, Kevin is still standing. All around, cries go up. People are calling Lennox names and booing. I'm one of them.

Gerald charges in, pressing his stocky body between the two of them. He straightens his shoulders and faces Lennox down. I bet if he had some of his tools with him, he'd make mincemeat out of Lennox.

Off to the side, I see Mom and Dad squabbling with Corbin, demanding he stop whatever this is. Threatening lawyers and calls to his producer.

By the look on Kevin's face, and the throbbing vein in his forehead, it's all he can do to stop from shoving his uncle aside and tackling Lennox. He might have the willpower to stop himself, but I sure don't.

Marching over to one of the food venders looking on, I grab the half-prepared hot dog out of his hand. I walk over to Lennox, draw the dog back like it's the most powerful spell ever created, and I let it fly.

The wiener soars true. It slaps Lennox across the face like, well, a soggy wiener. It leaves a streak of ketchup on his cheek like the first blood drawn in battle.

His face turns purple with rage as he searches for the source. When his eyes land on me, he starts like I'd just slapped him. Which I did. With a hot dog.

"A?"

The anger leaves his face, and I think he has a moment, a genuine moment, when he suddenly realizes he's been a total ass. He looks to Corbin as if for some cue, so he's turned away when the pizza slice hits him.

"Jerk," Keelie yells at him.

She raises a second slice and flings it like a throwing star at his head. This one sticks to his perfect matte black armor and slides down his chest. A moment later fries pelt him.

Kevin and Gerald back away to avoid being caught in the crossfire. Within seconds, it's too difficult to tell who's throwing the food. It's coming from everywhere. Hamburgers, pitas, wraps, tacos, churros.

Lennox dodges the food as best he can. He catches morsels to throw back at the crowd, but with the nonstop barrage against him, he looks like a dog chasing his tail. He can't win this fight.

Kevin grabs the squeezable ketchup and mustard containers from a stand and aims them straight at Lennox's head, spraying him like one of the overpriced abstract paintings Mom bought for the living room.

"Hey," someone yells close behind me. I spin to find Corbin picking a tomato out of his gelled hair.

He ducks to avoid a hamburger patty. I search for the source and burst out laughing when I see who it is. Mom!

Her high heels are digging into the soft grass, and she's pushed up the sleeves of her cardigan to keep it from getting stained. Her lips pursed, she draws back a sesame seed bun. Before she can toss it at him, he grabs me by the shoulders and cowers behind me, using me as a human shield.

Dad crosses his arms. "I think it's time you left, Corbin." This time, he doesn't have to tighten his tie to sound authoritative. He stares him down. "You're fired."

"But we have a contract," Corbin whines. "You can't fire me."

A man sporting a business suit and well-groomed goatee takes a step out of the crowd. "No, but I can."

Corbin's grip on my shoulders tighten. I'm guessing this is the producer.

"Mr. Bottom here tells me there have been some problems with filming," he says. "I gave you one more chance after our last meeting. I thought I would come out today to see if you've changed your habits. It appears as though I should have arrived a little sooner."

Corbin stands up straighter but doesn't come out from behind me. The crowd still has plenty of ammunition, and they look eager to use it.

He laughs. "This isn't what it looks like. This is all part of the plan. Isn't it, Adrianna? Tell them. You were in on it the whole time, weren't you?" He slaps me hard on the back like we're old pals playing a joke.

When I turn and scowl at him, he digs his fingers into my

shoulders. "Go on. Tell them," he hisses through clenched teeth. "Come on, kid. Help me out here."

I snort. To break free of his painful death grip, I jam the hilt of my sword into his gut. He grunts and lets go to rub the spot.

"You're on your own this time." I point my sword at him. "You had your chance to turn things around, and you blew it. You're done meddling with my life."

Dad walks right up to him until they're nose to nose and jabs his thumb toward the parking lot. "You heard the princess. Get off my property—before I call the police."

The food starts to fly again. This time it's an ice cream cone. It smacks him in the face and slides into the open collar of his shirt. He tries to wipe it away, but soon everyone has joined in the food fight. It's an onslaught. Even I'm getting hit by ricochet.

Harper suddenly appears from wherever she'd been taken down in the forest. The fight must be loud enough to resurrect the dead, since I see lots of fallen comrades are now joining the crowd to see what the commotion is.

"Lennox!" Harper yells at him. "What do you think you're doing? What's wrong with you?"

Lennox starts and gives her a look like he just woke up from a dream. He turns to Corbin. "Is this still part of the show?"

"What do you think?" he barks back.

"But you said this is what I was supposed to do. Why isn't anyone cheering? You said they'd be cheering. I was supposed to be a hero. That's what you said." Lennox turns to me, his black gauntlets reaching out as though pleading, bits of food dripping from them. "You knew about this, right? You were in on it, weren't you?"

He looks as confused as he did at the grand opening,

when he was looking at Corbin as though for instructions.

"No, Lennox. This wasn't supposed to happen. Why are you even here?"

Lennox's face contorts, his nostrils flaring, his jaw clenching. I suddenly have an intense sympathy for anyone who tries to tackle him on the football field. But then he turns that look on Corbin.

"You said! You said it was part of the show!"

Corbin quails. "It is. It is part of the show. I told you. They're all just acting right now. They're in character."

The frown on his face turns back to one of confusion. He looks from the angry mob to Corbin and back again.

"Lennox," I say. "You know reality TV isn't scripted, right? That's the whole point."

His eyes drop to his suit of armor as though processing this information and realizing how silly he looks. And for the first time, I realize this is total news to him.

I recall each blow-up event: the double date kiss, the grand opening, even today. Whenever he was causing problems, he seemed to be taking cues from Corbin, almost like he was being coached.

By the look on Lennox's face, he's recalling these moments, too, only a lot slower, like instead of a simple puzzle, it's a 3D one. I decide to throw him a bone.

"Corbin is setting you up," I say. "Can't you see that?"

The light bulb seems to flicker inside his brain, and his eyebrows shoot up in an "ah-ha!" moment before they draw together in an I'm-gonna-kill-you way.

Corbin realizes that look is meant for him, and he scrambles away. He trips over a mace lying on the ground and goes rolling backward until he hits a pita cart. Lennox hovers over him. Grabbing an entire container of *tzatziki* dip, he dumps it over Corbin's head.

Realizing he's on the losing end of the battle, Corbin finally makes a break for it. Wiping the dip out of his eyes, he scrambles through the line of larpers and into the parking lot.

Hugh tails his old director back to the van, documenting every cowardly moment of his retreat, laughing as he does so. Everyone follows in pursuit, continuing to attack Corbin.

As I pass a Taco Bell stall, I grab a handful of condiment packets. Keelie and I lead the chase and toss them at the network van as Corbin scrambles in and starts the engine. By the time he lays a patch of rubber on the pavement and races out of there, the van looks like a victim of a relish, ketchup, and mustard factory explosion.

As Corbin fades into the beautiful Hollywood sunset, a victorious cry goes up around us. We all hold hands and raise them up to the sky, the Seven Kingdoms of Asdor united against a common enemy. And when I look beside me, my hand is held firmly in Kevin's.

Chapter Forty-Three

My People

"Ouch." Kevin hisses as I hold a Popsicle up to his reddened cheek, but he doesn't pull away.

"I think you're going to have quite the shiner tomorrow," I say.

A swollen lump has already formed where Lennox punched him. Even in the dim evening light, I can see a shadow spread beneath his left eye.

"That's okay. It was worth it in the end. You could say I really *relished* it." His cheeks wrinkle at his joke. He winces at the movement.

I give him my most serious look. "On Monday at school, you *mustard*-ently try to avoid Lennox until he calms down."

"I'm not scared. He has to *ketchup* with me first."

We both break down into laughter now. Kevin's chuckles sound more like choking as each one causes him pain where he took Lennox's sword in the stomach. I pull the Popsicle away, but he covers my hand with his and holds it there.

"I'm glad you did this." He gestures to the scene around us. "It was pretty fun."

A few larpers mill about, eating snacks from the vendors and talking. The dismantled stage is being hauled away. The temporary shops are starting to pack up. The odd casual duel breaks out from time to time, backlit by the sunset over the green space. Many have already left for home, especially those from out of town, but most of the locals still want to hold onto their last day in Asdor.

"It was fun," I say. "I just wish it wasn't over."

"Me too," he says. "But it's not all over." He slides his hand into mine and I squeeze it.

Someone clears their throat nearby. It's Dad. I take a guilty step away from Kevin, and he drops my hand.

"Hey, princess," he says.

"Hey, Dad. Hey, Mom." I introduce Kevin officially, which feels super awkward. "How did things go with the producer?"

"It went well," Dad says. "He was very cooperative. We still have to fulfill our contract for this season of *Bathroom Barons*, but we won't be seeing Corbin again."

My entire body relaxes with the news until I think I might just melt into a puddle of goo on the ground. "That's good."

"As for next season..."

I instantly stiffen back up, and Dad smiles.

"We'll *all* decide what to do."

Mom yanks me in for a hug. "You did great out there today." She says it like I won a track meet, not just finished pretend-killing a bunch of people.

"Thanks, I think."

"I had a chance to talk to Mr. Carson after your show today. He was very impressed with your designs."

"The fashion guy?" I ask. "You mean he didn't think it was a joke?" I haven't had much time to think about it since the fashion show. I never thought I'd hear from him again.

"No. He said he quite enjoyed himself. However, he did say that costumes aren't his forte, so he put us in touch with a few of his contacts in Hollywood."

She grips my shoulders in excitement. "Just think, by this time next year, you could have your own shop, or have your line of costumes carried in the big-box stores. Or," she gasps as her mind starts to run away, and her fingers dig in harder until I think she might break the skin with her acrylics, "you could design costumes for movies. You could dress famous stars."

I gently brush her hands away. "That's great, Mom. We'll see." I give her a look.

"Oh, of course, dear." She gives a sheepish smile. "You know how I get carried away. I'm sorry if I've gotten wrapped up in the show lately." She grabs me for another hug. "I only want what's best for you."

"I know, Mom. Thanks."

When the hug starts to drag on too long and gets a little too mushy, Dad kindly pulls her back.

I straighten my tunic. "So, if the network wants a second season of the show, does that mean I haven't totally driven Bottom's Bathrooms and Accessories into the ground?" I ask in a joking way, although I'm totally not joking.

Dad chuckles. "No, nothing like that. I'm sorry we've been putting so much pressure on you lately."

I blink, more than surprised. "But the grand opening of the store…it was ruined. I thought for sure that what happened would affect sales."

Kevin crosses his arms. "I blame Lennox for that one."

I remember when I first met Lennox at school. He was nice enough. The major problems only started happening once Corbin stuck his nose in things. "Actually, I think that had more to do with Corbin than Lennox, to be honest."

Kevin looks at me like I've lost my mind. "You're not seriously defending him, are you?"

I hold up my hands. "I'm not saying he gets a free pass on everything. But, think about it, we already know that Corbin suckered him into showing up today. And when I think back to all the other stuff, it seems like maybe Lennox was being strung along."

Kevin snorts. "I think you're being too forgiving."

I tilt my head in a noncommittal response. Maybe I am, but Lennox isn't the sharpest weapon in the armory. Then again, who am I to point fingers at him when I'm not exactly the poster girl for good decisions lately. And he always seemed genuinely remorseful once he realized he'd done something wrong.

"Well, either way," Dad says, "now that Corbin's been sacked, I think things will be better. But I will give him this, after the episode he aired last night, I think it went a long way to repairing the damage he's done to both the company's and your reputation."

"The preliminary sales reports look very promising," Mom says.

"That's great," I say. Then suddenly, my shoulders sag. "So you're still going to open the second L.A. store here?" I try to hide my disappointment; it's not like I'm not happy that the business is doing well again.

"Well, actually," my dad begins, "we'd originally planned to use this lot— "

"Asdor," I correct.

"We had originally planned to use Asdor for my main warehousing location, in addition to the store being built here. But after the numbers showed us just how fickle the L.A. toilet market can be, we decided to stick to the one store for now." Instinctually, Dad reaches up to tighten his tie because he's talking business. "The shareholders feel it will be like putting all our eggs in one basket, so we're looking at opening another store in Montana instead."

"Wait," Kevin says. "So Asdor won't be destroyed?"

"Asdor is safe," Dad assures him. "And I can assure it remains safe, because I own it. No one will build on it."

"That's great news, Dad!" I tackle him with a giant hug like he just bought me a sports car. No. This is better than a sports car—but that doesn't mean I'm not still hoping for a car one day.

Strangely enough, while I've been so desperate to lose myself in Asdor since I arrived in Beverly Hills, the last few weeks made me realize something. While I'm happy that it's been saved, it was never Asdor that made me feel like I belonged somewhere. It was the people. My friends. And Kevin. Kevin made me feel like I belong, both in reality and in Asdor.

Dad glances back at the vendors still hanging around until the last stragglers go home. "Well, I'm going to go grab a hot dog. We'll be here when you want a ride home."

"Actually, sir," Kevin says. "I drove today. I could give her a ride home when we're all finished up here. I live only a few minutes from your house. It's no trouble at all."

OMG. Inside, I'm doing backflips. I'm breakdancing. I can't say anything since my mouth is stretched so wide by my smile.

I turn to Dad, who performs an awkward fatherly assessment of Kevin. After his protective once-over, he nods. Which really says a lot, what with his no-boyfriend policy and everything, not to mention the whole Lennox fiasco.

Mom's got a big grin on her face. She tugs on Dad's sleeve, trying to hint that they should go. I wish he would take that hint.

Finally, Dad relents. "That's fine. But no later than nine."

I don't argue. How can I argue? Everything's perfect. I nod, still too smiley to answer.

Spotting our group, Kevin's uncle walks up with a loaded hot dog in his hand. "Good job today, guys. You really kicked some make-believe butt."

"Thanks," Kevin says.

Gerald kind of lingers around, so I introduce him to my parents, and it suddenly hits me. "Hey, Dad," I say, in a completely casual, not-up-to-anything way. "With your second store falling through and everything, wouldn't it be a good idea to start moving some product through other stores? You know, smaller local stores that already have a good customer base."

"Actually, that is something being looked into," Mom says. "It would help decrease our overhead. At least until we grow big enough to justify opening another Bottom's store."

"Say," Gerald takes the opening I gave him like a regular salesman, "why don't I buy you two some hot dogs." He throws a neighborly arm around my dad.

They're already deep in discussion before they hit the vendors. Mom waves over her shoulder. I'm sure she will bombard me with excited questions about Kevin once I get home.

I hand Kevin the Popsicle, but it's mostly melted by now. "Thanks for the ride."

"The Kia's not the 'Stang,' but it gets me from point A to point B."

I wouldn't care if he drove me home in a canoe. "That's fine. The Mustang was an automatic anyway."

He laughs. "So, I guess you two are broken up now. You

know, since you hotdogged him in public and everything."

"It's hard to break up with someone when you weren't going out in the first place." I sigh. "I swear, there was nothing between Lennox and me. I can even show you the original footage of our date, before Corbin tampered with it."

Kevin holds up his hands. "Not necessary. If Harper believes you, then so do I." Something grabs his attention over my shoulder. "Speak of the devil."

I turn to see Lennox headed this way. He's dumped his costume somewhere, and has cleaned off the food stuck to his skin and hair as best as he could, but it still sticks up, probably stiff with ketchup. It's strange to think that only a couple of weeks ago I was washing ketchup out of my hair at school. Now Lennox is. Popularity is a fickle thing.

I'm surprised he stuck around. Hasn't he had enough? I know I've had enough of him for one day. And by the way all our friends gather around us, drawing their weapons, apparently so have they.

Harper stands next to me with her "You are in so much trouble" smile on. Keelie stands next to her with her "If you don't hit him, I will," scowl. I'm beginning to think there is more of her larping character in her than she realizes.

Lennox stares at his feet as he trudges up to us and shoves his hands into his pockets. "I'm sorry. I honestly didn't know I wasn't supposed to be here today."

"You expect us to believe that?" Kevin scoffs. "I'm thinking you really enjoyed it." He indicates the shadow beneath his eye that's growing darker by the minute.

Lennox winces. I think he's more of a punch first, ask questions later kind of guy. "I might have hit you harder than Corbin told me to."

"Why would you even go along with Corbin's plan?" I ask.

"Because he said it was for the show. That you were in on everything and wanted me to do it."

I snort. "Really? You still believed him even when I gave you a bloody nose? Even when I dumped slushie on you?"

Keelie suddenly giggles and grins at me. "That was awesome, by the way." Collecting herself, she resumes her scowling at Lennox. "Even when everyone started pelting food at you?" she asks him.

"I just thought that you guys were really good actors." He shrugs and when his shoulders come down, he looks like he's slumped over. "I guess if this were a movie, I'd be the bad guy."

I kind of feel sorry for him. I can see why Harper has a soft spot for him. I lower my weapon. "You're not a bad guy, Lennox. Just…" I look for some other word to use besides stupid. "Easily manipulated."

"Actually, you are the bad guy," Harper cuts in. "Why? Why would you do all this? Why would you hurt me like this?"

Lennox blinks. "Hurt you? How did I hurt you? I never did anything to you."

"Exactly. You never went on that date with me. You never kissed me. Instead, you kissed my best friend. You never asked me to the dance."

He blinks again. "But, but it's a Sadie Hawkins dance."

"Whatever. You've totally ignored me for months now. You dropped me with no explanation."

His eyebrows knit together like she was telling him the sky was green. "But why would you even care? You asked me to set you up on a date with Conner."

"Conner?" she screeches. "I was trying to set it up so Conner and Andy were on a date, so…" She hesitates and glances around. It still seems like she's afraid of being vulnerable, but she drops her voice and plows on anyway. "So it would be like you and I were on a date together."

I nudge her with my elbow. "Didn't you tell him whose date was whose when you were setting it up?"

"I thought I did." Although she doesn't sound so sure anymore.

"You wanted to go on a date with me?" Lennox asks her. "I wanted to go on a date with you, too. Actually, I never wanted to stop dating you. That's why I got so upset when school started and you were such a jerk to me."

Harper crosses her arms and stares at her feet. "Didn't seem that way when you were flirting with Andy right in front of me."

"I guess since Adrianna was popular and on a TV show and everything, I thought it would make you jealous if I started paying attention to her." He seems to catch himself and turns to me. "No offense. You're really nice and everything."

I hold up my hands. "None taken."

Everyone kind of grows quiet, but it seems like there's a lot left to say and figure out, because I know the whole story and even I'm getting confused. However, nothing is going to get worked out with so many onlookers and threatening weapons aimed at Lennox.

"It sounds like you two have a lot to talk about," I say. "We're just going to be over here." I point in the general direction of anywhere-but-here.

The others seem to take the hint and wander back to the grassy knoll where the last battle was won. Kevin and I walk slower than everyone else, lingering behind to have our own chat.

Kevin kind of laughs. "Looks like a lot could have been solved by them just talking things through."

I give him a sidelong glance. "They might not be the only ones."

"What do you mean?"

"Maybe you and Lennox have some things to hash out."

Now he really does laugh. "Yeah, right. Not in this lifetime. He's already proven himself to be a terrible friend. Why would I want to give him another shot?"

"Actually, here's the funny thing," I say, giving him a "stay with me" look. "He says the same thing about you."

"What?" He stops dead and turns to me. "You don't believe that, do you? I told you, when my parents were going through a divorce—"

"Lennox's grandmother was in the hospital dying," I cut in.

His mouth hangs open. "Gram-Gram Mary?" His voice kind of gets all high and squeaky as he says it, and something tells me Lennox isn't the only one upset by the loss.

I give him a sympathetic look. "The one and the same."

"We used to spend part of summer vacation at her house. She'd make us snickerdoodles." He shakes his head, like he suddenly remembers he's a sixteen-year-old and not a little kid anymore. "I had no idea."

"Apparently you didn't return any of his calls when she was in the hospital."

"My parents took us away on a month vacation over that summer. It was like their way of having one last big family vacation, to kind of deal with things, before the split. We didn't tell anyone we were going. My parents were kind of embarrassed about the separation. They didn't want all the neighbors talking, so they kept it all on the down-low." His lips purse, and he stares at the grass beneath his feet. "Lennox's Gram-Gram must have died around that time."

"I guess so."

Kevin kind of goes "huh," but in a deeply thoughtful way, and grows quiet like he's reviewing the last several years in his head.

He turns back to look at Lennox, and I follow his gaze to find him and Harper making out. I wrinkle my nose in both a disgusted and completely thrilled-for-her way.

"I guess you're not the only person I jumped to conclusions about," he finally says, and gives me a half smile, his cheek wrinkling.

I take it that means it's our turn to hash things out. "I'm sorry," I say. "About lying to you, for hiding behind the mask, and how I came off at school. I handled things badly."

"So did I." He shoves his hands in his pockets. "I'm sorry that I didn't believe you at the grand opening. After I saw the episode with you and Lennox kissing, I guess I was really hurt."

"I'm sorry that I was the one who hurt you."

"But I should have believed you," he said. "After everything you told me about Corbin. I should have given you the benefit of the doubt."

"I haven't exactly given you many reasons to. But from now on, what you see is what you get." I wave a hand over myself to indicate everything he'd get. "For better or worse."

Both his cheeks wrinkle this time. "Trust me, it's better."

I return his look, in case it's not clear by now that everything about him is better. "If I could do it all differently, from the start, I would."

He doesn't say anything for a moment, and I wonder if that's it. If that's all that we can say about it, because we can't go back. What's done is done.

Then he says, "Then let's do it."

"Do what?"

"Start again." He holds out his hand. "Hi. I'm Kevin. I work in my uncle's hardware store, I larp on the weekends, and I like weird, quirky girls with crazy hair."

I laugh, but it feels more like a relieved sigh. I shake his hand. "I'm Andy. I'm a weird, quirky girl with crazy hair. I like to sew, and larp, and I'm on a hugely embarrassing reality TV show called *Bathroom Barons*, because my dad invented the Bowl Buddy. I just moved to Beverly Hills, and I'm a little nervous that I won't be able to make any friends."

"Well, you've already made one."

We haven't let go of each other's hand yet, and the feel of mine in his is warm, and comforting, and hopeful.

Without either of us mentioning it, we wander over to the rest of the group. Keelie commandeered the yellow flag as a keepsake. It's tied around her neck like a superhero cape. Finn is tossing his beanbags to Eddie, who's knocking them out of the park with his broadsword.

I duck as a beanbag sails over my head from Eddie's sword.

"Oops. Forgive me, my lady," he calls, bowing deeply.

Harper and Lennox apparently decided to stick around, and since they're holding hands now, too, I'm thinking they had a good talk. She's sitting on Chad's shield so her butt doesn't get dirty. She waves me over and points to the spare slice of pizza she saved for me.

I sit down and lean closer so no one will hear. "Everything good?" I ask.

"Yeah. Everything's cool." She smiles her I'm-just-acting-cool-but-I'm-secretly-ecstatic smile.

I give her my don't-worry-it's-our-secret smile and take the slice of pizza she hands me.

Kevin sits down next to me and, because he's only two people away from Lennox and neither of them are yelling or throwing punches at each other, I think eventually things might actually be all right between them. Not like they'll be besties or anything, but at the very least, we won't have to pick McDonald's pickles out of our hair anymore.

Keelie bounces over to Kevin and me, wedging herself between us. She wraps her arms around our necks and drags our faces down to her height. "Finn. Take our picture."

Finn slips his phone out of his robes. He snaps a couple of cheesy action shots of the three of us in battle poses. When he's done, he calls Keelie over to show her the photos. I catch them tilting their heads a lot closer than they need to.

"I noticed you didn't get any prizes today when they drew names," Kevin says to me.

"I took my name out of the running for the prizes. It didn't seem fair." Actually, it didn't make sense to give up a car to help fund this weekend and then accept a few gift certificates in the end. But I don't tell him about the car. "I was the organizer, so it would seem like I didn't win the prizes fair and square."

"Well, I won a couple movie gift certificates." He pats his pocket. "I might be able to spare one. What do you say, Red? You free next weekend?"

My insides are now doing the macarena, the salsa, the disco. I think I even see strobe lights blinking in front of my eyes. Oh, wait. That's from lack of oxygen. *Breathe*, I tell myself. *Remember to breathe.*

Instead of jumping up and down or screaming like a five-year-old girl who got a pony for her birthday, I say, "I think that's doable. I'll check my schedule and have my people get back to you."

"Your people? Who are your people?"

I take in the ragtag group in front of me, take in the fuzzy good-time feelings from the entire day. And I take in Kevin's grin meant just for me.

I smile back as I realize *these* are my people.

Acknowledgments

It took a kingdom of people to make this fairy tale come true. This story all began with the hopeful musings of Simon Dovey, who is always trying to dream up the next big invention. Sorry the Bowl Buddy didn't work out for you, Simon, but thanks to you, it sparked the idea for the Porcelain Princess.

A big shout-out to those who read initial drafts of the book, including my sister, Wendy Slack, and my critique partners, Pat Esden and Claire Merle, and also to those who continued to give me feedback and moral support throughout the writing process—that means you Devin Smith, Rich Brown, Hayley Brown, and Debbie Callahan. And of course, there's my tireless agent, Pooja Menon, my knight in shining armor who championed this book through her guidance, support, and editing expertise. Thank you for finding my princess a home.

Hear ye! Hear ye! Stacy Abrams and Lydia Sharp at Entangled, I dub ye Editors of Most Awesomeness. Thank you for sharing my vision of this novel and for working so hard to help this book shine like a Bottom's Bathroom Buffer. You truly are royalty. I'd also like to thank the members of the royal court at Entangled for all their efforts in getting this book ready to ascend. Now that it's done, we can finally celebrate. Now let's potty! Err, I mean party!

Grab the Entangled Teen releases readers are talking about!

Proof of Lies
by Diana Rodriguez Wallach

Anastasia Phoenix's sister is missing, presumed dead. She's the only one who believes Keira is still alive, and when new evidence surfaces, Anastasia sets out to follow the trail—and lands in the middle of a massive conspiracy. Now she isn't sure who she can trust. At her side is Marcus, the bad boy with a sexy accent who's as secretive as she is. Nothing is as it appears, and when everything she's ever known is revealed to be a lie, Anastasia has to believe in one impossibility. She *will* find her sister.

Why I Loathe Sterling Lane
by Ingrid Paulson

537 rules hold Harper's world together, until spoiled, seditious, self-righteous Sterling Lane corrupts her brother. Worst of all, Sterling has perfected the role of a charming, misguided student trying to make amends for his past transgressions, and only Harper sees him for the troublemaker he absolutely is. As Harper breaks Rule after precious Rule in her battle of wits against Sterling and tension between them hits a boiling point, she's horrified to discover that perhaps the two of them aren't as different as she thought, and MAYBE she doesn't entirely hate him after all. Teaming up with Sterling to save her brother might be the only way to keep from breaking the most important rule—protecting Cole.

Romancing the Nerd
by Leah Rae Miller

Until recently, Dan Garrett was just another live-action role-playing (LARP) geek on the lowest rung of the social ladder. Cue a massive growth spurt and an uncanny skill at basketball and voila...Mr. Popular. The biggest drawback? It cost Dan the secret girl-of-his-dorky dreams. But when Dan humiliates her at school, Zelda Potts decides it's time for a little revenge—dork style. Nevermind that she used to have a crush on him. It's time to roll the dice...and hope like freakin' hell she doesn't lose her heart in the process.

The Replacement Crush
by Lisa Brown Roberts

After book blogger Vivian Galdi's longtime crush pretends their secret summer kissing sessions never happened, Vivian creates a list of safe crushes, determined to protect her heart.

But nerd-hot Dallas, the sweet new guy in town, sends the missions—and Vivian's zing meter—into chaos. While designing software for the bookstore where she works, Dallas wages a countermission.

Operation Replacement Crush is in full effect. And Dallas is determined to take her heart off the shelf.

THE SOUND OF US
BY JULIE HAMMERLE

When Kiki gets into a prestigious boot camp for aspiring opera students, she's determined to leave behind her nerdy, social-media-and-TV-obsessed persona. Except camp has rigid conduct rules—which means her surprising jam session with a super-cute and equally geeky drummer can't happen again, even though he thinks her nerd side is awesome. If Kiki wants to win a coveted scholarship to study music in college, she can't focus on friends or being cool, and she *definitely* can't fall in love.

OLIVIA DECODED
BY VIVI BARNES

This isn't my Jack, who once looked at me like I was his world. The guy who's occupied the better part of my mind for eight months.

This is Z, criminal hacker with a twisted agenda and an arsenal full of anger.

I've spent the past year trying to get my life on track. New school. New friends. New attitude. But old flames die hard, and one look at Jack—the hacker who enlisted me into his life and his hacking ring, stole my heart, and then left me—and every memory, every moment, every feeling comes rushing back. But Jack's not the only one who's resurfaced in my life. And if I can't break through Z's defenses and reach the old Jack, someone will get hurt...or worse.

Life After Juliet
by Shannon Lee Alexander

Becca Hanson was never able to make sense of the real world. When her best friend Charlotte died, she gave up on it altogether. Fortunately, Becca can count on her books to escape—to other times, other places, other people...

Until she meets Max Herrera. He's experienced loss, too, and his gorgeous, dark eyes see Becca the way no one else in school can.

As it turns out, kissing is a lot better in real life than on a page. But love and life are a lot more complicated in the real world...and happy endings aren't always guaranteed.

The companion novel to *Love and Other Unknown Variables* is an exploration of loss and regret, of kissing and love, and most importantly, a celebration of hope and discovering a life worth living again.

The Society
by Jodie Andrefski

Not everyone has what it takes to be part of The Society, Trinity Academy's secret, gold-plated clique. Once upon a time, Sam Evans would have been one of them. Now her dad's in prison and her former ex-bestie Jessica is queen of the school. And after years of Jessica treating her like a second-class citizen, Sam's out for blood. But vengeance never turns out the way it's supposed to...and when her scheming blows up all around her, Sam has to decide if revenge is worth it, no matter what the cost.

WAKE THE HOLLOW
BY GABY TRIANA

Forget the ghosts, Mica. It's real, live people you should fear.

Tragedy has brought Micaela Burgos back to her hometown of Sleepy Hollow. It's been six years since she chose to live with her father in Miami instead of her eccentric mother. And now her mother is dead.

This town will suck you in and not let go.

Sleepy Hollow may be famous for its fabled headless horseman, but the town is real. So are its prejudices and hatred, targeting Mica's family as outsiders. But ghostly voices carry on the wind, whispering that her mother's death was based on hate...not an accident at all. With the help of two very different guys—who pull at her heart in very different ways—Micaela must awaken the hidden secret of Sleepy Hollow...before she meets her mother's fate.

Find the answers.

Unless, of course, the answers find you first.